SVN and SERPENT

ALSO BY JON SPRUNK

THE SHADOW SAGA
Shadow's Son
Shadow's Lure
Shadow's Master

THE BOOK OF THE BLACK EARTH
Blood and Iron
Storm and Steel
Blade and Bone
Sun and Serpent

JON SPRUNK

SVN and SERPENT

THE BOOK OF THE BLACK EARTH
—— PART FOUR ——

Published 2019 by Pyr®

Cover photos by Shutterstock
Cover design by Jennifer Do
Text Design by Frank Wiedemann
Cover design © Start Science Fiction
Map by Rhys Davies

Inquiries should be addressed to
Start Science Fiction
221 River Street
9th Floor
Hoboken, NJ 07030
PHONE: 212-620-5700
WWW.PYRSF.COM

10 9 8 7 6 5 4 3 2 1

978-1-64506-002-4 (Paperback) | 978-1-64506-008-6 (eBook)

Printed in the United States of America

To my wife and son, who make my life a joy.
To my friends, who understand and support me
To my agents and publisher, my editors and copyeditors, my artists and printers.
But above all, I dedicate this book to my fans.

War marched upon the wasted plains,
his red eyes casting to and fro,
with the hounds of Pillage and Ruin
licking at his bloody heels.

—Excerpt from *The Ninety-Ninth Day*

PROLOGUE

She climbed to the top of the dune and collapsed on the summit, gasping for breath. Her son rolled free of her emaciated arms to lie beside her.

Heduma reached out to make sure he was still beside her. Her eyes no longer focused, half-blinded by the sun's fierce glare. Her tongue lay like a dead thing in her parched mouth. Every breath brought new torment to her burning lungs. Yet, fear of the hunters on their trail gave her the strength to rise from the sand. With stubborn strength, she lifted her child and began the descent down the dune's northern slope.

Flames danced across the sky as the sun blazed down on the desert. A faint zephyr blew over the hard-baked land, but its breath was like the heat of an oven and offered no relief. The season of rain was still months away.

In ancient times, it was said this land had been a lush forest, with hardwood trees that reached to the clouds. Now, only sand and deadwood existed in its place, with not a single sign of life for as far as the eye could see, except for the occasional serpent found basking on the dunes. Heduma was past the ability to care. A poisoned kiss would be a mercy and a blessing right now. Much better than the fate that pursued them.

Ahead, a chain of rust-red mountains marked the border between the Abyssian deserts and the lands of the north—Isuran, Haran, and even fabled Akeshia. If they could reach those peaks, they might find safety, but Heduma's hopes were vanishing quickly as her body grew weaker with each passing step. They weren't going to make it.

She looked down at her son. Through her gauzy eyes, she saw his clean limbs and hollowed chest, the noble cut of his jaw beginning to emerge from the softness of childhood. She had longed to watch him grow into maturity, but now she knew she never would. The mountains may as well have been on the other side of the world. They would never make it to them before they were caught.

SUN AND SERPENT

"Thirsty . . . ," her son murmured in her arms.

She soothed him with soft coos as she trudged up the slope of the next dune. Her legs gave out just as she reached the top, as the limit of her strength expired. Sobs wracked her chest, but she had no moisture left for tears. Cradling her son, she lay on her side, and waited for the end to come.

A sound reached her ears. Not the heavy trod of leather boots on sand, nor the hiss of steel sliding against leather, it sounded like creaking wood. She opened her eyes.

A hard-packed road lay on the other side of the dune. On it trundled a low wagon, pulled by a pair of oxen. The man in the driver's seat was wrapped in a long robe of plain homespun cloth, the hood pulled low against the sun's glare, and with a scarf wrapped around his mouth and nose.

Freeing one hand from holding her son, Heduma reached toward the wagon and called out in a scratchy warble, barely louder than the wind. The wagon stopped. Soft steps trod up the far slope, and a shadow cast over them.

"Haliel! Bring water!" The words were heavily stilted with a strange accent.

Heduma lifted her head, trying to pierce the shade under the hood's awning, but could not. "I am a priestess of the Hidden Temple," she said slowly, forcing out each word. "Please. Help us."

More footsteps on the sands, and then the nozzle of a skin was pressed to her lips. She drank greedily, groaning as the water met the parched tissues of her throat. After only a mouthful, she pushed it away, down toward her son. Strong hands dribbled water onto his lips. Heduma's heart almost stopped as her son lay unresponsive, the water filling his mouth and spilling out the sides. Then he swallowed, and relief surged through her.

"Take the boy," the accented voice said. "He'll fetch good coin in Pardisha if he survives."

Those strong hands reached down and lifted her son. She held on for a moment, but she didn't have the strength to resist.

"What about her?" another voice asked. A man's voice, but higher pitched and clearly subservient.

The boss-man in the long robe stood up, towering above her like a titan.

"She's too far gone. Leave her. She'll be dead before morning."

They started to turn away when the servant paused in his steps. "Look at his eyes."

The taller man leaned down over her son. "Strange. I've never seen eyes so gold before. Load him up."

As they left, Heduma tried to get up, but her arms and legs refused to obey. She crawled, down the far side of the dune toward the wagon, but her efforts were too slow. She could only watch as the two men lifted her son into the back of the wagon. The smaller one sat beside her son, while the other climbed into the driver's seat and flicked the reins.

Heduma slipped down the leeward slope and rolled to the bottom. Sprawled on her back, stricken by spasms of pain, she could only reach out her feeble arms as the wagon rolled away, north toward the red mountains and the lands beyond.

Her son's name was the last word she spoke before her head sank to the ground, never to rise again. *"Asta . . . ptah . . ."*

CHAPTER ONE

A warm breeze blew over the grassy crests of the hills, filling Mannu's head with the scents of foxtails and hyacinth. He stood at his favorite perch, a narrow finger of bare stone jutting out from the hillside, where he could look down on the river and watch the boats plying its languid waters. From here he could also keep an eye on his uncle's goats, grazing in the field to his left.

He was fourteen. Next year, or possibly the one after, he would marry, and then his uncle would give him half of the herd as a wedding gift to start his own life. He could taste the freedom of being his own man, as real to him as the mighty Typhon below. He wet his lips with his tongue, suddenly thirsty.

As he reached down for the gourd at his feet, plaintive bleating called from the field. He stood up fast, grabbing his staff with both hands. The goats were running away, down toward the riverbank. It might be a wolf or even a pack of hyenas. Such predators had become brazen this season, stealing chickens and poaching kids whenever they got the chance. He saw movement amid a clump of bramble bushes near the top of the field. The bleating came from there.

Mannu scrambled down from his perch, hopping from stone to stone, and then raced across the grassy slope. If he could drive off the animal, he might still save the goat. He was imagining how grateful his uncle would be as he ran up to the bushes. The goat was still crying out. That meant it was still alive, but it sounded like it was in an awful lot of pain. Mannu parted the thorny brush with the end of his staff, and then froze. A dirty man squatted over the goat, his head bent low to the animal's belly. The goat kicked weakly, but it could not get free.

Mannu lifted his staff, prepared to drive this vagabond off. The man turned, and Mannu's intentions faltered. Half of the goat-killer's face was falling off as if it had been eaten away by a horrible plague. Blood was smeared across his cheeks and nose and dripped from his lips in thick drops. Yet, it was his eyes that caught Mannu and held him fast. Black, wet orbs with no whites or irises. They swiveled toward him like the eyes of the damned.

Mannu took a step back, his insides turning to water. He turned to run and stumbled as the man tackled him from behind. Despite his afflictions, the stranger was fast and terribly strong. Mannu kicked and wriggled to break free, but he was helpless in the dirty man's grasp. He shrieked as broken teeth tore into his left cheek. Blood spurted in his eyes, washing the sky above in a scarlet patina.

Pumash coaxed his steed to climb the last few yards of the hill's steep slope, and then pulled back on the reins when they reached the summit. The Typhon wended below, cutting a path through these foothills. On the other side of the river sat Semira, the second oldest city in Akeshia, according to the tales.

A few yards away, one of the undead crouched over the splayed body of a young shepherd, feasting on the youth's innards. Tears ran from the young peasant's face, and his limbs trembled as the last dregs of life dribbled out. A blood-streaked hand lifted, possibly asking for help. Pumash looked away.

Beyond the city lay an ocean of wild grass, which, according to the scholars and explorers, extended hundreds of leagues until it reached the lands of Abatta, Oshan, Moldray, and the Jade Kingdoms beyond them. For a moment, the urge to keep on riding, past Semira and into the wilderness, gripped Pumash. Then, a voice called from behind him.

"Do you wish a drink of water, Master?"

Deemu climbed the last leg of the slope. The manservant halted beside him, puffing and sweating like an old sow.

Pumash didn't deign to reply as he picked at the thick layers of bandages wrapped around both his wrists. He had gotten drunk three nights ago and did something rash. He dimly remembered holding the knife and wondering how deep he could cut into his veins. Deemu had found him before he could finish the deed.

Afterward, as the manservant sutured and bound his self-inflicted injuries, Pumash had found himself viewing Deemu as more of a sentry than a servant. He was not here to obey, but to keep an eye on Pumash. *To keep me alive long enough to serve the* Manalish's *designs. I am still useful, it seems.*

He wanted to kill the manservant, but he could not. *I am broken and weak, a pale shadow of my old self. Gods and demons, just let me die.*

Hiding his true feelings behind a mask of indifference, Pumash indicated the city below. "Another jewel for the *Manalish's* crown. And beyond this, the great capital itself. Our journey is almost at an end."

"Yes, Master," Deemu said between breaths.

Pumash wished the horde was with him. It would have been far easier to stand here and watch the city fall from a distance. Although, no better for the inhabitants. They were already dead. Within a day's time—two at the most—Semira would be another necropolis. To the southeast, the flat plain of the empire's heartland reached to the horizon. Ceasa lay upriver, beyond his sight. *At least this nightmare is almost at an end.*

Was it, though? He was nagged by the fear that this existence would never end. After the empire had fallen, he would be sent out to repeat this farce over and over, until the entire world was dead. Pumash pictured himself as an old man, bent over the neck of this horse, approaching another city with the seeds of death growing inside him. The hilltop wavered as he swayed in the saddle. Hands reached up to steady him before he toppled over.

"Master!" Deemu cried, holding him up. "You need to rest."

Pumash shook his head as his vision cleared and his balance returned. "Not yet. Not for a long time, I think. Come, let us complete our task."

He urged his steed down the slope, past the corpse of the young shepherd, and tried not to think about the future.

SUN AND SERPENT

The palace's audience hall had been cleaned from ceiling to floor, but the faint smell of blood still lingered. Jirom stood before the dais, staring at the throne. Six days ago, a king had sat in this seat, ruling Thuum and its surrounding lands. Six days, and already the locals were clamoring for a new king to rule. So far, the alliance he had forged with the militia commander had held, but he suspected the pact wouldn't last once he and the rebels left the city.

No, not rebels any longer. Today they were setting out for Ceasa, to fight the one who threatened the survival of the empire. In the back of his mind Jirom wondered if the enemy of his enemy wasn't his ally, but he tried not to think on it. He had seen the devastation left behind by the Dark King's unliving hordes. There could be no peace with such a thing. It all seemed like a dream. Any moment he expected to wake up and find himself in a desert cave, still hiding from the Akeshians. It was an idle thought, crowded out by the myriad of uncertainties weighing on his mind. He worried they didn't have enough fighters for the task, that they weren't trained or seasoned enough, that they didn't have enough armaments in reserve, or supplies, and so on. The list seemed endless.

The door opened behind him. "Thought I'd find you here, Sarge. You know, you're getting awful morose in your old age."

Jirom smiled as Three Moons entered the chamber. The bent, wizened old man he'd known for years had been replaced by a strong-shouldered man just a few years past his prime. The physical change was radical, even without the color alteration. Three Moons was completely silver. His skin, his hair, his teeth—even his eyes were silver. It was bizarre, like watching a statue move and talk.

Three Moons had told him the story of how he and the Silver Blades— they'd renamed their company—had been transported to another world, where they fought strange creatures and drank from a silver river. It was incredible, but the proof stood before him. Besides, he had seen too much strangeness in his lifetime to disbelieve anything.

"So you think he'll take the big chair if we win?" Three Moons asked.

"Who?"

"The magician supreme. Your friend Horace."

Jirom looked back to the throne. Victory had seemed so remote that he hadn't much considered what would happen after. "I suppose. If we win."

"One last war."

We keep saying that. Just one more war, but it never ends. Though, if we lose, I can't see how anything goes on.

"Moons, did you see anything in that other world to make you believe we have a chance to stop what's happening?"

The wizard worked his jaw and made as if to spit, but then looked at the floor and swallowed. "It's not anything we saw. It's that we survived in a place where no human was ever meant to exist, and some of us returned. I've got to believe there's a purpose behind all of that."

Jirom considered that. Was there a purpose behind all this suffering and death? And, if not, what did that mean?

"When we were trapped in that Otherworld," Three Moons said, "I had no idea how we would get back. Then we found a portal, but there was no way of knowing where it led. It could have taken us to another realm beyond that one, or into the heart of a volcano. For all I knew, I was sending the Blades to their deaths when we went through the doorway."

"There was no choice," Jirom said. "Staying would have just as surely meant your deaths."

"Yes. And yet, I felt something familiar on the other side of the portal. A presence I had felt before. So, I took a leap of faith, and somehow we arrived in Thuum. I didn't understand how that was possible. Of all the places in the world, we landed exactly where we needed to be. How? That question has eaten at me ever since the battle."

"And have you found an answer?"

"Damned straight. It was Horace. He was the presence on the other side of the portal. He pulled us to Thuum from that other world. I can't explain how, but I feel it in my bones. He's like a magical lodestone, pulling power to him from all around."

Jirom understood what Three Moons meant. He had seen it for himself, how Horace affected things around him, sometimes without even realizing it. "What does it mean?"

"I wish I knew. There are powerful forces at work, Jirom. Far beyond my skills. To tell you the truth, part of me wants to get as far away from this shit as I can run."

I feel the same way, but there's nowhere to go. No place far enough to get away.

More footsteps caused them both to turn as Emanon appeared in the doorway. His expression was troubled.

"Problem?" Jirom asked.

His lover and second-in-command nodded. "Might be. I just got a report from a patrol in one of the temple districts. They found something we need to see before we leave."

"There's more than one?" Jirom asked.

"Thuum has a lot of temples. They pop up like mushrooms all over the city."

Jirom headed toward the doorway. "Show me."

They walked toward the front of the palace. Passing through the tall corridors and out the massive atrium, decorated with murals and ornamentation, Jirom thought again of the people who had lived and worked here. Kings, queens, courtiers, servants, and slaves—all of them dead now. All their accomplishments and dreams destroyed in a single night. He imagined their ghosts crowding these halls, crying out for justice. It reminded him of his grandmother, who had told him as a young child that he carried the spirits of his ancestors inside him, and he must lead an honorable life so as not to disgrace them. Were they satisfied with what they had witnessed up to now?

As they walked, soldiers fell in around them, forming an honor guard. Ralla, newly promoted to captain, gave him a firm nod as she took her place at the front of the unit.

Jirom ground his teeth at the necessity of it. It seemed like every day he took on more and more pomp. Honor guards, servants to see to his kit, even Mezim following him around looking for things to write down for "posterity." No matter how hard he tried to fight it, the bureaucracy of leadership crept into his life. It almost made him long for the simplicity of battle. Almost.

"Any word back on our message to Nemedia?" he asked Emanon.

"A reply arrived this morning. They say they're sending four legions, but those units are at least a couple weeks away."

Jirom sighed. Four legions could make all the difference, but they couldn't wait. "We'll stick with the plan and depart today."

"Maybe the Nemedians will arrive in time to avenge us," Three Moons said.

Jirom frowned at that, but let it pass. The old man was likely right.

The sun was just beginning to peek above the eastern ramparts, casting long shadows across the waking city.

Emanon led them to a neighborhood of short, neatly planned blocks, where the streets were lined with small shops and villas. The battle had touched only lightly here, as evidenced by the paucity of burned-out homes. A few roofs were scorched and some doors battered down, but otherwise the district appeared unmarred. Except for the silence. Where there should have been people shopping and cleaning and living their lives, there was only empty quiet, reminding Jirom that Thuum still had a long way to go before it was made whole again. *It may take generations before they fully recover, before there are enough people to fill these homes. Or, it may never happen.*

He didn't need to be reminded of the price of failure. The fate of the world balanced on the edge of a sword.

They turned a corner and entered a large plaza, just as empty as the streets that fed into it. It was lined with large, well-established buildings, their weathered facades showing the age of decades. Emanon pointed to a tall, narrow building with a high steeple midway along the western side of the plaza. A wall enclosed the temple's small enclosure, with a wrought-iron gate at the front. A squad of local soldiers stood outside.

Jirom recognized Captain Lesanep as they got nearer. The Thuumian commander was the highest-ranking Akeshian officer in the city. As such, Jirom treated with him as an equal, their two forces working together to rebuild the city and keep the peace. When the rebel army departed, Lesanep would take over governorship of Thuum. In return, he had agreed to lend Jirom eight hundred of his soldiers for the march against the Dark King. The city would be left even emptier.

SUN AND SERPENT

Lesanep came over to meet them. "I'm sorry to call you away from your preparations. I know you're moving out today."

Jirom gestured to the temple behind him. "What's happening here?"

"It's maybe better if I show you."

As they walked the path of flat stones to the main entrance, the Thuumian officer explained. "Some of my men found this on a routine patrol. I don't know what to make of it. At first, I thought perhaps there might be more ghuls loose in the city, and maybe they had done this."

Past the large, bronze front door was a long foyer. Their footsteps echoed off the gray stone walls and arched ceiling. More soldiers flanked the hall, all of them looking uneasy. Jirom found his skin crawling. He didn't have much use for temples. He'd been raised to believe the gods were best venerated in private or in small familial shrines, not in the grand palaces the northern peoples built for their deities.

Lesanep led them to another doorway. Jirom stopped at the threshold, looking into a vast round chamber. A massacre lay spread out before him.

"Fuck me," Emanon said.

"I'll second that," Three Moons added.

More than a score of bodies sprawled on the black marble floor. Priests and priestesses in fine white robes, their limbs contorted in death. The murder weapons had been left behind—daggers and knives of various sizes, and a long-handled candle snuffer, all drenched in blood. The smells of incense and loosed bowels hung heavy in the air.

Jirom noted how the bodies were arranged as he made his way around the chamber. After a few minutes of investigation, he made his way back to Emanon and Lesanep. "They killed each other."

"They what?" Emanon asked.

"It must have been planned." Jirom pointed to several cold braziers and a pair of long pipes. "They had been doing some kind of ritual, and then at some point, they simply attacked each other. All the wounds are from close-in fighting. They battled until there was only one left standing." He nodded toward a tall priest near the middle of the floor. "And he killed himself. The dirk is still lodged in his gut, stuck in from the front and thrusting upward. Suicide."

"But why?" Lesanep asked.

"Who knows? What god is this temple dedicated to?"

"Nabu," Lesanep answered.

"I don't know much about that one."

"He is called the Keeper of Secrets. His cult is . . . well, mysterious." Lesanep frowned. "But I've never heard of them using any violent rituals. In fact, they were perhaps the most peaceful sect in the empire."

Jirom looked to Three Moons. "Can you sense anything that might explain this?"

The old sorcerer was kneeling beside one of the bodies. He grunted as he stood up. "The spirits here are very strange. They say they come from the stars. No, the places *between* the stars. They're not easy to understand. I believe these priests were attempting a divination. Then, a powerful force entered this place from beyond. It took control of these people and made them do this to each other." He shook his head. "That's all I can glean. The temple spirits are fading fast, rising back into the ether."

Emanon came over to stand beside Jirom. "What do you think? It feels like a bad omen."

"There's nothing we can do about this. We're marching out. Have you seen Horace?"

"Not since the night we took the city."

Ralla spoke up. "I believe he's holed up in a Mourning House up by the Gardens."

Jirom frowned. He hadn't seen Horace since that night either. He had chalked it up to days and nights filled with planning sessions and logistics calculations and the other man's need for solace. The Gods only knew how he was taking Alyra's death. *Not well, would be my guess. But we need you, Horace. This entire operation hinges on you.*

"Mourning House?" Emanon said. "The only thing worse than a sorcerer is one with a death wish."

Three Moons grunted.

Is that what Horace had? A death wish? Jirom could understand that. For years as a gladiator slave he had held death's presence close like a lover, more than ready to feel her final embrace. Finding Emanon and the rebellion had saved him from that existence. What did Horace have left? *A burning need for vengeance.*

"Send someone to find him," Jirom said quietly.

Emanon replied, "I'll get him myself. We'll meet you on the road."

Jirom nodded. His mind was far away again, working on the problems of an army on the march. He hardly saw the slaughter before his eyes. With a sigh, he rubbed his hands together, as if wiping away invisible blood.

He called out before Emanon got out of the chamber. "Em? Don't rile him up."

His lover replied with a feral grin. "Of course not, Commander. By the book."

Jirom watched him leave. *Of course not.*

She was dying again.

Horace watched helplessly as she thrashed in his arms. Black bile dripped from her mouth and nose and ran across his wrist. It was boiling hot, but he held on tight to her. This was it. The last moment he would ever spend with this woman he loved. Despite his horror at what was happening, he struggled to memorize every detail. She looked up at him, pain written in her eyes. And then he watched those crystal blue orbs darken. Within seconds, they were completely black, and her thrashing ceased.

Horace swallowed painfully. She was gone. Whatever now occupied her body was not Alyra. It wasn't human at all. He Saw through her skin to the pulsing darkness growing within. It was concentrated in her brain and down her spine, but tiny branches of black energy were spreading swiftly through her torso and into her extremities, like a hungry parasite stretching out its tentacles. Her jaws opened, tongue reaching out as if to taste the air. Then she lunged at him. Her teeth slammed shut just an inch from his throat. He fought to hold her down, but she was getting stronger by the moment. He started to lose his grip.

I'm sorry, my love. So sorry.

He forced himself to watch as the stone spike pierced her forehead. There was no death throe. She simply shivered, and then slumped to the floor, black ichor running from the fresh wound.

A voice whispered in his ear. "You failed her, my love. Just as you failed us."

He turned his head, his heart thumping hard. She stood far off, on the other side of the vast chamber beneath Thuum's empty streets. He could barely see her in the gloom. "Sari? Where's Josef?"

His dead wife's voice floated in the air. "We are damned, Horace. All of us damned."

She started to retreat, fading into the gloom of the underground.

"Wait!" Horace tried to lift Alyra's body so he could run after Sari, but the corpse was too heavy. He couldn't get her off the ground. He struggled as he called out for Sari to wait.

Horace woke in a pile of twisted bedsheets, with his dead wife's name echoing in his head. He took a deep breath and let it out slowly. The dream was fading into the recesses of his subconscious, but it had left behind a painful ache.

Thirsty, he climbed out of the narrow bed. His room in the attic of this low-rent hostel was dark and cramped. It was called a Mourning House because it catered to the families of the recently departed, who would stay for days or even weeks as they mourned the passing. Thuumian culture tended toward fatalism. The detachment was exactly how Horace wanted it—far away from everyone, where he could be left alone. He found the pitcher on the floor beside the pile of his clothes and discovered it had a little water left in it. Taking a gulp, he sat back down on the bed and considered going back to sleep. The soothing embrace of slumber called to him, but it offered no peace. The dream returned every time he closed his eyes, every night since the fall of the city.

He looked down at his hands, tracing the waxy web of scars running across the palms and up the undersides of each finger. These hands had tried to dig his wife and son from the fires of their death, and they had held Alyra in her final moments. His failures were written all over them. He closed them into fists and squeezed tight, and the anger inside him made the power behind his *qa* begin to throb, eager to flow into him.

He was about to lay back down when a soft rapping came from the door. Horace reached out with the *zoana* and lifted the latch, swinging the door open. Mezim stood in the unlit hallway. The secretary looked worried. Horace supposed he had given the man enough reason to be concerned. Despite his anxious nature, Mezim had proven a good companion on their travels together. He was one of the few people on whom Horace could depend.

"I'm glad to see you are awake, sir." Mezim swept into the room, making it feel even smaller. "Captain Emanon is waiting downstairs. The army is departing."

"Well, I guess I had better get moving then."

"Yes, sir."

Mezim had brought fresh clothes and a full water pitcher. Horace got up from the bed and washed his face over the basin in the corner. He sighed as the cool water rinsed away his sweat and soothed his worries. The past was past. It was time to look to the here and now.

He allowed Mezim to dress him. The secretary had brought a tunic of gold silk chased with black stitched birds and a divided skirt—the kind Akeshians used for riding. Horace wondered idly where Mezim had gotten them but didn't bother to ask. Probably gifts from someone important. Thuum's higher castes—those few who had survived the night of terror—had been effusive in their praise for him and the rebels and their roles in saving their city. He had lost count of the number of triumphal feasts and parties to which he had been invited. Of course, he hadn't attended any. Mingling with the upper crust was the last thing he wanted to do, and since that night he had avoided the presence of other people as much as possible.

That solace had provided time to reflect, and the most pressing thing on his mind was Astaptah. He'd tried to remember everything he knew about Byleth's former vizier—the self-styled Dark King—and finally came to the realization he didn't know much at all. Most of his decisions up till now had been based on the desire to please Alyra and Queen Byleth while they lived, and later, on what he had learned from the woman at the ruins. Over the past six days Horace had concluded it was time he took control of his life. If he was meant to battle Astaptah for the fate of the empire, he would do it on his terms. Whatever that meant.

After lacing up his boots, Horace went downstairs. The common room of the house had an eating area with a couple of tables beside a low hearth. Emanon stood by the front door. The rebel captain wore his fighting leathers and carried his long spear. There was a sheen of sweat on his forehead.

Before Horace could say anything, Emanon called out. "The army is leaving. The commander requests you get your wizardly ass moving. With all due respect."

"You sound agitated, Emanon. Can't stand to be out of Jirom's shadow for even a few minutes?"

Emanon gave his famous twisted grin. "On the contrary, I get the privilege of escorting your magnificence."

Horace studied him for a moment. "But something has happened."

"Well, there's been a bit of a bad omen. Some priests killed themselves in the temple of Nabu."

"Why?"

Emanon shrugged. "No one knows. But we're marching out in any case."

"Good, because I've been thinking."

"Oh, lords of heaven. Why does that scare the shit out of me? Don't worry about the planning. Jirom and I have that covered. You just concern yourself with the sorcery. We still don't have a reliable answer to those walking corpses."

The undead army had fled Thuum after Byleth's defeat, but Horace recalled little else from the rest of that day. Only vague images of faces around him, voices swollen with victory and relief, but Horace hadn't been able to understand why. Had they really won? Yes, they lived, but the world had changed irrevocably. Nothing had been the same since. *I keep expecting Alyra to walk into the room and tell me all this has been a dream.*

"I don't either," Horace replied. "Not yet. But I know Astaptah will have all the advantages when we catch up to him. Most likely, he'll be ensconced behind the walls of the capital, with an army much bigger than ours."

"Like I said, let me and Jirom handle the planning."

"So, what's your solution?"

"You'll find out what you need to know, when you need to know it. Other than that, just try to follow orders and not get anyone killed."

"Listen, Emanon. I'm only interested in one thing. Putting a stop to Astaptah. Everything else is secondary."

"You listen to me. Don't burden Jirom with your cracked ideas. He has enough on his mind as it is."

"Jirom is dedicated to victory, whatever the cost. He knows what's at stake. We don't have time for petty insecurities."

"Insecurities?" Emanon stepped closer to him. "The only thing I'm worried about is that maybe you'll lose your mind and start killing our own troops, or just vanish again, leaving us to deal with this alone."

"You don't understand, Emanon. You're not waiting for me. I'm waiting for *you*. If I had my way, I would be facing Astaptah right now, instead of cooling my heels while you and Jirom decide how to get all the men and women under your command killed in a battle they can't possibly win. You're just a diversion, Emanon. A sideshow. So, for your own good, stay out of my way."

Horace pushed past Emanon and out the door.

Emanon had brought horses. Horace mounted one and waited. Emanon sauntered out of the Mourning House as if he had all the time in the world. Mezim followed with their belongings.

Horace reached down to take his pack. "Mezim, you should stay here in the city. These people need a lot of help, and where we're going . . . well, I don't expect we'll be coming back."

Mezim strapped his own pack behind the saddle of the third horse.

"Pardon me, sir, but I'd like to accompany you in any case. We've come this far together."

Horace nodded. "As you wish."

They rode toward the south gates, sticking to the main thoroughfares, which had been cleared of debris and bodies over the past few days, but many signs of the battle remained. Uprooted topiaries and smashed-in doors, bloodstains where bodies had fallen and then sometimes risen again. There were also signs of rebuilding, and Horace was heartened to see how the rebels and people of Thuum had begun to put their lives back together. A few homes had been restored to something resembling their original state. Horace saw occasional faces in their windows, but no one came out.

As they passed a rebuilt storefront, something hanging from the door caught his attention. It was a skull without the jawbone, dangling from a thin chain.

"I've seen a few of them," Emanon said, gesturing to the skull. "Here and there throughout the city."

"What are they? Wards against the return of the undead?"

"I suppose. I've heard people are appeasing those icons with offerings. Maybe they're trying to soothe the evil spirits." He rolled his broad shoulders in a shrug. "People do strange things after experiencing something terrible."

Staring back at the hanging skull as they rode away, Horace had a bad feeling. What if it wasn't just an icon to ward away evil? Akeshia was rife with cults, serving a plethora of deities. What if another sect was taking seed, here in a city that already worshipped death? What if people were embracing the evil to harness its power over others? *A cult dedicated to Astaptah's warped sensibilities.*

The idea terrified him.

They passed through the city gate and crossed the wide stone bridge to the hilly plains on the southern side of the Akesh River. The last elements of the army were far ahead, trailing a long cloud of dust. The sky was a sheet of molten iron above them, searing away the lingering coolness of the previous night. Birds soared in circles overhead, following the troops.

The rolling plain reminded Horace of the sea, and how he had once loved to look out over the endless waters and let his imagination wonder. Now he felt only melancholy at the sight of all this natural beauty, with the fear lurking in the back of his mind that no one might survive to appreciate it. He could imagine his own death, even make peace with it, but the thought of everyone everywhere dying thrust his mind over the edge of a vast abyss. It was too terrible to contemplate, and yet he could not stop himself, like a tongue continuously seeking out the pulpy space left behind by a lost tooth.

Burying that feeling deep inside, Horace set out on the dusty road with the other two men. The birds continued to circle high overhead.

CHAPTER TWO

Akeshia's heartland was a series of vast, rolling plains, dotted with copses of tall, straight cedar trees. The sky was a limitless bowl inverted above the grasslands, broken only by occasional wisps of clouds. Jirom stared at a flock of birds soaring high over the army.

They were two days out of Thuum, moving at a better pace than he had anticipated, considering that many of their troops weren't accustomed to an extended march. A settlement lay in the army's path, a mile or two ahead. His scouts had brought back sobering details, passed along with almost casual disregard. More destruction, more death, just like everywhere else. They were becoming numb to the horror. *What do we become when we lose our fear of death?*

He glanced back as Emanon rode up, with Horace in tow. They bore no wounds, which Jirom took to mean they hadn't come to blows. Yet. He hoped they had come to a mutual understanding. With the near-impossible task they had set for themselves, to save an empire thrashing in its death throes, the last thing he needed was discord between his lover and his friend.

Behind them stretched the column of the army, marching in companies. Eighteen hundred soldiers and former rebels—a little over a thousand rebels and six companies of Thuumian legionaries. More fighters than the rebellion had ever been able to field before. *And still too few, I fear.*

The Silver Blades were positioned around him in a loose formation, an unasked-for escort. He didn't have the gall to send them away, this bare handful of men and women who stood out like ancient heroes, their metallic skin matching the bright gleam of their armor. Three Moons was nearest to Jirom, though they had spoken little since leaving the city. Jirom's mind was focused on the road ahead. He wondered if Three Moons' was still back on what they'd found in the temple of Nabu. Of those who had seen the slaughter, the old sorcerer had been the most shaken. *At least, he hasn't lost his fear of death, despite all we've been through.*

SUN AND SERPENT

Emanon steered his mount alongside Jirom. "Something's wrong?"

"There is a village ahead, or what's left of one."

Emanon squinted as he peered ahead. Behind him, Horace faced the same direction. Where Emanon's expression held the ever-present suspicion of a military mind, always anticipating threats and seeking ways to neutralize them, Horace's face showed only calm determination. *The same look he had when we fought our way out of Erugash. The same look he had when we found him after the battle of Thuum. He's ready to die, but not before he gets his revenge.*

"I want to see it," Emanon said.

A chill settled at the base of Jirom's spine as they spurred their steeds into a canter, riding ahead of the army. The Blades accompanied them, of course. Horace came, too.

The ground before them had been trampled—a swathe nearly a bowshot across—by the passage of the undead horde. The grass was pounded into the mud, flowering weeds smashed flat by thousands of cold, lifeless feet. A trail of death. A few hundred yards ahead, the scouting team stood atop a low rise. Seng trotted down to meet them.

"What do you have, Captain?" Emanon asked as they reined in their steeds.

Seng's face was troubled. "It is not good, sir. Not good at all."

They started to move ahead, but Seng held up a hand. "Sirs, I suggest you leave your horses here."

Jirom nodded, and their party dismounted. The sour feeling roiled in his stomach as he climbed the short, steep slope on foot. At the top, he stopped. Behind him, one of the Blades uttered a loud curse.

The ground was flattened in a roughly oval area a couple hundred yards across. Swathes of dried thatch were stamped into the mud, and Jirom realized they had once been the roofs of simple dwellings. A few clay bricks stuck out of the mire here and there, but not a single wall still stood intact. Everything had been razed to the ground and crushed, as if a gigantic foot had come down from the sky to smash the village flat, and then ground its heel into the dirt for good measure. Beyond the village proper were the remains of fields, also utterly destroyed. Some sections were flooded from overflowing irrigation ditches fed by a swift-flowing stream.

Jirom forced himself to approach the devastation. He saw no bodies. No human bodies, at least. Pieces of torn hide and bone were mashed in among the wreckage, the remains of domesticated animals.

Emanon knelt and pulled a curved ox horn out of the morass. Its surface was gouged and pitted by teeth marks. "They had no fortifications. No walls. No guard towers. No way to survive this."

Jirom faced southeast, where the track of destruction continued. He imagined it running all the way to the gates of capital. The end of the road. "Emanon, order the army to swing wide around this site. We'll march another couple hours, and then stop for the night."

His lover dropped the ox horn back into the mire. "Will do."

As Emanon rode off back to the column, Jirom and Horace headed out, skirting the ruined village to take up the trail on the other side. They rode in silence, Jirom too preoccupied with thoughts of the coming days to start a conversation. Horace seemed reticent as well, but he had been that way for days.

The grasslands spread out before them, marred by the trail of death, running straight as an arrow.

They made camp at dusk. Emanon saw to the disposition of the troops, while Jirom retreated into his command tent. A soldier from Ralla's company brought the charts and laid them out on the table.

An old woman—one of the many camp followers marching with the army—came in with a covered plate, several cups, and a jar of wine. Jirom didn't know her name, but she brought him food and drink every night. She didn't speak, and she wouldn't stop no matter what he said, so Jirom had become resigned to the situation.

She reached for the jar to pour for him, but he grabbed it first. "I'll get my own," he said, with a bit more growl than he intended.

The old woman scowled, but said nothing as she departed.

"We're settled in for the night," Emanon said as he entered. He went to the side table and poured himself a cup of wine. "Double sentries, as you ordered."

Jirom nodded without looking up. He was studying their main map of the region, which Mezim had found in the Thuumian archives.

SUN AND SERPENT

The other unit commanders entered in a file and took places around the central table. His captains were Ralla, Silfar, Mamum, Pulla, Halil, and Seng—all veterans of Emanon's rebel outfit. The first five commanded companies, while Seng was in charge of the scouting units. With them came Captain Paranas and Three Moons, to represent the Silver Blades, and a grizzled old vet by the name of *Pradi* Naram who led the Thuumian soldiers. *Pradi* was an Akeshian rank roughly equal to a platoon sergeant. With so many of the Thuumian militia killed in the battle with the undead, there were no higher-ranked officers to lead, and it was said that Naram had refused a promotion when he was placed in charge.

Jirom traced a path from Thuum southeast through the Typhon River valley. "We're following the path of the horde that left the city. So far, they appear to be blazing a trail straight for the capital."

Emanon came over, chewing a hunk of bread. "I've been to Ceasa. The capital has several concentric walls and a full legion for its garrison. Not to mention it hosts the Master House of the Crimson Brotherhood and the largest school of sorcerers in the empire. Ceasa can hold out for some time."

"Perhaps," Jirom said. "But so far, the Dark King has marched through the center of Akeshia with hardly a pause, plucking cities like figs. We have to prepare for the eventuality we might be attacking a fortified city firmly in the enemy's control."

"Then we can assume they won't be using the walls and siege engines," *Pradi* Naram said. "Those mindless corpses will just come at us in a massive swarm. We would use that to our advantage."

"Lure them out," Ralla said. "And cut them off. Then we clean out the city."

"As easy as that?" Silfar asked with a hard laugh.

"Why not?" Ralla replied. "There might be a lot of them, but those ghuls are as stupid as a bag of rocks. Like some men I could name."

Mamum tapped the capital on the map with a thick forefinger. "If we attack from the north, we'll have to cross the river. Is there a bridge?"

Jirom looked to Emanon, who nodded. "Yes. A big stone one. It's big enough for half a dozen wagons to roll across, side by side. But the gatehouse there is going to be a bitch. High walls, battlements, and a huge gate. It would take a herd of elephants to get through with brute force."

"We have your friend, Sarge," Three Moons said. "He could take down an entire city wall without blinking an eye."

"Then why doesn't he just end the whole mess and save us the hassle," Pulla muttered.

Jirom stood up straight. "Horace will do his part. But it's up to us to buy him time."

"Buy him time for what?" *Pradi* Naram asked.

A voice answered from the tent's entrance before Jirom got the chance. "To take down the Dark King."

All heads turned as Horace entered. Everyone tensed. Jirom saw it in their faces and in the subtle change in their body language, as if a dangerous beast had just entered their midst. Jirom was aware some of his officers didn't trust Horace, including Emanon. The army was rife with rumors about him. That he was in league with demons. That he had killed Queen Byleth and tried to take her throne. That he was a western spy. Even though Jirom knew none of those were true, the truth was scary enough. Horace was a very dangerous man out for vengeance, and he wasn't going to let anything get in his way.

Horace came over to the table, and the captains shuffled away to give him space.

Emanon glanced over without an ounce of fear. "Any plans how to accomplish that goal?"

Horace leaned over the map. "Ceasa was always Astaptah's goal, but not for mere conquest. He's interested in something else."

"What else is there?" Mamum asked, and then clamped his mouth shut.

Jirom asked Horace, "What do you mean? When he has Ceasa, he has the empire."

"Conquering the empire is just a means to an end. Astaptah doesn't just want Akeshia. He wants the world." Horace looked around the gathering. "You should all know the truth. Astaptah isn't some rogue despot. He serves a pantheon of demonic gods who once ruled the world. I have seen them for myself."

The chill Jirom had felt earlier returned, despite the heat of the evening.

SUN AND SERPENT

He knew Horace had been through a lot. Something had happened after they fled the desert hideout. Horace had disappeared for days until he turned up again in Thuum, but he had changed. There was an evolution at work within the man, and it frightened Jirom.

It was Emanon who broke the silence after Horace's pronouncement. "You saw demon gods? Let me guess. They're coming back to kill us all."

"Yes."

The word hung in the air for several seconds. Emanon made as if to respond, but he closed his mouth without speaking again. The company commanders stood still, as if not sure whether to laugh or cry. Finally, Jirom rapped on the table to focus their attention.

"All right, Horace. Tell us what's going on."

Horace expounded in a voice without inflection or passion, as if he had no need to convince anyone. The chill ran up Jirom's back as he listened to Horace's description of a vision that took him beyond the boundaries of the mundane world, into a black void where monstrous nightmares lurked, eager to come back to the Earth and ravage its cities, as they had once before. Jirom saw the effects of the tale on his subordinates. Emanon and Naram appeared dubious, but the rest were worried.

When Horace was finished, silence had settled over the tent. The wind scratched against the canvas.

"All right," Jirom said when he could find his voice. "What can we do? How do we oppose such a threat?"

"Your army is just a distraction," Horace said. "The real battle will take place between me and Astaptah. I will try to protect the rest of you as best I can, but my focus will be on killing him, once and for all time."

"Well," Emanon said. "You're fucking full of yourself, aren't you, mageling?"

Horace held Jirom's gaze. "It's just the way of things. I know that now. We can't escape our fates."

I don't believe that. I can't.

Jirom cleared his throat. "Check in on your units. We're marching out with the dawn."

The commanders filed out, all but one walking past Horace without looking at him. *Pradi* Naram stared at him for a long moment before he followed the others.

Jirom waited until it was just him, Horace, and Emanon, then he let out a long sigh. "That could have gone better. What's your plan, Horace? What do you need us to do?"

"I don't know. It's possible we can't defeat Astaptah. This may all be futile."

"Fuck you," Emanon said, in the low tone Jirom knew all too well. It meant he was moments from exploding into violence. "Jirom has cobbled this army together with spit and sheer will. Then you stroll in here with your depressed bullshit, poisoning the minds of everyone who hears it."

Horace did not appear to take offense. "I'm just being honest."

"Maybe," Jirom said. "But we still must try. If there's a chance we can stop him, we have to take it."

"We need more soldiers. And sorcerers, too, if we can get them."

"Sorcerers?" Emanon frowned. "What are you talking about? There were none left in Thuum, besides you."

Horace tapped his finger on the map beside a city to the west of their position. "I've heard that Yuldir hasn't fallen to the enemy."

"The last report said they were attacked by an army of those dead things five days ago," Jirom said.

"Wait a minute," Emanon interrupted. "You aren't suggesting . . ."

"We need more allies if we're going to fight Astaptah," Horace pressed. "His army must number more than a hundred thousand by now. We have to recruit Yuldir and fight together."

"You're insane! Do you know that? The Yuldirans have no reason to help us."

"Of course they do. To save themselves."

"Bah!" Emanon cut the air between them with his hand. "They'll just kill our messenger and be done with it."

"I will go myself."

"Oh, I'd love to see that. Get yourself trussed up like a hog for the slaughter."

"Then you have no objections?"

Jirom glanced first at his lover, and then back to Horace. "We don't have the time or resources to divert for a rescue, or the negotiations that might follow. What about the siege of the dead surrounding Yuldir? Do you have a plan for that?"

"Actually, I do. I can get there quickly, break the siege, and make them an offer."

"They won't listen," Emanon said. "Even worse, they might strike against us while we're stretched out along the march. Then this entire plan is fucked."

Jirom stifled the sigh that threatened to show his angst over this idea. Now wasn't the time for second guessing. He tapped a cluster of hills on the map west of the capital. "Meet us here at the Black Gates in four days."

Horace frowned. "You're crossing the river to attack from the western side?"

"I told you to leave the planning to us," Emanon grumbled.

Jirom tapped the spot again for emphasis. "Four days. If you and the Yuldirans don't arrive in time, we'll make the assault without you."

"I understand," Horace replied. "This is the right move. I feel it. Every minute we delay, Astaptah's victory gets closer."

"I hope so. Without you, this attack doesn't stand a chance."

Horace left the tent. Jirom paced over to the sideboard and poured himself another cup of wine. He took a long sip, waiting for the inevitable explosion.

"What the fuck are you thinking?" Emanon finally blurted. "You just let our only chance walk out the door."

Jirom set down the cup. He was hungry, but he was too tired to eat. And he didn't feel like fighting his lover again. "He's right. We need help. We can't do this alone."

"The Akeshians are the enemy, Jirom. That will never change."

"It changed in Thuum."

Emanon looked like he wanted to spit, but instead he turned and stalked out of the tent. Jirom considered going after him but poured himself another cup instead. Holding the drink, he went back to the command table and looked for a better solution.

Horace found Mezim inside his tent. The former secretary was laying out Horace's clothes for the next day. A covered tray sat on a field chair beside a foldable desk.

"You are back sooner than I anticipated, sir. Did you dine?"

Horace opened the chest at the foot of the bedroll and rummaged through the meager contents. He found an old leather satchel and brought it out. He uncovered the tray. Ignoring the soup, he filled the satchel with bread rolls and a handful of dates. "Sorry, Mezim. I'm leaving. Do we have any water?"

Mezim handed him a stoppered gourd, which sloshed as Horace put it in the satchel. "Are we going to Yuldir, sir? I assume we will pack light. Perhaps just two changes of clothes. Oh, I will have to bring your good robe—"

"No, Mezim." Horace placed a hand on the man's shoulder. "Thank you. I know you would follow me anywhere, but I have to go alone."

"Sir, my place is with you."

"Not this time, my friend. Stay with Jirom. Help him manage this army."

Mezim turned and picked up a sheaf of papers. "Actually, I have some ideas about the management of stores. Particularly water . . ."

"Show him in the morning."

"I shall, sir. And may the Gods favor your journey."

"Yours as well."

Horace left the tent. Walking through the camp, he had the uneasy feeling he would never return. He might never see these men and women again. He glanced in the direction of Jirom's command pavilion, wondering if he should go say something. What else was there to say? This was how it had to be.

He passed through the sentry lines, down the sandy slope of a debouchment, and out onto the plain. Low hills made humps against the western horizon, silhouetted by the day's last light. The tall grass swished against his legs as he walked, until he felt he was far enough away, and then he stopped. He pictured the map with himself on it and tried to imagine his destination.

SUN AND SERPENT

When he was ready, he opened his *qa*. There was a momentary struggle for control as the magic poured into him like a raging river of ice and fire. He grasped hold of it and bent it to his will.

A moment later, he was gone.

"Gently, Princess. It requires a precise combination of wind and fire. There, yes. Just so and . . ."

Princess Dasha opened her eyes. A tiny spark flickered in the air between her and her tutor, Brother Kaluu. It flickered again, and then died.

She and the aged monk sat under a silk canopy in the orchid garden, an open courtyard of the imperial palace. High walls topped by leaf-shaped battlements surrounded the garden, yet the midday breeze found its way in to ruffle the blossoms.

She had been at this lesson for what felt like hours, and still she was no closer to achieving success. The princess looked at the spot of blood on the inside of her left wrist. The immaculata was small, but it hurt far worse than it looked. She bit her bottom lip. *I will not show this pain. I will be strong.*

"That was much improved, Princess. But you still used too much air and suffocated the ember before it was ready. Shall we try it again? This time add only a tiny thread of Imuvar to fan the flame."

Brother Kaluu gave her a consoling smile. He was ancient, with failing eyes and faded tattoos around the dome of his bald head. He had been her teacher of the magical arts since she was a child. Kind and patient, he was nothing like the other Brothers of the Crimson Order she had met, who were all stuffy and self-important. Despite her affection for the old man, right now Dasha wanted to strangle him.

"I can't do it. You know fire and air are my weakest elements. Let's try something else."

"We must persevere, Princess. Creating a light may seem trivial, but mastering this technique opens the way to a vast array of higher mysteries." He hesitated, wetting his thin lips with the tip of his tongue. "Is there something bothering you? You seem to be having trouble maintaining your focus today."

Dasha swatted at a midge buzzing past her face, stalling to consider an answer. She trusted Kaluu, who doted on her like a loving grandfather, but she had been raised in the imperial court for seventeen years and understood how a single careless word could cause calamity.

"I am concerned about my father," she replied in a neutral tone as she affected the 'silent lily' expression of complete passivity. "The news has been distressing."

"Ah, you speak of the usurper." Brother Kaluu bobbed his head in a dutiful nod. "Yes, it is distressing. However, our faith in the emperor, your father, may his name be praised for a thousand years, remains absolute."

"Of course."

Dasha dared not reveal her doubts, not even to Kaluu. The stories of the Dark King had first reached the palace a few months ago. At the time, she remembered laughing about them with the rest of the court. How could one king dare to take three cities at once? Everyone had been sure the upstart would be crushed by the other monarchs within a season. Instead, the Dark King's list of conquests had grown with uncanny speed, and just two days ago had come the news that Epur had fallen. The usurper was practically on their doorstep.

With each new report, Dasha had seen the toll exacted on her father. Before this, she had always seen him as the ruler of the greatest empire in the world. Immortal and all-powerful. However, over the past couple months he had shrunk, like a half-baked cake collapsing in upon itself. It was breaking her heart.

Dasha fought to keep herself from tearing up. "I will try to make the light again."

"Very well, Princess. Begin with a thin thread of—"

Running sandal heels slapped on the pavestones bordering the garden. Dasha stood up in the middle of Brother Kaluu's directions. He started to growl an admonishment, but she shushed him with a gesture. "Quiet. Someone is coming."

SUN AND SERPENT

Brother Kaluu turned around in his seat. "This is quite intolerable. They know this time is set aside for your instruction."

A blackbird erupted from a peach tree at the corner of the courtyard and flew over the palace roof, heading west to east. The running footsteps stopped, and low voices spoke at the edge of the garden. Dasha tapped her foot. After a few seconds, two persons approached on the path. One was Elia, her bodyguard. Tall—taller than many men at the imperial court—and strong, she always wore a suit of leather-and-iron-banded armor and a scimitar at her hip. Her long black hair was tied back in a soldier's queue. Her iron collar was barely visible under the armor.

The other woman was Muriah, one of her father's consorts.

"What is it?" Dasha asked as the women arrived. "What's happened?"

Muriah glanced at Brother Kaluu, who was struggling to stand up. She was a beautiful woman, graceful and elegant, and also blessed with a keen mind. It was no wonder she was the emperor's favorite. "May I have a moment alone with you, Royal Daughter?"

"This is no time—" Brother Kaluu started to argue.

Dasha silenced him with a hand upon his bony forearm. She was surprised to feel the tensile strength in the corded muscles beneath his skin. "Please, Honored Brother. We can continue our lesson tomorrow."

Brother Kaluu glared once more at Muriah and Elia, and then relented. "Very well, Princess."

As he walked away, his back straight with pride, Muriah leaned closer and whispered to Dasha. "Semira has fallen."

I knew it. I knew in my heart this news would reach us soon. The Dark King is coming for Ceasa.

Dasha needed to see her father right away. She started to leave, but Muriah stayed her, almost grabbing her arm but stopping inches from touching her. "Please wait," the consort said. "This is not to be shared with the others, but your blessed mother and the rest of the imperial family are going to the citadel tower."

Dasha glanced to the courtyard roof. There, just visible above the cornice stones, was the top of the citadel tower. It was said to be the most secure location in all of Ceasa, protected behind thick walls and steel doors. In times of dire emergency, that was where the imperial family resided until the danger passed. It had been used a few times in the past, during wars and periods of civil unrest, but never during Dasha's lifetime. Until today.

Dasha rested her fingertips on Muriah's wrist to acknowledge the woman's kindness. "Thank you. You should go to the tower at once."

"Princess, you are not coming?"

"Not yet. I must see my father."

The consort lowered her eyes. "He is meeting with his viziers in the Sun Chamber."

With a nod, Dasha left Muriah and the garden.

Elia fell into step beside her. "Princess, you should go to the tower with your mother."

"And be locked up with the rest of my brothers and sisters, cowering and praying? Not likely."

"This is not a time to be headstrong, Dasha. The emperor will deal with this crisis."

Dasha stopped at an intersection of halls and turned to her bodyguard. "How, Elia? Nothing has worked so far. City after city has fallen to this Dark King."

"And what will you do?"

"I'm not sure. But I can be there for my father."

She took off again, threading her way through the myriad of halls and chambers that made up the palace proper. Slaves bowed as she passed. The north wing was where the official business of the empire was conducted. She passed the scribes' chamber, where a dozen young men with shaved heads were bent over slanted desks, scratching at papyrus scrolls with quill pens. Past that was a series of lesser meeting chambers. Usually, they were empty, but today all the rooms were filled with men in noble garb. Men talking, arguing, even shouting at each other. Elia stayed close to her.

Finally, Dasha came to the door that led to a narrow corridor. A large slave holding a tulwar stood before it. He stepped aside as she approached. Elia and the slave exchanged brief nods as Dasha opened the door and went inside.

SUN AND SERPENT

The corridor beyond was dimly lit by a series of skylights that cast pools of light on the floor. It ran behind several antechambers and ended at a viewing area behind the Sun Chamber. A wooden screen divided it from the chamber within, carved with cunning little holes that allowed one to see and hear what transpired inside, but hid the viewer's identity. Voices could be heard through the screen as Dasha approached.

It was called the Sun Chamber because of its bright gold walls. The interior of the domed ceiling was a mosaic of lapis lazuli. In the center of the dome was a wide hole through which the sky could be seen. Her father sat in his throne at the end of the hall, on a dais of seven steps. Before him stood a dozen of his advisers and field commanders. Lord Virukuun, minister of the War Council, was addressing the court.

"—lost contact with Semira and its neighboring towns. All the western cities have fallen, and now we have rumors that Thuum may be lost as well. Ceasa, Your Majesty, now stands as the last bastion against this invasion."

Dasha's father was a man still in the fullness of his power. The touches of gray in his hair reinforced his imperial countenance. She expected a strong statement from him, a plan for how they would defeat this vile usurper and save the empire.

"Thank you, Lord Virukuun. I am authorizing the conscription of all able-bodied men, free and slave alike, below the rank of *zoanii*. The War Council will submit a strategy to defeat this threat before the midday hour tomorrow."

Conscription? Submit a strategy? Dasha felt her stomach tremble. Where was the fire? The imperial condemnation? He made it sound like they were planning a dinner party.

As the viziers filed out, Dasha opened the screen. Her father was resting his chin in his hand when she came around the dais and knelt before him.

"Dasha, I am glad to see you, child. Come here."

She climbed the steps and sat on the arm of the throne. He wrapped her in a warm hug. "I heard about Semira," she said.

"Yes." He sat back. His eyes were sadder than she had ever seen before. "Those poor souls, devoured by darkness. The empire is facing a dire peril."

"What are you going to do, Father?"

He placed a hand upon her back. "The people will be looking to our family for hope. We must present a good example. Will you go to the temple of Kishar and give an offering to the Earth Mother?"

"Of course, Father. But I want to do more to help."

"We are doing all we can. Our fate rests in the hands of the Gods."

Dasha bit down on her bottom lip as she struggled to put her ire into words. "Father, we can't be content with such gestures."

"Do not mock the Gods, Dasha."

His stern gaze made her want to shrink, but she pressed on, certain she was right. "Isn't it time for bold action, Father? The other cities tried to hide behind their walls and lost. Why don't we ride out to meet this usurper? Attack him before he reaches our gates?"

The emperor shook his head with a long sigh. "Dasha, my darling, you know nothing of war. What you say is not feasible. Please, do as I ask. Pray for the safety of our people, and let the ministers devise our defense."

She got up. "As you wish, Father. But I will not hide in the citadel tower with the rest."

He smiled, reaching out to touch her hand. "You were always the fiercest of my children. I lament that you were born into such dark times, but we shall need your strength in the days ahead. Go now, my daughter. Do as I have told you."

Dasha went down the dais steps and turned at the bottom to give the customary obeisance. Her father smiled down like a benevolent star, lovingly, but so remote now that she felt she hardly knew him. As she left the chamber, Elia pulled the screen shut behind her.

"There. You see?" Elia said. "Your Imperial Father and his counselors will deal with the enemy. Are we off to the temple now?"

Dasha looked back through the screen to where her father remained on his throne, staring ahead as if seeking wisdom from the walls around him. "Yes, I suppose so."

SUN AND SERPENT

Pumash stood atop the flat roof of the magister's tower, watching the *Manal-ish*'s minions assemble their diabolical machine of silver struts and girders. The tower jutted from the southern wing of the royal palace of Semira, at the end of a flying buttress. The gray-shrouded underlings worked in perfect harmony without exchanging a single word. It was as if they shared a single mind.

Pumash was observing their labor when the sound scratched at his ears. At first, he took it for buzzing insects, but after a few seconds he heard it more clearly as a low droning noise, like a chorus of distant moaning, rising from the city below. Disquieted, he stole to the edge of the roof and looked down.

The streets beyond the walls were filled with undead, tens of thousands packed together like teeming fish. The droning came from them, as if they lifted their voices in a macabre chorus. Pumash had never heard them make a sound before, and it horrified him. One fiend looked up in his direction, and the attention of the entire horde shifted to the tower roof. Pumash quailed under all those black gazes. He clutched the stone merlon as his legs shook. Taking shallow breaths, he backed away from the edge. An ominous crackle of thunder made him flinch. The master's henchmen had finished their work.

Pumash hurried down into the tower and across the long bridge. Deemu was waiting at the interior door of the palace.

"I was coming to fetch you, Master."

"Did you bring something to drink?"

Deemu produced a glass bottle. Pumash tore off the cork and took a long gulp, trying to wash away what he had witnessed.

"Master," Deemu said. "The Great One has called for you."

Pumash almost choked on the wine. He pushed the bottle back into Deemu's hands. "Is he . . . ?"

"At the temple of Nabu," Deemu finished for him. "Yes, Master."

Pumash straightened his shoulders. "All right. Take me to him."

He winced as thunder boomed overhead.

They walked through the empty hallways of the palace and out the front gates. Pumash hardly noticed the bloodstains on the marble floors where Semira's defenders had died. Died and then risen back up as mindless slaves to the *Manalish*. He told himself he was accustomed to such things now, but his insides quivered every now and then. The wine helped, somewhat.

They crossed the manicured grounds of the royal complex and entered the city. The avenue running from the palace to the temple district was vacant. Undead milled in the alleys and side streets and watched from the rooftops, but they left this route alone. *These dogs never slip their leash. The* Manalish's *control over them is absolute.*

For a moment, Pumash envied these living corpses for their ability to obey without questioning, without personal responsibility. Then he shuddered and banished those thoughts. Death would come for him soon enough.

The temple of Nabu sat in a secluded plot between the shrines of two lesser gods. The cult of Nabu, the Keeper of Secrets, had never possessed much political power, not even before the Godswar. As such, Pumash had never paid much mind to its adherents. As soon as he arrived in Semira, the *Manalish* had taken up residence in the temple, just as he had taken over the Keeper's temples in every city they conquered. *Working on another of his mystical projects, no doubt. Concocting some new horror to unleash on the world. Gods save us.*

Pumash swallowed his qualms as he arrived. The temple's outer gates hung open in silent invitation. Inside was a long courtyard with stone benches and a few shade trees. A double row of free-standing pillars led to a tall doorway. As they walked that path, Pumash noticed the pavestones were inscribed with indecipherable symbols. They twisted as he trod upon them, and Pumash felt they must hold some special meaning.

The interior of the temple sanctum was dark, lit only by a few windows in the domed ceiling. Deemu led Pumash to a stairway that he would have missed in the dim lighting, set along the edge of the inner chamber, and together they descended into the temple's lower reaches. What little light seeped in from above vanished within a few yards as the stairs turned in a slow circle. Pumash kept one hand on the wall to steady himself.

"Why didn't you bring a torch?" he hissed at his servant.

"Forgive me, Master. It is not permitted."

They descended for what felt like hours, around and around in an endless loop of stairs. The rhythmic slap of their feet became hypnotic, until Pumash's mind began to wander. What was the *Manalish* doing in these temples? Defiling them in the name of some infernal demon? Sporting with the dead? Pumash's stomach turned, imagining what he would see below. His foot almost missed a step. He grabbed the wall with one hand as he fought to regain his balance. He caught hold of Deemu's shoulder with his other hand and held on tight.

"Master, step carefully. We have reached the bottom."

Cold sweat formed on Pumash's brow as he stepped onto solid ground. Everything around them was black. "Where are we?"

"This way, Master. Take my arm."

As he held onto his manservant's bony elbow, Pumash wondered how Deemu was navigating this abyss so easily. *No doubt one of the* Manalish's *servants brought him down here just prior to summoning me. That would explain it.*

Despite assuring himself, Pumash could not entirely banish the nervousness settling in his stomach like a lead weight. He listened intently, trying to figure out their surroundings by the echoes of their footsteps. He guessed they were in a large passageway. The floor was smooth underfoot, but also gritty, as if coarse sand stuck to the stone. The air was still and dry and had absolutely no odor. He didn't even smell dust, which was faintly astonishing.

Just as he was about to ask how far they had to go, the passageway turned a corner, and pale green light blossomed in the distance. Its radiance painted the contours of the tunnel, which was about fifteen feet across with a ceiling arched equally high, reminding Pumash of a crypt. The walls were not faced in cut stone but carved out of the living rock.

Before them opened a large underground cavern. The green glow emanated from an orb hovering near the ceiling. The sight it revealed made Pumash stop at the entryway. The *Manalish* stood facing the far wall, inset with a massive stone door. More cabalistic sigils covered its face, resembling wriggling vines or serpents. In the center of the portal was a broad circle.

Half a dozen grey-hooded underlings surrounded the *Manalish*, holding black candles and swaying in a slow rhythm as they intoned a ceaseless mantra. It reminded Pumash of the horrible droning of the undead above.

Deemu started to enter the chamber, but Pumash held him back. "What is happening?" he whispered to his servant.

Deemu bent his head closer. "I have not been able to piece it all together, Master. But at every city we have conquered, the *Manalish* has found similar doorways under the shrines of the Wandering God. He opens them, and then leaves."

"What's behind the doors?" Pumash asked.

It was not Deemu who replied, but the *Manalish*, who turned to regard them. "The future."

Pumash released his hold on Deemu's arm and went down on one knee. "I have come, Master."

"Rise, Pumash." The *Manalish* gestured to the stone door. "For centuries, the priesthood of Nabu has served as guardian of the empire's most important secret. And its greatest sin."

All at once, Pumash understood what he was seeing. "The Gates of Death."

A harsh edge entered the *Manalish*'s voice. "Seven wards in the seven original cities of the Kuldean empire, erected by the misguided magi of that bygone age in a futile effort to prevent the Eldritch Lords from returning to this world and regaining their rightful place as its rulers. Once these wards are removed, the balance of the cosmos will be restored."

Pumash trembled as the quaking in his stomach spread out to seize his entire body. His knowledge of occult lore was slim, but he knew the old legends. How the world had once been dominated by ancient horrors, until the Gods were born and defeated their primal ancestors, flinging them into a bottomless abyss. Seven doorways—the Gates of Death—were built to guard their eternal prison. And the *Manalish* was tearing them down.

"Master," he said, his throat suddenly parched. "If the Old Ones return, what shall become of us?"

The *Manalish* smiled as he walked over. It was a terrible grin, filled with zealous rapture. "We shall rule at their sides. I have foreseen it in my visions. Imagine it. The entire world wiped clean of the filth and corruption of mankind. Made pristine once more, as it was at the beginning of time."

Fear clamped down Pumash's tongue. With great effort, he spat out, "What is the value of ruling an empty world?"

SUN AND SERPENT

"Empty? Not at all. On the contrary, the world shall be filled with perfect beings. Beings without the lusts of the flesh. Who never die. An entire world devoted to a single purpose."

The *Manalish* took his arm in an almost paternal way and led Pumash across the chamber. "I was orphaned when I was a young boy. Found by a traveling glass merchant and sold several times, until I finally became the property of a learned sage. He taught me how to read and write, taught me history and philosophy, and under his tutelage I discovered I had a powerful gift—the ability to summon power from the netherworld. And that is when I found true wisdom. I saw a vision of these Seals and the Eldritch Ones, and the glorious future that awaited the world.

"When I revealed this revelation to my master, he cast me out. I was exiled to the desert to die, again. Yet, I survived and eventually came to Akeshia, and that's when I realized everything was happening as it was meant to be. The vision was true. See here? The ward is cracking."

They had stopped before the door. Fine cracks snaked across its stone surface. Tiny flakes crumbled away as Pumash watched. With every passing moment, his dread grew, as if he were observing the slow, creeping approach of his own demise.

"There is only one last step to completion of our plan," the *Manalish* said. "The imperial city."

Pumash summoned the last of his courage and fell to his knees, slamming himself down on the hard floor. "Please, Master. Do not use me this way again. I cannot bear it. Not . . . again. Your armies are more than large enough to take the capital directly."

The *Manalish* reached down and grasped him by the back of the head. His strength was terrifying. "You must go, Pumash. So it has been written, that the emissary of the new prophet shall go to the kings of the world and cast them down, and a new world shall arise from their ashes. But there shall be no subterfuge this time. You go to Ceasa as my plenipotentiary, carrying the full authority of our crusade."

More underlings appeared, carrying items of apparel. As they took off his old clothes and dressed him in the new—fine silks, embroidered with gold and silver stitching—Pumash looked to the *Manalish*. "And when Ceasa has fallen, will I then be free?"

The *Manalish* placed the tip of his forefinger on Pumash's forehead, pressing the callused pad into his flesh so hard it felt like a bruise was forming. "When you complete your task, we shall *all* be free. So it is written, so it shall be done."

The *Manalish* pulled back his hand, but Pumash still felt the pressure on his brow. It flared with a fierce heat. Pumash tried to reach for the spot, but the grey-shrouded underlings held his arms fast. The burning sensation lasted only a few seconds. As it faded, a dizziness came over him.

Pumash was escorted out of the chamber and left at the threshold, where Deemu waited.

"Your belongings are packed, Master," the servant said. "We shall depart at once, yes?"

Pumash managed a shallow nod. His senses were slowly returning. He ran a hand down his chest, feeling the rich fibers of his new garments. "Yes. At once."

Deemu took his elbow and aided him up the passageway.

CHAPTER THREE

Horace leaned over, hands on his knees, as he struggled to calm his pounding heart. His first four magical jumps had landed him somewhere in a desert; no sign of civilization, just sand and sun.

After camping out on the wastes for the night, he had tried again. His first jump of the day had carried him up into the middle of the sky, looking down from a height of several thousand feet. Flailing his arms and legs, he had fought to weave the transporting spell again, as the wind whipped past his ears and images of a messy death crowded his brain.

That next hurried jump had carried him here, inexplicably—another spot in an unknown part of an unknown wasteland. Dry, cracked earth stretched before him to the horizon, dotted with withered trees and occasional mounds of red stone. *Great. At this rate, I won't even be able to find my way back—*

The thought vanished as Horace turned and spotted a long ribbon of brown water running through the countryside behind him. It had to be the Typhon River. And there, just a couple of miles downriver, rose a great city. He was sure he had never seen this one before. Its skyline was clustered with a forest of tall, slender towers capped with rounded domes. Its walls were high white stone that gleamed in the sunlight of midday. Was it Yuldir?

Bracing himself, he channeled his *zoana* again. Just enough for a short hop. An instant later, he appeared atop a short rise of bare rock less than a mile west of the city. A large crowd of people swarmed outside the tall gatehouse. The horde surged back and forth like a wild animal, and Horace knew, even from this distance, they weren't human. Not anymore. He could almost feel their feral malice from here. Atop the battlements, soldiers fired spears and arrows down into the mob with little visible effect. The gates were holding, but the strained timbers showed they could buckle at any time.

Horace was trying to determine how best to alleviate the siege when a few undead on the outer edge of the swarm turned in his direction. Like iron

SUN AND SERPENT

filings drawn to a lodestone, more and more undead faced toward him. Then, with long, loping strides, they started in his direction. *How in the hell . . .?*

Fighting down a surge of panic, Horace opened his *qa* and drew as much power as he could stand. There were at least a thousand undead in the crowd. He knew how to destroy them individually by unbinding the Shinar that animated them, but it would take far too long to deal with them one by one. Instead, he decided on mass immolation.

Fiery meteors rained down on the pack. The tiny balls of fire and stone exploded wherever they landed, sending red-hot shards tearing through corrupted flesh and bone in all directions. The undead fell in droves, writhing silently as they were ripped apart by burning shrapnel and consumed. They didn't try to flee, but simply kept crawling toward him until they were no more.

When the last of the undead were finished, the firestorm ceased, leaving behind a gulf of silence. Horace sent a fierce wind to clear a path through the sea of glowing ash as he walked toward the city. He made no attempt to hide from the sentries watching from the ramparts, trying to appear as unthreatening as possible. *Sure. As unthreatening as a person who just incinerated hundreds of walking corpses could look.*

Horace didn't really know what to expect. A shower of arrows? Pots of boiling oil? What if they refused to open the gates for him? Should he force his way inside? *I am here to negotiate. Don't piss them off unnecessarily.*

To his surprise, the gates opened. Then, a line of war chariots rolled out, shaking the ground with their iron-shod wheels. Spearmen stood in the cars behind the drivers, weapons raised to throw. Horace stopped. He was tempted to surround himself in a bubble of hardened air but did not. In fact, he let go of the *zoana* entirely and raised his hands, palms open, as the chariots approached.

At the last moment, the war vehicles swerved and drove in broad circles around him. The spearmen threatened but did not throw. Horace stood calmly amid the tumult. After a few circuits, the chariots slowed and turned inward. Men in deep red robes rode out from the city on coal-black horses. Their bald heads shone in the sunlight, red tattoos flashing like bloodstains. Brothers of the Crimson Order.

Horace tried to read their expressions as they approached, but their smooth faces revealed nothing. Ghostly fingers tickled the back of his neck—they were holding onto *zoana*, but they weren't wielding it. Horace took that for a good sign. He expected one of them to address him. Instead, they merely surrounded him, taking up positions like an honor guard but decidedly less than friendly. One Brother—a middle-aged man with thick gray eyebrows and an old scar running down the left side of his face—gestured toward the gates. With a congenial nod, Horace resumed his walk, and the entourage accompanied him.

As Horace passed through the gates, he was reminded once again how each city of the empire was unique in its own way. Erugash had been grand on a scale he had never seen before, with its massive palaces and monuments. Thuum was dedicated to its death cult. Yuldir was plainly different from either of them. First, its buildings were tall and slender, favoring delicate towers over stolid edifices. Narrow bridges high above street level spanned the gaps between some of the towers, making Horace dizzy just looking at them. Most of the homes and towers were built from milk-white stone. Tiny flecks glinted in the sunshine, creating millions of tiny sparkles throughout the city.

Few people walked the central boulevard down which the procession passed. Those Horace saw were much like the other citizens of the empire, copper-skinned and dark-haired. Their clothing may have been a little finer, with many of the men favoring white chitons and long skirts. The women wore slightly more colorful attire, adding dyed scarves and belts made from linked bangles. He saw no children, but reasoned they were likely being kept indoors while the 'foreign devil' traipsed past.

The thoroughfare followed a long curve around the rising slope of a hill. As they completed the turn, a tower sprouted from the top of the rise. It was huge and glorious, lofting higher than the city walls. Flying bridges connected the central bastion to six satellite towers, stationed equidistant around the middle hub. All seven towers were made from stone so translucent Horace took it for ice at first. The entire structure gleamed like a crystalline sculpture.

As they climbed, Horace spotted another building off to the east, even larger and more imposing. A ziggurat of yellow granite, it was capped by a golden dome that reminded him of the Sun Temple at Erugash. Despite the heat of the day, his skin pebbled at the memories.

In the grand court surrounding the palace, the brigade of Crimson Brothers dismounted and, surrounding Horace on foot, escorted him inside. The entire procession had a ritualistic quality that didn't make him feel any more comfortable. He was also faintly surprised they hadn't tried to restrain him in any way, or even question him. So, he kept quiet as he followed them into the central tower.

The interior was every bit as impressive as the outside. Light poured into the atrium from carved windows, shining on vivid frescoes covering the walls and a brilliant mosaic of cut glass cemented into the floor. Guards in silver mail flanked a grand archway into a long hallway.

The procession swept down the hall and into a large, round chamber. The chamber itself was three stories tall, with raised observation balconies where men and women in fine garb stood, watching quietly. A handful of old men in the silken robes of elder viziers and priests stood on the floor. All turned to watch Horace's arrival. As he entered the hall, Horace suddenly realized he did not know anything about the king of Yuldir, not even his name. The man in the throne was younger than Horace had expected, looking to be in his early thirties. His oiled hair was pulled up into a tight bun, held in place by long pins. He wore an unusually large number of necklaces around his slender neck—all gold, inset with sparkling jewels. The piece that immediately caught Horace's attention was a yellow orb the size of a fist, surrounded by a radiant corona. That, combined with the prominent temple outside and Crimson Brothers escorting him, made Horace feel like he was back in Erugash again. He looked to the priests standing on either side of the king, closer than anyone else. That did not bode well.

As Horace was brought before the throne, the Crimson Brothers stepped back to form a wide circle around him, but he could still feel their hold on the *zoana*. They were ready to pounce if he showed any sign of danger. He wondered idly if they would act first to protect the king, or their hierarchs on the dais.

A majordomo called out, "All hail His Royal Magnificence, Merodach et'Dazur, fourteenth king of Yuldir, Son of Amur, and Master of the Middle Cataracts."

Horace tensed for a moment. He didn't want to bow to this Akeshian king, but he was also conscious of the fact that he was here to negotiate. So, he settled for a deep nod that he hoped conveyed both respect and independence.

The king spoke first. "So this is the notorious *Belzama*. Murderer of a queen. Destroyer of Erugash. Slaughterer of the Akeshian people."

Horace frowned at those words and forced himself to remain calm. "I am Horace Delrosa of Arnos, Majesty. I don't know what you may have heard about me, but—"

"So, it is true," the king interrupted. "He does not bear the immaculata, just as the stories say."

"It is a sign of demonic possession, Your Majesty," the older of the two priests said. "This one is clearly their agent, sent to deliver us to ruin. Destroy him now is my advice."

The younger priest on the dais stepped forward. He was tall and strongly built. A string of gold beads hung from his belt. "We have heard much, Lord Horace. Enough to know you are an enemy of the empire."

"Then you are misinformed, Your Excellency." Horace dipped his chin slightly, indicating cautious deference. "With all due respect."

"How dare you?" another of the courtiers growled. He was an old man in a robe of deep burgundy. His bald head sported no tattoos, but instead was dotted with liver spots. "You should grovel on your belly before our holy lord!"

"I didn't come here to trade threats. I am here to offer you a truce."

Several of the viziers chuckled, some laughing openly. Neither of the priests so much as smiled.

The king wore a thoughtful expression. He tapped on the arm of his throne. "We need no truce. You are our enemy, and you have delivered yourself into our hands. If you are disposed of, the threat is ended."

"I am not the threat," Horace said. "I did not kill Queen Byleth or destroy Erugash. I did not conquer Nisus and Chiresh and the rest. I am not the wolf lurking at your door. Look just outside your gates, Majesty, and see the ashes of your true enemy. The Dark King will not rest until all of Akeshia is destroyed, until every man, woman, and child is corrupted into an undead mockery of human life. None of us can stand against this terror alone."

Horace waited as all eyes turned to the king. After several long seconds, with only the soft shuffle of feet and rubbing fabric to fill the huge chamber, the king regarded the two priests standing beside him. "Lord Thuvan, what is your perspective on this issue?"

Horace expected the older priest to reply. Instead, the younger man stepped forward. His gaze was cool and steady, like the eyes of a hawk on the hunt. "The Temple has placed a fiat on this man's head, Majesty. The faithful should do all in their power to bring him to justice. There can be no doubt of that."

Horace braced himself for an assault. The Brothers would attack first, opening with their most powerful sorcery. The soldiers would charge next, hoping to finish him off. Would the king participate? Horace started to reach for his *qa* in preparation.

Then Lord Thuvan continued, "However, matters have changed since the events in Erugash. The western and central cities have all fallen. But for the power of our sorcery and stalwart soldiers, Yuldir herself might be counted among the conquered. Majesty, I contend that perhaps the arrival of this man—hated though he might be—is fortuitous."

The king leaned forward, resting his chin on his fist. "As in . . . divinely inspired?"

"Perhaps," Lord Thuvan replied. "We could put it to the test."

"How so?"

Horace risked royal displeasure by cutting into the conversation. "What test?" He steeled himself for the answer, sure he would not like it.

Lord Thuvan waited until the king nodded, and then explained. "If you can perform a task for us, then it could be considered evidence that you have been sent to aid us in this dire time."

Horace bit back the temptation to tell the priest to go bugger himself. "You have a task in mind?"

Lord Thuvan turned to face the throne. "Majesty, when Nisus fell, the temple lost one of its most valuable relics—the Orb of Heaven. If this man would prove his intentions of peaceful alliance, he should bring the relic back to us."

"A relic?" Horace said. "In Nisus? That's insane. I won't risk my life to win you some religious bauble."

Lord Thuvan smiled at Horace, though there was no joy in his gaze. "The orb is no mere bauble. It is an artifact of great power."

"It's a weapon?"

"A reservoir of Amur's divine potency," Lord Thuvan corrected. "With it back in our possession, we will be in a much better position to rid the empire of this Dark King."

He did not include the phrase "and other threats," but Horace could read it in his mannerism. *Fine. I'll get back your toy, and we'll fight Astaptah together. After that, we shall see who rids the empire of whom.*

The king stood up. "It is decided. The foreigner shall obtain the Orb of Heaven from Nisus and return it here. If he can do this, we will entertain a truce between our city and the rebellious faction."

The court's members bowed deeply as the monarch walked out of the chamber. Horace made another nod of respect, but otherwise kept his posture. Most of the rest of the court left through the front entrance, leaving Horace alone with the Crimson Brothers, a few guards, and Lord Thuvan.

"You don't really believe I can get this relic back, do you?" Horace asked. "This is a just an easy way to see me killed without doing it yourself."

The young hierarch walked around the throne, eyeing the gilt-encrusted seat as if it held a great secret. "You may not be aware of this, but the king is my cousin. We grew up together. Of course, he wasn't called Merodach back then. Did you know it's forbidden to address a king by his former name? An offense punishable by public execution."

Horace rested his foot on the first step of the dais. The Crimson Brothers shifted to follow his movements but did not interfere. "Nisus is just a tomb now, crawling with the living dead. What makes you think I'll go?"

Lord Thuvan gave him an appraising glance. "I think you no longer have a choice."

Horace forced himself to smile through his indignation. "You would be wrong. I came here in a gesture of good faith, to make a proposal to our mutual benefit. You must have heard what is happening in the cities that have fallen to Ast—" He caught himself. "The Dark King. This is a matter of survival. We can work together, or we all die."

"Exactly, Lord Horace. We understand each other."

Horace stared at the priest, trying and failing to read the blank expression presented to him. "So, you are willing to die if I won't give in to your demand?"

"The king has spoken. The relic is housed in an underground vault. I will give you directions on how to find it and pass the safeguards."

"What safeguards?" This plan was getting worse by the moment.

"Defenses placed around the vault for its protection. Once inside, take care with the relic, Lord Horace. As you say, this is a matter of survival."

As Lord Thuvan detailed the vault's protections, Horace calculated the time available. Yuldir's soldiers had to leave within the two days if they were going to meet up with the rebels in time. Otherwise, they might miss the attack on Ceasa. Two days to get to Nisus, get this holy toy, and return. That was cutting it close.

"Do not touch anything else within the vault," Lord Thuvan said when he had finished his instructions. "There are curses on the temple's property that would blast your soul to slivers."

Horace nodded. The sooner he started this enterprise, the better. "Fine. I'm not interested in your treasures. Anything else?"

"Go with the Sun Lord's blessing."

Lord Thuvan reached up as if to touch his forehead, but Horace stepped back. "Thank you."

Lord Thuvan gave a shallow nod, and then departed the chamber, leaving Horace alone with the Crimson Brothers. The red-robed wizard-priests fell in around him once again, and then turned as a single unit toward the exit. Horace did not turn with them.

Giving the nearest brothers an insolent wink, he seized the *zoana* and wove it swiftly into a spell. He felt their power surge, but he was gone before they could react.

Along the southeastern border of Mehulha in the vast swampy delta at the headwaters of the Murgis River was a small village. The cluster of twenty or so mud-daubed huts had no name. The people living there were fishing folk for the most part, with a few hunters and root-gatherers among them.

Out behind the hut of Sag-Huar, the village's only priest, was a stand of moss-covered willows. As old as the swamp itself, according to the legends, that was where the bodies of villagers who had died were buried, deep in the wet mud under cairns of stones to keep their bones from floating away.

Since he had been a young boy, Three Moons had been drawn to those dark boles and the spirits who whispered to him from the muddy depths beneath their roots. On many a moonlit evening his mother had caught him down by the willows, talking to the darkness. Of course, it terrified her, enough to thrash him every time she caught him out by the willows. But one day, old Sag-Huar stopped her when she was beating Three Moons outside the door of their hut and asked why.

"He is possessed, Holy Man," she replied. "I beat the demons out of him." And she held up the sheaf of reeds to show him.

"No, woman. He is blessed," the old priest said. "The spirits of the next world speak to him. This is a gift from the Gods."

Three Moons looked up at his mother, and she looked down at him. "No, Holy Man. If the Gods want him, I will beat them out of him, too."

And she resumed the thrashing.

On his tenth naming day, Three Moons left home one night while his mother slept the sleep of the rush-wine in the arms of her possibly-fifth husband. He stole out like a shadow and he never went back.

He was a clever boy who knew how to catch fish with his bare hands and how to avoid the deep pools where lizard-fish lurked and the sticky mud that pulled you down and down until you drowned. He had never been more than a few miles from his village, but now he wandered far. He followed the sun, putting his back to it in the morning as its early rays stabbed through the swamp's green canopy. At midday he stopped to rest in the shade, drinking from clear streams and eating whatever he could find or catch. Then, as the sun started its homeward journey, he followed it to the horizon. From morning to nightfall, for so many days he lost count.

The spirits came with him. Whether curious about his sojourn, or drawn to something within him, they gathered around him as he trekked, so that he never felt lonely. They whispered things to him he would have never known on his own, like how far the wind that brushed his face had traveled that day or how to start fire with a special gesture. They played games with him, taking his mind off his weariness or thoughts of his mother, who must have loved him in her own way, certainly.

Eventually, he found the edge of the swamp and saw, for the first time, a wide plain of grass. And he thought to himself, "This is the entire world."

However, the spirits breathed to him, "No, child. This is just the beginning. Wait and you shall see more of this world and the next than you have ever dreamed."

For some reason, their words caused a chill to settle in his chest, but only for a moment. Then the bright sunshine coming down through the clear sky warmed his head, and he ran out into the sea of grass with the wild abandon of youth. But exuberance quickly gave way to worry as the boy discovered that this new world contained new challenges. Although the grasslands didn't have any lizard-fish, he heard the howls of strange animals at night and shook with fear. Finding water became a problem, and he might have died of thirst if not for the helpful spirits who found hidden springs and streams for him to drink from.

As he struggled to survive, Three Moons kept following the sun, until a new discovery crossed his path. He had never seen a road before, but his invisible guides told him what it was. At their suggestion he stepped upon it and headed north. That was how he came to the bustling trading town of Dawadar. Having never seen so many people living together, or buildings made of brick and stone, Three Moons wandered the streets for hours in amazement. He might have fallen victim to the city's many child-takers and ended up as a brothel slave. Instead, he was discovered by fate.

"Hey, boy."

He turned at the voice coming from the dim doorway of a tavern house and saw a short man standing there. A host of rich smells came from the doorway. He recognized one as wine, but the rest were alien and intriguing. The man had a bright red shirt, but otherwise his clothing was plain, and he wore no shoes. He was leaning on a broom. "Hey, boy. You know how to sweep a floor?"

Three Moons nodded.

"Here. I'll pay you two brassies a day and you can sleep in the back room. Deal?"

Those words changed the path of his life. With another nod, Three Moons accepted his first job.

He worked for Renatta for six years. He cleaned up and helped serve the customers, cooked and carried jars of liquors, but most of all he learned the ways of city people. He learned how to know when someone was lying to him and how to hide his own lies, how to duck away from a cuff and swear like a trader's drover, and how to drink potent spirits all night long. He might have stayed there for the rest of his life if Renatta hadn't burned his tavern down, killing himself in the process. The spirits whispered that Renatta's soul had died long before the fire, extinguished by a dire pain from his past. Three Moons had not wanted to understand what they meant, but he had, and that told him how much he'd grown since leaving the swamp.

So, out on his own again, Three Moons looked for another home, preferably one where he could drink and swear and lie with the best of them. When the recruiting sergeant for the Black Lions mercenary company found him, Three Moons didn't need the spirits' advice to tell him this would be a natural fit. He signed up before the sergeant even finished his enrollment speech.

Picking through his memories, Three Moons thought back to the boy he had been. All these years later, nearly a century by his reckoning, he could scarcely believe the winding path his life had taken, the choices that had brought him to this time and place. He wondered what the people of his homeland were thinking now, as they looked up at the eternally dark heavens. Did they cower and pray to their hundred thousand gods? Or were they already gone, victims of the never-ending hunger of civilization, the insatiable need to expand and devour all within its path?

Sitting on the ground beside his steed, Three Moons watched the combined army of rebels and Thuumian troopers as it crossed the Typhon. They were at a natural ford roughly midway between the city-states of Yuldir and Semira. The land on the other side of the river was just as barren as the country they had been passing through. Playful heat spirits danced above the hard-packed earth.

Watching the crossing of soldiers, horses, and materiel across the brown waters, Three Moons listened to the conversation of the army's commanders.

"—don't think it's worth the risk," Emanon said. A long scarf was wrapped around his forehead, the ends trailing down his back. "You shouldn't have let Horace go."

Jirom drank from his canteen and plugged the vessel. "How could I stop him?"

Emanon patted the head of his spear, which hung in a saddle sheath by his right leg. "Make a set of *zoahadin* manacles. Keep him locked up until we need him."

Jirom grunted.

Emanon growled at him, "Damnit, Jirom. We're going to need him before we reach Ceasa."

"A premonition?"

"No, damn you. Just common sense. We keep acting like we're going to catch the Dark King with his breeches down around his ankles, but he's been outsmarting us since Erugash. He'll have defenses in place."

"That's why we have Moons."

Three Moons looked over where they sat astride their horses, overseeing the crossing. Past them, a pair of rebels dragged a corpse from the river, heaving it up onto the riparian banks. The body was covered in silt, but only slightly decayed. The top half of its skull was missing. The innards had been scoured away by fish and other water scavengers.

While Emanon stayed put, Jirom got down from his steed and went over to the corpse. "Undead," he announced. "It died violently."

"The carved skull was a giveaway," Emanon called back.

Jirom returned, wiping his hands on his leather jerkin. "It's covered in slashes and punctures. If this was carried down from Yuldir, it could mean the city is still holding out."

"You know," Emanon replies, "I'm getting really tired of your optimism."

Three Moons grunted at that. Both commanders turned to stare at him. "What?" he said. "It was funny."

They continued their conversation with lowered voices, and Three Moons gazed across the river. He hoped Horace was right, that the Yuldirans—if they were still alive—would be receptive to his offer of alliance. This entire venture was one misstep away from destruction. They still had to pass the city of Semira, which they knew had fallen to the Dark King. After that was Ceasa, the unconquerable heart of the empire. Three Moons hoped Jirom knew what he was doing. *He's doing the only thing he can, putting one foot in front of the other and hoping everything works out all right. Poor lad. That dogged determination was always his greatest strength, and his inescapable weakness. Sometimes following one foot after the other leads you over the edge of a cliff.*

Getting up from the ground and hissing as his tired joints protested at the sudden activity, he took his steed by the reins. It was time to cross over.

It took the army an entire day and a half of the next to cross the river. Fortune shone upon them, and they didn't lose a single person or beast. Once they were assembled on the western side, Jirom sent them marching again. Time was another enemy now.

They marched south, back into the wastes. Beyond the Typhon's life-giving waters, there were few farms or settlements except for tiny enclaves clustered around natural springs where the earth was fertile enough to support life.

As always, Jirom was amazed that the Akeshians could build such a powerful empire, and yet most of their country lay unclaimed. Except for a few scattered tribes of herders and scrub farmers, most of these vast lands were empty. Akeshia's culture was concentrated in and around its cities. *Around its temples and palaces.*

That was the heart of the problem. An entire empire revolving around dueling seats of power, with the *zoanii* ruling and the rest of the people living in thrall to their desires. It was a cancer at the center of the realm. Jirom realized he had been fighting against such unmerciful authority his entire life, through his days as a sellsword, then a gladiator, and up to joining Emanon's rebellion. But this battle was different. Now he was fighting to save an empire. Was that why he couldn't find any peace with this decision? Even if they won, what would they accomplish? *If we win, we get to keep on living. That's something.*

Jirom turned around in the saddle to stretch. The army marched behind him in a decent semblance of a military column. *They can march, but how will they fight?*

In a departure from conventional military wisdom, he had mixed the ranks, combining seasoned veterans and new recruits in each company. The risk was that the greenhorns might buckle when they got into trouble and the units would crumble like weak brick under the first solid blow. He was gambling they would prove more resilient than that. *There are no perfect plans before a battle.*

That was something a former commander had told him a long time ago. You did the best you could, and the rest was in the hands of the Gods. He'd fought in enough battles to sense the truth in that sentiment. However, miniscule details about unit composition and training regimes kept him up at night. And Emanon's snoring didn't help.

Jirom's love rode near the middle of the column. He was gesticulating broadly as he talked to the soldiers. *Probably regaling them with war stories.*

Emanon caught his gaze and cantered forward.

As he turned back around, Jirom considered what might lie before them. Ceasa wasn't just another town; it was the center of the world. According to the stories, the capital had been conquered only once—by the barbaric Akeshii tribes as they swept over the previous empire. And he had to figure out a way to take it, without harming too many of its citizens. *And possibly without Horace.*

"Ralla's company wants to call themselves the Desert Hawks," Emanon announced as he rode up. "I was telling them about our first campaign at Omikur, how all the Akeshian legions had a nickname. The Hands of Death. The Bloody Fifth. The Queen's Legion." He laughed. "A couple of the men were talking about putting together a banner. Did you ever think this ragtag band would ever hoist colors?"

"We're a long way from Omikur."

"You can say that again. What are you brooding about? Going over your plans for the attack? Honestly, I never truly believed I would see this day. We're going to lay siege to the capital!"

"What happens if we win?"

Emanon clasped him by the arm and squeezed. "We'll change the course of history, love. No more slavery. No more kings and emperors. Just think of it—a free society of equal men."

"It doesn't sound possible."

"Not possible?" Emanon laughed. "We're on the verge of a new era."

"I've seen too much of this world to believe we can all live in harmony, Em. Violence and greed are bred into us from the womb. If we win this war, then we'll just be the next in a line of warlords that stretches back to the beginning of time. We'll tear down their statues and temples and replace them with our own. But the results will be the same. The powerful decide, and everyone must obey. At the point of a sword, if need be."

Emanon shook his head. "I've never heard you talk this way."

"Perhaps because I never believed we would get this far either." Jirom took a deep breath and held it for a moment before letting it out. "There was freedom in being the thorn in the lion's paw. We didn't have to be responsible for anything but ourselves. Now we're facing the most dangerous foe any of us can imagine, and I'm just as afraid of victory as I am to fail."

Before Emanon could answer, a call came from ahead. A forward scout was signaling caution. Jirom glanced at Emanon. *What now? Another ruined village? Or has the enemy made contact? If the Dark King has skirmishing parties out this far from the capital, we'll never get there.*

Jirom scanned the landscape. The ground became more broken as the rolling plains rose to meet a chain of barren hills, taller and rougher than anything else they had passed since leaving Thuum. The only living things in sight, except for his soldiers, were a pair of raptors circling high above. Jirom wished he could see what they saw.

Following the scout, they climbed through a gap between two bare hills and reined up suddenly as they reached the top of the narrow pass. Emanon swore and pulled his stallion back so hard it started to rear up. The land fell away just beyond the summit, plunging down in a steep cliff wall as if a giant blade had come down from the sky and cleaved off the southern half of the hill chain.

Beyond the plunge ran a vast canyon as far as Jirom could see, filled with dense, dark jungle. Treetops swayed with the wind as strange, bestial calls rang out beneath the leafy canopy. The entire woods had an alien cast to it. The leaves rippled in alternating colors of black and pale blue. What little of the ground below could be seen was dark and heavy with undergrowth, sprouting splashes of deep red here and there like pools of fresh blood.

"What the fuck happened here?" Emanon asked. "How did a forest just appear in the middle of the nowhere? And what's wrong with it?"

Jirom had no answer. It was unlike anything he'd ever seen before. He looked beyond the chasm to the far horizon, where dark clouds smudged the sky.

"It's not natural," Three Moons said as he rode up alongside them with Captain Paranas.

The two Silver Blades shared a glance, and the captain nodded. "Aye. It reminds me of a place I'd rather not remember, if you take my meaning. It's too much like that other place to be a coincidence."

Jirom understood. The "otherworld" Three Moons had told him about, where the Blades had found themselves on their return from Omikur. After hearing about it, he had given Paranas permission to offer his men a full discharge with honors and hazard pay. He hadn't been surprised when every Blade declined the offer. These were professional men and women, each of them personally invested in this war. Still, he'd had to make the gesture, if only to partially assuage his own guilt. "How did it get here?"

"There are holes in the fabric of the world," the old sorcerer replied. "And they are getting bigger. Things are starting to cross over."

Emanon sighed and slapped at a biting insect on his neck. "So we go around. We'll lose a week. Maybe more."

Jirom got down from his horse and began taking his gear from the saddle—his pack, canteens, blanket, and the black shield that hung from the saddle horn. "No, we can't afford to lose the time. We're going through. The Blades and I will blaze a trail."

Paranas looked uneasy at those words. "I don't mind telling you, I don't like this idea. We barely escaped that other place, and we lost some good people in the process."

Emanon climbed down from his mount and handed off the reins to a scout. "You know Jirom. He never avoids a problem when he has the chance to smash right through it."

"I learned from the best," Jirom replied. "Em, I need you to stay with the army."

Emanon slid his spear from the saddle holster. "To hell with that. If you're going, I'm coming with you."

Jirom opened his mouth to argue, but then closed it. There was no use. "All right. We're going ahead on foot." He called over Seng, his scout leader. "Keep the army moving, but don't push them too hard. We'll leave signs of safe passage. Send a rider if you run into trouble, but otherwise we'll plan to meet up on the other side of this."

"Yes, sir. Any message for Master Horace, if he returns while you are gone?"

"Tell him to stay with the army, too." Jirom gazed across the obscured landscape. "Just tell him to keep everyone safe."

Shouldering their packs, they started down the steep slope.

The palanquin rocked from side to side as it traveled down the broad avenue, making Dasha slightly ill. She pushed open the curtain to get some fresh air, and immediately wrinkled her nose at the smell of refuse and crowded bodies that assaulted her nostrils.

SUN AND SERPENT

Outside, people lined the avenue. Not well-wishers armed with rose petals—these were refugees by their look. Wearing the only clothes they owned, holding sacks and baskets that held all their earthly possessions. Children with dirty faces pressed to their parents' legs. All of them staring at the procession as if they were watching something from another world. Dasha started to shut the curtain but stayed her hand. *No. These are my people. If I cannot face them, how can I call myself their princess?*

Putting on a brave smile, she waved. Gazes stared back at her—some hostile, others miserable, but most simply dull with the acceptance of their fate. A small girl broke free from the crowd and raced past the cordon of soldiers. A woman cried out, her hand grasping toward the child, but she was held back by a wall of spears.

Dasha threw open the door of her litter and jumped out. A shock ran through the thin heels of her slippers as she landed on the hard stones of the road, but she caught the little girl one step before she ran in front of the palanquin. Elia barked a command to halt, and the bearers lurched to a stop. Clutching the child tightly, they both looked up at the large men who had almost trampled her.

Elia knelt beside Dasha and gently pried the child loose. "Come, girl," she growled, a little too harshly in Dasha's opinion. "Back where you belong."

The child grasped a lock of Dasha's hair as she was pulled away. Through the layer of grime and snot, there was a tiny smile. Dasha smiled back. Then Elia was carrying the child back to the sidewalk, past the spears to her desperately waiting mother. *Back where you belong.*

The words stayed with Dasha as she climbed back into her litter seat. As the palanquin got moving again, Elia came over to walk beside the window. "I'll say it again. This is a bad idea."

"I want to see him," Dasha replied.

Elia shrugged, making her armor creak. "It's just an emissary. You've seen hundreds of them."

"This is the Dark King's emissary. They say he has the power to kill with a glance."

Elia bristled at that but said nothing.

They arrived at the Grain Gate. A wide area was being kept clear of people by the Imperial Guard, but they allowed Dasha's retinue to enter without hesitation. As Dasha got out of the litter, a tall man in ornate bronze armor hurried over and knelt before her. Several scars ran across the weathered face of her father's First Sword.

"Princess," he said, "the emperor will not be glad you are here. It is not safe."

Dasha walked past him. "It is your duty to keep me safe, Amrah. Come. Let us see the visitor."

She climbed the steps leading up the side of the massive curtain wall, with Elia and the First Sword following her. The weather was exceedingly pleasant today, a cool breeze taking the sting out of the sun's bright rays. As they left the odors of the city below, Dasha breathed deep of the clean upper airs.

The ramparts rose more than fifty feet above the street level. The broad walkway atop the wall was crowded with soldiers. They made way for her with many bows and whispers of "Blessed Princess." Dasha beamed at them with kindness as she looked for her father. She found him at the elevated platform situated directly over the outer gate, surrounded by members of his court. She wondered how some of the elderly viziers had made the climb. *Probably rode up on some poor slave's back.*

With Elia and Amrah in tow, Dasha strode up to the high tier. Courtiers bowed as they parted before her, some with sharp glances of disapproval. Dasha smiled in their faces, silently daring them to say a word.

She walked over to her father and dropped to her knees with head bowed low. "Father, I greet you."

There was a moment of silence on the platform. Then he patted her shoulder with a light touch. "Rise, Daughter."

As she climbed to her feet, her father admonished her with a stern gaze. Then, he looked past her. "Elia, she should not be here."

Elia remained on her knees, eyes on the stone bricks. "Yes, Majesty. I told her so."

Dasha took her father by the arm. "Don't be cross with me. I had to see him for myself."

SUN AND SERPENT

The emperor bent his head close. "Dasha, you should be with your mother and brothers in the tower."

She waited for him to send her away, but he only regarded her with sad eyes.

"Since you are here to see," he said, "then look for yourself."

They stepped to the battlements and peered over. Dasha could not contain the gasp that escaped from her lips. A seething mass of people surrounded the city. They appeared ragged and dirty. Many wore no sandals, and some even stood in the nude. The nearest of them stood a couple hundred paces from the city walls—not moving, but merely watching, as if they were waiting for something. She expected angry sounds, perhaps even bestial howls—but they made no sound that she could hear.

"Are they . . .?" she started to ask.

Her father nodded. "They are the legions of the Dark King. The living dead."

Tears formed in Dasha's eyes, but she held them back. She could not believe such things could exist. It broke every law of nature she had ever been taught. "But how?"

"Old sorcery, my child. Very old and very dark. And now this evil has come to our doorstep."

Dasha gazed out over the sea of the dead, wondering why they just stood there. "What stays them?"

Elia pointed out over the crowd. "Perhaps that one."

The crowd of undead parted silently as a figure passed through their ranks. He sat on a horse, a gaunt, pale thing with a stringy white mane. Yet, he wore finery such as is seen only in royal courts—a robe of black silk, trimmed in gold, with wide shoulders and a long skirt. Dasha thought he looked quite serene, to be surrounded by thousands of undead creatures. She knew at once this must be the emissary. The servant of the Dark King. For months the rumors of conquest in the west had been just that. Rumors. But now it had come to their door.

The man himself was not as frightening as she had imagined. In fact, he was rather unintimidating, with his receding hair and weak chin. She wasn't sure what she had expected—demonic horns and a halo of fire?—but it surely wasn't this.

The emissary stopped before the gates and looked up. For a brief instant, Dasha felt his gaze upon her, and she trembled as the power of that stare pierced through her. A gelid horror formed in her stomach. She clenched her teeth tight to keep it down. This was no ordinary man. *He has been touched by a god. Lady Ishara, help us.*

The emissary spoke, and his voice echoed above the wall as if he were speaking from the sky. "I am come in the name of the *Manalish*, King of Kings, Ruler of the World. Open your gates and bow before his superior majesty."

The viziers on the wall stirred, many of them making signs to ward off evil as they shot furtive glances at the emperor. Dasha, too, watched her father.

The emperor leaned farther over the battlements with pursed lips, and a line of spittle fell to the sloping base of the wall far below. "There is the only obeisance your master will ever receive from us, dog! Begone from my city, lest I unleash my anger upon you."

Loud thunder boomed directly overhead. Dasha's mouth fell open as black clouds formed above the city in what had been a perfectly clear sky just moments ago. Down below, the emissary had not moved. Then he lifted his right hand and extended a finger at the battlements.

"Now," he said, his voice rumbling like the oncoming storm. "You pay the price for your obstinacy."

The mass of undead suddenly surged forward. They raced toward the ramparts like a pack of feral animals, clawing and snapping at each other in their haste. Dasha didn't see the point in their attack. The city's walls were solid stone, thirty feet thick at the base, built to resist massive siege engines. What could a charge by unarmed people do? True to her prediction, the undead fiends merely collided with the stonework, scratching and jumping as they tried to scale it without success. The fear inside her subsided. Everything was going to be all right. Her father had the matter well in hand.

Dasha was looking to him with a smile when a fierce wind blew over the barbican. A horrible stench came with it, making her choke and retch.

SUN AND SERPENT

Dasha was hiding her face in her sleeve when Elia grabbed her and yanked her away.

Dasha struggled to free herself. "I want to stay!" she hissed at her bodyguard.

Elia didn't answer, but unceremoniously scooped Dasha up and threw her over one brawny shoulder. Dasha clamped her jaws shut as she was carried swiftly back to the stairs. Each step made her bounce against the hard leather shoulder pad. Dasha stopped fighting and remained still, but inside she was furious. *How dare she manhandle me this way! I am the daughter of the emperor! I'll have her beaten.*

Even as she fumed, Dasha craned her neck upward to see what was happening above. The sky had turned black. Small arcs of green electricity shot through the clouds, accompanied by a chorus of ominous rumbling. Soldiers had moved to surround the upper platform, but Dasha couldn't see what they were defending against. It was just a thunderstorm.

She and Elia finally reached the street. Dasha was turning to demand again that she be put down when the entire world vanished in a flash of emerald fire. A tremendous crash filled her ears, making her cry out in pain and fear. She clung to Elia as the ground shook.

Dasha blinked as her vision slowly returned. Elia put her down in a corner between the inner curtain wall and a stone guardhouse, and Dasha caught her breath. A stench of burnt ozone clogged her head. She glanced up and a plaintive cry stuck in her throat. Flames leapt from the top of the gatehouse barbican. Tall and green, they licked at the underside of the black storm clouds.

Dasha tried to push Elia to get to the stairs, but the bodyguard held her fast. "No, Princess. We must go."

"No! My father is up there! We have to—"

Elia shook her, hard. "Princess, everyone up there is dead. Now we must go, before they get through."

Get through? Dasha shook her head, not understanding. Then she heard it, a vicious roar riding just beneath the rumble of the storm overhead. It came from outside the walls. "But they can't . . ."

"Don't bet on it," Elia growled as she spun Dasha around by the arm and escorted her back to the palanquin.

They arrived at the procession to find all the bearers gone. The crowd had dispersed, too, leaving the plaza inside the gatehouse vacant. Elia didn't stop, but strode swiftly down the avenue, back toward the palace.

Dasha allowed herself to be dragged along. None of this seemed real. People were running in fear as more fires sprung up around them. Every few steps, Dasha snuck a glance over her shoulder back to the gates and flinched as she looked upon the inferno raging atop the highest tier. Elia was right; no one could survive that. *Father, forgive me. I should have stayed with you. We could have perished together and met the Gods, hand in hand.*

"Come on!" Elia barked.

Dasha started as she realized she had been turning around, trying to go back to the pyre. Terrified, she hurried alongside Elia and thereafter kept her gaze planted firmly ahead. The palace seemed so far away, and in the distant part of her mind that wasn't paralyzed by fear Dasha realized she had never walked this avenue before, even though she had lived in this city all her life. *Stop it! Focus on what needs to be done.*

She took a deep breath to clear her thoughts. With her father dead, then the power of the throne passed to her eldest brother, Ralan, who was sequestered with her mother. He would have to contact the army commanders and the surviving viziers to organize the city's defense, or possible evacuation if it came to that. He should also secure the imperial treasury, just in case. "Elia, we have to reach the citadel tower."

Another cacophony of thunder shook the city. Dasha flinched as bright green light flashed behind them. She turned and stood aghast. Lightning had ripped the main gates off their hinges, leaving a smoking hole in their place. A rising sound spilled from the newly made aperture, and Dasha's stomach clenched tight as she realized it was the undead horde. Most of the soldiers at the gate had been annihilated by the lightning blast. The few remaining, dazed and stumbling with disorientation, fell immediately as the living dead poured through the gap.

Elia grabbed her by the elbow and pulled. "Run!"

SUN AND SERPENT

They sprinted toward the palace. Dasha kept her eyes on the tall spires and gold-chased domes. She was breathing hard as they reached the palace complex. The gate wardens fell to their knees in obeisance when they spotted Dasha and her guard.

"Get up!" Dasha commanded. "Secure the gates after us. There are invaders in the city."

As the guards hustled to follow her commands, Dasha followed Elia across the broad green, past the gardens and arbors, to the palace proper. Inside the big bronze doors, the grand atrium was empty. They crossed the expanse and entered the maze of corridors and halls that filled the main floor of the palace.

Though she knew the way to the citadel tower by heart, Dasha found herself becoming disoriented, more than once about to make a wrong turn before Elia corrected her. Finally, they reached the second floor of the north wing, which held the imperial residence. As Dasha reached the top of the stairs, she smelled the thick stench of ozone and burning metal. She ran to the nearest window and looked up. At the end of a long, elevated walkway stood the citadel tower. Dasha's mind went blank as her gaze lifted to the pinnacle of the tower. It took several heartbeats before she comprehended what she was seeing.

The tower was burning. Its roof had collapsed, and smoke poured out from the shuttered windows. By the scorched stonework and burnt spars, she guessed what had happened. *A lightning stroke from the heavens. It killed them all, just like Father.*

Dasha stared, unable to think clearly. It wasn't until a rough shaking jolted her body that she came out of the fugue.

"Princess!" Elia shouted in her face. "We have to leave."

Dasha could see from the panic in Elia's eyes that the bodyguard thought she might do something rash, like throw herself on the smoldering remains. She took a deep breath. "Yes, we do."

Now she was the heir of her father, but she could not hide behind these walls. Ceasa was going to fall like the other cities of the empire. They had to escape. And she knew the way.

Dasha hurried back down the stairs and through the warren of hallways. They were empty, which disturbed her almost as much as the horrors she had witnessed this day. These corridors were usually filled with people—slaves, servants, friends, and family. Now they were abandoned.

As she and Elia entered the hallway leading past the audience chamber, Dasha spotted a young soldier, pacing back and forth across the polished floor. She called to him. "What is your name?"

The soldier saluted. "Second Trooper Vasha, Your Highness," he answered in a strained voice. His face was covered in sweat, with damp locks of hair curling down from the rim of his helmet. He looked so young, even though he was probably a few years older than her.

"Vasha, listen to me. There is terrible danger coming this way. We have to get out of here."

"I'm not supposed to leave my post, Highness!"

Dasha put on her firmest frown, the one she used when her siblings were being difficult. The briefest thought of them flashed through her mind, but she shunted it aside. "Vasha, I am commanding you to accompany us out of here. Do you understand?"

"Yes, Highness. But where are we going?"

"We need a way out of the city," Elia said in a low voice. Her eyes moved constantly, back and forth, and even up to the ceiling occasionally, as if expecting danger to come from any direction. Dasha had never seen her so nervous.

Dasha closed her eyes for a moment and focused, as her tutors had taught her. When she opened them again, she was calmer. "I know a way. Follow me."

Not waiting for Elia to argue, Dasha led the way down the corridor and around several turns, heading to the south wing. She wished she could have returned to her rooms to pack a few things, but there wasn't time. Images of the undead horde pouring through the city gates kept flashing through her mind, driving her to move faster.

"Where are we going?" Elia asked.

"Down to the cellars." Dasha pushed open the heavy oaken door to the kitchens. She had discovered this secret way as a child, playing with her siblings. In fact, Ralan had been the one to show her. *Poor, sweet Ralan. May the Gods protect and guide your spirit, brother.*

Blinking back tears, Dasha led Elia and Vasha across the cold stone floor of the huge kitchen. All the cooks and serving slaves were gone, too. Word of the catastrophe traveled fast. She opened another door leading to the pantry cellars and froze as she saw several people huddled together inside the tight passageway. A few wore iron collars. Dasha recognized a tall man in the back, Rould, the kitchen steward.

"Rould! We're leaving the city. Bring these servants along."

The steward's long face was drawn with fear. "Forgive me, Highness, but we must not. We wait for the emperor's return."

Dasha steeled herself to say the words. "My father is dead, Rould. My entire family is—"

With a single wail, the servants and slaves fell to the floor, weeping and clutching each other. Dasha reached down and tried to lift one of the slave girls back to her feet, but the girl only wailed louder and held onto the other slaves tighter. Their cries rose louder, until Elia took Dasha by the arm and pulled her away.

"It's no use, Highness. Forgive me, but we must go."

Dasha couldn't stop the tears this time. "But we can't leave them here! They'll die."

Elia pulled with more force. "We have no choice."

Wiping her damp cheeks, Dasha looked back at the huddled people as she was dragged away. She knew Elia was right, but it seemed like a betrayal. *I will avenge you all. Someday. I swear it.*

The passageway led past several larders before reaching a set of old, stone stairs. A lantern sat on a shelf beside an iron bowl filled with faintly glowing embers. Elia lit the lantern and held it high. Side by side, with Vasha behind them, they descended into the lower chambers.

It had been years since Dasha had come down this way. The passages seemed smaller than she remembered, and there were several branches she didn't recognize at all. Pretending to possess confidence she didn't actually feel, she led them along the main corridor. It arrived at another set of stairs, and they descended those as well.

Those stairs descended thirty feet deeper underground. At the bottom, the stonework of the walls, ceiling, and floor appeared far older than the corridors above, the sand-colored travertine replaced by blocks of gray stone shot through with thick white veins. The air was dry and cool, smelling of ancient mortar and dust.

Dasha tried to remember exactly the way her brother had shown her, but the details escaped her. She thought there should be a turn ahead, but as they walked for several minutes, she began to feel they had missed something. Just then, the passageway came to a junction shaped like a T. She hesitated a moment, then chose the left-hand route.

"Are you sure you know the way, Highness?" Elia asked. Behind her, Vasha looked around with a nervous expression.

"It's been a long time, but I think this is it. It shouldn't be much farther."

They passed several pairs of small stone cells, each them no bigger than a few paces on a side, all empty save for pieces of broken wooden slats and a few corroded bronze hoops lying in the dust. Then the passage came to an end, and Dasha suddenly remembered this place. She went to the wall. There would be a hidden catch somewhere low. She ran her hands over the rough stone until she found it. Pressing the small indentation, she heard a faint click and breathed a sigh of relief. *Thank you, Ralan.*

Vasha leapt forward as if eager to help. He and Elia pushed, and the wall swung inward on grinding hinges, revealing a dark tunnel beyond. Elia held the lantern high as they started to enter. Just as Dasha crossed the threshold into the hidden tunnel, the walls and floor trembled with a violent quake. Elia grabbed Dasha and hugged her against a wall as bits of gravel rained down on them. The tremor lasted only for a couple seconds, but it made Dasha's heart lurch in her chest. Far above them, she thought she heard a distant boom. "Was that thunder?"

"Perhaps," Elia replied, releasing her. "We should get mov—"

A second quake, longer and more vicious than the first, shook the passageway. The upper part of the left-hand wall shifted outward with a loud cracking sound, and several blocks of stone tumbled to the floor. A loud noise exploded behind them, as if a burst of thunder had erupted in the corridor at their backs. The concussion threw Dasha forward. She struck the ground hard on her side and slid across the dusty stones before coming to a stop. The lantern had gone out. She thought she had heard breaking glass, but couldn't be sure. Plunged into absolute darkness, she lay on the floor and shivered as more thunderous rumbles echoed behind her, but eventually they quieted.

It was several long breaths before she summoned the courage to call out softly. "Elia? Vasha? Are you there?"

At first, there was nothing, until Dasha started to panic as the beating of her heart pounded louder. Then, Elia answered, "I am here, Princess. Are you hurt?"

Dasha sat up, running her hands over her body and legs. Although her head felt a little funny, as if she had drunk too much wine, she found no injuries. "I don't think so. Where are you?"

"Over here."

Moving in the direction of the voice, Dasha crawled on her hands and knees. She found Elia buried up to her waist under an avalanche of loose stone and dirt. "Oh, Elia. Are you—?"

"I'm fine, Majesty. But I can't move my legs."

"Where is Vasha?"

"I don't know. He was behind me."

Dasha sat back on her heels and fought to stop tears from forming in her eyes. It was her fault the young soldier was dead. She had insisted he come with them, and now he was entombed under a ton of stone and earth. *Second Trooper Vasha of the Imperial House Guard. Go swiftly into the arms of the Gods and know their love for the rest of eternity.*

She took a deep breath. There was no use in dwelling on it now. Just as with her family, the time for mourning would have to wait. "Where is the lantern?"

"I don't know. I think it's somewhere under this rubble."

Feeling with her hands, Dasha started pushing aside the debris, but it was difficult working in the dark. Sitting back on her heels, she focused on her *zoana*. As Brother Kaluu had taught her, she reached gently for her inner core—her *qa*—and coaxed it open. As the power flowed into her body, she attempted to mold it into the proper shape. In her mind's eye, she formed a stick of Girru surrounded by a thin shell of Imuvar. It held firm in her imagination, but the power collapsed as soon as she released it. Gritting her teeth, Dasha tried again. And again. Yet, after several attempts, she still couldn't produce a light.

Biting her bottom lip, she made one last try. A tiny spark flared into life. In that moment, Dasha glimpsed Elia laying before her with a pained expression. Then a burning streak sliced along the inside of Dasha's right wrist. Crying out, she clutched her forearm. The spark fizzled out.

"Damn this and damn me!" she shouted as the tears ran down her face and winced as her voice echoed in the tight passageway.

Driven by frustration and anger, Dasha flung open her *qa* and seized the power. She shaped it ruthlessly, not caring for finesse or proper technique. Suddenly, light exploded in front of her, brighter than a hearth fire. The pain flared again in her wrist at the same time, but she was prepared for it and didn't allow it to ruin her concentration. A quick glance showed a cut that ran about halfway down the length of her inner forearm. Blood flowed from the immaculata, but not a lot.

Elia shaded her eyes against the stark illumination. The inkling of pride Dasha felt shuddered and died as she glanced around. The passage behind them was completely blocked. Fortunately, the way ahead appeared open, so they weren't trapped.

Taking a deep breath, and instantly regretting it as she coughed on stone dust, Dasha started digging Elia out. It took less time than she thought, and within a few minutes the bodyguard was able to wriggle free.

Checking her legs for injury, Elia glanced down the only route available to them. "Can you lead us out of here?"

Dasha stood up and dusted off her hands. "I think I can. Are you all right to walk?"

Elia climbed to her feet without assistance. She checked to make sure her weapons were in place. "Yes. Let's get moving before our air runs out."

SUN AND SERPENT

A chill went through Dasha at the thought of dying down here in the dark, gasping for breath. "Yes."

Side by side, they limped onward, led by the floating light.

CHAPTER FOUR

I n his dreams, the avenues of Ceasa were shrouded in gray mist. He searched their paved byways for another living soul, but the capital was empty except for him. The last mortal left alive. He heard a noise and turned, but there was only the mist.

Then, a voice spoke beside him. Had he been awake, Pumash might have jumped or shouted. But here in the dream world, he felt only calm as he shifted his gaze.

A ghul stood beside him. Not hunched or walking on all fours like an animal, but standing upright, arms dangling by its lean sides. It had been a man in life, older than Pumash, with a white, lice-ridden beard.

"You don't belong here."

The thing's voice was rough like gravel tumbling down a rocky slope, as if it hadn't been used in many years.

Pumash looked to the skyline, where jagged shards of broken buildings jutted into the black sky. "I have nowhere else to go. What happened here?"

Although he knew the answer, he wanted to hear it anyway.

"This came to be because of you, Pumash et'Luradessus. You are the harbinger of death."

"I did not do this! I was a slave, just like you. I was compelled."

"Were you?"

"Yes!" Pumash shouted, and his voice echoed down the misty avenue. "I didn't want this! I just didn't want to die."

"And now you live. Only you."

Only me. Will I wander this nightmare alone for the rest of eternity?

"I had a family," the dead man said. "I was a father. A husband. A brother. A son."

"I don't want to know," Pumash pleaded. "Please, leave me be."

SUN AND SERPENT

"You must hear. You must know. You are the last. You must bear our memories, so they will live on."

"Our?"

The ghul gestured, and Pumash turned his head to see more undead, thousands of them, tens of thousands, filling the streets. Suddenly, he was looking down from a great height, and saw all the world was filled with undead. All of them faced him as they murmured their secrets. The words filled his ears until his head began to throb. Sharp pain ran down the center of his scalp, as if his skull was set to split apart.

"I can't!"

He sat up, suddenly awake.

He lay in a pile of blankets on a large, tiled floor. Looking around, Pumash took in the opulent murals on the surrounding walls, framed in gold, the tall pillars, and finally, the throne atop a low dais. He tried to swallow, but his throat was too dry. He was in the emperor's throne room.

He took a deep breath and regretted it instantly as a loud belch tore loose from his gut. The taste of stale wine filled his mouth, making him gag. An empty jar lay beside him, nestled in the blankets like a babe in swaddling.

His head ached, and his stomach was on the cusp of violent rebellion, but Pumash managed to climb to his feet. He recalled the sacking of the capital. He had sat on his pathetic steed as the undead swarmed the walls, watching them clamber over the ramparts like ragged spiders. Then, the *Manalish* had arrived from a cloud of shadows. With a mere sweep of his hand, he broke down the gates, and the horde flooded inside, with Pumash and his Master following in their wake.

They strode along the main boulevard penetrating the city. The barrage of green lightning had ceased, but the black sky still rumbled here and there, threatening to unleash its power again at any moment. All around them lay destruction, as the sounds of slaughter echoed from inside the homes and shops lining the street. The roofs of several taller buildings had collapsed, their innards smoldering. Their empty façades clawed at his heart. *I thought I was numb to this, after Chiresh, Nirak, Thuum, Semira . . . But it pains me just as fiercely as the first time I laid eyes on a city I helped to destroy. People lived in these buildings. They raised families. Now, they are dead, or worse. This was the heart of our civilization. Now, it is just another festering necropolis. Gods, why do you allow this? What have we done to deserve such a fate?*

They came to the Emperor's Round. Pumash pulled his steed to a stop as the *Manalish* paused, and they both gazed up at the statue of the long-dead first emperor of Akeshia, immortalized in bronze. Although centuries old, the statue possessed the crisp details of a fresh cast, no doubt due to sorcerous preservatives. Pumash felt a stirring in his chest, of pride in his people and the progress they had made since those early days of empire.

The *Manalish* made a hooking gesture with his left hand, and the giant statue was wrenched from its base with a resounding crash that made Pumash flinch. They continued past the mangled heap of metal, on toward the city's center.

"Go to the palace," the *Manalish* had said. "Oversee the demolition of the last resistance and wait for my instructions."

Pumash had wanted to fall to the pavement and beg that he be allowed to end his service then and there. Even if it meant his death, he had wanted to tell the *Manalish* it would be preferable to the hell he was living. His cowardice had won out, and after the *Manalish* vanished into a dark portal that appeared out of nowhere, Pumash rode onward as he had been bidden.

Now he was here in the imperial domicile, a place he had once dreamed of visiting as a favored courtier with the ear of the emperor, feted and lauded for his contributions to the empire's fame. He was here, but there were no honors to be found, no glories recounted, no life at all. Just death and desolation. The palace was an empty shell, and he was its final caretaker.

He was thirsty.

"Deemu!"

When he received no answer, Pumash exited the throne room. Out in the intersection of several hallways, he paused. Straight ahead to the west would take him out of the palace, and he didn't want to go out there. He glanced to his right, in the direction of the imperial residences. *No, too many ghosts lurking in those halls.*

So, he turned to his left and started his search in the southern wing.

SUN AND SERPENT

Passing by open doorways that led into salons and meeting chambers, Pumash saw many signs of the carnage inflicted when undead had seized the capital. Streaks of dried blood across the floor and walls, broken artwork, shards of shattered glass, a handful of long black hair that looked as if it had been yanked from a scalp and then dropped on the polished marble tiles.

Pumash had paused at the opening of a side hallway leading toward the imperial art wing, wondering if Deemu had gone wandering in that direction, when a sound reached his ears. A crash and subsequent clatter, almost like breaking pottery. He froze. Were there still ghuls lurking about the palace? He shouldn't fear them anymore, but he did. Even under the *Manalish*'s protection, Pumash dreaded every encounter with the rotting foot soldiers of His army. The way they looked at him, black eyes gleaming with savage, insatiable hunger. One day, he was certain, they would slip loose from the Master's leash and descend upon him, tearing him apart with their clawed hands while their teeth sought out his innards. He shivered and hurried deeper into the southern wing, away from the clatter.

Pumash turned several corners in his haste before realizing he had entered the servants' wing. Doors leading to small, nondescript rooms lined the walls, interspersed with common areas. He was about to turn and retrace his steps when a new sound echoed from ahead. A sharp, rhythmic staccato, like metal striking stone. He inched forward, putting one hand on the knife he wore under his outer robe. The familiar wooden handle felt reassuring against his palm. His father had given him the knife the day he took over the family business, and he had worn it ever since as a reminder of that trust. *Father, thank the Gods you are not alive to see what has become of the empire, or your son.*

Swallowing his guilt, he stole around another corner to the entrance of a wide chamber and found Deemu standing in a kitchen. The sounds came from his manservant pounding on the stoppered top of a large clay jar with a wooden mallet.

"Deemu! What are you doing?"

Startled, the servant missed the jar on his next swing and slammed the mallet's head against the tabletop. Eyes wide, he held out a hand toward Pumash. "Master, please! Don't come in here."

Pumash ignored the request, relieved to find another living face in this mausoleum. His relief turned to horror as he saw the stains of gore covering the kitchen floor. It looked like the inside of a slaughter house. His gaze travelled over the blood and brown matter sprayed up the walls and settled on a foot—a human foot—laying in a corner. Bare and pale, it sat upright as if waiting for its owner to retrieve it. Several wooden boxes and an overturned barrel sat behind the door, arranged as if they had been barricading the entrance.

Then Deemu was at his side. "Master, you needn't see this. Come, let me take you away, and then I will bring you some wine."

Feeling numb, Pumash allowed himself to be led out of the gory kitchen, back down the hall to a small room decorated with a fine hardwood table and two chairs. A narrow window looked out into a courtyard of flowers and fruit trees. Heavy rain pelted the leaves and pavestones, creating a soft susurrus in the background.

Deemu set him in a chair and left. A minute later, the banging continued unabated.

As he sat and gazed out the window at the rain, Pumash wished he had some *kafir* to smoke. He used to smoke it with his concubines, but that felt like ages ago, in another lifetime. Now, he felt dead inside. Just another ghul in a dead city. He could sense the presence of the *Manalish*, not far to the southeast, like a dark cancer nestled near him. Southeast was the temple district, where the great fane of Nabu was located. *When He opens the last Seal, this nightmare will finally be over. The world will end, and I will find someplace to die. Me and Deemu. Where is that wine?*

"Deemu!"

"Coming, Master!"

Horace stumbled as he stepped out of the void. His balance reeled until his feet landed on solid ground. Twilight had fallen, draping its purple shroud over the plain outside a great city. *I hope that's Nisus.*

SUN AND SERPENT

It matched the descriptions he had heard. The outer walls were thick and gray, with several tall towers peeking over the top. The tallest structure was an obelisk near the eastern edge of the city. That, according to the priests in Yuldir, would be the temple of Amur. Thunderheads brewed overhead, accompanied by powerful gusts that tugged at Horace's clothing. Occasional droplets of rain pattered the ground.

From outside, the city appeared dead. No lights shone from the walls or high windows. Horace considered transporting himself with a short hop into the city, but he didn't want to draw attention. If the rumors were true, Astaptah was in the east, but that didn't mean the Dark King hadn't left someone, or something, behind to watch over his holdings. Best to go quietly.

Horace walked across the empty plain to the nearest gate. Half a hundred small buildings clustered outside the entrance—travelers' houses, farrier shops, and more than a few hovels. All bore the faint aura of neglect that empty buildings took on when they had been left vacant for some time.

The outer gate was open, the portcullis lifted and the iron-shod doors yawning wide. A wagon with a broken wheel slumped over in the middle of the entrance. Its cargo had spilled onto the pavement, torn oilskin tarps revealing wooden furniture and crates within. The street leading into the city was as empty as the shanty town outside. Dark windows stared out over the vacant streets. Scanning the skyline to reorient himself, Horace set off toward the obelisk of yellow stone.

As he walked the clay-paved avenues, he felt more and more uneasy. It wasn't just that the city appeared empty. An unpleasant sensation nagged at him, as if something obscene lurked behind every corner. Then he realized what it was. The Shinar was present here. And not just the void, but its negative aspect—that half of the dominion that destroyed and corrupted—radiated from everything around him. It curdled his stomach. He gazed at the buildings and peered down the alleys between them, but there was no movement. The wind carried a stagnant odor, tainted with decay. Horace had smelled it before, in the crumbling ruins of the undercity beneath Thuum. It brought back painful memories of Alyra. Grinding his teeth, he put her out of his mind and quickened his pace.

He found the house of Amur at the end of a long street of temples. It was strange walking past so much marble and gilt, all of it empty and silent. All the holy places showed signs of damage: broken stonework and shattered gates, toppled statues. All except for one. One of the smaller shrines along the avenue was still in pristine condition. The modest building of gray stone stood behind a wrought-iron fence, without the gaudy ornamentation of the other temples. No signs of life showed from the gray building, yet the presence of Shinar was concentrated here. Horace could feel it pricking at the nape of his neck, a seductive lure with a poisoned sting. He considered investigating, but then reminded himself he was on a tight schedule. The silence was absolute as he passed by the shrine.

At the end of the avenue, surrounded by high walls, the Sun God's sanctuary was the largest complex in this part of the city. The front entrance hung open, the bronze gates askew and half-torn from their hinges. Slipping through, Horace entered a long arcade. At a different time, during the day, back when the city was alive and thriving, this must have been a beautiful sight that inspired awe in the Sun God's adherents. Now, the rows of ornamental trees were withered and brown. Refuse and debris were strewn across the pavement, and deep shadows lurked in the tall windows lining the gallery.

The yellow granite walls of the obelisk caught the moonlight and bathed the area around it in soft luminescence. At its apex, the four sides came to a sharp point, crowned with a gold orb. A flight of steps led up to large doors, closed tight. Horace had been told the relic was held in a vault under the temple. He had directions to find it, but little else, and every moment in this necropolis made him reevaluate the wisdom of this plan.

The temple doors were tall and arched, their panels chased with gold leaf. A scene of people from many walks of life standing under the glory of a halo-crowned sun was cast on the valves in bas-relief. The faces of the graven images were beatific. Horace studied them for a moment, wondering what that felt like, to completely surrender to something greater than yourself, asking nothing, content just to bask in its glory. He had never felt that. As a boy, his father had taken him to visit the basilica in Avice. He remembered the somber majesty of the huge building, with its marble statues and vivid paintings on ceilings so high it had made him dizzy to look up at them. That trip had begun his love of architecture and art. Despite his appreciation for the grandeur of the churches and cathedrals, he had never felt a personal connection to the True Faith, certainly nothing like the people depicted here were experiencing. Was that a flaw in him? Or was that kind of faith an illusion? Something people professed to ward off the emptiness they felt inside?

He shoved the doors, and they swung open smoothly until they slammed against the inner walls. A dull boom echoed down the hallway. *If anyone is lurking about, they know I'm here now.*

The long corridor was sheathed in sand-colored granite. More scenes were carved into the stone walls, of a long procession of people walking alongside him. They carried sacks and boxes, some led oxen by leashes, all of them heading deeper into the temple. After about thirty paces, he entered a large rectangular chamber. Tall windows admitted dingy gray light from the outside, which shone on the vast open floor. A row of pillars ran around the edge of the chamber, their capped tops supporting the high vaulted ceiling, which reminded Horace again of those cathedrals of his youth.

Beautiful frescoes covered the walls. They depicted a throng of people, of many stations and castes, all facing the chamber's rear, where stood a colossal statue of a handsome youth sitting in a white throne. Its head was crowned in golden spikes. The statue held a sword in its left hand, and its right hand was held out, palm facing upward as if accepting a gift.

Horace stared at the effigy for several seconds before he noticed the dark stains on the floor before it. Blood, judging by the color and pooling. A lot of blood. It looked weeks old. Long smears led around behind the statue. Horace followed them, as they were in the same direction as his objective.

In a large niche behind the throne's pedestal were rows of urns in cubby holes. The trail of blood led to the middle of this antechamber and then stopped. Horace suspected he knew what had become of the body; it had risen and joined the legions of the Dark King. Right now, it might be marching on the capital, killing and eating its former countrymen.

Horace went to the door at the back of the niche. It was half ajar and opened to a flight of stone steps leading down.

Before he started down the stairs, Horace took what he considered a reasonable risk; he reached for his *zoana* to create a magical light. But he didn't anticipate what happened next. Instead of a tiny trickle of power, his *qa* burst open and a tidal wave of energy filled him all at once. Lights exploded around him in a flurry of pyrotechnics as he bit back a growling scream. His insides were on fire, the magic scouring his veins. Finally, he managed to slam his *qa* shut with a small hiss of pain. The energy that had poured through still thrummed inside him, but he held onto it, not willing to risk another explosion of power. Slowly, it bled off until he was able to draw a full breath without shuddering.

What in the name of Heaven had happened? He had created light globes countless times without any problem. It had to be this place. Once again, the negative half of the Shinar pressed around him. Something had happened here, not just the killing of thousands of people. That may have been a part of it, or a result, but some dire sorcery had been practiced here. He didn't know what or how to combat it, and now he wasn't sure if he could trust his own powers.

Instead of risking another magical light, Horace searched the chamber for a lamp or a torch. He found a small room off the main chamber that had a box of candles amid shelves of cleaning supplies. He took a handful and a striker and returned to the stairs. Lighting the first candle, he held it high as he started down.

The stairs were constructed of dressed stone, well-cut and cemented with smooth joints. The air below was cool and dry, heavy with the scents of old earth and clay. It reminded Horace of his imprisonment in the dungeons beneath the Sun Temple in Erugash. Worse than that, the sense of the Shinar grew stronger the farther he descended. The urge to grab hold of his *zoana* for protection clawed at Horace, but he resisted.

After several minutes of slow descent, the stairway ended, opening into a wide chamber. The candlelight strained to show its sides and back. Bas-relief images were carved into the walls, of people standing straight and rigid like rows of pillars. Several passages branched out in different directions.

Horace took a moment to get his bearings. Lord Thuvan had described this chamber in his directions. Horace was supposed to follow the passage directly opposite the stairs, ignoring the other corridors. However, he took a minute to walk past each tunnel entrance. Two led off to the left and one to the right. All were faced in antique brick, set without mortar. He peered down one of the left-hand passages as far as his candle would shine. The arched tunnel led straight into the darkness.

Feeling the pressure of time, and wanting to be away from this place as soon as possible, Horace went to the specified passageway. From outside, it looked no different than the others. But as soon as his light hit the interior, glowing sigils appeared along its walls. Dozens of them, in differing shapes and sizes. They were completely foreign to him, not even resembling the mystical symbols he had seen in the tomes from Erugash's archives. Horace reached out his hand. Magical energy played across his skin like the heat from a kiln. Lord Thuvan hadn't mentioned anything like this.

Steeling himself, Horace stepped into the passageway. The energy surrounded him but did no harm. Satisfied, he kept walking. The feeling of negative power persisted, setting his nerves on edge, but he didn't sense it coming from the glyphs—though he didn't know what their purpose was, so he couldn't discount them. *Why would the sun cult install chaos-infused images in their catacombs? No, these must form some sort of protection for the vault. The dark energy has to be coming from outside.*

Then it hit him. *Not outside the temple. Outside the world.*

His mind flashed back to his vision of the great void beyond the veil that separated the natural realm from the Outside. *The barrier is weakening. Power is leaking through. This is Astaptah's doing. But what happens when the barrier collapses altogether?*

Horace suspected he knew. The titanic beings he'd glimpsed in the vision would awaken and enter the world, bringing destruction with them. Everyone and everything would die. *The end of existence.*

A branch split off from the main passageway on the right. Horace paused at the opening. It led to another tunnel, this one without the glowing symbols. Seeing nothing interesting, he kept going down the main corridor. After another twenty or so paces, another branch split off to the left. Horace ignored it as well and kept to the directions. Eventually, after a hundred paces or so, he entered a large, circular chamber with a buttressed ceiling. The walls, ceiling, and floor were all smooth, continuous stone. On the far side, directly opposite the entry, was a massive door. A single portal of bronze, dark with age. There was no handle or pull that Horace could see.

He shone his light into the cracks around the edges but could find no gaps. The door fit snugly into the frame. Lord Thuvan had only suggested using care when trying to open it. At the time he had received his final instructions before leaving Yuldir, Horace had felt there was something more the archpriest could have told him. However, Thuvan had elected not to share it, and now Horace regretted not pressing him further. *It's just a door. Do what you came here to do.*

He pressed on the surface, trying to swing it inward, but the door would not budge. He tried pulling on it, but without a handle he couldn't find a grip. He dug his fingernails into the side joins without success. Breathing a sigh, he knew he would have to chance using his magic again.

Horace went to the center of the chamber. Dripping some wax on the floor, he set his candle down in the hardening pool, and then lit three more candles and set them around the chamber. Then he faced the door. Closing his eyes, he reached for his *qa*. He could feel the power behind it, pushing to get through. He wanted to harness that energy, not be incinerated by it. The thought returned to him that the sun priests had sent him here to die. Using that anger for fuel, Horace carefully pried open his *qa*.

The power filled him instantly. Gritting his teeth, Horace held onto the flow, funneling it into a narrow stream, and sent it questing toward the door. The valve was solid, far heavier than he had assumed. He found the hinges recessed into the left-hand side; they appeared whole and remarkably free of corrosion. Horace felt that the entire door would swing freely with only a bit of pressure, but there was something else holding it in place. Then, he found it—a trickle of *zoana*, so slight he almost missed it. The energy ran around the door and through it. It wasn't reinforcing the structure. It was something else. A detection alarm?

As Horace delved deeper, following the lines of power, a sound caught his ear. It came from behind him. He turned, but the entry passageway was dark, the glowing sigils having faded to blend in with the walls. Why hadn't he noticed that? The sound didn't repeat itself. After a few seconds, Horace turned back to the door and continued following the conduits of power. They led away, into something on the far side of the door. He couldn't determine the source. It seemed unlikely it was a sorcerer. They would have been living down here, trapped, for the past few months. Still, he supposed it wasn't impossible. This could some be kind of emergency shelter for the temple priests. If there were people inside, including *zoanii*, he needed to be prepared.

Horace found the points where the magical energy entered the door. Bracing himself, he snipped them all simultaneously with blades of Shinar. A muffled boom sounded as the door shifted in its frame. Horace was so focused on his task he almost didn't hear the other sound coming from behind him, a soft clack like leather-wrapped wood falling on stone. He turned his head, and almost lost an eye as a ragged claw whipped past his face. Horace fell backward and landed on his hip. In the dim light, his assailant looked more animal than human as it fell on top of him, fingers scratching and fleshless jaws snapping. Horace managed to get his legs up in time to kick it away, but the thing leapt back on him. He tried to merely catch it in a grip of hardened air, but the invisible bands snapped shut like a bear trap, snapping bones and rending flesh as it crushed the undead inward into itself. Horace released the power. What fell to the ground in a sickening pulp no longer looked like it could have ever been human.

Strips of bloody cloth, once yellow, were woven into the remains. This must have been one of the temple priests, slain and corrupted by Astaptah's power and force to serve him in death. Though Horace had seen plenty of these living corpses before, the sight still sickened him. And yet, he was caught in a moment of curiosity. How did these things continue to live with such wounds? If he tore off its arm, would it feel any pain? Did it need to eat to survive? He was just getting back on his feet when more sounds came from down the passageway. Lots of them.

Horace hurried to the door, which swung outward at his touch. Not bothering to look at what lay within, he ducked inside and pulled the valve shut behind him. It closed with a solid thud. He looked for a latch, but just like the outer face, the inner surface was smooth with no handle to hold it shut. He was still searching when the undead reached the door. He heard their claws scrambling across the bronze surface. The door swung outward an inch.

In frustration, he grabbed for his power again. He only wanted to generate enough heat to fuse to hinges shut. Instead, his clothes burst into flames. With a shout, Horace dropped to the ground and beat his robes with his hands. After a few terrifying seconds, he managed to snuff the flames. Smoke stinking of burning cloth and hair rose in a cloud around him. He performed a quick check and discovered he wasn't seriously burned.

He looked to the door, and the uneasy feeling returned in the pit of his stomach. The massive portal sagged in its frame like a wax tablet left out in the sun. Lines of molten bronze ran down the inner surface to pool on the floor. The entire valve glowed red-hot and radiated more heat than an oven. Horace swallowed hard. He could have just as easily incinerated himself. However, the magic had accomplished its purpose. The melted sections of the huge door were hardening again as they cooled. Now, nothing short of a battering ram—or another magical burst—would get through it. *I just hope there's another way out, or I'll be testing that theory.*

Moving away from the barrier, Horace glimpsed the chamber before the glow from the cooling door faded. Its walls were lined with shadowed niches holding objects he couldn't make out. The ceiling was low for such a large chamber, supported by rows of wide columns. As the glow vanished, Horace dug into his belt for another candle and lit it with shaky fingers. *Get a hold of yourself. You're almost there. Get what you came for, and then you can leave this damned place.*

Horace headed to his right, holding the candle high. The niches on that side held several objects on display. There were a variety of weapons and armor along with more mundane items, like curio boxes and crystal containers. Some of the niches held stacks of clay tablets. One was piled with lacquered pipes about four feet long and capped at both ends with wax plugs, and another was filled from top to bottom with shelves holding amulets and icons of the sun. The candlelight reflected from the many golden surfaces and twinkling jewels.

SUN AND SERPENT

As he explored, Horace tried to estimate the value of these treasures, but quickly gave up. Here was a king's ransom, all locked up deep under the temple of Amur. And if every temple in the empire had such a vault . . . His mind boggled.

The chamber stretched more than a hundred paces. Past the forest of columns, Horace finally found the back wall. In the center was a stone archway with a short corridor to another circular room. Four doors confronted him.

The walls between the doors were unadorned, dressed stone, abnormally plain compared to the ostentation of the rest of the temple complex. Horace examined each door in turn. His instructions were clear; he was to take the second door from the left and not to touch, under any circumstances, the other portals. Lord Thuvan had been quite adamant about that. When Horace had asked what lay beyond the other doors, the archpriest had become reticent.

"That is not your concern," Lord Thuvan said. "You will be on temple grounds at our sufferance. You must agree to respect our restrictions or forget any chance of an alliance."

"But if there is something dangerous—"

"There is nothing dangerous within the vaults, as long as you follow my instructions to the letter. Do you understand?"

"Yes, but—"

Lord Thuvan leaned closer, forcing Horace to meet his eyes. "Do you swear it? That you will not deviate from my directions?"

Horace had sworn, on his "everlasting soul and hope for salvation"—the archpriest would accept no other vow. Now, facing the doors, Horace held to his oath. As much as he wanted to see what the temple hid behind the other doors, he went to the one he was instructed to open. According to Lord Thuvan, there was no security measure on this door, but he was dubious after what had happened so far. Bracing himself, he placed his hand on the handle. The bronze was cool to the touch. Did he feel a slight vibration in the metal? Maybe it was his nerves. He lifted the latch.

The door opened into a smooth tunnel with slightly rounded corners, almost like a natural tube. It ran straight for a dozen yards before entering a high chamber. More treasures were displayed here, along the sides like a museum showcase, but Horace looked past them to a tall exhibit at the far end. Gold.was hammered into the stone wall in the shape of a sunburst stretching almost to the ceiling, which was twice his height. Torches blazed on either side of the sculpture, their enchanted flames dancing in the golden surfaces. In the center of the sunburst sat a pedestal of alabaster, upon which rested a large golden icon. This had to be it.

Horace approached cautiously, reaching out with his extramundane senses. Besides the ever-burning torches, he Saw no other enchantments in the chamber. However, the icon itself foiled his magical senses, as if it were surrounded by a barrier. Curious, he walked up to the pedestal. The relic was an orb surrounded by a radiant corona, supported by a slender stand. The craftsmanship was amazing, showing finer details than any metal sculpture he had ever seen before. The entire thing stood a foot and a half tall. He reached out to touch it.

Just before his fingers made contact, a distant noise echoed behind him. Horace frowned. He was about to have company. The undead must have found another way around the bronze door. The shambling footsteps were drawing nearer. Horace turned, looking for another way out, but the chamber had only the one entrance. He would have to fight his way out.

Bracing himself, he opened himself to the *zoana* again. The power flooded into him, threatening to overwhelm him in its intoxicating euphoria. At the same time, the intensity of the magical power seared his insides. Every breath felt like swallowing fire.

Horace cut back on the power to keep from frying himself in the sudden surge, but there no time for subtlety as a large swarm of undead rushed into the chamber. Combining flows of Girru and Imuvar, he launched a fiery whirlwind down the center of the chamber that tore through the oncoming mass, throwing them backward as it shot out gouts of fire. Several undead appeared older than the rest, mere bones with a few strands of connective tissue holding the together. The flames incinerated those wights where they stood. The fresher ones withstood the flames, though it devoured much of their remaining flesh. They bounded past their fallen comrades, knocking over displays in their ferocity.

SUN AND SERPENT

Horace took them apart, one by one, by unbinding the ties of Shinar holding them together. But more undead flooded into the chamber from the tunnel beyond, until desperation began to constrict Horace's chest. The *zoana* was still swelling at the edge of his control, straining to break free. He needed a way out.

He was looking past the undead for an escape route when a clawed hand grabbed his shoulder and spun him around. The corpse of an old man, his skull showing through holes in his bare pate, stood behind him. The wight's talons slashed across Horace's chest, ripping through his robe and skin. Caught by surprise, Horace reacted out of instinct. He surrounded both fists in gloves of iron-hard air and shoved the undead away. His hands crushed the creature's ribs, which collapsed in puffs of moldering dust. He barely turned back around in time before the rest of the undead were upon him. He created a shell of hardened air around himself, but the *zoana* surged, and the shell shattered under the onslaught of cold flesh. Jets of fire and ice shot from his hands. He dropped one undead after another, but there was no end to them.

Horace fell back, stumbling to get away. His heel caught in the old corpse's remains and he started to fall. Horace reached out frantically, and his hand closed around a cool, firm object. Suddenly, his vision exploded in an incandescent flash. A terrible scream echoed in Horace's ears as he was picked up in a wave of pure *zoana*. He had no choice. He had to unleash it in every direction, as fast as he could, to keep the power from destroying him. Seismic tremors shook the chamber. He could hear the ceiling cracking open.

When he could see again, Horace looked down at the object in his hand. It was, as he had suspected, the golden icon. Somehow it was magnifying his power. Fighting through the pain, he got control of his *qa* and slowly closed the flow of power. Not entirely, just to the point where he could manage it. As his mind cleared, he understood he had to get out of this place before the entire catacombs collapsed.

Holding tight to the icon, Horace bent his knees and jumped. He flew straight up into the ceiling. The rock and earth parted before him, carved away by a channeled stream of Kishargal as a gust of Imuvar carried him higher. He finally burst free of the earth and plowed his way through the abandoned innards of the temple, not stopping until he exploded from the obelisk. Gravel and pieces of broken stone poured off him to pelt the ground far below. Horace took a deep breath of the cool night air. The icon glittered in the moonlight. He didn't understand how it functioned, but he marveled nonetheless. With this, he could bring down mountains, raise hurricanes, split the earth . . . *Or destroy a rival. This could give me the edge I need against Astaptah. Can I really give it over to the sun cult?*

I gave my word, but I didn't understand what I was promising. Doesn't that negate the oath?

With a deep breath, he pushed the question aside for now. He needed time to think, but he didn't want to hang around this dead city any longer. He knew where to go.

The transportation spell was tricky under the best circumstances, but now he had power to spare. When it was set, he channeled the magic. With a burst of icy cold that sucked his breath away, he vanished.

Dasha stopped to catch her breath. She was sweating, and her clothing—suited elegantly for palace life—clung uncomfortably to her damp skin. The sun beat down on the plain, so harsh it had left cracks in the soil. The few plants she saw were low and scraggly. Just the sight of them made her thirsty.

She and Elia had emerged from the escape tunnel into a ravine about a mile west of the city. The first taste of fresh air had been so intoxicating she had almost passed out just breathing it, but the relief had been short-lived as she and Elia started hiking. She let her bodyguard lead the way, of course. Dasha had been outside the city before, but only on supervised visits to neighboring estates. She remembered fondly those excursions to stately plantations with their olive groves and marble pools. They had been nothing like this. The land was so desolate once they got away from the river. So empty. She looked back.

The storm continued to rage over Ceasa, occasionally flashing with green lightning. It looked so remote, but she could still feel the rumble of thunder in her bones. "How far do we have to go?"

Elia turned her head. "We have another couple hours of daylight, then we'll stop. But we need to put as much distance as we can between ourselves and the capital."

A couple hours? Dasha quailed at the thought, but she pressed her lips together. Complaints were for children. She was alive and free, and she was grateful for both.

They traveled in silence for some time. To Dasha, time seemed to dribble by like grains through an hourglass as the sun slowly made its way down to the horizon. Her thirst grew with every passing minute, until it was the only thing she could think about. Even her sorrow over the loss of her family and friends became secondary to that privation. Her feet dragged in the parched soil, stirring up small clouds of dust.

After an hour, or perhaps two, Elia suddenly stopped and held up a hand, her fingers curled into a fist. Dasha halted beside her. "What is it?"

"I see a house up ahead. Might be a settlement, or just a lone homestead."

Dasha squinted against the glare. She could barely make out a tiny brown roof on the plain ahead. "Does it have water?"

"There will be a well in the vicinity. I'm going to scout ahead. You stay here. I'll be back in a candlemark."

"No, you don't. You aren't leaving me out here."

"Princess, it will be all—"

"I won't be left behind!"

Dasha clapped a hand to her lips, but the shout had already escaped. "I'm sorry," she whispered. "But you can't leave me here. I'm coming with you."

"Princess—"

Dasha raised herself to her full height, which was still a good handsbreadth shorter than Elia. "That is a command."

Elia let out a quiet breath that bordered on a sigh. "As you wish, Princess. But will you please do as I instruct? If there is anyone lurking about, we don't want to draw their attention."

"Of course. I'll follow your every footstep exactly."

Elia looked dubious but had the good sense not to voice it. The bodyguard walked with a hunch, keeping her head down, and Dasha—true to her word—did the same, following over the broken ground toward the building. Dasha was priding herself on her stealth when she ran into Elia's rear end. And then, she almost compounded the error by blurting out a question but stopped herself in time. Instead, she crept up beside the bodyguard and whispered, "See anything?"

The house was closer now, a bowshot from where they stood. It appeared to be a single-family home with a couple small outbuildings. There was a paddock and a barn, but no sight of any animals. Or people.

Elia pointed to a small stand of nut trees near the right front corner of the main house. She and Dasha moved forward together, angling behind the trees. Dasha kept looking around, listening for the slightest sound, but they reached the edge of the house without incident. She tried to peer into the closest window, but the interior was dark and partly obscured by a loose curtain. The curtain was embroidered with little flowers, which she found endearing. She wondered who had lived here. She imagined a farmer and his family—a wife who ran the home, children helping their father in the field. "Where are the people?" she asked.

"Perhaps they ran off," Elia responded in a low whisper. She drew her sword. "With the war coming, they may have sought safety elsewhere. Come."

Dasha followed Elia around the side, past a neglected vegetable garden, to the main door of the home. The bodyguard opened the door and walked in, sword extended. Dasha held her breath and waited outside. When there were no sounds of fighting, she followed.

The inside of the house was better lit than she imagined. There was only one floor to the structure, and most of it was a single room, which served as kitchen, dining room, and sitting area. There were personal effects everywhere—a basket of flax beside a spinning wheel, a pair of heavy gloves on the mantle over the small hearth, even a company of wooden toy soldiers on the floor. All signs that people had lived here recently, but there was a hollowness about the home that said this family had left for good.

Elia went into the back room and returned a minute later with a homespun dress and a pair of plain leather sandals. "Put these on. You stand out like a prize calf at market."

Dasha looked down at her clothes. The hem of her gown was tattered and stained with mud—hardly pristine any longer—but she understood what Elia meant. "You want to disguise us. In case there is pursuit from the city."

"If we run into anyone out here, I don't want them knowing who you are."

"Why not?" Dasha asked as she started to undress. "People need to know I am still alive, that their empress lives."

"Your father is dead. Your family is dead."

Dasha blinked back tears as the words stung an already-fresh wound. "Why are you speaking to me this way?"

"Because you have to understand, Princess. The world outside the palace is not so nice and protected. Times of turmoil bring out the worst in people. Out here, any man who wants can make himself your master. And all your manners and pretty words won't make a damned bit of difference."

"I have you to protect me."

Elia's laugh was more like a grunt. "I'm one person, Princess. We're out here on our own. We need to use our wits, or we won't last a week. So, until we're back safe and sound in the capital with you firmly planted on the throne, no one needs to know who you are. Understand?"

Dasha put on the borrowed dress. It was a loose fit, but there was a cord to belt it. The sandals were exactly her size, but worn and hard. She stood up in her new outfit, feeling out of place. It was odd wearing someone else's clothes. "How do I look?"

"Like any other peasant girl. Now check the larder for anything we can take with us. There won't be any imperial banquets in the wild."

Dasha was about to demand to know why she must do the search but held her tongue. Elia was right. She needed to learn to do things for herself if she wanted to survive. They stripped the place bare of anything edible, which barely filled the bottom of a makeshift bag Elia made from an old blanket. They also took a clay jar with a lid.

As they left the house, Dasha had the odd feeling she was leaving home again. She blinked back a sudden burst of moisture in her eyes as she followed Elia across the bare yard to a small well. "What's our plan?" she asked.

"We'll hide in the countryside until the danger passes."

"And if it doesn't?"

"I don't know, Princess. I'm acting on instinct. My first priority is to keep you alive. Beyond that, I just don't know."

Dasha nodded fiercely. *But I will avenge my family and take back my throne.*

Elia tried the draw some water, but the bucket came up filled with mud. "It's dry," she stated, dropping bucket back down the hole. "That's probably why this place was abandoned. We'll find a spring and refill there." She pointed ahead. "We'll head northwest, away from the river. It's hard country, but it will take us far from hostile—"

The bodyguard stiffened and muttered something under her breath.

"What is it?" Dasha asked, trying to see what the other woman saw. But the landscape was much the same—dry, brown earth and clumps of low brush, a few trees scattered about.

Then she saw it. Them. A group of people moving this way from the north. They were still a long way off, but Dasha could see the jerky, lumbering way in which they walked. They weren't human. At least, not anymore. "Elia . . ."

"Move slowly, Princess," Elia replied, stepping backward. "Nice and easy, back around behind the farmhouse."

It seemed to take forever for them to retrace their steps the twenty yards back to the house. Dasha's eyes never left the advancing undead. Elia led her around the back. Once in the shade at the lee of the house, Dasha took a deep breath. She was covered in sweat, not all of it from the day's heat. Elia took another glance around the corner.

"Are they still coming?" Dasha asked. "What are we going to do? Run?"

Elia hefted her sword, as if weighing a decision. "Running will only draw their attention. And there's too many to fight. No, we have to sneak away and hope they don't notice us."

Dasha nodded. She was suddenly very thirsty again. "Okay. Let's do that."

Elia went first, her head bent low as she left the shade and crossed the open ground to the barn. Dasha kept watch. The undead didn't seem to notice, but they were getting closer. Taking a breath and holding it, Dasha emulated her bodyguard and trod carefully across the yard. Sweat rolled down her back, making her want to scratch or scream or both. Finally, she made it, joining Elia by a large paddock attached to the barn.

"There's no more cover after this," Elia said. "Just keeping moving, no matter what."

"What if they see us?"

"Run. As fast as you can, as long as you are able."

Dasha understood what that meant. Elia was going to do something *heroic*, which was another word for suicidal. "We stay together. Understand? If you stop to fight, I stop with you."

"Princess—"

"That's an order."

Elia held her gaze for a few seconds before she nodded. "As you wish, Princess. We stay together. Remain low and quiet. We're just a couple of field mice."

Side by side, they left the barn, heading to the east into open territory. Elia took them down into every gulley and ditch she could find, keeping as low as possible. Every so often Dasha stole a glance over her shoulder, but she couldn't see the undead anymore. She hoped that was a good sign. Still, her heart didn't stop thumping until they had traveled a full mile from the farmstead. By then she was tired and hot, but they continued hiking.

Dasha thought she was going to die of exhaustion by the time twilight arrived, darkening the sky to shades of deeper purple. When she tried to speak, the dry air and the exertion forced her to croak out the words, "Can we stop soon?"

Elia paused. They were traveling through a flat depression between several low hills. She pointed ahead and to the left, toward the base of one hill. "We'll look over there for some shelter."

Dasha trudged along in her bodyguard's wake. Her feet felt like nails were being driven up through her soles. Her chin rested on her chest, her gaze focused only on the steps right in front of her. She thought she could collapse at any moment. *Just keep going. There's no choice. We flee or we die. And I must live. I have to free my people. I have to keep going . . .*

Finally, as the sky had deepened into somber purple, Elia found a shallow niche under an outcropping of rock at the base of the hill. Dasha huddled against the stony wall. The temperature had fallen off as the sun set, and a cold wind blew across the wasted landscape.

"I'll be right back," Elia said. "Stay here."

"What? Where are you going?"

"Just for a look around. Don't worry. I won't go far."

Dasha nodded as she rested her forehead on her knees. She was starving and her throat ached for a drink, but more than anything she just wanted to sleep. She was drifting off when Elia woke her with a light shake.

"Here," the woman said. "Eat this."

Groggy, Dasha took the offering. It was a thick rind with a mass of pulpy fruit. She licked it tentatively and recoiled at the bitter-sharp taste. "What is it?"

"Cactus. Eat it. It will keep you alive."

Dasha finished it in a couple bites. The juice felt wonderful on her throat, but after she finished it, she was thirstier than before.

Elia seemed to read her mind. "We can live off this for a while, but eventually we'll need to find water."

Dasha put her head back down and tried not to think about it. Her lips and tongue were growing numb.

"Might've been something in that cactus," Elia slurred as she huddled beside her. "Feel . . . weird."

Dasha could only nod as she closed her eyes. She wanted to sleep for a thousand years, sleep until this nightmare was open. She imagined she would wake up tomorrow, back in her bed in her room, and everything she had witnessed this day would be just a bad dream. The thought made her smile as she drifted away on a cloud of spun sugar.

The sun disappeared above the thick canopy of intertwined branches, its light only showing through in wan dapples between the layers of broad, dark leaves. Jirom stood in one of the sunlit spots for a moment as he uncorked his canteen. The rest of the company filed past him, heads swiveling back and forth, eyes constantly tracking for threats.

They were traveling light and fast, cutting their way through the dense jungle. The ropy vines that hung from the trees resisted cutting and leaked sticky, red sap that soon covered everyone, making the Silver Blades appear to have just emerged from a slaughterhouse. The air inside the jungle was close and hot and made Jirom almost long for the clean, dry heat of the desert. Almost.

As he put away the canteen, he considered the route ahead. They were traveling through a vast canyon. Now and again they would catch glimpses of the steep black stone walls, rising past the treetops. An hour ago, he had sent Niko up one of those trees for a bird's-eye look around. The report back hadn't been encouraging. More jungle for as far as he could see.

"I should have stayed in Thuum." Three Moons came to stand alongside Jirom. "Wine, women, and cool shade to rest my old bones. What was I thinking?"

Jirom glanced over at him. "Who gave you a choice?"

"True enough. I've been dragooned. Well, consider this an official complaint, Commander. I want out of this rotten outfit."

"Sorry, old man. You're enlisted for life."

"Is that all? Hell, I'll just plop down over there under the shade of that tree and wait for death to take me."

Jirom reached over and plucked a hairy spider the size of an orange off the sorcerer's back. Holding it by one leg, he flung it into a clump of thorny bushes. "It wouldn't take long. This place is crawling with unpleasant surprises."

Three Moons grunted. It was the same sound he always made whenever he sat or stood up, a low grunt that sounded like an abbreviated expression of countless years piled upon a body. "You said a mouthful there. Underneath all these roots and vines and dirt is a lot of bad mojo."

"What do you mean?"

"This place ain't natural. It's almost . . . well, it reminds me a lot more of that Otherworld than I'm comfortable with. Corruption seeps right up from the ground and infuses everything. It's all polluted."

Jauna came jogging back from the forward scouting position. "Sir, there's a waterway ahead, running across our path."

"Can we ford it?"

"Perhaps, but Niko said you would want to see it first."

"All right. Lead the way."

As they followed Jauna through the moss-bearded trees, Jirom shared a look with Three Moons. "Reminds you of that other place, eh?"

The old sorcerer swatted a vine out of his way, and then flinched away when it swung back toward him. "A bit too much."

Two hundred yards brought them to the bank of a slow-running stream. There was no sign of Niko when they arrived. Jirom went to the edge and looked down. The stream was pure black. Not deep brown with silt or mud, but black like squid ink. He knelt in the wet mud and sniffed. There was no odor rising from the liquid, but he sensed the unnaturalness of it. The thought of wading across made his skin crawl. There were, he noted, no animal tracks in the mud along the bank.

Niko returned from upstream. His boots were wet, but the rest of him was dry. "I followed it for half a mile but couldn't find the source. Going around could take a long time."

Jirom stood up and took off his sword belt. The rest of the Silver Blades were gathering. "Stay here."

Niko made as if to block his way. "Commander, I wouldn't—"

Jirom pushed him aside with a gentle nudge. "I'll take the risk."

Holding his sword above his head, Jirom walked out into the stream. The water's bite through his leather boots was frigid, which was soothing at first but quickly became uncomfortable. As he waded deeper, moving slowly to be sure of his footing, numbness crept up his legs as if the water was leeching the strength from his muscles. The stream came up to his chest at its deepest part. Biting his lip as the frigid chill infected his torso, Jirom was heading toward the far bank when he paused, standing still in the moving water.

"Sarge?" Three Moons called over to him. "You all right? Niko, get in there with him."

SUN AND SERPENT

Jirom held up one hand for silence as he turned his head, trying to pick up the sound he had detected just a moment ago. He thought he'd heard movement on the southern side of the stream, a soft swish as if something moving through the underbrush. His gaze wandered upward, and a hoarse cry was torn from his lips. "In the trees!"

He drew his sword as several huge, hairy shapes dropped from the branches on the far side of the stream. At first, he took them for great apes, like the kind from his homeland, but if anything, these creatures were more massive, and four arms sprouted from each one's muscular shoulders. Long fingers ended in curved talons. With a host of bestial screams, they landed with disturbing grace and charged toward him.

Crossbows fired as the demonic beasts leapt into the water. The thick quarrels thudded into furred flesh, but not one of the creatures stopped or even slowed down.

Jirom attacked when the first monster splashed down in front of him. It stood a head taller than him but was whip-thin beneath its mat of ruddy fur. The edge of his blade bit into the top of the beast's shoulder and stopped. A sharp vibration ran up through the hilt into Jirom's hands like he had hit a rock. The thing struck back, and Jirom was thrown backward. He lost his grip and his tulwar tumbled into the stream. The beast's claws had ripped through his leather jerkin and scored the skin of his chest. Dripping blood, he stood his ground as the creature charged at him again, its four fists raised to strike. He caught two by the wrist they descended, but the other pair hammered into his shoulders, driving Jirom to his knees.

Submerged under the icy black water, Jirom twisted the thick wrists sideways. The beast was incredibly strong, but a bestial force rose within Jirom. He strained until the beast toppled under the water with him. He let go of one arm to draw his dagger. Then, clamping his legs around the creature's torso, Jirom drove the poniard into its chest, blindly guessing for a spot just below the breastbone and shoving all his weight on top of the thrust. The dagger's point halted for an instant, and then punched through. Warm blood swirled in the water. The beast thrashed, trying to throw him off, but Jirom held on tight with his thighs. Inch by inch, the dagger's blade slid into its body. After several violent seconds, the beast's struggles lessened. Then it gave one final convulsion that almost threw Jirom off before it sank down into the darkness and did not rise back up.

Blood dripped from Jirom's neck and chest as he stood up in the stream, gasping for air. The Blades had closed to engage the rest of the demon creatures in a fierce melee of silver skin and red fur. Claws scrabbled across steel shields, blades bit deep, and shouts arose. Blood—both red and black—spilled into the frigid dark water.

Holding his dagger, Jirom rushed to Emanon's side. His lover had poked several holes in a demon beast's chest and abdomen, but the thing kept coming. Emanon bled from several cuts, including a long scratch across his forehead. Splashing through the stream, Jirom came up behind Emanon's foe and thrust his dagger into the thing's side with all his strength, aiming for a lung. Matted fur and the flesh underneath parted, and the blade sank halfway up its length into hard muscle. The beast cried out and wheeled on Jirom, which gave Emanon the opportunity to stab his spear into its back. The beast thrashed and stumbled to the ground. Its arms articulated around to clutch feebly at the spear protruding from its spine as it died.

"You good?" Jirom asked.

Emanon swiped at the blood running down his face. "Yeah. You?"

The Blades were hacking at the last of the beasts, taking them apart limb by limb. Two of his people lay on the riverbank, unmoving. Lamnot's neck was twisted almost the whole way around, his head tilted at a sickening angle. Nothing remained of Meghan's face and upper chest except for masses of red pulp as she lay on her side, partially curled up. Jirom went to stand over them for a moment. They had survived so much, just to end up here.

Swallowing his angst, Jirom investigated the corpses of their foes. He'd never seen such creatures before. Although bestial in appearance, they displayed cunning that was almost human. If there had been more than a handful of them, they would have overwhelmed the mercenaries. What other surprises did this dark jungle have in store?

Jirom and Emanon crossed the stream to the southern bank. Jirom was glad to get free of the icy water. The deep tissues of his legs quivered as feeling returned. He checked his injuries. His chest was still bleeding. Finding a clear spot of ground, he sat down and rooted through his field kit.

Three Moons stood over him. "The rest of this area seems clear now."

"Any idea what we just fought?"

The old sorcerer shook his head. His face was scrunched up like he was constipated. "Not exactly, no. Anything I say would just confuse you more."

Jirom threaded a bone needle, tied off the ends, and started sewing up his wound. "Try me."

"All right. If we operate under the assumption that this stretch of territory touches the Otherworld, that it's a weak spot in the barrier between realms, then things are starting to bleed through."

"Did you see creatures like this in the other realm?"

"No, but that doesn't mean shit. We were too busy running for our lives to take a tour."

"Settle down. I'm just trying to suss out some answers."

"Well, Sarge, I'm in short supply of those. But I know this much: if it's happening here, then it's happening other places, too. And if it gets much worse . . ."

"Aye. I understand. We're running out of time, again."

"Sorry I don't have any good news."

Jirom finished the sutures and inspected his handiwork. The slashes were bound up as tight as he could get them. The flow of blood had ceased. He put away the gear and stood up.

Emanon came over, carrying Jirom's tulwar and sword belt, both dripping wet. "Everyone can still march. What's the plan?"

Jirom took back the weapon. The hilt was freezing cold to the touch as he slid it back into the scabbard. "We keep moving. Make some marks for the army, then we press on."

Niko chopped a trailblazing sign into the trunk of a nearby tree while the rest of the Blades headed out. Everyone marched in silence, eyes scanning the canopy above. The hairs on the back of Jirom's neck bristled. Every shadow seemed to hide a deadly threat. Shield strapped to his forearm, he walked with a light step and strained to hear every sound.

"Sarge," Three Moons said, walking on his shield-arm side. "We're getting close to something. I can feel it ahead. Big mojo."

Jirom growled under his breath as he drew his sword. *Why couldn't anything be easy?* "Can you tell what it is? More of the four-armed creatures?"

"No. It feels like . . . like the portal we used to escape the desert."

"The one that took you into the Otherworld?"

Three Moons nodded, his gaze focused ahead.

Jirom felt the muscles in his jaw bunching together, the strain rippling down his neck and into his shoulders. He longed for a clean fight, but more than that, he wanted an end to all this mayhem. With every life he took, he felt more unclean. Over the course of his life he had bathed in a sea of blood, and he feared it would never wash away, that he was tainted by its stain on his soul. Sweat dripped down his face and covered his body, and he couldn't stop imagining it was more blood, oozing out of him. With a grunt, he bit down on his tongue to focus his mind.

Jauna appeared from behind a wall of undergrowth thirty paces ahead of them and gave the signal for caution. The Blades fanned out in pairs, crossbows ready. Emanon took the left wing, leading half the troopers around to flank. Three Moons stayed with Jirom as he took the remaining Blades straight ahead.

Long thorns snagged in their clothing and armor as they moved through the brush, forcing them to hack their way through. Jirom didn't worry about making noise. His role in this position was to draw attention. As he cut away branches of brambles, he began to feel something. A vibration running through the air. It itched like a million ants crawling all over him.

He glanced sideways. Three Moons' face was pale and drawn like he was seeing his worst nightmare. "Moons, what is it?"

"Power, Jirom. So much power."

Jirom couldn't suppress a shiver that ran down his spine. Three Moons never called him by his name. He tightened his grip on his sword.

He led the Blades past a line of close-set trees, and then halted.

SUN AND SERPENT

Three Moons was having difficulty walking straight. His head felt like he'd just come off a six-day bender at his favorite smoking den. Hazy and unable to concentrate. It had started when they entered this unearthly jungle and got worse with every step. The worst part was the feeling that he was failing his brothers and sisters. He hadn't been able to help them fight the four-armed monsters, couldn't even summon a single tiny sprite, for all the buzzing interference inside his skull.

But now a single note was cutting through the buzzing and the haze, a high-pitched tone as clear as a bell's chime. It made his teeth ache, and he was fairly certain he was the only person who heard it. The only thing he could tell was that its source came from directly ahead, and not too far in the distance.

Jirom chopped his way through a hedge of briars and stopped, sword hanging loosely in his hand. Three Moons swallowed hard as he followed. Beyond the next row of trees, the ground fell away in a broad basin, about twelve to fifteen feet down at its deepest point. The ground of the basin was bare rock, which glistened like raw obsidian. At the very center stood a vertical slash, as if a knife had cut open the air to reveal its guts. It pulsed with harsh energy. From one angle it was black as midnight, but when Three Moons moved his head slightly, the rent throbbed with more colors than he even knew existed. He shivered as the power washed over him in waves, pounding at his inner defenses.

"What the fuck is that?" Emanon asked.

Jirom looked over. "Moons?"

Three Moons shook his head. "I don't . . ." He swallowed. *No, they deserve to know the truth.* "It's a hole between worlds. And before you ask me, no, I don't know how it got here. But somehow, the barrier between us and the Otherworld is weakening. It's getting thinner and forming tears like this. I'm guessing this is what caused this jungle to grow out of nothing and where the four-armed apes came from. And it's probably going to get worse."

"Worse?" Emanon said. "How much worse can it get?"

Three Moons let out a long breath. "End-of-the-world worse."

"Fuck me," Captain Paranas whispered.

Three Moons could only nod in agreement. *Indeed. We're all fucked. Every man, woman, and child in the world.* He tried to imagine a future where the realms were conjoined, and his mind recoiled from the vision of darkness and horror it evoked.

"So how do we close it?" Jirom asked.

Three Moons noticed everyone was watching him. *Like I have any fucking answers.* Steeling himself for the looks of disappointment he was about to get, he shrugged. "I doubt we can, Sarge."

"Come again?" Emanon said.

"Just what I said. I don't think there's anything we can do about it. Oh, maybe if your pal Horace the Storm Lord was here."

Emanon passed a fierce glance at Jirom, who ignored it. Mostly.

"But I doubt even he would have enough juice to close it for good," Three Moons continued. "The barrier is shredding itself to pieces. It would take more power than you can imagine to stop it."

Jirom glared at him as if he wanted to strangle someone. "And how do we get that much power?"

Three Moon fought the urge to shrug again. "Blood, maybe. There's power in blood. The spirits respond to it. But you would need a lot of blood, Sarge. I mean a fucking ocean. And that means human sacrifice."

Emanon looked pensive, staring at the color-shifting hole.

Jirom shook his head. "All right. You've made your point. If we stop the Dark King, does this barrier go back to normal?"

"I imagine so."

"Good. Now that we have that settled, let's keep moving. We have more ground to cover while there's still daylight. Niko, lead the way but don't get too far ahead. We don't know that might be lurking out there."

As the Blades filed out, heading south, Three Moons stayed where he was for a few seconds, staring into the pulsing rift. Its power ebbed slightly and then rushed back at full force, like the tide rushing in and out. Did this hole lead to the same Otherworld he and his brethren had visited before? He didn't think so. The energy pouring from it had a more sinister feel.

He had been in the command pavilion days ago, standing quietly in the back, when Horace told his tale about the ancient gods lurking in the darkness beyond this world, waiting to return and reclaim their hegemony. He had believed the young mage then, and the feel of this tear-between-realms only reinforced that belief. Forces beyond his imagination were at play. After all, he was just a backwoods shaman with a few tricks. What could he do to change the world?

"Moons!" Jirom called back to him. "You coming?"

Three Moons nodded as he left the rent. *Aye, Sarge. I'm coming. One more journey for these old bones.*

CHAPTER FIVE

Dasha sat on a rock with her eyes squeezed closed. She focused on the spot of ground before her, questing down into its hard soil with her inner vision. Or tried to. She was having trouble locating her qa. A trickle of sweat ran down her cheek past her right eye as she tried again. After several minutes, the mystical gateway to her power remained closed.

With a growl of frustration, she gave up and opened her eyes. The earth before her was bone dry. Still. She didn't understand. She was descended from a long line of great sorcerers and sorceresses. This should be child's play. Yet, again and again she failed. They needed water but couldn't summon so much as a thimbleful.

You must remain calm, Princess. It will come when you are at peace. In control of your emotions.

Brother Kaluu's words echoed in her mind but gave little solace. She was worn out, physically and emotionally. Her nerves were frayed from both the knowledge of what had happened and the perilous path that lay ahead.

Elia had left at first light to search for food. In her absence, Dasha had been hounded by her memories of yesterday. It didn't seem real. It couldn't be. She prayed she would close her eyes and open them again to find out it had all been a terrible nightmare. She would call out, and Elia would enter to assure her all was well. *It was just a dream.*

Blinking away tears she could not afford to shed, Dasha stood up. The night in the wastes had been cold and terrifying. Huddled next to Elia, she had shivered all night, sleeping only in small snatches when her mind became too exhausted to fight it off any longer. Each time, she awoke in the dark, startled by some unfamiliar sound, and she would have to begin the long journey to slumber again.

Why had she been the one to live, when so many others had died? *Father, you would know what to do. Mother, I miss you so much. I'm all alone out here and I can't find my way.*

Dasha heard soft footsteps approaching. Her heartbeat quickened as she crouched down against the rock wall of the hillside. Then Elia appeared from behind an outcropping of stone. *No, I'm not alone. I have one friend left.*

Elia carried a long tube that looked like an elongated melon. Setting it down beside Dasha, the bodyguard sliced off a section and handed it to her. Dasha devoured the juicy pulp, not minding the bitter taste at all or how it burned her chapped lips. This was survival.

"I saw some taller hills," Elia said as they ate. "Northwest from here. It's possible we could find better shelter. Game to trap."

"And water?"

The bodyguard shrugged. "It's possible. There were trees, and trees mean water."

Dasha licked the juice from her fingers. "Let's go."

Her feet were sore from the previous day as they started off, but within a bell's time they felt better. Dasha felt stronger, despite the physical tolls she was suffering. Fatigue, hunger, and a raving thirst that seemed like it would never be sated again. Still, there was something else. "I feel . . . I know it's going to be strange to say this, but I feel good. Better, at least."

"It's partly relief at still being alive," Elia said. "You feel guilty at first, but then relieved."

Yes, that's it. I'm alive and thankful for that. So many died, but I'm still here. "Partly?"

"The other part is freedom."

Dasha frowned, confused. "What do you mean? I've always been free." Then she glanced at the iron collar Elia wore. "Elia, I'm sorry. I didn't mean—"

The bodyguard waved off the apology. "That's not what I'm talking about. Out here, you're finally, truly free, for the first time. No parents, no tutors, no one watching your every move. No one telling you where to go and how to behave."

Dasha thought about it. Elia was right, in a way. Her entire life had been planned out for her. She had been groomed to be a princess, and perhaps eventually an empress. Taught to speak and act a certain way, how to walk and dress, even how to eat in a way that was dainty and dignified. If her instructors could see her now, dirty and disheveled, with cactus juice running down her chin, they would be aghast. "You're right. It feels scary, but it's also . . . nice.

"Now, about your collar."

Elia shrugged. "We have bigger things to worry about, Princess."

"Still, it's important. We have to get it off."

"Did you happen to bring a set of smith's tools?"

Dasha stopped in her tracks. "Elia. Are you smiling?"

The bodyguard hid her expression behind a scowl. "No."

"You were! I've never seen you smile before. You know, you're quite pretty."

"Don't go getting any ideas, Princess."

Dasha put a hand to her mouth. "Oh, Elia. No! I didn't mean—"

The smile crept out on her companion's lips again.

Dasha hurried to catch up. "But seriously, I'm declaring you are no longer a slave. I can do that, right?"

"I suppose you can."

"All right then. You are free."

This time it was Elia who halted. "Truly?"

"Yes. I give you your freedom."

Dasha felt good saying that. She had been surrounded by slaves her entire life. She hadn't seen them as any different than free servants, until now. Until she had tasted true freedom for herself for the first time.

"So, what if I want to leave you?" Elia asked. "Just walk off and go my own way?"

Dasha took a deep breath and held it for a moment before exhaling. "Well, I couldn't stop you before you were free. I certainly can't stop you now. And . . . I wouldn't try. You are free to choose for yourself."

Another shrug. "Let's go. We're wasting daylight, and I'd really like to find some water before we shrivel up."

As they walked, side by side, Dasha said, "We'll get that collar off as soon as we can."

"That would be nice. It clashes with all my fancy dresses."

Dasha imagined Elia in a pretty dress, with her hair done up in a fine coiffure, and burst out laughing. After a moment, Elia joined her. She had a warm, rich laugh. "You wouldn't really leave me. Would you, Elia?"

"I made a promise to your mother, Princess. And it had nothing to do with this collar. I'll see you safe. After that, we'll see."

The sun was rising fast, bringing with it a terrible heat. Dasha found herself sweating unbearably, and her thirst returned like a living thing, clawing at her throat. They were crossing a trough of ground between two low hills when Elia stopped, again raising a closed fist above her shoulder.

"What does that mean?" Dasha asked.

"Stop," Elia replied in a whisper. "Movement ahead."

Dasha's mind went back to the undead they had found at the farm, and a shudder ran through her. "More of *them?*" she mouthed.

Elia shook her head and pointed ahead. Dasha squinted until she saw them, a group of several dozen people moving through the wilderness. Many of them carried large sacks and baskets. "My people," she said.

"No one can know who you are, Princess. Not until we are back in Ceasa."

"Surely, you don't think my subjects would betray their empress? I am their sole remaining link to the Gods."

Elia frowned, which caused deep lines to form across her brow. "Until you are installed on the throne, you are nothing but a . . . a girl lost in the wilds with her aunt."

Dasha couldn't suppress a smile. "So, you'll be my Aunt Elia?"

"Yes. But you must have a new name. Pick one."

Dasha chose the first name that came to her mind—her mother's. "Sepharah."

"No, it must be something more removed from the imperial family. How about Yura?"

"Yura? No, that sounds like—"

"Like an everyday peasant girl. Yes, that will work."

"But you get to keep your name?" Dasha grumbled under her breath.

Elia beckoned her forward. They angled toward the group. As they got closer, Dasha noticed the worn, tired look of the people ahead. Many were bent over by their burdens, but a few walked tall among them. These men carried weapons—spears, mostly, and a few bows. They prowled along the edges of the group with wary eyes. It was one of these armed men who first noticed them approaching. He whistled, and the group froze, with several of the bearers dropping to the ground.

Dasha froze like a startled mouse. Taking a deep breath, she tried to calm her nerves. *These are your people. You have nothing to fear from them.*

Two men separated from the group, coming in their direction. They were both tall and broad-chested. One had long, curly hair, while the other was so close-shaven he was almost bald. They wore plain tunics and leather sandals in the manner of common people. The man with the long hair held a spear. The nearly bald man had a sword; it was bare in his hand but held low in a nonthreatening posture.

"Let me be the one to talk," Elia whispered.

Dasha nodded. She could play the demure peasant girl. *Yura. Don't forget your name is Yura.*

Elia hailed them with a raised, open hand. The two men stopped a dozen paces away.

"Are you two alone?" the bald man asked.

"Yes," Elia replied. "Our home was attacked by the dead. My niece and I fled. Is that your family beyond?"

The bald man gestured to the weapon at Elia's hip. "That sword belt looks like it fits you well. Are you a soldier?"

"No," Elia replied. "I took it off the body of a man I killed. Along with his armor."

The men exchanged a glance.

"I am Harrid, and this is my brother Ohan," the bald man said. "Those people are strays we found, survivors from the city and surrounding farms."

"Where are you going?" Elia asked.

"We're leaving this place. The living dead are everywhere. You can travel with us, if you like."

"North?" Elia asked.

"West," Harrid replied. "Do you wish to come with us? We have food. And water."

The mention of water made Dasha's mouth want to cry. She looked to Elia, but the bodyguard ignored her, focused on the men.

"Semira has fallen as well," Elia said. "We don't know about the northern cities. They may still be standing."

Harrid seemed more at ease now. "We heard that as well. But there is a great jungle north of here, blocking that route. We go around. Though if the north has fallen, then perhaps no place will be safe."

"Jungle?" Elia's tone was suspicious. "There is no jungle within a hundred leagues of here."

Harrid shrugged his wide shoulders. "There is now. Much has changed since the waking of the dead. Come with us. You will see for yourself."

Dasha nudged Elia. Maybe they would find shelter until the war was over. "Yes," she said, deciding to take a chance. Then she suddenly remembered her role. "I mean, we should go with them, Aunt. You said we needed protection."

Harrid smiled, showing strong teeth. "We'll keep you safe, little dove. What do you say, auntie?"

Elia's frown didn't waver, but she nodded. "For the time being."

Harrid and Ohan led the way back to their group. As they got closer, Dasha saw signs of desperation. These people were dirty and tired, and fear haunted their eyes. Even their protectors with the spears looked on the verge of panic. There were a few children among the score and a half of refugees, but they huddled close to their parents. Dasha's heart ached for them, torn from their homes and forced to flee. *We are the same now, imperial daughter and her subjects. And together we will face this threat to our country.*

"Walk with me," Harrid invited. "Are you hungry? Thirsty?"

Dasha almost leapt at the mention of thirst. "Water, please."

While Ohan got the people moving again, bellowing like a cattle driver, Harrid took a capped gourd from a passing man. The man gave a look of panic, but Harrid ushered him along with a smile. "We all share here. Please, young lady. Have a drink."

Dasha took the gourd with a nod of thanks. It was half-filled, but she almost drained it in a single sweet gulp. Panting a little as she lowered the container, she passed it to Elia, who smelled it first before taking a measured sip. Harrid produced two wilted figs, and Dasha chewed on hers as they followed the group. She felt much better. She and Elia were no longer alone, they had food and water, and they were heading away from the war zone. Fortune was smiling on them.

"Where are you from?" Harrid asked Dasha. "You dress like country folk, but your way of speaking reminds me of the capital."

"I am from a good family," she answered.

"We had a farm," Elia said. "My brother's daughter was visiting from Ceasa when the disaster came." She lowered her voice. "He's a scribe for a banking house."

Harrid nodded sagely, as if that information was important to understanding their situation. "We had a cousin who tried to become a priest in the House of Amur. He ended up cleaning the temple middens."

He looked to Dasha again. "So, you didn't see what happened in the city? We were all wondering how it fell so swiftly."

Her thoughts reached back to the horrors of the previous day. She could still hear the screams echoing in her mind, and see the explosion of the gatehouse, all over again. "No," she answered softly.

"I told you," Elia cut in. "She was with me."

Dasha blushed and lowered her eyes. She wasn't practiced at lying. At least, not to strangers. She wanted to tell the truth. She imagined these men going down on their knees and making grand vows to defend her with their lives. This might be the beginning of an army to purge her city of evil.

They came to a faint road cutting through the wastelands. Harrid's men ushered the people onto it, which made walking a little easier. Dasha addressed Harrid directly. "What is this road we follow?"

His smile returned. "It's an old caravan route. I was once a salt trader. I made this journey twice a year from Ceasa to the western cities on occasion. I've been to Hirak and Chiresh, even Erugash a time or two."

He launched into a tale of battling bandits on this road, gesturing wildly with his hands as he described the actions, but always his gaze remained on her. He reminded her of a hawk, proud and strong. And hungry. Rather than being afraid, Dasha found she enjoyed his attention. She made appropriate comments to spur his storytelling, and his smile grew as he went from one tale of harrowing adventure to another. He seemed to have lived an exciting life. When Harrid excused himself to go check with the head of the group, Dasha watched him leave.

"We need to separate ourselves from this band as soon as possible," Elia said, keeping her voice low.

"Why? This arrangement seems ideal. And we're going in the right direction, more or less."

"I don't trust this Harrid," Elia growled. "He is not what he seems."

Dasha pulled Elia to a halt and waited until the rest of the group were far enough away that they couldn't overhear. "This is my decision. We are staying with these people until a better situation presents itself."

Elia's frowned deepened, but she lowered her head in a slight nod. "As you say. But do not allow yourself to be alone with Harrid."

Dasha lifted her chin. "Of course not."

They fell in at the end of the humble procession. Dasha walked beside Elia, but her gaze was cast far ahead to the front, watching the object of her fascination.

They hiked for the rest of the day, but time passed by quickly for Dasha. Harrid came to see her and Elia occasionally, staying to share another story or ask polite questions about her past. On Elia's advice, she kept her answers vague, so she didn't get tripped up on a falsehood. She tried not to think of it as lying, but more like playing a role in a drama. She had loved the theatre back in Ceasa, and now she imagined herself on the grand stage, playing for an audience of one.

Harrid was in the middle of a tale about when he had been left for dead by a tribe of nomads in the wastes of the Iron Desert when his brother came back to find him.

"There are some rocks ahead," Ohan said. His voice was very deep, and he had a slow way of speaking that made him seem more ominous. "A secure place to stop."

Harrid looked to the horizon. The sun was less than an hour from setting. "Good enough."

Ohan nodded and, after a lingering glance at Dasha, went back to the front. Dasha watched him go. She noticed a dark smudge on the sky, far ahead. "What's that?" she asked.

Harrid shaded his eyes. "Could be a storm rolling in. We'll camp in some shelter tonight and hope it passes."

As he left them again, Elia gave Dasha a sharp look.

"What?"

The bodyguard only shook her head and kept walking as the sun slipped down toward the horizon.

Horace stepped out of the void and onto the hot sands of the Iron Desert. Blinking against the brilliant sunlight, he took a deep breath to cleanse the stench of Nisus his lungs, and almost choked as the superheated air seared the back of his throat. Wiping away a layer of newly formed sweat above his eyes, he turned in a slow circle.

An ocean of sand surrounded him. After the cloying passages of the catacombs under Nisus, the open desert felt like a whole different world. Looking up at the vast sky, while breathtaking, was an experience also laced with apprehension, as if he might lose his footing at any moment and be swept up into that blue expanse. He remembered feeling the same way whenever he had looked out over a calm sea.

He felt certain this was the spot where the city of Urabul had once stood. He had walked its ancient streets with Mezim and met a most spectacular spirit. The Mother of Chaos herself had spoken to him and shown him things. Terrible things. Now, there was nothing left to see. The ruins had been swallowed by the dunes, back into antiquity from which they had climbed. Had it all been just a dream?

He wasn't sure why he had come here, unless it was the vast emptiness inside himself, a nothingness that had plagued him since the night of Alyra's death. He was rudderless and alone on a great black sea. Looking out over the desert, Horace didn't see what used to be; he saw the world to come. An empty wasteland, populated only by the dead and the damned. The oncoming evil seemed impossible to stop. He could delay its progress, but eventually his strength would falter. He would stumble, and then Astaptah would win.

He hefted the sack in his hand. That was another thing on his mind. Somehow the relic enhanced his powers, allowing him to draw far more *zoana* than he could without it. He imagined what he could do with such a weapon in his possession. Should he return it to the Sun Cult? He couldn't afford to trust them. Yet, without them, the rebels didn't stand a chance. With either choice, he foresaw doom.

Horace was about to leave when he heard Her voice.

"Now, you are the one waiting for me, Horace of Tines."

She stood at the crest of a tall dune to his left, wrapped in a red gown and shawl, so dark they were almost black against the desert's brightness.

"I wasn't sure what would be here. Nothing, I suppose."

Suddenly, She was standing beside him. "But you would be wrong. The past is never as far away as it may seem."

Horace looked over his shoulder and saw the city laid out behind him. Its sweeping walls and grand towers rose from the dunes like something from a dream. *Which it is.*

"Are you so sure of your perceptions?" She asked, the coy tone he remembered all too well reflected in the words.

"No. Isn't that the point? We're never sure that what we're seeing is real, or just some figment."

Eridu smiled. "You have learned."

"But I still don't know enough. Mulcibar studied this his entire life, and he barely scratched the surface. What chance do I have?"

"So, you give up? Defeated before you even begin?"

"That's not an option. I know that much. But it would be nice if things weren't so fucking mysterious. For example, where are the gods of Akeshian in all this? Why don't they intervene?"

She inclined her head. "Maybe they are, in ways that are not easy to recognize or understand."

Horace turned to Her. "The incomprehensibility of God? Sorry, but I heard enough of that philosophical claptrap back in Arnos when I was growing up. Ask the wrong questions, and the answer always comes back to the same dead end. The mind of God cannot be understood, so we just have to accept everything that happens is part of some divine plan? Bullshit.

"I'm not asking for the secrets of the cosmos. I just want to know why these gods of yours won't step in to save their own hides. It makes all this bloodshed and suffering sound like a game. Is that the riddle at the heart of this disaster? The gods are bored?"

The Woman regarded him for a long moment, Her expression showing nothing except a wan trace of concern. Then it faded, and She smiled. "Come with me."

Together, they went into the city. They strode along the broad streets, flanked by picturesque palaces and temples, statues of queens and conquerors.

As they crossed a long bridge spanning a canal of green waters, She stopped and turned to him. "I wanted to walk these avenues one last time. I thank you for that."

"Surely you didn't need me for that."

"But I do, Horace. You are my tether to this time and place."

"That doesn't sound right. You brought me here the last time."

"Not at all. I merely waited for the one who would be sent. We all have our parts to play, Horace. You were the Seeker, and I was the Guide. Now, my part is done."

Looking down at the cool waters with a swathe of lilies floating against the slow current, he said, "So what part am I to play now? The Warrior? The King? Or the Destroyer?"

"Perhaps all of them. Perhaps none." She leaned over the railing. "We cannot see what lies before us. Only the paths at our feet, and the choices in our wake. Those are the building blocks of the future, which we fashion with every step and every decision."

"I'm not sure why I came back here."

SUN AND SERPENT

"You are searching for something."

Horace couldn't stop himself from a small laugh. All his life he had been searching for something. And every time he thought he had found it, the feeling slipped away like sand through his fingers, until nothing was left. He had rebuilt his life after Sari and Josef died, and then again when he crashed on these shores. Now, since Alyra's death, he felt abandoned. Shipwrecked once again in a strange land. Only this time, he didn't know if he had the strength to carry on. The task was too great.

"I miss her. It feels like there's a hole inside me."

The Woman nodded, leaning back as Her gaze swept across the bright azure sky. "Her spirit lives on. Part of it resides in you. That which you feel is not a hole, but a link. The memories you shared are a connection nothing can sever, not even mortality."

"It's not the same."

She continued to walk, and he followed. They came at last to the great plaza at the center of the city. The pyramid rose above the skyline, its apex blotting out the sun.

The Woman stopped before the steps that led up to a massive door in the front of the pyramid. "Death is a shore between the land of the living and the endless sea beyond. Once you pass beyond the surf, the currents will take you places you have never dreamt of, where you will meet old friends and loves once again. I have been trapped on that shore for a long time, watching the other side but unable to reach it. Until now. Now I am free. And you, Horace of Tines. You could come with me."

It almost sounded good to Horace. He let his gaze wander up the steep sides of the structure to the top, to the quad-pointed crest surrounded by a halo of golden light. "I'm going after Astaptah. Isn't that what you wanted? The cosmos needs balance."

"The cosmos has survived eternity, and it will continue on long after you and I have faded from memory. The choice is yours, as it has always been."

Horace felt the pull of the next world, tugging at him like ankle-high waves on the shore, pulling him forward even as they eroded the sand beneath his feet. He could lose himself in oblivion, and none could blame him. *That's*

*not true. Sari, Alyra, Mulcibar, Ubar. I could never face their shades if I ran away
from this trial.*

"I must face him," he whispered.

A chill brushed against his arm, and Horace looked down to see Her hand
on his elbow. It was the first time She had touched him. The feeling was like a
cold draft under his sleeve. "The Adversary is close to breaking the final Seal.
You know what will happen if he succeeds."

He swallowed hard, recalling the vision She had shown him. The endless
frozen void. The vast beings floating within, sleeping giants waiting to wake
and feed their immortal hunger. "I won't let that happen."

The Woman removed Her hand, though the chill lingered on his flesh.
"We shall see."

They stood in silence for a time, gazing upon the ephemeral city. Horace
didn't want to move, didn't want to break the spell of this moment. He knew
he would never return here. He took a deep breath and savored the taste of
clay bricks and dolomite statuary and the distant tang of the people. Then he
lifted the rucksack with its holy burden. "Should I give to this back to the
cult? There's so much at stake. It seems a shame to . . ."

He turned his head to the empty space beside him. She was gone. Not
just vanished. He felt a vacancy in the atmosphere. She was truly departed, off
to whatever afterlife she had earned.

"Farewell, Eridu."

A warm breeze blew at his back, ruffling his clothing and making the
loose ends of the sack flap like a bird's wings. Slowly, like a fading dream, the
city vanished around him, until he was once again standing on bare sand. The
wind whistled around him.

Exhaling loudly, he opened a portal and stepped through.

Harrid's group of refugees entered the broken land in a huddled mass. As the
sky darkened, they passed through a series of arroyos. High cliffs blocked out

sight of the wastes beyond, for which Dasha was glad. The endless flats had
been exhausting, and there was some comfort to be found behind stony walls.

Just as twilight arrived, they found a cave large enough for everyone.
Following a brief exploration by Ohan, it was proclaimed safe, and everyone
filed inside.

After a day's marching under the sun, the cave's coolness was a blessing.
She and Elia found a spot where they could sit with their backs to a wall, and
Dasha luxuriated as the cold stone leeched the swelter from her skin. Outside,
a low rumble of thunder echoed in the canyon beyond, but they were safe now.
She closed her eyes and felt herself drifting off. A soft elbow in the side jarred
her awake. As she opened her eyes, she saw that a fire had been built in the
middle of the floor. The smell of woodsmoke filled the cave.

A woman came over with a gourd and a small bundle wrapped in muslin
cloth. Elia accepted them with a nod.

"Thank you," Dasha said. "I'm . . . Yura."

She had to think for a moment to remember her assumed name. The
woman nodded without a word and turned to leave.

Dasha leaned forward. "Wait, please. We would like to talk to you."

The woman was older, about the same age as Dasha's mother, with gray
streaks running through the wisps of hair that had escaped the tightly bound
scarf covering her head. She hesitated a moment, but then shook her head and
scurried away, back across to the other side of the cave.

Dasha noticed no one was sitting close to her and Elia, as if they were
considered dangerous or unclean. Elia opened the gourd and tasted the contents before passing it to Dasha. Then she opened the parcel, to find two
large pieces of unleavened bread. She tried to give them both to Dasha, but
the princess took only one, pushing the other back into her bodyguard's
hand.

"You need to keep up your strength," Elia said.

"So do you." Dasha dropped her voice to a whisper. "That's an order."

The others ate in small groups, and Dasha could see their familial ties. A
few of the fighters walked among them, taking what they wanted, whether
it was an extra helping of bread or a drink. Watching them, a chill that had

nothing to do with the cave's coolness invaded Dasha's blood, as she realized how vulnerable she was. *I am depending on Elia's skills and Harrid's good manners, out here where the rules and laws of society have no place.*

Directly across from where she sat, an older couple huddled close together, sharing their meal. The man wore a soldier's tunic that looked as if it hadn't been worn in decades, with faded fabric and tarnished buttons. After he finished eating, the old man used his spear to help him stand up, and then he walked out of the cave.

When Harrid entered a few seconds later, everyone stopped what they were doing to watch him. Dasha watched him, too, as he strolled about the cave as if observing all that was going on. His tunic was soaked with rain, and his bare scalp glistened in the firelight. Then his gaze slid to her, and he sauntered over to sit with them.

"Did you get enough to eat?" he asked.

"Yes. Thank you." Dasha placed a hand on Elia's arm and felt the rigid muscles under her sleeve. "My aunt and I were wondering how we can help these people."

Harrid smiled at her. "You have a kind heart. I can see that. Perhaps your aunt would like to walk outside. The canyon is sheltered from the worst of the storm, and the rain is exhilarating."

"I'm fine right here," Elia said.

"What if we found a farm," Dasha said. "Someplace big enough for everyone here. We could grow food and maybe build walls around it, and . . ."

"That won't work," he interjected.

Dasha sat back, stunned. She wasn't accustomed to being cut off by anyone, except her family members. This action by a man she hardly knew was jarring.

"There are too many living dead near the capital," Harrid continued, as if nothing was wrong. "They would find us, and no barricade could stop them. No, we must keep moving. Until we find a free city, or the coast."

"The coast?' Elia snorted. "That's a journey of weeks, maybe months for this group. You'll never make it."

"The strong will make it," Harrid replied with a shrug. "The rest . . ."

Dasha was struck by the callousness of that reply. *He's not what I thought he was. He's a predator.* "Still, we would like to help."

"Well, Ohan and I are taking a party out tomorrow to scavenge for food. These hills may have some game, or perhaps even a wayward flock of sheep. Perhaps your aunt would accompany us."

"I'm not leaving Yu—"

Dasha put a hand on Elia's wrist, silencing her with a touch. "We'll both go. At first light?"

Harrid nodded, his gaze passing between her and Elia. "Yes. First light." He rose to his feet with effortless grace. "Until tomorrow. Rest well."

As he stalked away, through the cave and out the entrance, where occasional flashes of lightning played across the stone walls, Dasha suppressed a shiver. *He's a serpent, and I am his prey.*

"I still don't trust him," Elia said, softly so no one else but Dasha would hear.

"I know, but we need him, at least for now. We must stay close to him until we can leave."

She looked around at all the shivering people. They were terrified, and not just of the undead. They were trapped by Harrid and his gang, and they knew it. But she wasn't going to allow that to stand. *These are my people. I will save them.*

Dasha leaned back and rested her head on the stony wall. The food had made her drowsy. She needed to sleep and regain her strength. There was much to do.

Dawn arrived with a cool breeze that entered the cave, carrying the scents of the dwindling night. Dasha awoke with stiffness in her shoulder and hip from lying on the hard stone floor. The storm had died sometime before midnight, passing by after dropping a deluge of rain and thunder over the hills.

Elia was already awake. She had procured more bread and water. Dasha looked around as she ate, wishing she had some extra water with which to bathe. She felt dirty, but then, everyone was dirty. A bath was an impossible luxury. She tried not to think of the many pools and streams of the imperial gardens, surrounded by an acre of fragrant blossoms and carefully sculpted shade trees.

Harrid's warriors were assembling at the cave's entrance. Dasha watched them, their movements tense as they checked their weapons several times. "What do you think of them?"

Elia had been watching the men as well. "There isn't a professional soldier among them. I'd wager they were all farmhands and shepherds until a couple weeks ago."

"Can they protect us?"

Elia shrugged. "Without training, they could break at first contact with a real enemy. A lot depends on their commander."

"And what do you think of him? Besides not trusting him, I mean."

"He's ruthless. I wouldn't trust him at my back. Nor at yours. But he wears that sword like he knows how to use it. His brother, too. They are the ones to watch out for if things go bad."

If things go bad. How much worse could they get? We're living on the edge of complete destruction. When the food stores run out, and there are no crops to harvest, what are people going to do?

She imagined the entire empire returning to its barbaric roots, living off the land, moving with the seasons to follow the migratory herds, reduced to the basic problem of just staying alive. *Until the Dark King hunts us all down and kills us, more grist for his ever-growing and eternal army.*

The thought frightened her so much she started shivering, which is how Harrid found her when he came over. "You're freezing, young one," he said. "Come outside. The sun is rising."

"What are we hunting for today?" Elia asked him.

Harrid responded with a broad smile. "Whatever will fill our bellies, Aunt. These hills are filled with—"

Ohan entered the cave, spotted Harrid, and rushed over. He said something in Harrid's ear. The refugee leader frowned for a moment, and then nodded. "Prepare everyone."

"What's happening?" Dasha asked.

He returned to his smooth smile. "Nothing for you to worry about. You will stay here with the others while Ohan and I take the warriors out."

"We said we're coming with you."

"This is no longer a hunting trip, young one. Armed men are approaching."

Dasha's heart beat faster. Soldiers? Perhaps they were survivors from Ceasa's garrison. "Perhaps they are refugees, too."

"Not likely," he answered. "Ohan says they look dangerous. They are probably marauders. It is time to fight for our freedom."

Dasha wished she had a good argument against it. She almost took the chance of revealing her true identity but held back. Now was not the time. "Still, my aunt and I will go with you."

"I can't allow that. It will be too dangerous. People are going to be injured, possibly die. You don't want to see that." He shifted his gaze to Elia for the first time since he came over to them. "Please, tell her. A battle is no place for a young woman."

The muscles in Elia's jaw bunched as if she wanted to explode, but she merely nodded toward Dasha. "My niece can go where she wishes."

Harrid shook his head. "No, you will remain here."

Dasha tried to complain, but he walked away. He and Ohan spoke briefly, and then they left the cave, leaving one warrior behind at the entrance.

"So that's that," Elia said. "Now you know where we stand."

Dasha sat against the stone wall and drew her knees up to her chin, while Elia stood over her, with one hand on the hilt of her sword. Dasha tried not to shiver but couldn't help herself. They were prisoners. She had no doubt that Elia could defeat the single guard watching over them, but then what? Wander the wilderness until the living dead found them? She needed a solid plan.

As the sun's early light crept up to the edge of the cave entrance, she tried to think of one.

CHAPTER SIX

Years ago, the Company and its couple hundred mercenaries had been hired to protect the city of a rich but foolhardy nobleman in northern Isuran. It had been a dream ticket, until a full Akeshian legion arrived at the doorstep, bent on conquest. Most of the Company's members had died in the subsequent battle—not for their homes or families, just for coin they would not live to spend. Jirom had been one of the few survivors. Sometimes he wondered whether the most vital part of him had died at Pardisha, or been born.

His days as a mercenary had forged him into a weapon, year after year of relentless marching and fighting, going from battle to battle, passing from one master to the next, until the only consistencies were the need to survive and your faith in the comrade by your side. He had been anesthetized to the horrors of war, and that numbness continued during his years as a gladiator slave. It hadn't been until he met Emanon that he started to feel authentic emotions again. And then, like vast waters breaking through a dam, he had been deluged by all the feelings he had kept pent up for so long, until he could barely control them.

We're just human jetsam, Three Moons had said to him the night before they left Thuum. *Caught up by forces we barely understand, thrown this way and that. And, in the end, what? A peaceful death? Not likely. Not for ones like us.*

Jirom wiped his forehead with the back of his hand. They had left the jungle one day ago and were now traversing the hardpacked wastes of the south-central empire. He loosened the ties of his jerkin as the sweat rolled off him. Their team had been attacked twice by packs of undead the night before. Now, as the sun sank toward the western horizon, tension mounted throughout the group. Weapons were checked and rechecked, straps tightened, and every eye became more alert.

"It's gonna be a bad one."

Jirom raised an eyebrow as Three Moons walked over. The old sorcerer was looking to the south, a grim expression creasing his silver-hued features. "Storm?"

"It's coming fast."

Jirom eyed the path ahead. The cluster of broken hills known as the Black Gates lay less than a league to the south. "The army will have to hunker down until it blows over. We're going on ahead."

Whistling to the Blades, Jirom started out. Emanon appeared over a low ridge, coming back from the point.

"I was beginning to think you were lost," Jirom said when his lover arrived.

"I sent Niko and Jauna ahead on a long-range sweep, looking for a good place to make camp."

Jirom rubbed the stubble on his chin. "Knowing Niko, he'll pick the highest, most exposed peak in the chain. That man hates not to see everything."

"Maybe not a bad idea out here. We're a long way from Thuum."

"We're a long way from anything."

Emanon nodded as he sipped from his canteen. "True enough."

They walked side by side, near the tail of the column. Watching the mercenaries marching ahead of them, Jirom remembered traversing the stretch of desert between Sekhatun and Erugash, back when he had still been a gladiator slave. Horace had been chained behind him. The bond they formed on that harrowing trek remained between them, stronger and more immutable than those iron chains and collars. "I know you have doubts."

Emanon looked over. He walked with his spear propped on his shoulder. His hair was getting shaggy. "You have to be more specific than that."

"About this mission. About Horace." *Maybe about my ability to lead.*

A striped serpent lay off to their right, sunning itself on a rock. A raptor cried overhead.

Emanon said nothing for a while. Then, "We didn't pick this fight, but we're going to finish it. Because no one else can. It's not about wanting to. It's just a fact.

"As for your friend, you place too much faith in him. But just like this war, we don't have a choice. Still, if anyone can lead us through this, it's you, Jirom. I knew that the first time I saw you in that cage. Live or die, we're with you. Anyway, it's all long odds. The Gods make no promises."

"Really? All I hear from them is promises, but they never seem to pay up."

"That's the priests. String 'em all up and the world would be a better place."

Emanon held a straight face for a moment before he cracked his famous lopsided grin. Jirom chuckled. Their mirth lasted only a few seconds before it fell away, drained by the solemnity of the task before them. A lot of people were going to die. *We need you, Horace. Don't let us down.*

A flurry of wings beat behind them. Jirom turned in time to see the raptor flying off, the serpent hanging limp in its talons.

After an hour of steady hiking, they reached the edge of hills, which broke through the crust of earth in towering, sheer cliffs, like stony fists thrust up into the air. None of the peaks on the northern face had much vegetation— nothing taller than waist-high scrub—but Jirom hoped they found some trees farther into the cluster. Trees meant fresh water, and maybe something better to eat than salted meat and flatbread.

Ino found the small pile of stones Niko had left, marking a crease between two tall hills. The Blades started up the winding, jagged path. Scree crunched under their boots. The trail led into a narrow ravine. High cliffs of dun stone streaked with white veins rose on both sides. The floor of the defile was covered in tumbled stone, but the way was mostly flat and even.

Emanon took half the platoon ahead, marching as quiet as ghosts.

They hadn't gone more than a hundred yards before Three Moons dropped back to walk with him. "Trouble coming up."

"The spirits are talking to you again?"

Three Moons made a face. "No, Jauna told me. She says there are some hostiles up on the heights ahead."

Jirom peered along the clifftops. "Undead?"

"Not this time." The old sorcerer smiled. "Flesh and blood enemies, just like the old days. You want me to rustle up something to flush them out?"

"No. We'll spring their trap. Is Emanon in place?"

Three Moons nodded, his smile reminding Jirom of a lion about to pounce.

Up ahead, Emanon's squad was marching through the center of the canyon, seemingly unaware of any lurking danger.

Jirom's squad tightened up their lines and held their crossbows ready. Three Moons stuck close by. As for himself, Jirom had to fight the temptation to keep checking his sword to make sure it was loose in the scabbard. He tried to relax, but his heart was beating faster, and the old pre-battle excitement was thrumming in his blood.

Jirom had just sighted a gap at the end of the ravine, which looked to lead into another canyon, when he heard the rattle of tumbling rocks above. High up on the cliffs on both sides, men rose from their hiding places. Many of them had spears held ready, but a couple held short hunting bows. The Blades aimed their crossbows upward, fingers on the triggers, but did not fire.

A voice called down from the heights. "Drop your weapons! Or die where you stand."

Jirom looked up, squinting against the sun's dwindling glare. The speaker stood at the highest point of the right-hand cliff. Wearing a dingy homespun tunic with a leather baldric, he didn't have the look of a soldier, but he held a sword. His bald head glistened in the sunlight. Jirom knew what these men were at once. He'd seen their like in every part of the world. Brigands, preying on everyone who crossed their path. With how the empire had turned upside down, he could almost understand their plight. Most of them had probably been farmers and shepherds, driven from their homes by the ravaging undead. Now they survived the only way they could.

But this was war, and he couldn't afford any distractions from his goal. These men could just as easily be spies for the Dark King. Better not to take any chances.

Jirom reached for his sword but didn't draw it. He could give them a chance to surrender. Mercy increased the risk to his team, but he didn't relish the idea of slaughtering these peasants. "We're scouts for the army following us. Stand down, before you get hurt."

The speaker laughed. "An army marching through the Gates toward Ceasa? Nice try. But if it's bloodshed you're after . . ." The speaker raised his arm.

Jirom whistled. A dozen quarrels flashed through the air. Most found targets on the heights. Bandits crumpled, their shoddy weapons clattering on the rocks. A handful of arrows sailed down. Most of them targeted Emanon's squad and passed through them, causing no injury, to thud into the rocky ground. One missile struck Jirom in the right shoulder, but it lacked the power to penetrate his hardened leather cuirass.

The bandit leader, who had survived the first salvo, raised his sword as if to order a charge. Before he could complete the command, Emanon's squad appeared on the heights behind the ambushers, rising from the clifftops like silver wraiths. Jauna came up behind the leader and put a knife to his throat. His man's sword wavered for an instant, and then dropped in surrender.

At the same time, the illusion of Emanon's team on the ground vanished in swirling wisps of mist. Jirom glanced at Three Moons. The old man had his eyes squeezed shut and his lips were moving, mumbling something under his breath. As the illusionary mercenaries faded from sight, his eyes opened. Something shone within their silver depths, a raw power Jirom had only seen in one other person. Horace. And now, just as then, it set the hairs on the back of his neck to standing up. His hand wanted to inch toward his sword hilt. He forced himself to remain outwardly calm. "Good work. Very convincing."

The spectral gleam had faded from the sorcerer's eyes. "I do what I can."

Emanon's squad brought their prisoners down, marching them weaponless with their hands behind their necks, fingers laced together. Nine bandits had survived the attack. None of the Blades in Jirom's squad had taken any injuries. He sent Ivikson and Pie-Eye to watch the route ahead, just in case, and then went to greet the other squad.

Emanon escorted the bandit leader down and shoved the man with his spear as they reach the canyon floor. Jirom hid a smile. He enjoyed watching his man work. Composing his face into a stern mask, Jirom approached, one thumb hooked into his belt by the hilt of his sword in a not-so-subtle threat. He was glad to see the bandit chief didn't miss it either.

"These two are the brains," Emanon said, gesturing to the leader and another man, also tall and broadly built, but with a full head of hair.

Jirom looked from one man to the other. "You're brothers."

The bald bandit's eyebrows rose, as if surprised Jirom had noticed. "Well, I'm not one to ignore when the tables have turned. You've got us, dead to rights."

He's smart. Probably too smart to trust. He'll start off defiant, and then try to worm his way in our good graces, probably by insisting he can be valuable. But he'll turn on us the first good chance he gets. He's a scavenger, not a hunter.

Emanon leaned on his spear. "Let's just kill them now and be done with it. Filthy jackals."

The bald man lifted his hands in surrender. "Hold on! I know this looks bad, but we're the victims here."

Jirom tapped a finger on the pommel of his sword. "What are your names?"

"I'm Harrid, and this Ohan. As you said, we're brothers." The bald man's gaze focused on the brands on Jirom's cheek. "Four diamonds? We don't see many like you outside a gladiator pit. Let me guess. You killed your overseer when the world went upside down, and now you're roaming the wastes, just trying to survive. Not so different than us, eh?"

Without blinking an eye, Jirom stepped forward and drove his balled fist into Harrid's stomach. The man doubled over and fell to one knee.

Jirom backed up a step. "I ask. You answer. Understand?"

The leader got up on shaky legs. "Yes."

"Where are you from?"

"A little village about twenty leagues east of here. Nothing left of it now."

"Along the river?"

The man replied with a cautious nod.

"Are these all your men?"

Harrid started to nod, but then changed his mind. "No. I have a couple more back at our camp, protecting the others."

"What others?"

"A group of misfits. Women, children, elders. We were heading west, trying to find somewhere safe."

"How many?" Jirom asked.

"Thirty or forty. Listen, I know we were trying to rob you, but we need to eat. We need weapons to defend ourselves. You know what's out there. You've seen them, right? It's madness."

"Them?"

"The dead. They're everywhere."

Jirom felt a pang of sympathy, remembering the destruction of the village from a few days ago. "I have. Go on."

"There's nothing left to say. We're just trying to survive."

Behind Harrid, Emanon was frowning. *He knows me too well.*

"Take me to them," Jirom said. "These people you are protecting."

"Of course." Harrid held out a hand. "Can I know the name of our rescuer?"

Jirom ignored the gesture and motioned for the men to move. "Lead on."

As the Blades marched the bandits along the canyon floor, Emanon pulled Jirom aside. "What are we doing? We can't take on prisoners. We'll be marching for the capital as soon as your magician shows up. *If* he shows up. What are we doing to do with these idiots?"

"I want to see what they're up to. Indulge me." Jirom winked at his lover.

Emanon breathed a melodramatic sigh. "Don't I always? And just watch where it gets me."

"Come on, old man."

Emanon raised his eyebrows but followed without further comment.

They hiked through a series of winding canyons. The hills were more expansive than they had appeared from the north, extending for miles to the south and east. The shale stone was shot through with veins of white and pale gold, showing in many layers where the rock had sheared away from the cliff faces over countless centuries. The valley floors were bedded in tumbled stone, interspersed with tall weeds and thorny brush. These Gates were a desolate location and no place for the army to stop for an extended period, but the locale did possess one redeeming feature in Jirom's estimation—you could hide an army ten times the size of his motley band amid these cliffs and hill peaks. *If the enemy hasn't noted our approach, we may still possess the element of surprise. And we need all the advantages we can get.*

SUN AND SERPENT

Harrid and his men marched without conviction, like they were walking to the gallows. Jirom resisted the impulse to give them hope. He didn't know what to do with them. *We can't turn them loose to terrorize others, and we can't trust them.* Still, he didn't want to embrace Emanon's cold-eyed solution. *But will I have a choice?*

Following Harrid's directions, they exited a narrow defile and passed around a pair of sharp bends turning back on each other before entering a deep box canyon. Jirom's gaze swept the cliff tops, searching for another ambush, but all appeared quiet. Then a mewling cry broke the silence, coming from the end of the canyon.

"They're right this way," Harrid said, flashing a smile. "Just like I told you. I might be a thief." He made a small laugh. "But I'm no liar."

A cave was nestled in the back of the canyon. A guard leaning on a spear stood at the entrance. He was little more than a boy, half-starved and wrapped in dirty rags. When he saw the Blades, he grabbed his weapon with both hands and made a brave show.

Harrid called out. "All is well, Gann. We found new friends. Gather everyone."

"Where did you find these people?" Jirom asked as the boy disappeared back into the cave.

"We just picked them up here and there. They didn't have any place else to go. Most of them used to be serfs. A couple escaped the capital before it fell."

"You have people here from Ceasa?" Emanon asked.

"Aye. Two women. Take them as my gift." Harrid touched his chest. "From one leader to another. They are strong and healthy, and the younger one is quite a beauty. You'll be pleased, I'm sure—"

"You're all coming with us," Jirom said.

Harrid hesitated, his smile fading. "It is a kind offer. Truly. But we don't want to burden you."

Jirom signaled to Captain Paranas. "Get these people moving."

"We're falling back?" Emanon asked.

"Yes. We'll regroup with the main army and resupply."

As Paranas and a few Blades entered the cave, Harrid sidled closer to Jirom. "Sir. Commander. If I may? These people are timid creatures, broken by deprivation and horror. Leave them in my care, and I will continue to watch over them as if they were my own children."

Jirom considered feeding the man his own teeth, one at a time. He knew exactly what 'protection' Harrid offered these people. The same kind that a rancher offered his cattle. "You won't have time for that, Harrid. You and your men will be joining our army."

Harrid stared at him. Jirom met his gaze impassively, a part of him wishing the man would do something stupid. After several seconds, Harrid smiled again. "We would be honored to join your host. My men are excellent fighters, you'll see. Tell me, Commander. What is our target?"

Jirom allowed himself to smile. "Ceasa. We're marching to take down the Dark King."

Harrid was slow in responding. "Excellent. Most excellent. Would you excuse me? I will gather my things."

Jirom nodded.

Harrid stumbled a step before recovering his balance. He gestured to his brother, and they hurried into the cave.

"We can't trust him," Emanon said, watching the bandit leader depart. "He'll turn on us the first chance he gets."

"Probably. We'll split up him and his men, keep them under close watch. Maybe they'll come around. If not, we'll discuss other options."

"Assign Harrid to Ralla's unit. She'll break down this trumped-up little warlord in no time."

Jirom glanced around the canyon. The sky was getting darker, although it was still an hour away from sunset. He remembered Three Moons' words. A storm was coming. And they were directly in its path.

He was debating whether to march in the incoming weather or wait it out when Jauna appeared atop the southern cliff wall. She flashed eight fingers and dragged a finger across her own throat, and then pointed west before she vanished again. Jirom's gaze shot in that direction. A force of undead was approaching, at least eighty strong. *Fuck me.*

"Everyone out here!" he bellowed into the cave. "Hurry!"

Emanon was eyeing the western end of the canyon, which was their only way out. "You think they trailed us?"

"It's more likely they found the tracks of these refugees." Jirom scanned the cliffs, gauging how difficult they would be to climb. He and his Blades could make it, no trouble.

All thoughts of the refugees climbing anything were dashed as people started to file out of the cave. They were in worse condition than he had imagined. Many were old enough to be his parents, or grandparents. The younger people were hobbled with injuries or maimed. Except for two women who exited at the tail end of the group, accompanied by Harrid and his brother.

The first woman was as tall as Emanon, with rugged shoulders and a fighter's build. She wore a homespun tunic, but with a wide leather belt that held a shortsword and a combat knife. Her eyes swept over Jirom, paused for a moment, and then moved on with the practiced evaluation of a professional. If she wasn't military, she was exceedingly well trained.

The other woman was younger and much shorter, almost petite, but she moved with an easy grace that spoke of confidence beyond her years. She wore a similar tunic to the taller woman's, though it was too big for her. Jirom supposed she would be considered beautiful, with her high cheekbones and fine complexion, but there was also pain in her eyes. Pain she was trying very hard to conquer.

"Commander," Harrid said, coming forward. "These are the two women I was telling you—"

"There's no time for introductions," Jirom snapped.

"You have a habit of cutting me off," the bandit leader said in a jesting tone.

"Tell it to the undead coming our way," Emanon told him.

Harrid's face paled slightly. "The dead are here?"

"It seems they may have followed you," Emanon said. "Please tell us there's a back way out of this deathtrap."

Harrid turned to his second. "Ohan?"

His brother shrugged. "Not likely. We picked this spot because it is easily guarded. No one can sneak up on you."

"Fucking morons." Emanon started to lower his spear.

Jirom clamped a hand on his lover's forearm. "No. Harrid, get your fighters assembled at the canyon entrance. Hug the walls. Use whatever cover you can find. Rocks, ditches, whatever." He called to Paranas. "Give them back their weapons and assemble with them at the mouth!"

Jirom lowered his voice to a growl as he leaned closer to the bandit leader. "And if a single man of yours runs or refuses to fight, I'll stake them to the ground and pull out their entrails for the buzzards to eat. You understand?"

Harrid nodded several times. Then he and his brother hustled out, shouting for their men to follow.

"What's the plan, Jirom?" Emanon asked, as the refugees huddled around them outside the cave entrance.

"There's no time for subtlety. We either break through the enemy force, or we die here. Leave a couple Blades to guard the people. The rest of us will try to hold the center."

"Where do you want me?" Three Moons asked.

Jirom drew his sword. "Right by my side, old man. We'll need every imp and djinn you can conjure up if we're going to survive this."

Three Moons frowned as he looked up at the darkening sky. "I'll do what I can. But things are going to get nasty, Sarge. And real quick."

Of course they are. Nothing is ever easy.

Horace winced as the heavy lid of the golden chest slammed shut with a boom that echoed through the royal audience hall. The gaggle of priests from the Sun Temple lifted the wooden rods supporting the chest and carried it out at a somber pace. And just like that, the relic he had risked his life to rescue was taken away.

"I must say." Lord Thuvan stood beside him—the only person besides his escort of Crimson Brothers who was willing to stand anywhere near Horace in the vast chamber. "I am more than a little surprised you managed to accomplish it."

Horace was tired and wanted nothing more than to finish here and be on his way. He imagined the rebel army had reached the Black Gates by now. Jirom would be impatient to move on the capital. "You meant for me to decline the task. Or to die in the attempt. Either way, you win."

Lord Thuvan tilted his head slightly to one side. The corners of his mouth twitched in a faint facsimile of a smile. "Yet you prevailed."

"And your cult still wins. How convenient for you. I know what the relic is. What it does."

Lord Thuvan's narrow eyebrows rose a fraction of an inch. "Perhaps it would be best to discuss that elsewhere."

His meaning was clear. *Or nowhere at all.*

The court majordomo called out as King Merodach rose from his throne. His Majesty hadn't said a word since Horace's arrival. His expression bordered between angry and indifferent, moving firmly into concern as the relic left. His gaze, too, lingered on the door after their departure. *Probably wondering if giving them more power was a smart move. I'm asking myself the same thing, Your Excellence.*

Preserving his silence, the king came down from the dais and left the chamber by a different doorway, escorted by his phalanx of guards. Once he was gone, the noble assembly began to break up.

"Now what?" Horace asked.

"Now we are allied," Lord Thuvan replied. "The city will send envoys to the insurrectionists."

"What about troops? My friends are approaching the capital right now."

"Soldiers will be forthcoming. We can send cavalry and chariot units first, but the infantry will obviously take longer to reach them. Will your army wait?"

"I'm not sure. Perhaps if your envoys reach them soon enough. But if Jirom thinks he's taking on the city by himself, he won't hesitate. He's counting on surprise to give him an edge."

Lord Thuvan nodded, his mouth pressed into a firm line. "There will be a feast here in the palace tonight to celebrate your return and cement our joint pact. You will attend, of course?"

Horace suppressed a grimace. He wanted to be away from here as soon as possible, but he couldn't risk insulting these new allies. "Of course. But I don't have any spare clothes to wear."

The priest showed his teeth. "I shall send you my tailor."

Hours later, Horace was standing in a lavish chamber atop a tower in the royal grounds, swirling wine in his cup as he waited for his host to arrive. Lord Thuvan's tailor was extraordinary, and the suit Horace wore tonight was a gorgeous robe of black silk embroidered with swirling designs in silver thread at the cuffs, hem, and collar. This all felt very familiar, in a way that made him anxious.

The feast room had no walls, only thick pillars at the corners that held up the roof. A cool breeze whispered through the chamber, carrying the scents of the gardens below. The sun hung low above the city's western expanse like a burnished gold coin as the afternoon slowly dwindled. The smells, the wine, the smoothness of the silk he wore—it all reminded him of his time in Erugash. As First Sword, he had felt trapped in an impossible situation. *Not so different from now.*

The sound of clinking glasses made him turn. The gathering was small, with only a dozen people in attendance. They wore the finery of the city's elite and made polite conversation among themselves. Horace stood alone by one of the pillars, wishing he had a good excuse to leave early, but the king was expected to arrive soon. Horace braced himself for an evening of inanity, a useless gesture of civility while the rest of the empire writhed in agony.

A tall man in a military uniform came over. By his shaved head and the two golden knots displayed on his shoulder, he was a high-ranking member of the *hekatatum* military caste. "The wine is quite good, isn't it? Royal vintage."

"I suppose so," Horace said.

The *sarleskar* bowed his head. "I am Istaran Punanu, Commander of His Majesty's First Legion."

Horace introduced himself, and then asked, "Is the king going to arrive soon?"

Istaran smiled slightly, his eyes crinkling as if he were indulging a petulant child. "His Majesty has many weighty matters to attend to. We worthless subjects must wait for His arrival like the blossoms wait for the rain."

"Pardon me. There is a fly in my wine."

Horace walked away from the commander and went to another corner of the chamber where he could stand alone. He was grateful no one else approached him, except for the serving slaves who filled his cup at regular intervals.

Finally, the majordomo appeared to announce the king's arrival. Everyone else dropped to one knee as King Merodach entered the chamber with Lord Thuvan, but Horace remained standing. At first, the king did not seem to notice him. However, as he made a magnanimous gesture for his people to rise, Merodach stole a glance in Horace's direction. His smile faltered for only a moment before it was fixed back in place.

Horace stifled a sigh. *So much for a warm reception. Maybe we can at least get through this charade without anyone trying to kill me.*

The king lifted both hands as if to welcome an embrace. "We gather to honor Lord Horace of Erugash for his service to our city. In liberating the sacred icon of the Sun Lord, he has delivered unto us the means to protect Yuldir forever. Let us celebrate this new friendship and pray that together we may free the empire of the darkness that threatens our very way of life."

The attendees applauded with restraint. Horace forced himself to smile as he raised his cup. As the feast began, he was seated between the *sarleskar* and a heavyset noblewoman who kept addressing him as 'the man from the West.' He tried to avoid conversation as much as possible. What he really wanted was to drown his annoyance in wine, but he didn't trust his company. They seemed to all be watching him with suspicion, so he saw everything they said and did in the same light, which made for a tense meal. He hardly touched the fare, despite its excellence. By the time the first dessert course was served, he had had enough.

Excusing himself, Horace got up from the table and went out through the western window to a narrow terrace that surrounded the top of the tower. The city below looked like a painting. People walked through the streets. From up here, they appeared to pursue their lives as if nothing else were happening in the world, as if peace and safety were assured forever. Perhaps that was the key to Akeshian thinking, an unshakable faith in their rulers. Beyond the homes and businesses rose the city walls, where sentries walked their rounds along the stout ramparts. Everything was oddly calm, but Horace saw it for the illusion it was. Beyond these walls, the world was about to end.

"Not one for feting?"

Horace turned as Lord Thuvan joined him on the terrace. The sun priest wore a fine robe of gold with black trim. His scalp tattoos glittered in the waning sunlight. "No, it feels strange. We're celebrating here while people are fighting for their lives elsewhere."

Lord Thuvan came over to the balustrade. "It can be difficult living with such onus, but that is the life we were born into. Nothing can change that. Even if we turn away from our responsibilities, they still remain to haunt us."

Disturbed at how closely the priest's words echoed his own thoughts, Horace tried to change the subject. "Thank you for supporting the alliance."

The hierarch's face was impassive. "My office deals with the acquisition of information from around the empire and beyond. I understand full well the danger we face. However, all are not convinced. This alliance, I fear, may not last long."

The embers of rage, which lurked close beneath the surface of Horace's emotions, flared to new life. "Are you saying the king won't honor his word?"

Lord Thuvan adjusted the left sleeve of his robe as if nothing were bothering him, but Horace knew enough about Akeshian cues to see the man was perturbed. "It is a royal prerogative to interpret words as one sees fit. His Majesty—Amur bless his name—is a good and wise ruler. However, he is still bound to certain laws and traditions."

"He's under pressure from his nobles."

"Yes, but more importantly, there is dissent among the cults. Anti-rebel sentiment and—forgive me again—feelings of hostility toward your person are still very high. For instance, the master of our local chapter of the Crimson Order declined an invitation to this evening's fete. It is a powerful statement, as I'm sure you know."

"But we worked together in Thuum. Akeshians and freed slaves fought side by side. They are marching together as we speak, all of them prepared to sacrifice their lives to save this country. If Yuldir sits idly by, there is no guarantee we won't all be dead soon."

"All we can do is pray for deliverance, and that our leaders receive the proper guidance."

"With all respect, my lord, I don't think—"

A powerful surge of energy interrupted him. Horace and Thuvan both turned to the south. There, far beyond the horizon, he felt a sudden surge of *zoana*. He held his breath. For him to feel the power so strongly from so far away meant it must be titanic in scope. *It's Astaptah. I know it in my bones. What is he—*

Thirty-eight refugees crammed together around half a dozen small fires inside the cave. The smoke hung in the close air, making Dasha's eyes water. The walls and ceiling seemed to press in on her.

It is strange. Before, all I wanted was shelter from the world, and now I long to be outside. The freedom of the open land, with no boundaries or limitations.

The short time she had spent with Elia in the wastes had been terrifying, but also liberating. Elia was right. It had been the first time in her life she was actually, truly free. Her dreams this night had been unpleasant, rousing her from sleep several times with images of dead people coming back to life and chasing her through the streets of Ceasa.

This morning when Harrid announced that he and his men were leaving to attack the people they had discovered, Dasha had seen him in a different light, seen the naked lust lurking in his eyes. He was not the gallant rescuer she had taken him for. She had spent the hours since keeping to herself, lost in thought. She and Elia couldn't stay with these men indefinitely. They needed a plan.

Elia brought over a pair of brown biscuits and a clay cup. Dasha accepted her share with a nod.

"You're overly quiet," Elia said as she sat down beside her, their backs to the cave wall.

Dasha took a bite of the hard bread and chewed slowly. "Just thinking."

"Now is a good time."

Dasha blinked and focused on her bodyguard. "A good time for what?"

"To make our escape. While Harrid and most of his men are out doing murder."

"What if these others are as Harrid said? What if he really is protecting us?"

Elia shrugged as she tore off a hunk of biscuit. "When two wolves fight over a rabbit, whichever one wins, it's still not good for the rabbit."

"We would need food and water. Enough to get us far away."

Elia winked and opened the flap of her belt pouch. Inside were more biscuits. "It's not much, but it should do. We'll grab a couple water gourds on the way out. There's only one guard outside the cave. I'll take care of him first. Then we run."

Dasha looked around the cave. "What about these people? Elia, we can't leave them to Harrid's mercy."

"Pri—Yura, how are we going to transport this many people all the way across the empire? Your heart is in the right place, girl, but—"

"No!" Several people looked over. Embarrassed, Dasha averted her eyes until they lost interest. "I won't leave them. We're taking everyone with us."

Elia looked as if she would continue arguing, but instead she chewed quietly on her bread. After a minute, she said, "Still, we should go now. While the others are away."

Dasha stood up. Her stomach fluttered as the prospect of action flooded her mind. "All right. What do we do about the guard outside?"

Elia finished her bread, wiped her hands on her tunic front, and loosened her dagger in its sheath. "I'll handle him."

"Elia, he's barely older than I am. Perhaps we can convince him to come with us."

Her bodyguard's face became grim. "We can't risk it. If he changes his mind and runs off later, Harrid's entire band will hunt us down. I'm sorry, but I can't take the risk with your life."

Dasha nodded, trying not to feel bad about the decision.

Elia continued, "You gather everyone together. Take all the food and water. It should be enough to get us to—"

She fell silent as swift footsteps echoed at the cave entrance. Everyone turned as the young guard ran into the cavern. His expression was worried. "Harrid is back," he said. "And more men have come with him. Fighting men. We're supposed to come out."

"Fuck," Elia whispered.

Dasha didn't have time to be surprised by her bodyguard's profanity. Her stomach dropped, the anticipation of breaking free dashed to pieces. They had lost their chance. Or was it really too late? In the confusion of meeting the new arrivals, she and Elia might be forgotten. They might still slip away unnoticed. It was a slim chance, but better than none. But then they couldn't take the other refugees with them. Tears formed in her eyes from the frustration. She *would* see these people free and safe.

The refugees milled about, obviously afraid to leave the cave, until the young guard began shouting at them. He, too, looked frightened.

"What can we do?" Dasha asked Elia quietly.

Any reply was stifled as more men entered the cave. Many voices gasped as the light of the crude torches fell upon them, and Dasha's was among them. The strangers were silver. Their skin, their hair, even their eyes—all completely silver as if they had been dipped into a whitesmith's foundry. Dasha looked to Elia. Were these 'men' human? Elia's gaze was steady on the strangers. Her hands, though, stayed close to her weapons.

The silver men wore armor and weapons. As the young guard had said, they were obviously fighting men. One of them spoke up, and his voice filled the interior cavern. "I'm Paranas, captain of the Silver Blades. Danger is coming this way, so we need everyone to exit the cave."

Confused voices rose from the refugees, but no one moved.

Dasha spoke up. "What danger, Captain?"

The man—Paranas—looked relieved to have someone to address directly. "The dead. Many of them. They will be here soon, so we must go."

An icy tremor ran through Dasha. For a moment, she imagined the undead pouring into this canyon, dragging down the people one by one and devouring them like wild animals. She tightened her hands into fists. *Get a hold of yourself. Think!*

"Come on!" she shouted to the people. "Take food and water and leave the cave."

With Elia beside her, they joined the group as it filed out. The silver men stood by, merely watching. It made Dasha feel strange, like a beast being led to market. Yet, the silver captain had a kind voice. She hoped they could trust him.

Outside, she blinked as the late afternoon sunlight struck her eyes. The sun hovered over the lip of the canyon, casting long shadows across the floor. Harrid's men stood outside the cave, but only a dozen or so. Where were the rest? A few of them bore injuries, and Dasha guessed they had been in a fight, and lost.

Then she saw more strangers. Two of them were not silver-hued like the others but had the appearance of normal men. Both were tall, but one was bigger than all the rest. He looked to be a few years older than her. Muscles bunched and rippled under his leather jerkin. A big sword hung at his hip. Then Dasha saw the brands on his cheek—the marks of a slave who had killed—and her legs suddenly felt weak. Had Harrid been right?

The big man was talking to Harrid. Curious, Dasha sidled closer, with Elia close beside her.

"Get your fighters assembled at the canyon entrance, half on each side," the newcomer was instructing. And, to Dasha's amazement, Harrid was listening. "Hug the walls. Use whatever cover you can find. Rocks, ditches, whatever. And wait for my signal."

The massive stranger leaned close to Harrid and said something Dasha couldn't make out. Harrid nodded vigorously and ran off, calling his men to him. Dasha couldn't believe it. Who was this stranger? Perhaps a local warlord. Harrid obviously respected him a great deal.

The other stranger stood close to the boss. He had a wolfish look about him. "What's the plan, Jirom?" he asked.

"There's no time for subtlety," the big man said. "We either break through the attack force, or we die here. Put the others at the canyon entrance. We'll try to hold the center."

Elia pulled Dasha's arm, forcing her to step back. "Let us go now," she whispered. "While they are distracted."

"Not yet," Dasha replied, moving with the refugees as they were herded toward the canyon entrance behind the fighters. "Did you see what he did? The new one?"

Elia hissed a soft curse. "He's just another bandit wolf. As soon as the danger is passed, he'll turn on the rabbits."

Dasha wasn't so sure. In either case, she had made up her mind. She wasn't leaving these people—her people—in the clutches of dangerous men. "Either we all escape, or we all stay. Work on a plan for that, until we know more."

Elia growled in her throat like she wanted to snap at Dasha, but she remained quiet as they tagged along with the others. The fighters assembled at the end of the canyon, as ordered. The new leader—Jirom—stood at the center with his lieutenant and an older silver man, speaking quietly among themselves. Dasha wished she could listen in, but the refugees were spread out along the canyon wall and told to remain still by a silver woman. Dasha asked her name.

"I'm Jauna," she replied. Her voice was husky, as if she didn't use it often. "Stay quiet. When we break their line, we'll all rush out as one. Stick together. Hold hands if you must. Stragglers are liable to get picked off."

Dasha shivered, remembering her first sight of the dead ones at the gates of Ceasa. The mindless, hungry horde. Was there any hope of defeating them? She looked around for another route out, but the cliff walls were tall and sheer. A feeling bubbled in the pit of her stomach like she would soon be ill. She kept her hands clenched into tight fists. *I will not lose control. I am the daughter of Manishtushu-Amur, Twenty-Eighth Emperor of Akeshia. I fear nothing.*

Ignoring a look of warning from Elia, Dasha edged forward, until she was near the fighters. Harrid and Ohan squatted with a handful of their men. A quiet debate was underway. Dasha inched closer.

"—when the fighting gets fierce, you get behind the big one," Harrid was saying. "If we take him out, the rest of his gang will fall in line. We'll have more men, and their weapons."

"What about their army?" Ohan asked. "He said it was nearby."

Harrid spat on the rocks under their feet. "A lie. A trick to put us under his thumb."

"I don't know. He sounded convincing to me."

"Dammit, Ohan! Listen to me. If we cut off the serpent's head, the rest will follow us. That's how we handled Uricho."

"But these silver warriors—"

Dasha held her breath as Harrid cursed and stood up. She was only a couple paces from them, but neither man looked in her direction.

"You don't know anything," Harrid muttered mockingly. "See how far that gets us with this new commander."

He strode off, toward the front of the group, and knelt behind a low clump of boulders. Ohan joined him, and they waited together without talking. Dasha was wondering what to do with this information when sounds echoed from the west. At first, they sounded like horses, galloping toward the canyon. Then, as they got closer, she could make out the difference. These weren't hooves pounding on rock, but the slap of feet. Lots of them. She snuck back to Elia.

"That was a foolish risk," her bodyguard whispered.

"They are planning to murder the big one. Jirom."

"If he has the wits of a goat, he already knows as much." She dug her fingers into Dasha's arm. "This is no game. Blood will be shed, and people are going to die. If you are among them, then I have failed in my duty. I won't let that happen."

Meeting her bodyguard's gaze, Dasha felt the lump in her stomach double in size. "I understand. I'll do as you say."

Elia grunted. "That will be the day. Now, stay close and try not to rouse suspicion. The fighting will be fiercest at the onset. We'll wait for our chance, and then run. Are you ready?"

Dasha nodded, feeling bad for lying, but it was for the greater good. Elia would see. She watched Jirom speak to his comrade with the spear. There was a closeness between them. She saw it in the way they stood near each other, hips almost touching, heads bent together as if discussing something heartfelt. Sudden pangs wrenched her heart as she found herself desperately missing her family, but there was no time to grieve. The noises were racing closer.

The numbing claws of paralysis sunk into her limbs when she saw them. A loose mass of things that had formerly been people sprinted through the pass. It was easy to think of them as still human, if one ignored the feral glint in their dark eyes, or the unnervingly silent way in which they snarled, dirty fingers extended like talons. She felt like she needed to be ill. That's why she was astonished to see Jirom and his comrade charge forward together, *into* the mass of undead. It seemed insane. She kept expecting to wake up, as if this was all some horrible nightmare. She couldn't feel her hands, even though she was clasping them together, so hard her knuckles had turned white.

Just before the pair met the enemy, sharp twangs echoed from the silver warriors. A dozen undead fell where they stood, their skulls transfixed by long crossbow quarrels. A moment later, Jirom and the other man crashed into the horde. Their weapons—Jirom's tulwar and his comrade's spear—lashed out in a frenzy, chopping through the enemy with startling swiftness. The crunch of splintering bones, blurs of flashing steel, half of a human head rolling in the dust—these images seared themselves into Dasha's memory.

As Jirom and his second pressed into the melee, they were quickly surrounded by dozens of the living dead. They fought like demons, and the silver warriors struggled to keep up with them, but there were too many foes. This battle could have only one conclusion.

The black shield burst into view, lifted by an upswing that had bashed in the face of an elderly corpse. This was followed by a savage chopping of the tulwar that separated two more undead heads from their bodies. For a second, there was an opening in the horde, and Jirom plunged into it like a man possessed, with his battle partner so close behind they almost seemed like two halves of the same person. The two men evaded all attempts to grab them and pull them down. Any undead who ventured too close with chomping jaws were sent reeling back with smashed-out teeth and severed limbs. Slowly, the fighting style of the newcomers fell into a rhythm Dasha could make out. Block of the black shield, a hard shove to make space, followed by slashes so quick she could barely follow them with her gaze. Jirom's comrade guarded his back, his spear's point seeming to be everywhere at once—knocking clawed hands away, tripping up awkward feet, punching through eye sockets and open mouths. It was gruesome and thrilling at the same time. A growing pile of unmoving bodies lay in their wake.

Along the edge of the canyon wall, Harrid and his men waited, not joining the battle. Dasha might have considered it cowardice, if not for what she had overheard. *They plan to use this battle as a chance to eliminate their new rivals.*

Her heart beat hard in her chest as she tried to come up with a solution.

"Now! Follow me!" Jauna raised her sword like a banner as she ran through a narrow gap created by the other warriors.

The refugees followed in a ragged file, running for their lives. Dasha held her breath as she and Elia hurried through the narrow corridor of safety. She couldn't help looking at the undead. She wanted to see them up close, but the sight was worse than she had imagined. The closer she got, the less human they appeared. Many were missing sections of skin, on their faces, arms, and bodies. One woman had almost no face left, just bare tendons controlling the opening and closing her jaws and a pair of black eyes. The eyes—they were what drove home the terror in Dasha. Large and glassy like wet marbles in these ravaged, bestial faces. The undead fought like wild animals, tearing at each other to get to the silver men holding the pass. Yet, when they died, their expressions melted into something calm, almost blissful in its serenity, as if death was a blessing. Seeing it happen, again and again, shook Dasha to her core.

Then, suddenly, the refugees were free, running past the melee and into the open canyon beyond. Those who were able broke into a sprint, while the old and weak were left behind. Jauna didn't run; she stayed with the slower people, her eyes casting about in all directions for more foes.

Dasha stayed with the slower people, too, and watched the battle with her heart in her throat. The undead were many, but the fighting men slowly them whittled down. The silver warriors were invincible. Even so, they were slowly pushed back by sheer numbers. One enemy flung itself high into the air, trying to leap past the bottleneck. Jirom speared it through the stomach with the point of his sword and dropped it to the ground, and then smashed its forehead open with the rim of his shield.

Harrid's men stayed on the edge of the fighting, moving only to surround and cut down the few undead who managed to squeeze past the silver warriors. Dasha wanted to cry. If Harrid and his gang joined the battle in full, everyone might have a chance to survive.

Looking back over her shoulder, Dasha ran into an old man in front of her. The line had stopped. The people at the front were turning back in terror. Dasha looked past them and felt her legs tremble. More undead were coming. They filled the other end of the canyon, closing in fast.

"Go back!" Jauna shouted. The silver woman didn't fall back with her charges. She faced the enemy, clearly intent on holding them off while the people escaped.

Elia tugged on Dasha's sleeve. "Now is the time," she whispered as she pointed to a steep trail that climbed the southern cliff of the ravine. "Let's go."

Dasha stopped with a small shake of her head. She could barely see Jirom through the press of bodies, but she knew he had to be alive from the flying blood. She took a step in his direction.

"Stop!" her bodyguard hissed.

Dasha met Elia's gaze with an expression she hoped looked resolute. *I'm not abandoning them.*

With a terse sigh, her bodyguard relented. "I hope this doesn't spell our deaths."

Dasha called to her *zoana*. It fluttered like a spark behind her *qa*. There was no time for subtle manipulations. She grabbed it, and the magic writhed like a living serpent in her mental grasp. Holding on tight, she wove it into the shape she needed. Kishargal wasn't one of her stronger dominions, but she was desperate. Sharp pains lanced across her stomach as she worked. Biting her bottom lip to stay focused, Dasha finished the weave and, with a prayer to Enkath, ancient protector of the earth, she let it go.

The ground rumbled. At the precise instant, the pains in Dash's stomach exploded into agony. She grabbed Elia's arm for stability. They both watched in awe as the south cliff of the canyon mouth came tumbling down in a massive rockslide. The rockslide collapsed on top of the newly arriving undead, burying most of them under tons of stone and gravel. A few survived, still loping toward the refugees.

"Go," Dasha said, pushing Elia weakly. She could hardly draw breath. "Help them."

Elia hesitated a moment, and then went, drawing her sword as she ran. The bodyguard joined Jauna in meeting the oncoming undead. Side by side they fought, a two-woman bulwark against the tide of death. Dasha leaned against the canyon wall and struggled not to clutch her stomach. She could feel blood running down her belly and feared what she would find if she looked under her clothes. In her mind, the *immaculata* were massive tears exposing her innards. Fortunately, no blood had appeared on her loose tunic.

In just a few minutes, the last remnants of the undead horde were slaughtered. Dasha took a long breath, freeing herself from the terrible stress that had gripped her during the battle. They were going to live. The fighters had suffered only a few injuries, and one death. The young man who had been guarding the cave lay on the ground, his throat torn out, white cartilage dangling from the ghastly wound.

Elia returned, her sword covered in black blood. "You need to rest."

"What's wrong with her?" Jauna asked. The silver woman wiped her own blade with a tattered cloak she had stripped from a corpse.

Dasha looked up at Elia, pleading with her eyes.

"She's having her cycle," the bodyguard said, her gaze lowering to Dasha's stomach, where the blood was cooling on her skin. "That, combined with the fright of battle."

Jauna eyed them for a moment, and then slipped off her satchel and tossed it to Elia. "There's cloth in there you can wad up to staunch the flow, and bitterroot to ease the ache."

"Thank you," Dasha said.

"We could use some privacy," Elia said.

"You'll have some when we get where we're going."

"Where's that?" Dasha asked.

Jauna cocked her head toward the spot where Jirom stood with his lieutenant and a couple of silver warriors. "Wherever the commander decides. I expect they're coming up with an answer about now. Let's find out."

Dasha took a step in that direction. The pain in her abdomen was receding, making her think the worst was over. She regained strength with each step and was soon standing on her own, but Elia hovered close beside her as they stepped over the multitude of corpses. The smells rising from the dead made Dasha gag.

As they approach the cluster of men, Dasha overheard Jirom talking with the old silver man.

"—wasn't me, Sarge. I was too busy trying to save my own skin."

"So what caused it? Cliffs don't collapse on their own."

The tan-skinned lieutenant shrugged, leaning on his spear. "Maybe it was an act of the Gods."

As Jirom shook his head, Dasha saw Harrid approach from behind the commander. He had a bared knife, held in a reverse grip so the blade lay hidden against his forearm. Ohan walked beside his brother and looked to also be palming something in his large hand. Dasha froze in a panic as Harrid and Ohan walked with languid slowness, closing in on their targets. Dasha could see what was going to happen, but the terrible paralysis had returned, locking her in place. Suddenly, just as the bandit leaders stepped behind the newcomers, she broke free and exhaled a loud shout.

"Behind you!"

Jirom and his friend whirled about faster than Dasha thought was possible. Their weapons were blurs, arcing out as they turned. Harrid fell on his back, holding his severed throat with both hands, his knife fallen to the ground. Ohan staggered back a step and dropped to his knees, the point of the spear protruding from his breastbone. A line of blood spilled from his mouth as he collapsed.

Jirom and his comrade stood over the dead bandits. Dasha trembled at the looks in their eyes as they shifted their gazes to the rest of Harrid's men, and then to the refugees. Would they decide to kill them all for this betrayal? Dasha stepped ahead of the other refugees, still bent over and staggering with each step.

"Yura!" Elia hissed as she moved toward Dasha, sword in hand.

All eyes were focused on them. Then the sky exploded.

Looking down at the two dead men at his feet, Jirom wondered what the point was. *It's a waste of life.*

Beyond Harrid and his brother lay a mass of slaughtered undead, who had once been living, breathing people. Now they were just meat for the carrion birds. He and Emanon, and the army under their command—they were in a war against death, and every lost life was a defeat. If they were going to continue to fight and kill each other in the end, then what was the point of it all?

His gaze rose to the girl who had shouted a warning. He had felt the two would-be assassins coming up behind him, and seen that Emanon noticed them too, but her cry had alerted everyone else. Now she stood there, trembling beside her protector. Trembling, and yet unafraid. Her eyes, though slightly clouded with some distress he couldn't pinpoint, were fierce and undaunted. Who was she? Surely not some impoverished farm girl, judging by the way she spoke. Clearly, she had some education. Perhaps she was a tradesman's daughter.

He was debating how to approach her and what to say when a boom like every thunderstorm in the world's history all combined into a single blast detonated behind him. He ducked his head as he turned around, and what he saw turned his insides to ice water. The sky was being devoured. That's how it appeared as arms of inky black stretched across the firmament. They originated in the east, behind the canyon's high cliffs, and extended to the horizon in every direction. Each arm of darkness thickened as it reached out, filling in the gaps between and swallowing the daylight like a plague of locusts sweeping through a grain field. No stars shone through the spreading darkness, nor any moon—it was all pure black.

More rumbles echoed overhead, shaking the ground, and in that moment Jirom felt insignificant. What was the point of resisting?

As the last rays of sunlight dwindled and died, that question echoed in his mind.

"My lord," Lord Thuvan said behind him. "Is something—?"

Horace didn't hear the rest of the priest's words as a massive boom echoed from the sky. It came from the southeast. Squinting, Horace thought he saw a distant burst of bright green light in that direction, like the twinkle of a shooting star, too fast for the eye to follow. Then the light vanished in an explosion of darkness. Black tendrils shot across the sky, radiating from that point in the southeast and stretching to every horizon. Like a sudden eclipse, daylight faded as the darkness blotted out the sun, and with the dark came a rushing wind that guttered out flames and knocked loose tiles from the rooftops. The feast's attendees cried out as the gale abruptly overturned their dinnerware and whipped through their fine attire. Thunder rolled and boomed overhead.

The itch of sorcery ran down Horace's spine. A moment later, the gale was held back as several of the guests summoned their *zoana* to surround the tower in walls of hardened air. Horace was too distracted to lend assistance. His gaze was focused on the origin of the preternatural storm, which had spread to cover the entire sky within the span of a dozen heartbeats. Far away, perhaps a hundred leagues or more, the sky was stained a darker shade of night, and that deep abyss of total black was spreading out like a cancer. Another gale struck the city, this one so strong that trees were knocked over and doors slammed open. The tower's defenses withstood the blast, but Horace could feel them straining.

Finally, the wind died down, leaving behind a swirl of haphazard zephyrs that resolved themselves into a multitude of tiny dust devils. Across the sky, all was darkness. No sun or stars shone through.

Horace was still studying the phenomenon when he noticed Thuvan had left. The archpriest had fled the tower, along with most of the revel's guests, including the king. The only ones left were Horace, Istaran, and a few servants cleaning up.

Horace called over to the *sarleskar*. "Tell the king he had better not waver on his promise. If he does, I will personally return and demolish this city, until there's not a single brick left standing. Tell him that."

Istaran bowed his head. Fear was etched into his expression. "I will tell him, *Belzama*."

Then Horace was gone, wrapped up in the void and carried away. As he traveled the winds of sorcery, he couldn't get the image out of his mind of a sky gone completely dark. The dying light had shoved an icicle into his chest.

The horde was hungry.

Pumash stood atop a tower in the imperial palace, looking down over the capital. The dead prowled the streets and alleys for something to kill and devour. The gates of the palace were flung open in silent invitation. He had nothing to protect him. No guards. Nothing except for the surety of the *Manalish*. So far, that had been enough.

Watching the dead roam the benighted streets, Pumash wondered if this was what victory looked like. *From here, it looks much the same as defeat.*

Thunder rumbled overhead as arcs of green lightning flashed amid the mantle of clouds. The storm was a constant presence, night and day, until he could no longer tell the time. He slept, woke, and wandered the halls of palace, eating and drinking to sustain himself—mostly drinking. The entire contents of the wine cellar were at his disposal, and he intended to drink it all. Sometimes—most times—delirium was all that kept him from jumping off one of these high towers. He imagined the fall would feel like flying, as his mortal body was freed from the constraints of gravity, right until the final moment. And then, blessed oblivion.

Perhaps tomorrow.

He was turning away from the macabre tableau when a titanic crash of thunder boomed over his head. Pumash dropped to his knees and hugged the tower's battlements. With the smooth ashlar blocks pressed against his cheek, he looked up into a maelstrom of horror. The sky had split open, and a giant vortex raged within the heart of the storm, surrounded by a funnel of black clouds and flickers of green lightning. Pumash held on tight as the wind whipped around him, trying to pry his fingers from the stone.

Above him, the darkness of the storm was spreading out in long arms, like the tentacles of a vast undersea beast, across the sky in every direction until all was black. *Eternal night, just as the* Manalish *promised.*

Something broke inside Pumash as the vista above stripped away his last bit of fear. This was the end of everything. Soon, the entire world would be dead, and nothing would remain except great masses of animated corpses, forever roaming under a midnight sky. *Forever and ever.*

After some time, the winds died down. Pulling himself upright, Pumash brushed the bits of gravel and grit from his skirt, and then headed toward the stairs. He needed a drink. *Several drinks. Jars and jars of wine, until I fall into a deep, dreamless sleep.*

With every step downward, he saw the spreading darkness in his mind's eye, and the roaming dead. Death and undeath, embracing at the end of the world.

Elia's mouth moved, but Dasha couldn't hear what she was saying as the tremendous explosion in the sky drowned out all other sounds. Louder than any thunder boom, it ripped her breath away, sounding like the entire world was being torn apart. The late afternoon sky dimmed as dark clouds washed across its previously unflawed expanse. The refugees cried out as they clutched each other. Dasha wanted to collapse under the powerful hopelessness that crashed over her. The explosion came from the south, and she knew without seeing that it had originated in Ceasa. Her home. And this gloom spreading from it like blood from a wound must be a harbinger of the end.

As the sky dimmed, the canyon reverberated with aftershocks of the crash, each echo shaking the rock faces around them. Small avalanches rolled from the heights. Somewhere far below, the earth groaned in torment. Within a few heartbeats, the last of the daylight had been extinguished, leaving them in absolute darkness, silent except for the sobs and moans of the frightened people.

Then, Jirom's voice rang out like a clarion call. "Torches!"

The silver warriors jumped into action, pulling brands from their rucksacks and lighting them. Dasha took a deep breath. The illumination banished some of the futility she was feeling.

"All of you," Jirom addressed the refugees. "We are returning to our army, which marches on Ceasa. The way will be dangerous, but we have food and water. Those who wish are welcome to come with us. Or else, you are free to go."

Without another word, he headed out of the canyon, followed by his men. The old silver man looked around. Dasha stiffened as his strange gaze lingered on her for a moment. Then he turned and left with the others.

"Well?" Elia asked. "What shall we do?"

The refugees trudged along after the silver warriors, looking as pitiful and downtrodden as when they had followed Harrid. This was their lot, and they accepted it, for better or worse. But they were still her people.

"We go with them."

CHAPTER SEVEN

There was no dawn. The sky remained a uniform black—no stars or moon. Dasha recalled some tidbit of ecclesial education from her childhood foretelling of the end of the world. It had mentioned a sky 'as dark as night.'

"What was the name of the village you say you're from?"

Dasha looked past the large woman standing before her, outside the tent where she and Elia had slept. After waking, she had come out to look around and stopped, gazing at the sky, when the tall woman who called herself Captain Ralla accosted her with a series of probing questions.

"It was called Seven Roads," Dasha answered.

Torches lashed to spear shafts, thrust into the ground, illuminated the camp. Their flames danced in the cold wind. By this time, approaching mid-morning, the temperature should be getting much warmer, but the chill of night remained. Dasha wondered how cold it would get.

The camp itself was much larger than she had expected. The commander, Jirom, had said he and his silver men were an advance force for a larger army, but she had thought he might be exaggerating. If anything, he had been downplaying it. There had to be at least a couple thousand men under arms here, plus a sizable group of nonfighters—civilians, as the soldiers called them. For the first time since they had fled Ceasa, she actually felt a measure of security, nestled among so many. She couldn't believe a former slave led this army. Even more incredible, there was a detachment of Akeshian soldiers from Thuum here, taking orders from him. *Perhaps this is the end of the world. All previously held beliefs are coming undone.*

"Was?" the captain asked.

Dasha focused back on what the woman was saying. "What?"

"You said it *was* called Seven Roads."

"Oh. It's gone now. The dead attacked and destroyed everything."

SUN AND SERPENT

Captain Ralla frowned, which pulled down a long scar across her forehead. Dasha thought it made her look more attractive, in a rugged sort of way. Comely or not, this woman was obviously every bit a soldier, from the sturdy leather armor and weapons she wore as straightforwardly as a noblewoman wore her jewels, to the way she stood—legs stiff and planted far apart, arms crossed across her chest. Everything about her screamed that she was no one to trifle with. Dasha wondered idly who would walk away from a brawl, her or Elia.

"How far from the capital was it?"

"Hmmm? Oh, sorry. I'm still a little tired." Dasha did a quick calculation. "It was about ten miles from Ceasa."

"So you've been there?"

"The capital?" Dasha hesitated, sensing a trap. "Um, yes. But just once or twice."

"Was it once or twice?"

"Well, I was just a girl when papa took me." Dasha plunged into the story she and Elia had invented. "He was a farmer. Was, because he's dead now. My mother and brothers and sisters, too. All I have left is my aunt. I think she's still sleeping. Where is this army from?"

"When you went to Ceasa, did you get a good look at the walls and gates? Could you draw them on a parchment?"

"I'm not sure. Maybe."

The flap of the tent opened, and Elia stepped out, adjusting her weapons belt over her homespun tunic. "What's going on here?"

Dasha put on her best smile. "Captain Ralla was asking me some questions. About our history."

Ralla and Elia eyed each other for a moment, and then suddenly seemed to lose interest.

"The commander was hoping you could provide some intel on the capital," Ralla said.

"Commander Jirom?" Dasha asked. "What is he like? And who are those silver soldiers? Why do they look that way?"

Ralla hitched a thumb over her left shoulder. "Chow wagons are that way.

You eat after the fighters. Latrines are to the east. Stay out of the way. You know where we're going. So, if you don't want another visit to the capital, I suggest you take your free meal and be on your way."

With that, the captain walked off with long, forceful strides.

Dasha glanced at Elia. "What do you think?"

"I could eat."

"No, about her?"

Elia cast her gaze after the departing woman, and then shrugged. "Capable."

Dasha made sure to hide her smile. "Let's go find this chow wagon."

"How are you feeling?"

Dasha placed a hand on her stomach, which was wrapped in layers of bandages. The *immaculata* were shallow—thank the Gods—but they had appeared in a tender place. "Sore, but I'd like to walk around a bit. I feel like we've been cooped up for days."

"Just go slow. If those cuts start bleeding again, we'll have to sew them shut."

Repressing a shiver at the thought, Dasha started off with Elia at her side. The camp reminded her somewhat of a crowded street market, with a mixture of peoples, sights, and smells. The torchlight made everything feel clandestine and more exciting, and Dasha found she enjoyed the freedom to walk among these people as one of them. There were no ranks among these refugees and camp followers, at least none she could see. Just people trying to survive.

They found the food wagons, which served as mobile kitchens. Sweaty men and women ladled out bowls of soup and crusts of bread. Dasha and Elia got in line with the rest of the camp followers. When they had received their portion, they found a spot out of the way where they could sit and eat. The soup was lukewarm and watery, but Dasha savored it, sopping it up with her heel of barley bread.

"Well, out with it," Elia said.

"What?" Dasha looked over, caught in her train of thoughts.

"I can see it in your face. You're plotting something, so you might as well tell me."

"All right. It's Jirom."

"What about him?" Elia paused, and then a concerned look crossed her face. "Oh, Pr—Yura. Don't tell me . . ." She lowered her voice. "You're not falling for him, are you?"

Dasha almost spilled her soup, shaking her head. "No, no. It's not that."

Elia returned to her meal. "Good. He's a good-looking man, I'll admit. But did you see how he stands next to his second-in-command? I'll wager they share a bed."

Dasha felt her face heating up. "I think we can use him to get back Ceasa. From the—" She lowered her voice to a whisper. "—Dark King."

Elia put down her bowl and looked straight into Dasha's eyes. "I understand. You lost everything. Your family, your home, and your status. You want revenge. But this army isn't going to take back Ceasa. Not for you. Not for anybody. You were there when the dead broke the gates and slaughtered the garrison."

"But you saw what Jirom's men did against the undead in the canyon."

"Against a few score. The Dark King has legions of those fiends. Yura, it's time to face the truth. The empire is fallen. Now we must survive the best we can. We should get back to our original plan."

"Hiding again? Running away?"

"Yes, if it will keep you alive."

"No. I told you, Elia. We are not abandoning my people. This is my father's empire, and I will not rest until it is freed from this curse."

"So, what do you expect to do? Strap on a sword and join the army?"

"If I have to."

A man stood beside the water wagon across from them. Not very tall, he had a dark bronze complexion and a prominent nose. His head was shaved and shiny with sweat. And he was looking in their direction. In fact, Dasha was sure he was looking at her. His face had gone pale, as if he were seeing the dead. Dasha didn't move. Who was he? Why was he staring at her?

Abruptly, the man walked away at a swift pace.

Elia watched him go. "What's wrong?"

Dasha swallowed the lump that had formed in her throat and stood up.

"Come on! Follow him."

They hurried after the man. Elia made sure people got out of their way, usually with a hard look but also sometimes with a firm push. Dasha tried to keep up, one hand held to her abdomen.

"What is this about?" the bodyguard asked as they rushed through an aisle of low tents.

Dasha stopped at the end of the row, looking around. She had lost sight of him. The torches threw long shadows down the gaps between the tents. "I think he recognized me."

Elia loosened the long knife at her hip. Dasha noticed the gesture. "We won't need that."

"If he knows who you are, he's a threat."

"We can't kill everyone who knows my face, Elia."

Dasha caught a glimpse of a shiny bald head, heading away from them. She raced off in pursuit. After turning down another row of tents and pushing under a rope fence, Dasha realized Elia was gone. She stood up on tiptoe to look for her bodyguard, but the woman was nowhere to be seen. *She'll find me. I can't risk losing this man.*

Dasha turned past another tent and found herself facing the canyon wall. The steep cliff rose more than a hundred feet before her. The man stood in front of her, gazing up those heights as if thinking to scale them. He turned and backed away as he saw Dasha.

"Leave me alone. I have done nothing to you."

He edged to his right, toward an opening between the cliff and a large tent. Dasha sidled that way as well, mirroring him.

"Wait," she said. "I just want to talk."

The man ran toward the gap, and then pulled up short, quickly backpedaling. Dasha saw why as Elia appeared in the space beyond, her knife drawn.

"You have no right to accost me," the man said.

"Like she told you." Elia grabbed him by the collar. "We just want to talk."

Elia looked around, and then cut an opening at the rear of the large tent. Motioning for Dasha to follow, she shoved the man inside.

The shelter held stacks of crates and barrels. Elia pushed the man against a wall of wooden boxes and held him there with a hand on his shoulder. He looked terrified and refused to meet Dasha's eyes.

"You know who I am," she said, speaking softly, as she would to a frightened child. "It's all right. Tell me."

"No!" he shouted.

"Quiet!" Elia hissed. She held up her knife so it caught in the light coming from the entry they had made in the rear canvas wall. "Tell her the truth."

"Start with your name," Dasha said.

"Mezim. I'm no one. Just a simple clerk."

Elia arched an eyebrow. "What does an army of slaves and Thuumian troopers need with a clerk?"

"I keep records. Supplies, arms, and what not. I used to work for the First Sword of Erugash, but that was before the city fell."

Erugash. The first city to fall to the Dark King, if the rumors were true. "What do you know about the Dark King?" Dasha asked.

"More than I wish to," he replied. Then panic filled his eyes. "But not much, actually. I know he was vizier to Queen Byleth. He accused my master of killing her, but it was a lie. *He* killed her, and then took her place during the Battle of the Four Kings."

"And how did you recognize me?"

Mezim licked his bottom lip with a darting tongue. "I wasn't sure. I saw drawings of the likenesses of the imperial family in the palace at Erugash. I thought you looked like one princess."

"Which one?" she pressed.

He was shaking now. "Princess Dasha." Suddenly, he dropped to his knees. "Please, forgive me, Highness. I will tell no one. I swear it."

He looked up at her in alarm. "If you are here, it can only mean . . ."

"Yes," Dasha said. "My father, the emperor, is dead. Along with the rest of my family, as far as I know."

"Then we have no hope," he whispered.

"What are we going to do with him?" Elia asked, still holding her knife where he could see it.

Dasha came to a decision. She knelt beside the man and took his hand. "Mezim, you are going to help us. First, you will swear on your family and by the Typhon not to reveal my presence here."

"I swear it," he replied. "By my family and the Typhon."

"Second, you're going to help us get close to the leaders of this army."

Mezim looked bewildered. "Highness, if you wish an audience with them, you need only tell them who you are. I am sure they would receive you with the honor due your station. Commander Jirom is a good man, although a little short-tempered at times."

"I cannot take that risk. I need to get close to him, without him knowing who I am. You will set it up so I can join his household."

"What's this?" Elia growled. "A new plan?"

"We need information, Elia. And for that we need access."

"Forgive me, Highness," Mezim said. "But the commander has no household to speak of. He won't even keep a manservant or personal steward."

Mezim's tone made it plain he did not agree with that situation. Dasha was surprised. Most leaders kept a large contingent of servants and slaves. However, this man—Jirom—fought to free the slaves. Perhaps his humble roots did not allow him to use others this way. "Does he have no assistants at all? Does he cook his own food? Mend his own clothes?"

"Often, yes, Highness. He is a barbarian, after all. Not like my master—"

"Nevertheless, you shall arrange a duty that gets me into his presence daily. His cupbearer, perhaps. All men enjoy having their wine poured by a beautiful woman, yes?"

Mezim looked dubious, but he nodded. "Yes, Highness. He may decide to dismiss you, but I will get you the position."

Elia gestured with the knife. "Out with you."

"Don't forget your oath," Dasha said. "This stays between us."

Mezim bowed his head. "I won't, Highness. May the blessing of the Gods be upon you."

"And you as well."

Elia put away her knife as the man slipped out of the tent. "I don't trust him."

Dasha nodded, considering how events might play out. "Because that's your job. My job is to get back control of my empire. If this clerk can help me, I will use him."

"You are becoming more like him."

"Like Mezim?"

Elia gave her a slow smile. "No. Your father."

"Shall I take that as a compliment?"

Elia shrugged as she headed for the rear of the tent. "Time will tell."

Dasha frowned as she stepped back out into the eternal night. Yes, time *would* tell, for better or worse.

Staring down at the collection of maps of the region and the capital, most drawn from memory by soldiers who either had not been to Ceasa in a long time, or were going off second- or third-hand information, Jirom wanted to toss the entire lot into a fire. His reports were sparse and often conflicting, which made planning a campaign based on them virtually impossible, but he had two thousand men and women depending on him to do just that. And not just any campaign—he needed the most brilliant military plan ever devised, to crack the most well-defended city in the world held by an unstoppable army and an insane sorcerer who had stolen the sun.

And he had to do it soon.

Jirom reached for his cup and found it empty. He thought about going to find more, but decided he was too tired. *I won't discover any answers at the bottom of a wine jar.*

As he picked up a map of Ceasa's outer defenses, drawn for him by a retired legionnaire who had visited the capital once, twenty years ago, and evidently remembered few details, strong hands came to rest on his shoulders from behind. They kneaded the tired muscles at the base of his neck, thumbs working deep into the tissues. "I hope that's you, Em. Or we're both going to be in a lot of trouble."

Emanon stopped the massage and came around to stand beside him. "Good answer. Any luck yet?"

Jirom dropped the useless drawing on the table. "No. And I'm starting to think this was a terrible idea."

"Don't look at me, lover. I wanted to stay in Thuum." He picked up two of the maps and held them side by side. "We need better intelligence."

Jirom hesitated. "I know. That's why I sent the Blades out to scout the capital." When Emanon glanced over, he said, "Yes, it smacks of the debacle at Omikur, but like you said, we need information."

"What have you come up with so far, Oh Wise Leader?"

Jirom sorted through the papers until he found the most complete map of the capital's outer defenses. "This shows at least four walls, each with its own towers, gatehouses, and barbicans. The report says Ceasa is at least half a mile across at its widest point. That means we can't attempt a traditional siege. We don't have the manpower."

Emanon leaned over the map and tapped the separate walls. "The undead aren't going to sit behind these ramparts and wait us out. They'll pour out like a swarm of hornets from a kicked nest."

"That's the other problem. We can't attack them like a living enemy. Feints and intricate maneuvers won't work on them."

"And once they close with us, we're finished. They must outnumber us five to one."

"I'm assuming ten to one, at the least. The Dark King has been gathering fresh troops from each town, village, and city he's conquered."

Emanon shook his head. "And they're all packed together in the capital like a tumor filled with pus. Okay, can we use their ferocity against them?"

Jirom pulled out a map of the surrounding territory. "I thought about that. We could use a decoy force to draw them out."

"Lure the cold bastards away on a merry chase while the rest of us hit the city and cut off the head of the snake."

"Exactly. But the problem—again—is sheer numbers. Even if we could get the attention of all the undead inside the capital, or even most of them, all at the same time, and get them moving, it would take hours for them to leave through the gates. During that time, if they get distracted or simply stop following the pack, the plan is ruined. We're still left assaulting a well-defended position occupied by an overwhelming force. It would take a couple full legions working in concert to lure them all out."

"So, what do we do?"

"I'm working on it. Round up the unit leaders."

"You sure? We have time."

Jirom knew what he meant. Horace hadn't returned, and without him they didn't stand much of a chance. "We can't wait. We have to prepare with the resources we have on hand. Bring them in."

Emanon placed a hand on his shoulder. "Come on. We'll hit the chow line first. You haven't eaten since we got back."

"I had a biscuit."

Emanon pulled him away from the table. "Even glorious commanders need food. And maybe a bath."

"Are you saying I smell?"

"Never, my love. But you want to knock the captains over with your spectacular planning, not your odor."

Jirom allowed himself to be pulled away from the table, but his mind was churning with plans and tactics as they went out into a cool darkness.

Perhaps, Jirom thought as he and Emanon strolled past the rows of tents and their guards, standing watch with torchlight flickering across their armor and the points of their spears, he was overthinking it. Complicated strategies had never been his forte, neither as a mercenary nor a gladiator. Perhaps he just needed to do what he had always done.

Hit them first and hard, and let the Gods worry about the outcome.

The table was set for a conference. The various maps were rolled up and neatly stacked. The overhead lamps were lit. She had opened the jar of wine so it could breathe, cups ready to be filled. Incense smelling of sandalwood burned in a small brazier. All was ready.

Mezim had made good on his promise. She was now the commander's official cupbearer. Dasha walked around the tent, checking everything for a third time. She was nervous and excited. She had never served before. Oh, she had played 'servant girl' with her siblings as a child, but nothing like this. What if she did something wrong? Would they know her pedigree at once? Everything hinged on her learning what kind of man this commander was, whether she could trust him or not. If she couldn't, then she might have no other choice than to heed Elia's advice and flee this army of former slaves.

Lightning flashed outside, and she could not resist the impulse to listen for the thunder, counting to herself. *1 . . . 2 . . . 3 . . .*

Dasha jumped as a voice spoke behind her. "Yura."

At that moment, thunder crashed. Dasha turned to the speaker, trying to compose herself. "Yes, Purna."

The old war widow held out a square of plain linen. "Tie up your hair."

Dasha accepted the cloth and bound up her hair. Purna had shown her into the tent and told her what to do. Evidently, the old woman had very strong feelings on decorum and proper service. "Thank you."

Purna looked around, moving things slightly, and then left through the rear. For a moment, Dasha saw the sky outside, a solid sheet of black, and shivered. It was midday.

The front tent flap opened, and the commander entered. He looked bigger in person, almost too large to fit inside the pavilion. His gaze brushed across her, barely pausing, before he walked to the side table and poured his own wine. Then, taking a deep quaff, he went to the map table. He stood there, silent, unmoving except to lift the cup to his lips occasionally.

Dasha felt her face warming. She felt like a piece of furniture, or a decorative vase, for as much attention as he paid her. She felt the need to say something to fill the space between them, but she reminded herself that she was here to observe and learn. The tent-flap opened again, and the commander's friend entered. She had heard his name was Emanon. He was like Jirom in some ways. They were both large men and powerfully built, but Emanon had a more wolfish look, while Jirom reminded her of only one thing—the tiger her father had received as a gift from a king in the East. She had been only seven at the time, but she remembered being fascinated by the creature. How regal it looked, how powerfully it moved, and its eyes were like matched pieces of golden opal. She had loved the beast, until it had escaped its pen only a few weeks after it arrived and killed one of its keepers. Then her father had been forced to order its elimination. Jirom had the same magnetic attraction, beautiful and dangerous at the same time.

Emanon stopped at the table and stared at her. Dasha was used to men looking at her. It had been happening since she was a girl. Some of them looked because of lust, others because of her lineage. Emanon merely looked at her.

"You been picking up strays, Jirom?"

The commander didn't look up from the map. "Another servant. Mezim seems to think I need civilizing."

"That man lives for mucking with other people's lives. She doesn't look like much. You should toss her out on her narrow ass."

Dasha gritted her teeth to keep from snapping back at him. She reminded herself how the servants in her father's palace had acted, always poised and accommodating. Suddenly, she was very embarrassed for her behavior as a child, of how she had spoken to and treated the palace staff. *This is no more than a small taste of my just desserts. Just relax. You are here to learn.*

"Leave her be," Jirom said. Then the two men bent their heads together over the map, speaking in low tones.

Dasha itched to move closer so she could overhear what they were saying. After a minute, she picked up the wine jar and a cup and went over to them on the pretext of offering a drink to Emanon. He took the cup, sipped, and thereafter ignored her. Dasha waited a moment, watching as they traced their fingers over the map's drawn contours. They were planning the final leg of their march.

More unit leaders entered and surrounded the table. They were a diverse crowd, including both old and young, men and a couple of women, and people obviously from all walks of life.

As they discussed which route to take, Emanon traced a route straight to Ceasa. "I still think we should cut across this pan. It might be rough terrain, but it will save us time. If we set out tomorrow morning—whatever the fuck *that* means anymore—and keep a fast pace, we can reach the city within seven or eight hours."

Jirom shook his head. "I won't launch an attack on the heels of a forced march. No, we'll take it slow and give the troops from Yuldir time to reach us. We can camp here at these tors. They command the road west, and the open land around them will make it hard for the enemy to approach unseen."

A heavyset Akeshian who wore the stripes of a *pradi* stamped his blunt finger on the map. "That's a long shot." After a short pause, he added a barely audible, "Commander." After clearing his throat, he continued, "How long do we to wait for these supposed reinforcements? A day? A week? Longer? Every day the enemy gets stronger, yes? Our best chance is to hit them as fast as possible, punch them right in the mouth before they solidify their position."

Jirom straightened his back as if working out a kink. The gesture made him loom above everyone else, and in that moment, he reminded Dasha of a patient teacher standing over his students. "This isn't about a land grab, Naram. This Dark King doesn't care about territory or resources, or even subjects."

Dasha wondered at that. How could the Dark King not care about territory? He had seized most of the empire already. What else was there?

"You've been talking to Horace too much," Emanon mumbled, loud enough to be heard.

Jirom turned to regard his second-in-command. "In every place he's conquered, the usurper does the same thing. He converts all the people into his undead slaves, and then moves on. He doesn't bother with garrisons or food or even gold. His legions travel like animals, driving from one target to the next. No, he has what he wants, and he doesn't think anyone can stop him."

"He might be right," Emanon said.

Dasha hated to admit it, even to herself, but she agreed. This army was not capable of defeating the horde that had taken Ceasa. Not to mention the supernatural storm raging over the capital. She couldn't help herself from making a little sound, partway between a sigh and growl.

Emanon looked at her, one eyebrow raised. "Have something to say, girl?"

Dasha dropped her eyes to the floor. Her stomach was trembling.

"Anyway," Emanon continued, "Horace is probably dead. Going alone to Yuldir was a mistake."

Jirom frowned, and Dasha saw the concern in his eyes. It surprised her. There was more to this 'barbarian warlord' than met the eye. She wanted to know more about this man Horace. She had heard of him, of course. The foreign devil who had seduced the queen of Erugash. Now he was allied with the rebel slaves, and apparently, he had gone to the city of Yuldir to find more allies in their fight against the Dark King. But why? Her father had spoken of him only once in her presence. She had been hiding behind the audience chamber's partition while he met with his foreign ministers.

"This outlander is a demon," one of the lords said to her father.

"It is true, Majesty," echoed another. "He is known to conjure entities from the nether planes and send them to do his bidding."

"Strange noises have been heard coming from his home at all hours of the day and night," chimed in a third. "And he is very close to the queen. I have it on good authority from the royal household staff."

Her father held up his hand to stop the litany of accusations. "My lords, I caution you not to make rash judgements. What we know and what we suspect, or wish to believe, are often very different things. Gather proof, and then we can discuss the matter in full."

Remembering that moment made Dasha miss her father so intensely she couldn't stop a lone tear from escaping her left eye. She wiped it away quickly and took a deep breath to steady her nerves.

"No," Jirom said. "Horace is alive. And he will return to us."

Emanon shrugged. "I wish I had your faith."

Dasha took another deep breath. She had decided to reveal her identity. She could help them with their plans to take Ceasa, if they promised to leave the capital as soon as the Dark King and his minions were defeated. She was about to speak when the tent flap opened, and a young soldier appeared.

"Commander, Lord Horace has returned!"

Jirom looked to Emanon, who merely shrugged. "So, I was wrong."

"Let's go hear what he has to say."

The commander and his captains left the tent. Dasha started to follow, but Purna appeared in the entrance to stop her. "Put away the wine and clean the cups, girl," she growled.

Dasha shoved the ewer into the old woman's hands. "You do it."

As the other woman sputtered angry words, Dasha pushed past her and rushed outside. A sheet of rain met her at the entrance, drenching her thin tunic and headscarf. Dasha lowered her head and ran out into the weather. Angry clouds rolled across the dark firmament. Lightning flickered in the distance.

Jirom and Emanon had gone only a short way, stopping at the other side of a large open square inside the camp. Dasha slowed as she saw the man standing with them. She shielded her eyes for a better look. Yes, it must be him. The one they'd been talking about.

Horace. He's back.

Wrapped in his wet robes, Horace stepped out of the void. Rain pelted him, but he was already soaked to the bone, so it made no difference. Through the leaden haze he Saw the tall cliffs on either side of him, forming a deep arroyo silhouetted against the black sky.

As his foot touched down on the muddy ground, Horace took a deep breath and let it out. The humid air carried the smells of animals and people in tight confinement, a mélange of musk and sweat and dung that caught in the back of his throat. The canyon continued north through the wastelands called the Black Gates. Half a mile up a narrow trading road was the camp of the combined army.

He had been searching for the camp for the better part of six hours in this weather. First, he'd arrived at the southern edge of the Black Gates only to realize they were much vaster than he imagined. He used his sorcery to travel east in small jumps, stopping every mile or two to look around. This was the eighth canyon he had searched. With a deep-felt sigh, he released his power and walked toward the encampment.

Jirom's military orderliness was obvious. Hundreds of squad tents were pitched in precise rows, organized by companies. Patrols roamed the perimeter, crossing paths and exchanging call signs. Along the heights of the canyon cliffs, Horace's sorcery-enhanced eyesight picked out more sentries, wrapped in cloaks to protect them from the weather.

Walking up the old path leading through the camp, Horace could not tell where the rebel tents ended and the Thuumian military camp began, which he also attributed to Jirom's insistence on uniformity. He hoped the discipline paid off when they met the enemy. *They've been stalwart this far. I have to believe they can hold fast to the end. There is no other choice.*

He had a hunch that taking Ceasa would be far more difficult than any of them imagined. Even knowing Astaptah's abilities and the ferocity of his undead legions, Horace suspected they were in for more surprises. On top of it all, they were running out of time. Every hour put Astaptah closer to his goal of freeing the Ancient Ones. *If he succeeds, the world will be plunged into an age of darkness, maybe without end. Millions will die, and those who survive will envy the dead. We should have burned Erugash to the ground and buried Astaptah in the rubble. I don't know if even that would have prevented this. There are unseen forces working. They want a showdown, but we're the ones who suffer the consequences.*

"Halt and name yourself!"

A patrol of Thuumian soldiers approached him with spears extended.

"It's Horace." He grimaced as he added. "The Stormlord."

The soldiers surrounded him, half of them keeping their eyes on him while the others fanned out. "Are you alone, sir?" the sergeant asked. Horace didn't recognize him, but they seemed to know him.

"Yes. I need to see the commander at once."

The sergeant sent one soldier off with the message, and then waved Horace through. "You are cleared to pass, sir."

Nodding, Horace followed the hastening messenger. As he entered the camp, he felt a new kind of tension wash over him. Troops gathered around campfires. Heads turned to watch him, their eyes questing for answers, possibly for a reassuring word. Horace kept his gaze forward. Once again, he felt like the outsider, an intruder into this brotherhood of comrades. He was relieved when he spotted Emanon and Jirom striding down the track toward him.

"You haven't left the Gates yet," he said as they came together.

"You're observant as fuck," Emanon said. "No wonder Jirom puts so much faith in you."

Ignoring the temptation to wrap up the rebel second-in-command in bonds of iron-hard air, Horace focused on Jirom. "What happened?"

"We ran into some trouble. Undead comb these hills. What happened in Yuldir?"

Horace ran a hand through his sodden hair. "They are sending troops."

"Holy shit," Emanon said. "I can't believe it. What did you do? Seduce their queen?"

"I did them a favor. Now they're committed to defeating Astaptah." Horace hoped that was true. After his last talk with Lord Thuvan, he had some doubts, but he had to believe self-preservation would outweigh King Merodach's misgivings about aiding the rebel slaves.

Jirom's frown spoke volumes, but he remained silent.

"We need to call a war council," Horace said.

"We love it when you tell us little people what to do," Emanon remarked.

"Yuldir is sending troops, but we can't wait for them."

"Why not?" Jirom asked.

"I'll tell you with everyone assembled."

Jirom shared a look with Emanon, and then nodded. "We just sent the captains back to their companies. Give me an hour to round them up again. Get something to eat and meet us at my tent."

"Now," Horace replied, wanting to take the edge out of his voice but failing anyway. "I can eat while we talk."

"Fine," Emanon said as he turned and strode off, back into the heart of the camp. Jirom followed.

SUN AND SERPENT

As they left, Horace saw a young woman some distance behind them. She had been watching their conversation intently, but she ran off when Emanon and Jirom turned around. Just another camp follower. Yawning, Horace headed after the rebel leaders.

Half a bell later, Horace leaned over the table in Jirom's command tent, chewing on a piece of unleavened bread while he studied the map before him. The drawing was crude and incomplete, especially the plain around Ceasa, which appeared as merely a large blank expanse bisected by the river.

Jirom and Emanon stood on the other side of the table, while the various officers crowded around. The air was close from so many bodies packed together. Jirom was talking about overland travel speeds and ensuring the proper amount of rest for the soldiers. Horace barely listened. He was focused on the region around Ceasa, trying to measure the lives that would be required to get inside its walls and take the fight to Astaptah. There had to be a better way. *Maybe I should just ask him to come out for a duel?*

He accepted a cup of wine with a nod. Then he glanced sideways and noticed who was pouring. It was the girl he'd seen watching his conversation with Jirom and Emanon outside. She was watching him intently until he noticed her. Then, she dropped her eyes and disappeared into the crowd. *Strange. Do I know her? She seems vaguely familiar.*

"All right. Everyone is here," Emanon said. "You mind telling us why we're in such a hurry?"

Horace took a sip as he considered his words. There was no value in keeping secrets at this point. "Because Astaptah—whom some of you know as the Dark King but was once the main vizier to Queen Byleth of Erugash—is breaking the Seals that protect the world from destruction."

There was complete silence in the tent. Someone in the back dropped a cup and cursed quietly. Horace's pulse thrummed loudly in his ears as he waited for his words to sink in.

Finally, Jirom said, "Explain that."

"Without going into too much detail, everyone knows about the Kuldean cities of old, how they were so great and mighty. Well, their magi punched holes in the fabric of reality, and beings on the Other Side took notice. Or

180

perhaps the magi summoned them. It's difficult to know what really happened. But we know the results. These Ancient Ones entered our world, at least partially, and they brought devastation."

He paused to look around. The faces watching him intently were filled with doubt and confusion.

"Where did you learn this?" Jirom asked.

"It's not common knowledge, but the *zoanii* know parts of it. I pieced the rest together from clues I picked up here and there. That's not important right now. What you need to understand is that these Ancient Ones were evicted from the world, and the passage between the two realms was sealed with sorcery."

"And the Dark King is attempting to break those seals." Jirom leaned forward and put his hands on the table. "Why?"

"He serves the Ancient Ones. I've seen these entities—in a vision. They are vast—"

"Visions?" Emanon asked. "No offense, Horace, but we're trying to plan a campaign, not put the kiddies to bed."

Jirom held up a hand to his lover. "Peace, Em. Let him speak."

Horace took up where he was cut off. "They are beings of vast power, drifting in a black sea." He paused as he remembered the vision. For a moment he was in that great void again, floating before the awesome majesty of the powers outside the veil.

"And they want to return to rule again," Jirom finished for him.

"Apparently so. I got the impression they existed solely to destroy, caring nothing for the lives they take or the damage wrought. They felt more like forces of nature than anything else." Horace looked around the tent again. "Nothing and no one will survive if they return. The world will be a barren husk."

Horace expected outcries and condemnations, accusations at the least. Yet, the assembled crowd was quiet. Calm. Disciplined. *You've done well, Jirom. These women and men are ready to follow you anywhere. I just hope we don't lead them into catastrophe.*

The moan of the wind filled the tent as the front flap whipped open. Rain poured in as a pair of sentries wrestled with the flap. Finally, they tied it back into place.

Jirom had leaned back from the table, his face drawn. "We've all seen the undead. Seen the darkness in their eyes. It takes no great imagination to see what's in store if their maker conquers all. So, how do we defeat him?"

"I don't know." Horace finished his wine and set down the empty cup. "I wish I had a simple solution, but I don't. We have to get inside the city to confront Astaptah, and he's surrounded by thousands of undead."

"Try tens of thousands," Emanon said.

"What about your ability to come and go unseen?" Jirom asked. "Can't you get inside?"

"Has Mezim been talking while I was away?"

Jirom smiled. "Only a little. He's been worried about you. Anyway, he wouldn't tell me where you two went, but he told me how. If you can move yourself and a few fighters into the city—"

Horace shook his head. "Astaptah would sense it immediately and send his creatures to intercept us. No, we need a way inside that doesn't draw attention."

"I can help."

The small voice rose from the back of the tent. Heads turned and bodies parted, revealing the serving girl. She looked frightened by the sudden attention.

"What?" Jirom asked.

The young woman cleared her throat. "I can help you get inside the capital."

Emanon stalked over to loom over her. "You think this is funny, girl? It's not a game. People are putting their lives on the line."

She shook her head fervently. "No, I'm serious! I know how to get into Ceasa. A secret way."

Emanon took her by the arm and led her to the table. "Tell us this secret. And I warn you—if I find out you're just spinning tales you'll be the sorrier for it."

"I am . . ." She hesitated. Then, seeming to gather her courage, she blurted out, "I am Princess Dasha et'Murannumur."

"All right. That's enough." Emanon grabbed her by the arm again.

"Emanon," Horace said, calmly despite the tremor inside him. He had suddenly remembered why she looked so familiar. He'd seen her face before, in a drawing of the imperial family that Mezim had shown him, back in Erugash when he was the First Sword. "Let her go."

Emanon frowned, but moved back, hands at his side.

Horace nodded to the young woman. "Go on."

"I was in Ceasa when the Dark King attacked," she said. "Lightning came down from the sky and destroyed the city gates, and then the undead legions swarmed inside. I ran." Her voice trembled slightly, but she held it together. "I managed to escape with a bodyguard. We went through a secret tunnel under the city walls. Very few knew about it. Very few outside my family, that is."

"The emperor?" Jirom asked.

She shook her head. "I believe everyone who was inside the city is now dead."

Or worse. Horace could tell she was thinking it, too.

"How do we find this secret tunnel?" Jirom asked.

"I'll tell you," she answered. "But I have some conditions."

Emanon's eyebrows rose. "Conditions? We're at war, or didn't you understand that?"

"I understand. Nevertheless, you will agree to my terms, or I won't tell you how to get inside the capital."

Horace half-expected Jirom to insist on her cooperation. Perhaps even threaten her. Instead, he merely asked, "What do you want?"

Her chin lifted slightly in an expression that was both regal and heartbreaking in its sincerity. "When the enemy is defeated, you and your army must leave Ceasa. You cannot pillage or loot. You may not remain as conquerors. Promise this on your lives."

"What?" Emanon said. "You think we'll fight and die, and then you'll re-establish your empire of slavers? You can go—"

"I swear it," Jirom said.

"I swear," Horace said.

SUN AND SERPENT

They both looked to Emanon, who frowned like he wanted to spit in their faces. Finally, he snarled, "I swear it. And may the Gods burn me for it."

The princess visibly relaxed. "Thank you."

"With a way inside the city," Horace said to Jirom, "we might be able to find Astaptah without alerting his legions."

"How big is this tunnel?" Jirom asked.

"It runs a little more than a mile," Princess Dasha answered. "But it's not very wide, if that's what you're asking. Enough for two people to walk abreast for most of its length, but it narrows in a few places, and we had to squeeze to get through."

"With such a tight space, we won't be able to get the entire army inside in short order," Emanon said. "But we could send a strike team with you, me, and the Stormlord here."

Captain Ralla stepped up to the table. "My squad volunteers to be part of that team, sirs."

Jirom smiled at her. "I had no doubts. Captain Paranas, care to join us?"

The silver-skinned mercenary chief looked up from his study of the map. "Why not? We've come this far together. Might as well see it through to the end."

"But we'll leave Three Moons with the army."

"He won't like that," Paranas replied.

"He doesn't have a choice. The troops will need some magical support, and he's all we got."

"Getting inside won't do any good if we're facing the undead," Horace said. "They'll swarm us like a colony of ants. We need a diversion."

"Like an all-out attack on the city walls?" Emanon offered. "We'll hit from the outside with everything we have. That should draw the attention of the undead and give the team an opportunity to get to where we're going. Where are we going anyway?"

All eyes looked to Horace. He looked at the map for inspiration but found none. "We will make for the palace. Once we're inside the city, I should be able to feel Astaptah's presence and lead us right to him."

"But won't he be able to sense you just the same?" Jirom asked.

"Not if I don't use the *zoana*."

"Gods be damned," Emanon muttered. "A handful of troops and a wizard without magic against an army from Hell."

Jirom mumbled something. To Horace, it sounded like, "It was always thus."

The princess spoke up. "One last thing. I will be going with your team."

Everyone looked at her, until her cheeks turned bright red. "I insist," she said. "It is my city, and I will fight for her. Also, there are twists and branches in the tunnel. You'll never find your way without me."

Jirom nodded to her. "Agreed."

Emanon's sigh was louder than the wind roaring outside. "We're being punished for a past life."

As the war council broke up, with the various company and squad commanders talking over the details on their way out of the tent, Horace stayed to study the map again. They were casting darts in the dark, hoping to strike a bull's-eye, and every step felt like it balanced on the edge of complete disaster. They had found a way into the city, but after that the dangers only increased. He couldn't help thinking that Astaptah must have foreseen all this and would be waiting for them.

"It will be like the attacks we made in the desert," Jirom said. "Hit hard and fast, and be gone before they know what happened."

Horace shook his head. "No, it won't."

"No. But we'll do what must be done."

Horace nodded. *That's what I'm afraid of.*

Dasha took a deep breath behind the tent. The rain beat down on her, but she didn't care. She couldn't believe she had done it.

"Well?" Elia emerged from the foggy gloom. "How did it go? Did you learn anything important?"

"I told them, Elia. I told them who I am."

SUN AND SERPENT

The bodyguard's face turned ashen, more horrified than Dasha had seen her look even during the attack on Ceasa. "Why would you do that? You've placed yourself at their mercy. Now they control the empire."

"No. The Dark King—this Astaptah—controls the empire. If I want to save my people, I must have allies. And alliances require trust. We can't just keep running, Elia. Eventually, there will be no place to hide."

Elia stood before her, the rain turning her short-cropped hair into a droopy mess. "Come on," she said. "We need to get you some dry clothes and something warm to eat."

Nodding dutifully, Dasha followed her protector through the rebel camp. As she thought about the days ahead, she considered all the risks they would undertake and all the people who might die, and she knew in her heart she had made the right decision. For better or worse, it was time to cast the die.

CHAPTER EIGHT

Pumash shivered underneath his robe as he climbed the long, winding stairs. Each granite step was worn smooth from the countless feet that had trod this path before him. It was less than an hour past midday, but the sky was black as night. A damp cold hung in the air. It leeched through his clothes and skin to settle in his bones, creating a chill that wine could not warm. He would have preferred to sit by a fire, but necessity had forced him to come.

The *Manalish* had summoned him.

Since the taking of Ceasa, Pumash had been mostly ignored by the Master's servants, allowed to wander the palace as he wished. He had spent the last couple days walking its empty halls in a fugue, sometimes so overcome with misgivings he couldn't remember where he was or how he had gotten here. In those moments, he came closest to feeling this was all just a terrible nightmare, and he would stand very still, waiting to wake up in his bed in Nisus. As the time slipped by, minute after minute, he would be gripped by a terrible palsy, shaking his body with such force he would lose his balance. More than once, he had come to his senses on the floor, bewildered and distraught. And then the horror would return, slinking into his veins like gelid serpents.

He had been on one of his meanderings when one of the Master's grey-shrouded minions found him, standing in the main audience chamber and staring at the emperor's throne. The hall was pristine, exactly as it had been at the time of the city's fall. No blood or viscera. No signs of violence, like an island of peace within the destruction that had consumed the rest of the capital. He had been thinking about power, about how it was gathered by some, and transferred from one to another. From parent to child, from emperor to heir, from heaven to humanity.

When he was a child, his father had taken him to the slave auctions in Nisus. He remembered the vast crowd and all its new sights and smells, and the roar of their many voices. A vast wooden stage stood between the tall buildings, looming like canyon walls all around. The sky had been flawless blue that day. *The slaves were brought up on the stage, sometimes one by one, but other times in groups. Their eyes downcast, they walked up and stood there, as the crowd roared and bid upon them.*

He remembered seeing the winners step forward to claim their new property, and the slaves being led away in silence. This auction was held every spring, and he recalled how his perception of it had changed over the years. *As my innocence fell away, I saw the event for what it truly was. An exchange of power. The slaves had none. Prisoners of foreign wars, debtors, those born into bondage—they had nothing to offer society except their labor. And so, it was forced from them with shackles and whips. The buyers and sellers held the power, and they haggled over its price the same as any two merchants in the marketplace, and the property went meekly where it was told.*

That is the lesson of power.

Once he had learned it, he saw it in every human interaction. Between master and slave, between lord and subject, between parent and child. All exchanges of power. Everyone wanted it, but not all could obtain it. For some, the price was beyond their means. So, he had learned another lesson. *Far better to hold the whip, or the coin, than to taste the other side.*

He recalled another piece of that early memory. A family, mother and two small children, had been brought upon the stage. All of them had thick black hair and olive-hued skin, making him think they might be Akeshian. The mother looked regal, despite her nudity, which he thought ought to shock him but had not. The children were tall and clean-limbed, a boy and girl, about Pumash's age.

The bidding for them was fierce, with the men all around Pumash and his father shouting to be heard. While this went on, by some strange coincidence, the boy and Pumash made eye contact. For a moment that seemed to last much longer, they saw each other. To Pumash's adolescent mind, the boy's eyes seemed sad, but more than that, they were resigned. He had no power to affect what was about to happen, and neither did Pumash. They were both flotsam in life's great river. Then, the auctioneer banged his staff butt on the stage, and the slaves were sold. The boy looked away after one last glance, which seemed to Pumash to hold a special message.

See me, those eyes said. *I am here. I am not to be forgotten.*

Pumash stood quietly in the imperial audience chamber and wondered what had happened to that boy. Had he ever earned his freedom, or had he lived his entire life as a slave? Had he been bought and sold, switching hands again and again? Perhaps, in some accident of fate, Pumash had been one of those buyers or sellers. Perhaps that boy, as a man, had been among the many he had owned in his lifetime. Where was that slave now? Dead? Or worse, a slave for all eternity to the *Manalish? Perhaps he is out there right now, prowling the capital with a slavering hunger that can never be sated. Another victim of an imbalance of power.*

Pumash considered that as he followed his hunchbacked guide through the city. The streets were empty. Signs of devastation were many, but the most unnerving part of the journey was the silence. Block after city block of empty homes and shops, except for flocks of carrion birds picking at the remains. He wondered where the living dead were at, but then buried the thought. He didn't care. He just wanted to avoid them, with their unnatural vitality and their ink-black eyes. If not for the Master, they would tear him to shreds. Or worse, welcome him into their unfeeling ranks. *No, better to die than that.*

His hand closed around the smooth handle under his robe, clasped it once to make sure it was there, and then let it go.

Pumash and his guide came to the temple of Nabu. It wasn't the largest temple in Ceasa—that honor, of course, went to the house of Amur the Sun Lord—but this was by far the biggest temple of the Wanderer in the empire. The front gates yawned open, and they entered a long courtyard. To the left of the temple sanctum, a gigantic bronze statue lay in a twisted heap. Although it was malformed, Pumash had seen many of its kind in his lifetime—an impossibly tall man in a hooded robe, only a smooth, blank space where his face should have been. *All your secrets are laid bare for the* Manalish, *Keeper. Do you tremble in your celestial abode? Or was all this foreseen?*

The temple's interior was dark. Pumash kept his eyes downcast as he

SUN AND SERPENT

followed his guide. He sensed the presence of things—entities, not persons—and did not want to risk meeting their inhuman gazes.

They came to stairs and began to climb. The steps wound outside the wall of a grand tower that rose through the heart of the temple. The view of the city, revealed to Pumash in occasional flashes of lightning, was phenomenal. Ceasa was one of the oldest cities in the empire, perhaps the world. It followed no single plan, but instead had grown up over the centuries as its population grew. The imperial palace and residence were in the eastern half, in what was known as the City of Antiquity. A city in and of itself, it housed the empire's oldest and most well-connected families.

Ceasa expanded outward in a series of neighborhoods. Unlike some other cities, where the trades were confined to separate parts of town, in Ceasa merchants and artisans and commoners all lived together. Rows of small homes were interrupted by vast estates and tenement buildings. Jewelers and potters and stonemasons lived side by side.

The only section of the city reserved for special use was here, a long stretch of ground south of the Imperial Palace where the city's great temples and shrines were built. As Pumash neared the top of his climb, a loud rumble shook the sky. He winced, expecting thunderbolts to come raining down as they had several times a day since Ceasa's fall. Expectation hung in the air. Something momentous was about to happen, and he had a deep-seated belief he would rather be anyplace else when it did.

The top of the tower came into his view. The roof was a flat circle about fifty paces across, covered in slabs of gray stone. Where the statue of the Wanderer had stood in its center, now towered another of the *Manalish*'s silver machines. This one, though, was much larger than any of the others Pumash had seen. Its apex reached more than three man-heights above his head. The thing hummed ominously as it was ministered to by a half-dozen gray minions. Overhead, the sky answered with similar rumbles.

The *Manalish* stood at the northern edge of the roof platform, gazing off into the darkness.

Pumash carefully went over to stand beside and slightly behind him. "You have won, Master. The empire is yours."

190

"Yes."

"The other cities. The ones not yet conquered. Will you go after them now?" Though he dreaded the answer, he was compelled to ask. He had to know if this nightmare was over.

"No. Once the Great Ones return, those places will fall of their own accord. All will surrender themselves or be destroyed."

Pumash struggled to swallow. "And what of your humble slave, Master? What shall be done with me?"

A hand fell upon his shoulder and moved to rub across the back of his neck. It was firm, but not unkind. *The way you would caress a beloved pet.*

"A new era shall soon shine across the world," the *Manalish* replied. His voice was rich and deep, its tones reverberating in the air. "The old decadences of liberty and choice will be crushed, replaced by the serenity of total subjugation."

The *Manalish* turned his head to look down at him. "However, even I am only a servant, Pumash. We shall both be absorbed by the totality of chaos when They come. And it shall be glorious."

Emboldened by this sudden affection, or at least the absence of punishment, Pumash spoke up again. "And we had to conquer the empire for this to happen? I don't understand why. All this death and misery, did it mean anything?"

"Oh, Pumash. It means everything. Suffering purifies the spirit. As for why we came to Ceasa, the answer lies beneath our feet." The *Manalish* spread his hands toward the sky. "And above our heads. Here, in the vaults of this temple, lies the final Seal. The last clasp holding shut the veil between the worlds. As it is broken, the new age shall come."

Pumash glanced back at the great machine. The last link in the chain dragging the world to its end. He imagined the Seal as a large wax circle down in the dark depths of the temple catacombs, pieces falling to the floor as it began to crack. Suddenly he was overwhelmed with panic. He didn't want to see the end of humanity. He would rather be dead. *Blessed are those who died and never returned.*

"Master, I—"

SUN AND SERPENT

The roof trembled as a thundering sizzle erupted behind them. The *Manalish* turned, his grip forcing Pumash to turn with him. They gazed upon the machine as it awakened. Arcs of green electricity snaked through the silver lattice. Its hum vibrated in Pumash's chest like a swarm of hornets.

Pumash clasped his hands before him and trembled as the machine rumbled and spat. Only the *Manalish*'s hand on his neck kept him standing upright. *I am witness to the end of the world. Oh, Gods. Why have you forsaken us?*

Horace floated, lost and alone, in a sea of infinite darkness. Mountainous waves threatened to drown him. He gasped and kicked and fought for every breath of air. Even as one part of his mind knew this was only a dream, that was no comfort. Dreams could be just as deadly as the waking world. Dreams could betray you.

He sensed titanic shapes lurking in the water, moving closer, hungering for him. Horace tried to swim away, but they lay in wait in every direction, hedging him in, drifting closer. Silent green lightning etched the sky without the faintest rumble of thunder. In that instant of illumination, he saw the prow of a ship looming above him, moments from sailing over him. Horace kicked hard and managed to get out of its way just in time. The rotting planks of the ship sailed past, hung with dead seaweed and frayed nets. Then he saw the name on the side of the hull.

Bantu Ray.

A face peered over the side gunnels. Lean and framed in shaggy hair, its visage was partially obscured in shadow. The ghoulish green lightning crackled again, and Horace gazed up into his own face. Then the illumination vanished, and he was plunged back into darkness.

Stricken by terror he couldn't explain, he kicked and pushed himself away from the ship and its revenant pilot.

He was still thrashing when he awoke. Opening his eyes, he lay still on his back, looking up but seeing nothing. The black sky encompassed the entire firmament, just like the dark ocean in his dream. *Eternal night reigning over a dead world.*

The ground was hard underneath him, but it crumbled as he shifted. He could feel the layer of grit covering him, carried by the evening winds. Although he couldn't see with his eyes, Horace Saw the landscape around them. A few miles to the north across the broken pan of flat earth, hills rose in uneven clumps of sharp-edged hummocks, as if they had been sculpted with a knife. What little vegetation that remained was stunted and leafless, its darkened trunks and stalks bent low to the ground. Everything about this land screamed dissolution and lifelessness. All was dying, and soon nothing would live here. When all the plant life was gone, the insects would die out, and then the larger animals, until nothing was left. A dead zone, and it was spreading.

Movement alerted him that others were stirring. Horace sat up and reached for his field pack. Tied to the side were a pair of bulging waterskins. He opened one and took a sip, swishing the tepid water around his mouth before swallowing. Next, he found the wrapped bundles of rations and broke off a piece of hardtack bread. While he chewed, he considered what lay before him.

Two days ago, they had left the army at the Black Gates and headed south. After several hours of marching, they turned east in a broad sweep that would eventually take them to the capital. There were no roads here, not even trader tracks.

Footsteps crunched on the ground as Jirom came over. "Horace."

"I'm awake."

By Jirom's order, they lit no torches or lanterns. Theirs was a mission of secrecy, conducted in complete darkness. Horace was their guide, and his compass was the throbbing tumor of corruption he felt at all times, even in his sleep. Ceasa, the seat of Astaptah's power.

Jirom squatted down beside him. His black shield was slung on his back. To Horace's extraordinary senses, it felt like a magnet, drawing in all the *zoana* around it. He was uncomfortable being this close to the object, as if it were a deep hole and he was teetering on the edge, about to fall in.

"We should be about six hours from the city," Jirom said. "Does that sound about right?"

"Yes. I don't see any major obstacles ahead, just some scattered ridges."

"Any idea if we're being watched?"

The thought had occurred to Horace as well. He didn't know the true extent of Astaptah's power. It was possible their every move was under surveillance. "No. But we don't have much choice."

"If this mission goes bad, Horace, you should—"

"I'll do what I have to. Whatever it takes. This must end today."

Jirom nodded calmly, as if they were discussing gardening tips. "We're leaving in five."

As the big man got up and walked away, Horace thought of Alyra. Sometimes he woke up expecting to see her, or he imagined hearing her voice, only to remember she was gone. What would she say if she were here now? *Stick with the mission, Horace. We are expendable, but the task must be completed.*

He shook his head. No, that was his own fatalism talking. Alyra had never been so pessimistic. She always saw the brighter possibilities in things. *Including me. That's one of the things I loved most about her. She made me a better person.*

The Silver Blades broke camp and headed out. They hiked in a loose diamond formation, with the mercenaries at the sides ranging farther out, watching for trouble. The princess and her ever-present bodyguard marched at the front with Jirom. Horace saw them talking often, heads bent together to hear each other over the constant groan of the wind.

"An interesting pair," came a comment from over his shoulder as Captain Paranas appeared beside him.

Horace greeted him with a nod in the dark. He wasn't comfortable in the presence of these mercenaries. It wasn't just their silver skin. They all shared a look in their eyes, as if they saw through things. "This war has made a lot of strange alliances."

Paranas grunted. "That's the truth. This reminds me of the old days. A small band of seasoned vets out on our own."

It reminded Horace of when he had been a slave, being driven across the desert to an unknown fate. Except this time, he wasn't wearing chains. *Well, none that I can see.*

"Like Omikur?"

Captain Paranas made a spitting sound, although nothing left his mouth. "That's when everything went to shit. We never should have accepted that commission, but our previous captain had a soft spot for the plight of the downtrodden."

Horace recalled the view of that town from the deck of Queen Byleth's flying ship, how the battle had seemed so remote from the air, like it wasn't happening to real people. He could imagine how it must have felt to those involved. After all, he had seen his share of battles. *Sekhatun, Erugash, Thuum. More than enough for one lifetime, yet these mercenaries—and Jirom—have experienced far more. How do they do it? How do they keep going?*

"You don't share those sensibilities?"

The mercenary leader shrugged, eliciting a squeak of leather and rustling metal from his armor. "I've learned that you don't mix business with personal feelings. When you make it personal, you lose your perspective. You start making decisions based on how you want the world to be, rather than how it really is."

"So why are you here? Why didn't you take the Blades and leave after Erugash? Or Thuum?"

Captain Paranas smiled, revealing rows of metallic teeth, as he stared ahead. "Well, it got personal. You see that man up there?"

"Jirom."

"He's one of us. Oh, not officially. But he's part of our family. So here we are, following him into the maw of death, as it were."

Horace couldn't agree more. That was an apt description of this mission. "And if it comes down to deciding whether to follow Jirom or complete the task, what will you choose?"

"We took the job. We'll see it through."

Horace heard the expectant tone in the mercenary's voice. *Here I was trying to determine if he was reliable, when all along they've all been worried about me. If I'll follow through when the time comes.* "I think we understand one another, Captain."

SUN AND SERPENT

Paranas nodded in the dark, and then dropped back to the rear of the formation. Horace was glad for the solitude. His gaze wandered back to Jirom and the princess, still conversing close together. The imperial heiress made him uneasy. She had escaped the destruction of Ceasa, found the rebels on the march, and wormed her way into Jirom's personal retinue. That spoke of her intelligence and capability, but all her stipulations before she volunteered to aid them made him suspicious of her motivations. Did she really believe the rebels would fight and die to regain her city, and then she would just take up where her father had left off as ruler of the empire? Worse, would Jirom allow it to happen?

For once, Horace wished Emanon were here. He had been left in command of the main army, but his gruff impertinence would be a welcome counterweight in this party. For himself, Horace couldn't summon the ire to interfere. All his energy was focused on the battle ahead. In his grimmer moments, he mused there was no need to worry about the princess's machinations. Even if they managed to get inside the city undetected and get to the palace, and find Astaptah, he wasn't sure he could conquer his rival one-on-one. He had failed before in Erugash, and that was before the vizier had consolidated his power. Now, he could see for himself how Astaptah's powers had grown. What could he do against such might?

Horace was musing about their chances when a sharp tingle clawed down the back of his neck. He stopped, straining his extranormal senses, but the source of the sensation was difficult to pinpoint. It felt like it was coming from all directions. Horace looked down. He was opening his mouth to shout a warning when the ground erupted beneath his feet.

"We should get to the Hall of Ancient Kings and follow the corridor past the Blossom Garden to the audience chamber," Dasha told the rebel commander. "It's the most direct route from the servants' wing."

The darkness was oppressive. Even though her eyes had adjusted to the gloom enough to make out nearby shapes, Dasha still resented the unrelenting night. As if the sun was a gift that had been stolen from her. Talking to Jirom helped distract her from her own thoughts. And she found he was much more intelligent and interesting than her initial assessment. *Certainly, he is no dumb brute, despite the brands on his face.*

"Hall of Ancient Kings. Blossom Garden," he mused. "Are the streets of Ceasa paved in jewels?"

Dasha allowed herself a slight smile, although none could see it. "We, ah, have a penchant for colorful imagery, I'll admit. But Ceasa is a beautiful city. Or, at least, it was. And it will be again."

He leaned closer, trying to see her face. She looked away, but only for a moment. This was a singular opportunity, to speak with this leader of men and make him an ally. He and his officers had sworn the oath she insisted upon, but she knew from years of spying upon her father's court that promises were merely air. They held no surety unless they could be enforced, and her leverage here was scant. If Jirom decided to betray her once the fighting was over, she would have little recourse.

When the fighting is over . . . if we are all still alive. I saw what happened in Ceasa. I saw the undead sweep through the streets in their thousands. What chance do we have? Are we just marching to our deaths?

He looked ahead, and she followed his gaze. A small light flashed in the distance. Three times, and after a short pause, two times.

"What is that?" she asked.

"Our scouts. They're calling back that all is clear ahead."

"That light? Is it sorcery?"

"No. It was Emanon's idea, actually. The scouts carry a hooded lantern. There's a door on one side. When you open it, the light shines out, but only in one direction, so it can be used to make a signal."

"Clever. I also noticed your mercenaries are spread out. Why is that?"

Jirom gestured at the Silver Blades marching at the flanks of the party. "To cover more ground. Also, if we are attacked, they aren't clumped together." He pointed out the two mercenaries nearest them. "They train to fight in tandem. It allows the unit to be more flexible on the battlefield, especially in close quarters fighting."

"And Emanon is your partner?"

Dasha wanted to swallow her tongue. The words had just slipped out. After Elia had mentioned it, she noticed how close the two leaders of the rebels were, how they seemed to mirror each other, in action as well as mood. "I didn't mean—"

"He is my mate," Jirom said, without hesitation. "And we fight well together."

Dasha nodded, glad he hadn't been offended by her question. "He didn't wish to be left behind with the army."

"No. Em always wants to be where the danger is greatest."

"That reminds me of my brother, R—"

A shout from behind made Dasha jump. She turned as something crawled up from the broken earth near the center of their formation. Revulsion surged within her when she saw the withered specters rising with grasping hands to attack the Blades. Perhaps because they had lain under the dry earth, these undead were more wasted and shriveled than those Dasha had seen before. Desiccated skin and fragments of old clothing hung in tatters from their frames, but they fought with the same eerily silent ferocity that cast her mind back to the battle in the canyon. Their grimy talons tore through leather and flesh, drawing dark blood. Then the stench hit her, its putrescence almost driving her to her knees.

Elia was at her side in an instant, sword out and eyes searching the ground for more threats. The Silver Blades reacted with a composure that was nearly as shocking to Dasha as the sudden attack. Swords were drawn and wielded with preternatural calm. The weapons rang out like axes chopping into hardwood as they cut into emaciated limbs and bodies.

Jirom waded into the thick of the combat, delivering devastating blows with his tulwar that shattered limb sockets and skulls alike. An undead latched onto his ankle, its fleshless jaws seeking his foot, but he stomped on its head to hold it fast and then severed the thing's neck with a downward stroke. Without wasting a moment, he moved on to assist a Blade fending off three undead assailants.

Because of the mercenaries' calm, Dasha felt they had the matter well in hand. However, as the seconds passed, she saw more and more of the undead rise from the ground. The initial dozen turned into thirty, and then twice that number in the span of a few heartbeats. She edged closer to Elia.

Horace stood alone at the center of the melee. At first, Dasha expected him to unleash a magical attack to drive off the undead, but then she remembered he couldn't use his *zoana*. Neither could she. Horace had warned them the Dark King would sense the use of magic even from far away. In her case, it didn't much matter; her miniscule power wouldn't be of much use in a battle. But she had heard so many stories of the Stormlord's prowess, part of her wanted to see it in action. The other part wanted nothing to do with him.

Elia recoiled abruptly, shoving her back. An undead had lunged, trying to grab her bodyguard's throat. Elia pivoted away from its grasping claws and shoved her sword into its body to hold it in place. Then she finished it with a dagger punch through an eye socket. The thing collapsed, dying again at their feet. Elia breathed hard as she pulled her weapons free.

Over her shoulder, Dasha saw the mercenaries being pushed back by sheer numbers. They had formed a crude line, trying to corral the undead, but there weren't enough of them. Another corpse slipped through the line, and Elia batted it back with a pommel to the forehead followed by a kick in the stomach. The undead stumbled to one knee, and one of the Blades—a stocky man with wide-set eyes—hacked off its head with a sword like he was cutting wood.

Dasha had never seen a rout personally, though she had heard her father's war ministers use the term. Despite their orderly withdrawal, the Blades were in danger of being overwhelmed. She felt so helpless. She tried to think of something she could do to help, but without her magic she was defenseless. She wished she had Elia's combat training. And her muscles. *You've got a brain, so use it! What can I do?*

Then Dasha remembered the lantern signal. The scouts! Niko and Jauna traveled ahead of the main group. They were only two, but they might be enough to turn the tide.

The nearest pair of Blades was fighting off a stubborn undead that refused to die. They had dropped their rucksacks to the ground as they battled. Dasha ran over and rummaged through the closest bag until she found a bundle of torches. Praying she hadn't jeopardized the entire mission, she pulled out one of the torches and held it before her. She looked deep inside herself for her *qa*, and found it lying inert and quiet at the base of her consciousness. She forced it open and sought the power within. It was evasive, as ever. Dasha focused her will on the task. She found the threads of *zoana* and quickly wove them together.

The torch flared alight. After seeing only darkness for so long, Dasha was momentarily blinded. She released her magical energy and took off, holding the burning torch aloft as she ran as fast as she could in the direction of the scouts.

"Princess!" Elia called behind her, but she kept running, all the while waving the torch over her head.

The torch shed only a small circle of light, not revealing the way before her until she was almost upon it. Time and time again she spotted a dip or a sinkhole just a step before she reached it. There was no time for careful navigation; she leapt these obstacles one after another.

Dasha risked a glance over her shoulder, and immediately wished she hadn't. Several undead had broken off from the fighting to follow her. They loped after her with long, shambling strides. She tore her gaze away and ran harder. Her heart beat ever faster, until she could feel it pounding against her ribcage as if trying to break free. *Where are the scouts? Don't they hear the fighting?*

Dasha scrambled up the side of a steep hillock. Her lungs burned, and her feet were getting heavier with each stride. She was about to call out for help when a shadow rose from a crevice in the ground—she swore it couldn't have hidden anything larger than a cat—just a few feet off to her right. Dasha held in a yelp as the shadow formed at the edge of her torchlight into the shape of a young woman. Jauna's silver skin gleamed in the wavering torchlight.

"Whoa," the mercenary woman said, softly but with conviction as she held out a hand to stop Dasha. "What are you doing out here?"

"Fight!" Dasha burst out as she gasped for breath. She thought she might pass out. "Back. There. The dead are . . . coming."

After a moment staring into her face, the mercenary turned and called out. "Niko! Trouble at the rear! And we're about to have company!"

A few seconds later, Niko appeared. He held a loaded crossbow and the hooded lantern. Looking back past Dasha, he set down the lantern. "Douse that torch. No, better yet, give it to me."

She handed him the torch, and he hurled it off to the north, over the side of the hill.

"Why did you—?" Dasha started to ask, but then she saw the group of undead following her had turned away, heading toward the direction of the torch.

Niko and Jauna aimed their crossbows and fired. A pair of undead staggered and dropped in their tracks. The scouts reloaded their weapons and fired again, and again, dropping more foes with each volley until none remained standing.

"Stay here," Niko said as he and Jauna drew their blades.

They went down to finish off the undead who had clambered toward the torchlight, and then raced off, back toward the main group.

Dasha hugged herself as she watched them go, wanting to run with them but understanding she would only be an impediment. As the light of the torch dwindled and then sputtered out, the darkness returned, deeper and more awful than before, and she could only listen to the sounds of combat. She heard shouts and curses, but—thank the Gods—no screams of anguish.

She didn't know when the noises stopped, for she had drifted into a state of mental numbness. Her mind wandered, wondering if there was some island out in the sea where the horrors of the empire did not extend, where one could languish under the ebon sky in idle ignorance, unknowing and uncaring of the world's troubles. Elia's voice started her from the reverie.

"Princess!"

Taking a deep breath, Dasha hesitated for a moment before she responded. The battle din had ceased, leaving behind an eerie silence. "I'm here."

Elia topped the ridge, breathing heavily. "Are you all right?"

"Fine. Was anyone hurt?"

"A couple are wounded. I don't know how seriously. They were all alive when I left."

They returned together to the battle site and found the mercenaries huddled together. The sheer number of corpses astonished her. There were at least a hundred, maybe more, fallen in poses of disarray. She couldn't stop herself from looking at their faces, which appeared so calm in death, except for the all-black eyes. They almost appeared like dolls.

Jirom stood amid his fighters, covered in dark blood and looking like a prehistoric god of war. Horace, too, had been splashed with gore. He held a broad-bladed dagger, which he cleaned on his sleeve and tossed back to one of the Blades with a nod. Dasha wasn't quite disappointed to see him alive, but she had assumed he would be cowering behind the troops, not fighting alongside them. She watched as he went over to stand beside Jirom. *There's more to him than is easily seen.*

The Blades were standing around one of their own, the short man called Raste. Pie-Eye held a bloody cloth to Raste's right leg where the leather leggings had been torn open. When Pie-Eye pulled back the cloth, fresh blood spurted from the wound. Captain Paranas swore as he, too, knelt beside the injured mercenary.

"He was bit," Pie-Eye explained. "Looks bad."

"Leave me." Raste's face was pale as he spoke and sweat covered his forehead. "You can't be slowed down."

"Shut it." Jirom ran a hand across his bald head. Then he beckoned to a nearby mercenary. "Light a torch."

Dasha blinked as another light was struck. Ivikson handed the brand over, and Jirom held the edge of his tulwar in the flame. "We'll need a flat iron. Heat it up."

Captain Paranas was already holding a small camp skillet over another torch flame. "I've got it. Give me a few moments."

Niko took off his belt and tied it around Raste's thigh, cinching it tight above the knee. "Someone give him something to bite down on."

Jauna offered a leather dagger sheath.

"What are they doing?" Dasha asked Elia.

"You don't want to see this."

Elia tried to turn her away, but Dasha held her ground. She wouldn't be protected and hidden away anymore. These men and women had fought to protect her. The least she could do was share their pain. *I am not a child any longer. Life is misery, or so my teachers said. Now I will see it for myself. I must not flinch away.*

"They have to amputate," Elia said. "Or he'll die. The undead carry an infection in their bite. It spreads the disease."

Raste sat completely still, except for an occasional shiver. Dasha was shuddering now, too, in sympathy.

Jirom lifted his sword with two hands. Ivikson grabbed Raste's foot and pulled the leg straight, holding it down. There was no preamble or warning before Jirom chopped downward. Raste convulsed as the blade sliced completely through his leg with a sharp crack, just an inch or two below the knee. Ivikson fell back, holding the severed limb. Bright blood leapt from the wound. Dasha felt her gorge rise as she saw the white bone. Then Captain Paranas was kneeling beside the young man, slapping the red-hot underside of the pan against the raw wound. A horrible smell of burning flesh cut through the miasma of battlefield stenches. Dasha turned and staggered a few steps before she was on her knees, throwing up the remains of her breakfast.

When she had recovered, Raste lay quietly. His eyes were closed, but she could tell he was still conscious by his long, even breaths. Paranas and Ivikson were wrapping the stump in thick bandages.

Jirom had put away his sword. His face was impassive, showing no sign of what he was feeling. Dasha imagined he was devastated for his soldier, but he had to hide that in order to maintain the air of command. Their lives depended on his decisions. They had to trust him beyond all logic or fear, and that responsibility placed a barrier between them. The distance of command. *Father was the same way. He never showed his warm, loving side to his viziers and officers. He kept that reserved for us. To the rest of the world, he was the resolute monarch, hard and unyielding. Can I be that way?*

When the wound was bound, the big Isurani named Ino hoisted his injured comrade over his shoulder. Raste coughed once, and then lay still.

SUN AND SERPENT

Ivikson held up the remains of his leg, but he shook his head. Ivikson dropped it on the ground.

"We're ready to move," Captain Paranas said.

Jirom nodded. "We'll tighten up the formation. Niko, I want you and Jauna within eyesight at all times."

The scouts saluted and set off ahead. The Blades fell in behind them, snuffing the torches.

"This was a bad idea," Elia said. "We shall all end up dead before this is through."

Dasha could only nod. "Probably."

"That thing you did, running off by yourself to get Niko and Jauna."

"I know. It was foolhardy."

"No. It was smart and very brave. You may have saved all our lives."

"Thank you." She didn't feel smart or brave, but she appreciated the words.

They started after the troopers, leaving the dead and Raste's leg lying on the broken soil behind them.

CHAPTER NINE

The wind lashed them like a living tormentor, beating them with rain and filling their heads with its incessant roar. Jirom ran his hand across his head, and the rough stubble made a satisfying rasp. Saying goodbye to Emanon hadn't been easy. Since Thuum, they had scarcely been apart.

"I won't say it," Emanon had said, not meeting his eyes, as they stood alone in the command tent. The smoke from the oil lamp filled the pavilion with a fragrant haze, mixed with the vapors of several open wine jars.

Jirom came over and caressed his lover's chest. "Nor I. We can leave it unsaid, until . . ."

Emanon turned into him so that their stomachs touched, seeking each other out like hungry beasts. "Yes. Until."

Their kiss seemed to last forever as they pulled each other down to the carpet. At least, that's how Jirom remembered it. They hadn't spoken again, letting their bodies speak for them. Come the morning, they split up after a brief kiss; Emanon to see to the army's disposition while Jirom went to find his strike team. Walking out of the tent had felt like leaving behind everything he wanted, but they had done it. Without a word.

Wiping the rain from his face, Jirom tried to survey the way ahead, but the dark made it difficult. He stood on the edge of a shallow ravine while part of his team explored ahead without the benefit of a light. It was slow going, and this was the third ravine they had found today. Somewhere among these rills and canyon, according to the princess, was a hidden entrance to Ceasa. Jirom was starting to think they would have an easier time scaling the walls.

Speaking of the imperial princess, he heard her struggling up the slope toward him, and the soft clank of her bodyguard's weapons following close behind. When she finally made it up, Jirom handed over his canteen, and the princess drank.

SUN AND SERPENT

Lowering the container after several deep swallows, she said, "I think this is it."

This close to the storm, the wind howled around them, tearing up through the gulch and racing along the plains beyond. "So you said at the last ravine."

"I know." Even covered in grime and wearing travel-stained clothing, she carried herself with a poise beyond her years. "But I really think this is it. The tunnel entrance will be at the eastern end, nestled between two rock walls."

"I've sent Niko and Jauna ahead to investigate. We'll wait here until they report back."

The rest of the Silver Blades were situated along the top of the ravine. They were spread out more than he liked, but there was no choice in the matter. They had chosen to bring a small group for speed and stealth. Their only chance in this gambit was to enter the city undetected. Still, he felt exposed out here, as if the darkness hid a host of unseen eyes.

"Have you thought about my idea?" Princess Dasha asked.

"It won't work."

"Why not?"

Before the undead attack, she had been bending his ear about a scheme she had concocted. According to her, the idea had just 'come' to her, but it smacked of long planning to him. The imperial palace was laid out in a series of wings, each almost a separate building in and of itself. The palace had grown over the centuries as each emperor added his own flourishes and pet projects, forcing the compound to expand. Old wings were abandoned or built over, until the palace had become a warren of twisting passages and chambers. There was no way, she'd argued, the usurper could have learned all the ways around the palace.

The princess's idea was to split up the strike team once they got inside. While one group made a frontal attack on the audience chamber—where they assumed the Dark King would be headquartered—the other would take another route to attack from a flanking position. It was sharp tactics, but he didn't think they could use it.

"We don't have the manpower," he replied, looking past her. Horace was now climbing the slope behind them. His friend had been quiet since the undead attack, doing nothing more than following at the tail of the small troupe. *Saving his strength for the battle to come.* "We chose a small team for stealth and swiftness, but our strength is limited. If we split up and the timing of the attack is off by even a little, the enemy will carve us up one at a time."

"Listen to him," Elia said. Her voice was gruffer than usual.

"But he won't be expecting a second attack from the rear," Princess Dasha argued. "We would have the advantage of surprise."

Jirom shook his head and took another sip from his canteen. "We're already counting on that. Emanon and the army are going to arrive outside those walls in a matter of hours. They'll only be able to hold the enemy's attention for so long. We have to find and eliminate our target as soon as possible. We don't have time to add another wrinkle to the plan."

"But . . ." She stopped what she was saying as Horace came up to them.

He waved away Jirom's offer of a drink as he reached the top. "Raste's in considerable pain."

Jirom had heard the groans, echoing down from the cliff. "There isn't anything we can do for him, unless . . .?"

Horace made an uneasy grimace. "No, sorry. I don't know the first thing about healing magic. But even if I did . . ."

"We can't risk using it this close to the city."

Lightning flashed to the north, throwing the rugged contours of the ravine in stark relief. The far end, maybe a mile away, was shrouded in deep shadow. He didn't see his scouts, but he hoped they had found something. A constant count ran in the back of his mind, like the sands of an hourglass, telling him they had to hurry.

"Pig-Eye is with him now," Horace said.

"Pie-Eye," Jirom corrected.

"Whatever. He gave Raste some leaves to chew, says they will dull the pain, but we can't do anything about the blood loss or risk of infection."

Jirom nodded but did not reply. There was nothing more to say on the matter. People were going to die. He couldn't change that, but those around him kept looking to him for answers. He didn't have the heart to tell them there were no answers, just a dwindling supply of poorer and poorer choices.

SUN AND SERPENT

"Once we find the tunnel, we'll set him up with some food and water in a nook where he can wait."

"He still wants to come with us," Horace said. His tone was decidedly neutral.

He's become harder than stone. Losing Alyra almost broke him. I can see Death lurking behind his eyes. Life doesn't hold much appeal anymore. How many friends have I seen go down that path? Too fucking many.

Horace's gaze swept to the east, as if he saw something through the gloom.

"What is it?" Jirom asked.

"There's a massive concentration of power in that direction."

"I feel nothing," Princess Dasha said softly.

"It's raw and hungry," Horace continued. "Like an open sore on the land."

Those words lodged in Jirom's mind. He didn't have Horace's abilities, but he'd felt the *wrongness* of this place, getting worse with every step. "Can he sense you from this far away?"

Horace slowly shook his head. "I don't think so. I don't feel his attention in this direction, but Astaptah wouldn't tip his hand that way. In any case, he's waiting for me."

Ideas ran through Jirom's mind. If the enemy knew you were approaching his position, show him exactly what he expects while preparing an attack from another direction. If the Dark King knew Horace would come, they could use that against him, though it would mean using Horace to bait the trap. Perhaps the princess's plan had more merit than he'd originally thought.

A small light appeared, coming back down the ravine floor. When it neared, Jirom made out Jauna's lithe form.

"We think we found it, sir. A broad cave in the eastern edge of the ravine, with a tunnel in the back. Looks like it goes pretty deep."

"That's it," the princess said.

Jirom ordered Jauna, "Go back and tell Niko to stay put. I don't want any exploring until we're all there."

Jauna took off back down the slope, with the princess and her bodyguard following her. Jirom had seen the eagerness in the young woman's gaze in the glow of the lantern. She wanted her city back, but he sensed there was more to it than that. There was pain in her, too. She hid it better than most, especially considering her age, but he saw it in the occasional look and heard it when she spoke of the night she had fled Ceasa. Unlike Horace, she took strength from her pain. *She will be a formidable woman when she is older. If any of us live long enough to see it.*

Jirom whistled to the Blades, loud to be heard over the wind, and they set off, coming down the ravine wall in pairs. He waited until the entire team was ahead of him. Pie-Eye and Ino carried Raste between them.

"There will be no way to notify Emanon if we fail," Horace said.

"He knows. He'll do what is necessary."

"It's not too late to back out. You and your people could leave now, and I'll go in by myself."

Jirom stared hard at the other man. "You think I'd let you do this alone?"

Horace's smile was rueful. "I had to try."

Jirom reached out and clasped him by the shoulder, squeezing hard enough to make Horace flinch. "We're going to see this through to end. Together. Now, come on. They're waiting."

Leaning into the wind, they traversed the steep decline down into the ravine. The floor of the canyon was smooth, except for occasional clumps of broken boulders. The walls showed scores of strata in bands of brown, red, and yellow. The stone had been quarried in several places, leaving behind large, clean-cut gaps. Oddly, he saw no fortifications. The rulers of Ceasa must have known this would be an easy route for an attacking army to take. Then he wanted to smack his own forehead. The rulers were all *zoanii*. Of course, this ravine must be studded with magical defenses invisible to the normal eye.

He mentioned that to Horace, who nodded. Horace had a far-off gaze as if he were concentrating hard. "There used to be wards here, all over the valley. But they're gone now. Nothing but ghosts left behind."

"Ghosts?"

"Sorry. Not spirits. Just residues of past sorcery, like footprints in sand. The wards have been wiped away."

"Perhaps Astaptah did it when he took over the city."

"Perhaps. But the protections wouldn't pose a danger to him or his minions. They only serve as an early warning system. Why would he want that dismantled?"

Too many questions. And too few answers.

They arrived at the eastern tip of the ravine where the canyon walls pinched together in a V. At the base of the crevice yawned a wide cave mouth. The Blades were arrayed outside. Niko came over.

"She went inside." His mouth twisted in a frown. "I didn't have orders to stop her."

Jirom didn't have to ask who. "Understood. Light the lanterns. We're going straight in."

The mercenaries stowed their crossbows and unpacked storm lanterns and flasks of oil. Jirom blinked as they flared to life. Everyone was assembled, except for the princess and her bodyguard. Jirom peered into the dark cave, but it was dark as pitch inside.

"They're in an awful hurry," Captain Paranas said.

"They aren't the only ones," Jirom replied. He gestured for Niko to lead the way, and the Blades started to file inside, holding their lanterns high. "We have no time to waste. There's an entire city between us and our goal."

Paranas looked at him with an expression Jirom had never seen on him before. The martial stoniness was gone, stripped away until all that was left was a look of pure sorrow. "You don't have to keep up appearances anymore, Jirom. We're not raw recruits. Everyone in this team knows we're not coming back from this. But I'll say this much. It was damned good serving with you. And don't take this the wrong way, but Three Moons is right. You've turned into quite a commander."

Jirom's composure threatened to crack for a moment before he got it back under control. He placed a hand, gently, on the captain's shoulder and steered him into the cave. "We'd better get moving. Before the others claim all the glory."

The cave wasn't very tall, its roof just scant inches above Jirom's head, but a tunnel opened in the back, wide enough for two men to walk abreast. Lights shone within, showing him the path the others had taken.

The tunnel ran about seventy paces into the earth, at a slight decline, before it opened into a broad underground cavern. The rest of the strike team waited there. Jirom saw the strain in their eyes, the tense readiness that came before a battle. Nerves were taut, but everyone was keeping it under control. He spotted the princess near the back, near the entrances to three more tunnels. Her bodyguard held a lantern on one hand, and a bared sword in the other. The two women were having an animated conversation in low whispers.

Jirom moved up to stand by Horace. "What's going on?"

"They appear to be discussing which is the right way."

Stifling a growl, Jirom went over to the women. He glanced pointedly at the bodyguard's weapon. "Expecting trouble already?"

"Just being cautious."

"Which way leads to the city?"

The princess indicated the middle tunnel. To Jirom, it looked no different from the others. "This one."

Jirom looked to the bodyguard, but she said nothing. "All right, Princess. You're our guide from here on in."

She nodded, looking a little nervous as she strode into the next tunnel. Her bodyguard followed on her heels. Jirom went over to Pie-Eye and Paranas, who stood over Raste. "You all set up?"

He wanted to soften his tone, to let this man know they cared about him, but he kept a hard edge to his words. Because that was what was expected of him.

The young Blade cradled a crossbow in the crook of his arm. His stump was stretched out before him beside his whole leg. Some blood had seeped through the bandages, but it was mostly stopped. Beside him sat a knapsack, three waterskins, a full quiver, and a lantern. The light reflected off Raste's skin, casting small points of light across the cavern ceiling. "Yes, sir. Nothing will get past this position."

With a firm nod, Jirom turned away and pulled Paranas aside. "I want two Blades with the princess at all times. They are not to let her out of their sight for a moment."

Captain Paranas nodded. "Do we have a contingency in case this is a trap?"

"If the Dark King knows we're coming, this is going to be a short attack."

"I mean the girl."

Jirom glanced down the tunnel, at the line of bobbing lanterns traveling through the stone warren. "What of her?"

"What if she made a deal with our adversary? She helps end the resistance in exchange for something."

Jirom frowned. Mercenaries were notoriously paranoid, but that didn't mean he was wrong. "So, keep an eye on her. Isn't that's what I pay you for?"

"We haven't been paid in months, Commander. And you fucking know it."

"Just get after her, old man. But don't let her know she's being watched."

With something between a salute and a fuck-you, Paranas grabbed Pie-Eye and they ducked into the tunnel after the others. Raste waved goodbye with one hand while he packed a pinch of dark green leaves into his mouth with the other.

Jirom took one last glance around the cavern. Horace came over. He had been listening the entire time.

"She's *zoanii*," Horace said as they entered the tunnel together. "Her spark is low, but I can't tell if her talent is weak or she's keeping it turned down on purpose."

That made sense. Most Akeshians of the noble class were sorcery-wielders. Though it was odd she hadn't mentioned it. "And? You think Paranas's concerns have merit?"

"That's she a spy for Astaptah? No. But she doesn't trust us, and that makes her unpredictable."

Jirom raised an eyebrow. "That's interesting, coming from you."

Horace regarded him with a sober gaze. "I don't know what's going to happen once we get inside the city, Jirom, but I will do whatever it takes to finish Astaptah. You need to understand that."

Jirom nodded as they continued after the rest of the team. *I do, my friend. Trust me, I understand completely.*

Thunder crackled. A cold wind blew across the empty plains surrounding the capital. A scant mile to the southeast, the sky above Ceasa was blotted out by a cauldron of black storm clouds. Flickering green lightning etched their underbellies, erupting every few heartbeats in a jagged lance that stabbed the ground. A palpable malice rode the wind.

Three Moons shivered and pulled his cloak closer around his body. He suddenly felt his age again, as if all the vigor he'd found in the Otherworld had been stripped from him. He had seen how these storms appeared in that mystical realm—a hundred massive, amorphous limbs surrounding a hungry maw. The image appeared in his mind's eye every time he blinked, like a scar on his soul that would never fully heal.

Three Moons bent his head to spit on the ground, but his mouth was as dry as the desert breeze. It was no fun pondering existential questions while sober. He'd been up most of the night communing with the spirits. Just like at Omikur, the spirits were reticent this close to the imperial capital, but he'd been able to coax a few into talking. As they'd sipped from the bowl of fresh blood he set out, they told him of the evil doings inside the walls. Their words didn't bring him any comfort. *Death. The imprisonment of many souls in cold shells. Power beyond imagining.*

By morning, he'd been tempted to open his wrists. Instead, he decided to face one last battle, to stand with the men and women of this self-styled rebellion. *One last spit in Death's baleful eye. And then, I pray I don't feel anything else. Gods, just let me sleep.*

The low hill where he stood was the only elevation on the plain for miles around. Plots of black earth—deserted farms—stretched along the banks of the river to the east, all the way to the city. Empty houses and storage hives dotted the landscape amid the expanse of withered crops. The capital's walls rose from the plain in concentric rings. Seven walls, it was said, though Three Moons could only see two from this vantage. Those broad curtains were pitted and stained black as if the stone had decayed, their jagged ramparts reminding him of rotting teeth, like a titan's jawbone thrust up through the earth.

Soldiers talked about Ceasa like a thing out of legend. The center of the world, impregnable and eternal. To Three Moons, it looked like just another city. He'd seen big cities fall before. *But never to a force so paltry.*

The rebels were divided into two armies, positioned to the north of the capital. Eighteen hundred men and women sounded like a lot of people, until you saw them lined up for battle on such a vast plain, saw them dwarfed by the magnitude of the task set before them. If they had ten times as many fighters, he still wouldn't feel confident. The eight hundred troops from Thuum were on the left flank with their outside shoulders against the river.

Doing his best to mask his unease, Three Moons walked over to Emanon, standing with the Thuumian *pradi*. Emanon had been in a black mood ever since Jirom left with the strike team. It was a point of honor with him to be in the heart of every battle, to throw himself into every perilous endeavor. Personally, Three Moons suspected the man had a death wish, but he kept that to himself. They were all in dark moods these days. *Who can blame us, after all we've seen? It's a wonder we can even function.*

"Are you ready?" Emanon asked him. The rebel leader's eyes were surrounded by dark circles, as if he hadn't slept in days. Yet, there was no fatigue in his gaze, only feverish intensity.

Three Moon shrugged under his cloak, feigning nonchalance. He'd been doing the act for so long, he saw Emanon accept it at once. *More's the pity.* "As best as can be expected. I can raise a little ruckus out here on the plain. But once we get inside the city, there's not much the spirits will be able to do for us."

Emanon nodded as if he expected nothing more, still staring at the capital. Then he asked, "What if we made a sacrifice?"

Three Moons started to shrug again but stopped himself. This deserved a proper answer. "I don't know if it would get the spirits' attention. At least, not enough to stick out their necks. They're terrified of what's inside those walls." *And we should be, too. Damn you, Jirom. Why didn't you let us run when we had the chance?*

"What would it take to get them to fight alongside us? All the way to the end."

Three Moons looked to the Thuumian, but the *pradi* had turned away.

"Are you suggesting human sacrifice? Hang up a few of our men by their heels and open their throats? Sure, that would get some serious attention. It might also draw out what's inside those walls—" He paused a moment as it sank in. "I see."

Yes, I see all too well. Draw the enemy out from behind those walls and fight them here. But would that be any better?

Three Moons didn't fancy himself an expert strategist, but the plain before them was flat and largely featureless. Their smaller force would be dwarfed by the armies of undead inside, surrounded and devoured in short order. Fighting inside a city, house to house, was as ugly and dirty as it got, but at least the cover of walls gave them a chance of surviving long enough for Jirom to achieve his goal. *After all, we're just the diversion.*

"I'll take care of it," Three Moons said. "When the time comes."

Emanon said nothing more. Sensing his dismissal, Three Moons started to turn away. Then, a vicious crack sounded from the capital. The afterimage of lightning seared his peripheral vision, followed by a deep rumble. One of the towers flanking the city's west gate started to crumble, hunks of masonry and battlements tumbling down in a spill that became an avalanche. A minute later, the tower was gone.

"We can't wait any longer," Emanon said. "We have to advance now."

With a nod, *Pradi* Naram climbed onto his horse and rode off.

"Come on," Emanon said as he started out toward the army's central body.

Three Moons followed them down onto the plain where the army waited. The rain pelted on armor and helms and turned the ground into a morass.

As they passed through the ranks, troopers turned and nodded toward Emanon. Some of them had been following him since he started the revolution. Others were new recruits from the slave pens of Thuum. One and all, they honored him. Emanon ignored them as he strode past, his gaze focused on the walls of Ceasa. As they took their place at the front of the army, Emanon raised his spear. Lightning reflected from the silvery head.

"Advance!"

Muted horns bleated mournfully into the gloomy air, and the host began its march. The Thuumian force had the heavier mail and tower shields. As planned, they marched slightly ahead of the rebel cohorts, which were mostly lightly armored skirmishers with a couple platoons of archers and slingers in the mix. They had no cavalry to speak of, and there were no auxiliaries. If the lines broke, the battle would be over.

Watching the army advance toward the walls, Three Moons missed the Blades. Even though they had been whittled down over the years until they were hardly enough to form a decent honor guard, they had emerged from the Otherworld with something extra, a vitality he couldn't rightly explain. Even more than that, he wished for the original Bronze Blades, as they had been at the siege of Pardisha. Five hundred battle-hardened mercenaries, worth a dozen times their numbers in a fight like this. Now, he could only stroke his fetish bag and pray to his own patron gods.

The army crossed the intervening distance in a bell's time, on routes that would hit the three northern gates of the capital. Just before the Thuumians arrived at the riverside gate, figures appeared in the shadow of the half-ruined gatehouse. A few at first, running out onto the plain, but they quickly grew in numbers. Three Moons gazed intently as the first undead threw themselves against the army's battle line, only to be cut down like so many stalks of wheat. The Thuumians knew their business from hard experience. The living corpses were beheaded and chopped to pieces. The advance became more grueling as more enemies arrived. The frontline units slowed and then ground to a halt as more undead poured out of the capital.

Three Moons felt the central cohort slow as well, preparing itself to meet the enemy. Emanon pointed his spear ahead, and they charged. Three Moons winced as he ran with the army, feeling old aches reawaken in his knees and hips. Then there was no time to think of such things as they collided with the first wave of undead. He stayed a few rows back from the fighting as thousands more undead emerged from the city.

He mumbled under his breath. "Work fast, Jirom. We aren't going to last long out here."

As Emanon led the center, the right flank of the cohort swung around to engage the enemy. The undead mob was pinched between two walls of soldiers, but the creatures didn't care. They attacked indiscriminately.

Emanon's presence rallied his fighters enough to push back the horde, but it was slow, bloody work. Foot by foot, the army advanced again. Too slow, Three Moons saw.

Ignoring the voice in his head that told him to stay put where it was relatively safe, he pushed ahead through the ranks of troopers. He found Captain Ralla's company on the frontline, which was no surprise. Every fifth trooper held a torch instead of a shield, and the light of those brands shone on grim faces.

"Emanon!" he shouted over the din of the fighting. A rebel soldier fell just a few feet in front of him, screaming as he clutched his throat, blood spurting from the wound in all directions. The soldiers on either side closed ranks in front of the fallen trooper. "Emanon, we have to secure the gates! Too many are getting through!"

Emanon half-turned and raised his bloody spear again. The army surged forward in a single massive wave, through the sea of ravaged faces. The sounds of swords and axes chopping into cold flesh mixed with shouts and cries from the living.

Three Moons held his position and let the troopers flow past him. It was time to do his part. The spirits could leach the moisture from a person, boil their brain with a fever, or pack dust in their entrails—all pains which could render a person incapable of fighting. Yet, these undead weren't affected by such bodily indignities in the least. So, he had to do what he was loath to do. Taking out his belt knife, Three Moons slashed the edge across his palm. Warm blood flowed out to drip on the ground. He closed his eyes and whispered his plea.

A handful of heartbeats later, a score of undead massed in front of the cohort collapsed, falling in a jumble as the ground suddenly went as soft as quicksand under their feet. The troopers chopped them down and advanced, and the soil firmed up for them once again. A dozen yards at a time, Three Moons sent his spirits head of the host, fouling the earth beneath their enemies and restoring it when the army pushed onward. Sweat ran down his forehead as he concentrated. With each step, blood was pulled from the wound in his palm as the thirsty spirits took the price for their service.

SUN AND SERPENT

After a bell and a half, the combined army reached the gates. Three Moons was gasping for breath as he released the spirits. He was drained and exhausted, but it had worked. Emanon sent recon squads into the nearby buildings as the main host passed through the bottleneck of the gatehouse.

Captain Ralla found Three Moons leaning under the inner gate, binding his hand in an old rag. "You all right?" she asked.

Her arms and breastplate were covered in black blood, her face spattered with flecks of the same. The blade of her saber was notched, but she had taken the time to wipe it clean.

He nodded as he used his teeth to tie off the field dressing. "As well as any of us. What's the next step?"

"Emanon says we're heading straight for the palace."

"To cut off the head of the snake."

"That's the plan. Tell me, old man. What are the odds Jirom is going to succeed?"

Three Moons used his good hand to wipe the rain from his face. "Probably about as good as ours. What's your point?"

She shrugged her armored shoulders. "Don't have one. I was just wondering."

Yes, as are we all. Wondering if this was an impossible task from the start. We could be back in Thuum, drinking ourselves into a stupor behind those walls while the world collapsed around us, until it eventually came for us, too. If the end is unavoidable, then why bother fighting it?

Instead of speaking his mind, Three Moons tried to imagine how Jirom would respond. "We don't have a choice. We're soldiers. At least, some of us used to be. We fight because that's what we do when someone needs killing. Even if the odds are long and the night seems to last forever. We just keep fighting."

Ralla stared at him, the rain running down her cheeks and mixing with the blood spatters to make a dingy gray mélange that dripped from her chin in heavy drops. "Damn, old man. I was just shooting the shit while we took a breather. Come on. We got work to do."

Crashing thunder overhead drowned out his reply, which was—in afterthought—probably for the best. Three Moons shook his head as the boom rolled off into the distance. More undead were stampeding toward them. The troopers formed a wall across the avenue, shields up, spears ready. The clash of bodies against armor and steel echoed the thunder's roar.

Three Moons shivered as an icy chill ran through him, starting in his chest and spreading out to his arms and legs, until his entire body was numb. The spirits whispered in his ears. He couldn't make out the words, but he knew their intentions. They wanted more blood, and they would do anything to get it. The presence of the chaos storm, mixed with the alien flavor of his life essence, had made them crazed with hunger. He wanted to send them away, but he could not. Jirom needed them.

Steeling himself against the pain, he tore off the bandage and reopened the wound. *Come get it, you little devils. Feast and grow strong. There's work to be done.*

CHAPTER TEN

"**T**his is a fine fucking mess." Pie-Eye kicked a hunk of rocky debris across the uneven ground. "Remind me whose grand idea this was."

Jirom stood before the cave-in that filled the tunnel before them, completely blocking the passage. Part of him wanted to throttle Pie-Eye so the man would shut up, but another part agreed with him. This mission was fucked.

He turned to the princess, where she stood with her bodyguard, both staring at the mountain of fallen rock as if they could wish it away. "This happened after you came through?"

Princess Dasha's face was pensive in the wan lantern light. "During, actually. There was an explosion from above. I assume it came from the fighting in the city, or perhaps the lightning. We barely escaped with our lives."

"And you didn't think to tell us this detail?"

Pie-Eye snorted. "They didn't want to ruin the surprise."

Jauna stepped up behind the mercenary and cuffed him across the back of the head. With a dark glare at her, he quieted down.

The princess turned away from the cave-in, both hands on her hips. "We were already committed to this plan. I hoped that an alternative would present itself."

Horace spoke from the other side of the tunnel where he had been crouching down to examine the loose scree. "But you knew I couldn't invoke my magic or reveal my presence to our adversary."

"So now what?" Niko asked.

"We leave," Captain Paranas said. "And regroup with the main army. A concerted attack may be our best option."

"Our only option," Pie-Eye quipped, and ducked his head as he stepped away from Jauna.

Jirom turned to Horace. "Are you sure using your power would alert the enemy?"

SUN AND SERPENT

"Yes. Remember the battle at Sekhatun? I could sense Three Moons using his magic even before he entered the town. I couldn't pin him down to a precise location, but I knew he was out there. Astaptah will detect it, too. And his senses may be more precise than mine."

"So that's it," Captain Paranas said. "We must go back."

"Not all of us." Horace turned to Jirom. "Take everyone else back to the army. I'll keep going on alone. After you've gone, I can clear this passage and make my way into the city. I'll keep Astaptah distracted during the main attack."

Jirom considered his options. Going back to rejoin the army seemed pointless. Even if they could get back in time, a couple dozen swords weren't going to sway the battle. They needed a strike force inside the walls. "No," he said. "We're going on together."

Captain Paranas gestured at the wall of rubble before them. "Shall we begin digging with our hands?"

"We passed by other tunnels on our way down here. One of them might lead around this blockage."

"It's too dangerous," her bodyguard said, standing close to the princess, as if daring anyone to take her away.

Jirom motioned for Paranas to get the company moving. "It's all dangerous. We'll search the side passages, as the princess suggests. Now get going or get left behind."

"Commander! It is not proper to address—"

Jirom saw the movement behind the bodyguard just before it struck. A long shape emerged from the rubble. Moving like a whip, it lashed itself around the bodyguard's neck. Jirom drew his tulwar and leapt forward, but before he could reach her, another tentacle erupted from the wall to his right and slammed across his chest, knocking him back as it coiled around his torso. Made of rock and earth, it squeezed the breath from his lungs. Jirom slashed downward with his sword. Sparks flew as the tulwar's edge bounced off the tentacle's stony surface.

A score of tentacles sprang from the tunnel walls and ceiling. They wrapped themselves around anything they touched. Captain Paranas's face grew a darker shade of silver as he was lifted by an appendage around his neck.

The tentacle around Jirom was yanking him back and forth as it constricted. His ribs cried out under the pressure, and he couldn't breathe. He was still hacking at the appendage when Horace appeared beside him. Horace grabbed the end of the tentacle and pulled. Jirom dropped his tulwar and added both hands to the effort. Together, they strained, but the tentacle's grip was too strong.

Horace gave up tugging and wriggled out of his backpack. Dropping the sack to the floor, he reached inside to retrieve a bulging leather pouch. He pulled out handful of rust-red powder. "Hold your breath!" he commanded, sprinkling some of the dust on the base of the tentacle where it jutted from the wall.

"No sorcery!" Jirom gasped. Black and yellow spots appeared before his eyes.

"I got it from Three Moons," Horace said, "but it's not magic. Some kind of alchemy. I need a light."

He ran over to a pair of Blades battling a tentacle and snatched the lantern from one. He brought it over, stripping off the hood. "Turn away."

Jirom turned his head. Something sizzled behind him. Then there was a bright flash accompanied by a low thump, as if a giant had clapped its hands together. Suddenly, the tentacle fell loose from his waist. He risked a glance over his shoulder. The stony appendage had been severed cleanly at the point where it joined the wall. The wall itself was scorched black.

Freed, Jirom rushed to help the princess and her bodyguard. Amazingly, they had almost managed to wrestle free of their tentacle on their own. Jirom added his brawn, and together they unwound the appendage. Once Elia was free, the loose end slithered out of their grasp, whipping back and forth in search of a new victim. Meanwhile, another small explosion flared on the opposite side of the tunnel where Horace was liberating Paranas. Most of the team was free now. Jirom directed them back down the way they had entered, with him and Horace being the last ones out.

A dozen paces down the tunnel, Horace tied off his pouch and held it up to the lantern's flame. "Everyone away!"

Jirom barked for the team to keep moving as Horace set fire to a corner of the pouch. Then he tossed the bag behind him toward the cave-in. "Run, damn you!"

Jirom raced back up the tunnel, skinning his elbows against the rock walls along the way. A dull thump echoed behind them, followed by a gust of hot wind carrying streams of smoke and a powerful stench of chemicals. Coughing and wiping their eyes, he and Horace caught up to the rest of the team in a small widening of the tunnel.

Captain Paranas handed Jirom his sword, hilt first. "So, this 'secret' passage wasn't undefended, after all," the mercenary said. "We have to assume the Dark King now knows of our presence."

Horace waved a strand of smoke away from his face. He still held the un-hooded lantern. "Not necessarily. The spell summoning those things could have been set to trigger automatically. It's possible Astaptah doesn't realize it went off yet."

"Yet?" Jirom asked. "How long before he does?"

"There's no way to know for sure. But I'd say we have some time. Enough time to try your alternate plan."

Jirom signaled for the Blades to continue back up the passage. "We'll take the first side branch we find. Blaze a trail and keep a sharp eye for more surprises." He added under his breath, "Who knows what else we'll find hiding down here."

The tunnel wound on and on, a rocky tube that never ran straight, always twisting and turning as it took them deeper into the earth. Horace tried to focus on remaining alert for danger, but memories of the catacombs under Erugash and the undercity of Thuum kept sapping his concentration. He found himself reliving his captivity in Astaptah's torture chamber, of having the life sucked from his body under excruciating duress. *Use that fear. Feel the anger lying under the surface. Remember what Byleth did to Alyra.*

He could hear Jirom and Captain Paranas discussing the way ahead from the front of the party. He wished he could help, but there wasn't anything he could do without using his magic. He was sorely tempted, as all this waiting was killing him, but he had agreed to bide his time, and so he would. For now.

He didn't realize he had company until she spoke beside him. "The black sky overhead," she said. "Do you believe it extends to every corner of the world?"

Princess Dasha was shorter than he imagined she would be. The top of her head didn't even reach his shoulder, and she looked so damned young. "Perhaps. It wouldn't be wise to underestimate our adversary."

"If it does, I wonder what the people of Arnos think about all this?"

Horace glanced at her again before returning his gaze to the rough floor beneath their feet. "Some are probably clustered in the churches, praying for an end to the darkness, but it's probably just another day for most of them. The king will have issued an edict, telling the people not to fear. God will overcome the darkness, eventually."

"They are quite religious, your people?"

"Somewhat, but not like yours. They don't believe their rulers are descended from God."

She snorted. "I've always had difficulty believing that one myself. My father was many things—wise and very kind, a doting parent—but he wasn't divine. He used to cheat when he played stones with me."

Horace didn't know how he was supposed to respond to that, but her words triggered a host of memories of his own father, who had been a complex man, both a stern shipbuilder who commanded dozens of men, and a devoted family man who had nursed Horace and his mother back to health when they both caught an ague. The princess's question about Arnos got him thinking. What would his father think of these events if he were alive today? Horace thought back to when he was eight or nine years old and his father had taught him how to row a longboat.

Focus on what you're doing, Horace. It's not about brute force. There's a technique to everything in life. Once you master it, things will come easier.

SUN AND SERPENT

Just mind your course and keep an eye out for the weather. Squalls can turn up fast, and you don't want to be out on the open water when that happens. When the sky gets dark, you turn about and head for safety.

"Horace?"

The princess's voice brought him out of the reverie. He cleared his throat. "Yes?"

"Can we defeat the Dark King?" She looked up, and her eyes burned with ferocity that took Horace aback. "Can we win?"

"I don't know." When she did not respond, he took a deep breath as he ran a hand through his hair, feeling the grit embedded in his scalp. "I fought him once before, and it didn't go so well."

"In Erugash? I've heard this tale. You killed Queen Byleth and tried to take her throne."

Horace ground his teeth together. "I did *not* kill Byleth."

For a moment, his *zoana* surged and threatened to break free. He tamped it down with some difficulty. When he was firmly back in control of himself, he continued. "Astaptah played the two of us against each other, and then he killed her when I wouldn't."

Horace told her about how he had been taken captive and held in the catacombs beneath the royal palace, until Jirom and Alyra had come to rescue him. He found himself fumbling for words when it came time to describe his fateful battle with Astaptah. He didn't like thinking about that encounter, as it filled him with recriminations. "We fought until the walls shook. I couldn't defeat him, no matter how much power I used. He was just too strong. Alyra and I were going to die."

"What happened?"

"I remembered something a friend gave to me."

Horace smiled at the memory. The princess stared at him until he elaborated. "Some kind of magical device. I infused it with my power and threw it, and the explosion destroyed Astaptah." His smile wilted. "Or so we thought at the time."

Princess Dasha's face was pinched in a thoughtful frown. "Where is the friend who gave you this device?"

JON SPRUNK

"Long gone, unfortunately. I wish he was here. Maybe he would know how to finish this nightmare."

"I understand. I wish my father was here. Though not a great *zoanii*, he was a great leader."

Horace didn't say anything. From what he had seen during his time in Akeshia—slavery, cruelty, power-hungry kings and queens—the empire wasn't the beneficiary of what he would call 'great leadership.' However, he understood the way people often saw their family differently than the world viewed them, and there was no good to come from tarnishing her memories. They were all she had left.

They caught up to the scouts. Jauna and Niko were waiting in a broad cavern with a low ceiling. The tunnel continued on the other side, back toward the surface, but there was an offshoot branch in the left-hand wall, where the rough stone was replaced by ancient fired bricks. A couple yards farther up the main passage, a second side-tunnel split off to the right.

Niko approached Jirom. "I was going to check both tunnels, but we waited for you."

"We could wander down here for days." Jirom turned to the princess. "You navigated these tunnels before. What do you think?"

Princess Dasha approached the brick-lined archway with her bodyguard. "The histories say Ceasa was built upon the bones of older cities, but I never dreamed any of them were still intact." She ran her hand across the bricks, smearing the dust.

Yes, cities built on top of cities. Nations on top of nations. It's the story of the world.

Suddenly, Horace was struck by an image, of the world that he knew lying buried beneath the stones of the earth. And on top of it, the foundations of a new world, a world of complete darkness where nothing lived save for a lone tower. Inside that tower, Astaptah sat upon a throne of bones. The last king. He couldn't tell if this was just his imagination running away from him, or a true vision of the future to come.

At the princess's insistence, they took the new passage, through the constructed wall and down a long tunnel lined with more brickwork. It ran straight for a hundred or so paces. Horace could feel antique pavestones beneath the thick layer of dirt underfoot. The ceiling overhead was made of broad blocks of solid stone. Horace wanted to reach out with his magical senses to quest through the material, to feel how far it extended. Denied the use of his powers, he felt partially blinded. He was studying the stonework above when the team halted again. Through the press of bodies, he saw the corridor abruptly slanted downward at a steep angle. The bricks in the wall were replaced by rough bedrock once again. Jirom signaled an advance, and they kept going.

A fine layer of gravel made the slope's footing treacherous. Horace reached out to the walls on either side to help him navigate. The slanted tunnel descended far longer than he anticipated, until he estimated they were at least a couple hundred yards beneath the blocked passageway. Eventually, the tunnel leveled off, but it remained rocky and unworked. They passed a pair of side branches, but Jirom deemed them too narrow to traverse, so they kept going.

After another fifty or so paces, the tunnel arrived at an open space, roughly rectangular, about thirty yards wide and half as long. Lantern light reflected off walls of mud-brown brick. A stone obelisk stood in the center of the space, its upper half broken off. The ceiling here was a perfect vault of stone. A closer look revealed it was made of compacted dirt and rubble. There were no windows in any of the walls, but two narrow alleys exited the strange plaza; one to their left and the other traveling almost straight ahead. Jirom was discussing the routes with the princess when the scouts reported that the left-hand branch came to a dead-end about fifty paces in, so they were forced to continue straight.

No one talked as they marched through the subterranean passages, but Horace could feel the tension mounting among the fighters. The frustration of tramping through this subterranean labyrinth with no end in sight. Worse, there was a growing possibility they might have to turn around and retrace their steps at some point, and then what? *I know what I'll do. Jirom won't like it, but I don't have a choice.*

After several hours of hiking, Jirom called for an extended rest. They had discovered a long cavern with two exits. Sentries were assigned, and everyone else fell out along the cavern's chalky walls. All lanterns except one were doused to conserve fuel.

As the lights winked out, Horace found a spot to sit by himself. The Blades opened wrapped packages of food. Boots scuffed over the hard, stone floor. Leather creaked as the team tried to find semi-comfortable positions.

Horace wasn't hungry. He sipped from his waterskin before putting it away. It was useless, he knew, to try to sleep. He was too focused on what was to come. There would be killing and intense suffering. Many of the people here with him would likely die in the next few hours. *If we fail, they will be the fortunate ones.*

As he sat in the darkness, Jirom came over and sat down. The big man moved with barely sound. "It's not going to work," Jirom said. His voice was low, so as not to carry.

Horace sighed, his solitude evaporating. "Probably not, but what choice do we have?"

"Not this. Your plan to sacrifice yourself to the Dark King while the rest of us fight his army. You think you'll buy us time, but it won't work."

"Is that so?"

Jirom leaned back against the rock wall. "It's written on your face. You're marching to your death. You think I haven't seen that look before? Many times, my friend. Many times."

"Aren't we all?" Horace flinched as he said those words. "This is a one-way mission. We get in, create havoc, and then hope Emanon can somehow achieve the impossible. We're all hoping for a miracle, but there isn't one coming. We're going to die."

"Mayhap, but you can't fight the Dark King alone. We're all in this together. You need us, and we need you."

Horace clenched his jaws tight and listened to the beat of his pulse in his ear drums. "No, you need me and Astaptah out of the way. That's the only way this scheme works. I take him out, and you and Emanon deal with the rest."

"We can't always see the path before our feet, Horace. We think we know where it leads, but we're fooling ourselves. We go off on a tear, assured in our convictions, and end up right back where we started. I'm just saying that when the time comes, don't just follow what you've been led to believe. There might be another way."

Leather creaked again as Jirom stood up. "We're all here together for a reason. You're not shouldering the burden alone. I've got to take a piss."

As Jirom walked away, the silence resumed. Horace couldn't hear anything now, as if everyone and everything around him had frozen in place. The darkness was suffocating. He took a deep breath and let it out slow. *I appreciate your concern, but when it comes to this battle, I am alone. When we get inside the city—if we ever get inside—we're going to risk everything on one roll of the dice, but I'm the one making the cast. Astaptah will come at me with everything he's got. I've seen what he can do. He'll raze this city to the ground and trample its ashes as easily as snuffing a lantern wick.*

A vibration interrupted his thoughts. The ground buzzed underneath him, and a burning itch like tongues of fire ran up Horace's back. He felt a massive spike to *zoana* nearby. He almost reached for his own power to form a defensive measure but stopped himself. The magic wasn't aimed at him. Instead, it felt like the foundation of the world was being ripped apart. Fear struck through him, leaving him unable to breathe. Astaptah was opening the final Seal.

After a few moments, the rumbling quieted, and Horace finally managed to take a breath. The Seal, he felt certain, was still intact. But for how long?

Horace got up. Lights were being relit. Following their pale glows, he sought out Jirom and found him with Captain Paranas.

"We've got to get moving," the mercenary commander was saying. "These caverns could collapse on us at any time."

"It's Astaptah," Horace told them. "He's close to his goal."

Jirom signaled to the group. "Let's move. Horace, stay with me."

The Blades formed up and proceeded down the tunnel with haste. Horace's attention was divided. Part of him remained with these men and women who were risking their lives alongside him, but the other part combed through his memories. He tried to recall everything he had seen and heard in the desert ruins, about the ancient war between pantheons, about the central conflict between life and death. The mere thought of death made him think of

Alyra, which triggered deeper remembrances of Sari and Josef, his lost family. He almost stumbled on an unseen crack in the ground as the old pains sliced through him.

Jirom's hand steadied him. "You all right? Do you need to stop?"

Horace shook his head, pushing the hand away.

Farther down, the tunnel branched again. Horace didn't hesitate but pointed in the direction closer to the emanations of power, which continued to ebb and flow as they marched. They found an intact building, possibly built centuries ago, and had to crawl up through its partially collapsed innards, but they found another system of tunnels at the top and kept going. They came to a rough cavern with several choices, and again Horace guided them, all the while hoping he was doing the right thing. He imagined them stumbling into Astaptah's clutches. Slowly, the passages began to angle upward, and that brought enough relief to banish his doubts.

They were traveling along a long tunnel with flecks of crystal embedded in the rock walls when Princess Dasha spoke up excitedly.

"I know where we are!" she said. "This is the route we used to escape."

She looked to her bodyguard, who nodded hesitantly. "Yes. I believe it may be."

Jirom called a halt. After a short conference with Paranas, he sent the scouts ahead while the rest of them waited. The Blades stood or sat down, taking sips from their canteens and checking their weapons, while Jirom spoke in low tones with their captain about how they would deploy when they got topside. The princess stood facing a wall, staring as if she could see through it.

Horace stood by himself as time crawled by, ignoring the urge to pace and fidget. Pangs of anxiety attempted to chip away at his resolve, but he resisted their lure. After so much pain and sorrow, he would finally have the chance to put things right, to address the evils of his enemy. Astaptah. Even the name held no dread for him anymore. He said it aloud to prove to himself it had no more power. Several of the Blades looked up, eyebrows rising on their silver foreheads, but none said a word. They simply continued their preparations.

SUN AND SERPENT

The *zoana* pushed against his *qa* as if eager to be released. He wanted to move. He was ready for all this waiting to be over. *Be calm. It will all be over soon.*

Jauna returned to Jirom. "It's clear, sir. We are inside."

"Where does the tunnel enter?" Captain Paranas asked. "A sewer channel? Warehouse?"

The scout scratched her grime-caked forehead. "No, sir. By our best reckoning, we're inside the palace."

Jirom glanced over to the princess before he signaled to the Blades. As Captain Paranas led his men down the tunnel, Jirom came over to Horace. "Are you ready?"

Are any of us? Horace watched the backs of the departing mercenaries. "We're as ready as we can be. Jirom, whatever happens—"

The big man rested a hand on his shoulder. "Before a battle, we say, 'I'll see you on the other side.'"

Horace nodded. "See you on the other side."

Jirom smiled, but there was nothing glad about it. Together, they followed the others.

Dasha tried once again to push past Elia for a better look, and again she was gently but firmly pressed back. Her stomach was tied in knots as they emerged from the hidden passage and entered the cellars beneath the palace. It was a homecoming she hadn't imagined would come so soon, and she faced it with mixed feelings.

The stone cells and corridors of the lower level gave way to the narrow stairs she and Elia had come down only weeks ago, rising to the larders and storerooms that had once fed the palace. The silver-hued soldiers entered first, searching each room and hallway as they went. Everyone remained completely quiet, so quiet Dasha cringed every time she accidently dragged a sandal across the floor or brushed against a corner. But then a gigantic crash of thunder exploded above them, shaking the walls and floor. Dasha drew a shuddering breath. The storm still raged above the city.

Captain Paranas held up a fist, signaling a halt, as they reached the steps leading up to the kitchens. Niko and Jauna darted up the stairs alone, while the rest of the team hugged the walls of the staircase and corridor, weapons ready.

Dasha dreaded what they would find above. She imagined a slaughterhouse strewn with the bodies of people she had known her entire life. Then she thought of the bastion tower. Was there a chance her family still survived? The tower was designed as a last-ditch refuge in case the city was conquered, with provisions and its own cistern.

She gripped Elia's arm and whispered into her ear. "We need to see the bastion. No matter what happens, I must be sure."

Her bodyguard's gaze never left the stairs. "I understand."

Finally, after a short eternity, the scouts returned. They spoke to Paranas, who turned as Jirom came to the forefront, with Horace at his side. The three of them conferenced for a minute, and then Jirom nodded. Captain Paranas's mercenaries stormed up the stairs. Dasha started to follow, but Elia held her back with an arm.

"What did they find?" Dasha asked Jirom.

The rebel commander's face was stern. "Nothing. The chambers above are empty."

"No sign of any servants?" She was thinking of Rould and the kitchen staff. They had been hiding down here when the invaders attacked.

Jirom shook his head as he followed the Blades. Elia waited until he was up the stairs before she allowed Dasha to follow.

True to the commander's word, they found the kitchens vacant. Pots and pieces of cutlery lay on the floor as if dropped in a hurry. A broken clay pitcher lay beside the wine cellar door. More thunder sent rumbles through the walls and ceiling. The shutters on the tall windows rattled, pelted from the outside with incessant rain. Then she saw the entrance. Tables and benches had been stacked against the doorway from the inside, but the crude barricade was shattered, along with tearing the door half off its hinges.

SUN AND SERPENT

Weeks-old stains showed where blood had spilled. A lot of it. Dasha's heart swelled, threatening to choke her, as she thought of the palace servants, how they must have huddled in here while the undead pounded at the door, until the barrier finally gave way and they were slaughtered. No corpses remained to give proof to the ghastly incident. *Of course not. After they died, they rose again to join his shambling army.*

Dasha stood on the hard tiles, shivering with her thoughts. While the Blades fanned out through the exit, she decided to peek inside the wine cellar door, which hung open. The cellar was a long, narrow room filled with wooden racks holding hundreds of jars. Some of them, Rould had once told her, were more than a century old. The air inside was sweet and cool.

"Princess." Elia stood in the doorway. "We're leaving. The servants' wing is empty."

"The bastion?"

"We should tell the commander."

Dasha shook her head. "He'll want his fighters to search it while we wait behind. No. If anyone is still alive, mine should be the first face they see."

Elia looked unconvinced but remained silent.

They left the wine cellar and rejoined the Blades in the hall connecting to the main body of the palace. Horace and Jirom stood off to one side, talking quietly. Perhaps they were arguing, but Dasha couldn't focus on them. Too many memories were returning now, crowding out her thoughts as they drew her deeper into the palace. Her stomach fluttered as she walked through this place where she had grown up. Everything was quiet now, just room after empty room. In the south library, the paintings of lotus flowers on the wall were all hanging askew, a detail that bothered her like a loose tooth. She felt compelled to right them, one by one.

When Elia caught her eye, she shrugged. "I couldn't help myself."

They entered the imperial quarters in the northern wing. The long hallways were floored in light wood, scuffed in places and showing a little dust but otherwise unmarred by the conquest. Dasha recalled the times spent playing in these halls, playing chase-the-hare with her brothers and sisters.

"What time is it?" Horace asked.

Jirom held his tulwar in one hand, with his black shield strapped to the other arm, as if expecting to be attacked at any moment. "If everything is going according to plan, the army will commence its assault soon."

"We need to hurry," Horace said. "Time is short."

Dasha didn't hear the reply. She had stopped by the private solarium where she had eaten breakfast almost every morning for her entire life. The table and floor cushions were still in place, everything in its proper position. Then she noticed the glass tumbler lying on the floor by the sideboard table. A dark red stain surrounded it. Dasha's heart hammered in her chest as she walked over on stiff legs and bent down. The stain was spilled wine. She found the empty jar behind the far end of the table. Who would have been drinking in this chamber on the day of the invasion? *Or did it happen afterward?*

Her senses suddenly alert, she left the chamber. Elia stood in the hall, somehow watching in both directions at once. The Blades were searching room by room while Niko and Jauna stood guard at the end of the hallway.

"I think someone is here," Dasha said quietly.

Elia's gaze sharpened as it fell on her. "Undead?"

"No. Someone alive. Maybe it's my mother and the others."

Elia indicated the stairs that led up to the second floor. From there, a roofed walkway led beyond the walls of the palace proper to the bastion tower. Dasha nodded. Without a word, they left the mercenaries and headed toward the stairs. Captain Paranas called after them, but Dasha ignored him as she raced up the polished marble steps. Her heart beat faster. She desperately wanted to hope that her family was still alive but dared not let herself believe it. Losing them once had been almost too much to bear. To have it happen again . . .

Elia reached the second-floor landing first and motioned for Dasha to stay back as she searched the upper hallway. On this level were several meeting rooms and her father's private den, as well as her parents' chambers. Dasha silently urged Elia to hurry, hearing boots on the stairs below, coming after them. Finally, the bodyguard beckoned, and Dasha hurried to join her. Passing the emperor's suite, Dasha felt an intense urge to stop and look inside, but she resisted. With the Dark King in control of the capital, her family—if any of them survived—would still be hiding in the inner fortress.

Together she and Elia hustled to the corridor that broke off from the main hall, angling northeast. This passage lacked the fine wood molding and geometric borders of the others. Instead, its walls, ceiling, and floor were all plain stone. There were no windows along its forty-pace length. Through the walls, Dasha could hear the steady susurrus of pounding rain and the faint echoing rumble of thunder.

Dasha froze at the end of the corridor where it made a short bend before coming to the heavy bronze door that had once held it secure. Now that door lay on the floor, torn from its hinges. Its surface was warped like a sheet of discarded papyrus. The edges of the doorframe were blackened. Just inside the threshold were the burnt remains of several palace guards, their banded armor half-melted and twisted, weapons fused to their skeletal hands. The hope that had bloomed in Dasha's heart fell to pieces that stank of scorched flesh and metal.

Dasha stood mute as Elia edged past her. The bodyguard led the way, stepping over the burnt corpses to investigate the bastion's interior. Dasha's skin crawled as she followed. She couldn't keep herself from staring down at the ruined faces as she walked past. She didn't recognize the guards, even though she must have known them when they were alive.

After a short antechamber of bare stone, the frame of an inner door was completely empty, its paneled portal gone. Beyond, the private suites of the bastion lay in ruins. While Elia checked the adjoining door, Dasha looked around, fighting off a deluge of reminiscences. The chair where her mother had sometimes read to her was smashed, its legs snapped off. The fine carpets where her brothers had pretended to sword-fight with wooden rods were stained with wide swathes of blood. She kept expecting to see the corpses of her family everywhere she looked, and yet—besides the guards at the entrance—there were no remains here.

Elia emerged from the last bedchamber and shook her head. They both looked to the narrow stars; one set led down to the private kitchen and armory, the other up to the revelry hall. Dasha had never been up to the top chamber. It had been forbidden to her. Secrets passed among her sisters spoke of all-night orgies and other decadences enjoyed by the adults of the imperial court. Dasha started toward the steps, intending to investigate the lower floor first, when she heard a shout from the upper level. It was clearly human. She heard words but couldn't make them out.

Elia charged up the steps ahead of Dasha. As they reached the upper landing, both women froze in place. The tableau before them was jarring in its contrasts. Amid incredible opulence, a man in a loose robe stood, repeatedly kicking a second man who knelt on the floor and bent over a third, older man. The marble floor tiles around them were slick with blood.

Dasha watched in mute horror as Elia approached them with her bared blade.

"Deemu!"

Pumash walked the halls of the palace. He was hungover and hungry, but he couldn't find his manservant anywhere. He had searched the kitchens, stopping for a quick nip to ease his aching head, and the galleries where Deemu sometimes lingered. The old servant liked looking at the paintings, though Pumash had no idea why. They were all of people and events of a past that was lost to them. There would be no more emperors, no more feats of architecture, no grand conquests bringing tribute to these lands. The future held only death. He needed a drink, but he could hardly hear himself shout over the near-constant roar of the lightning storm outside.

"Deemu!"

He wandered into the northern wing, checking doors as he passed down the vacant hallways. Between the booms of thunder, the silence was absolute. *As quiet as a tomb.*

The thought made him chuckle, but the laugh turned into a hoarse cough that irritated his throat. Where was this damned man?

Pumash started to call out again when he passed by a corridor he had never noticed before. Almost at the foot of the imperial residence, it branched out from the main hallway. Curious, he explored, and discovered it ended in a fortified doorway, but the door had been torn off its recessed hinges. The skeletal remains of soldiers lay inside the threshold. They had been incinerated by a great heat. When had this happened? He didn't recall any fighting inside the palace. However, admittedly, he had been quite inebriated at the time. He may have passed out.

Pumash paused at the threshold, not sure he wanted to enter. The place reeked of death, and why would Deemu come here anyway?

He was about to continue his search elsewhere when a faint cry reached his ears. It seemed to come from inside. *Leave it alone. It's none of my business.*

Pumash turned to go when the cry called out again. This time he was certain. It was Deemu's voice.

Lifting the hem of his robe, he stepped over the scorched corpses. He had never been inside a palace retreat, the place where the ruling family would be sequestered in times of upheaval, but he recognized this as one. The main floor consisted of a large central chamber, suitable for leisure, surrounded by several suites. A quick search revealed they were empty. There were some signs of violence—overturned furniture, a streak of blood on the floor here and there—but otherwise he imagined this refuge had looked much the same before the city had fallen. It was probably little used, since the capital hadn't been seriously threatened in generations. Pumash took to the stairs to the next level. As he arrived above, he paused.

The upper floor was one massive chamber, floored in fine marble with dozens of cushioned divans and seats all around. Lush curtains draped the walls in warm colors. At the far end rose a short dais, upon which sat two padded couches, upholstered in red silk. Deemu sat in the center of the floor, ruining the marble with his blood as an undead crouched over him, tearing at the flesh of the older man's shoulder.

The manservant looked over, only moving his head. "I am sorry, Master." He indicated a dark brown bottle lying beside him. Spots of blood spattered the glass. "I was looking for some spirits for you when it surprised me."

Pumash shouted as he rushed over to them. "Away! Get away from him, you filthy beast!"

Overcome with revulsion, Pumash kicked the undead as he would have a stray dog on the street. The creature fell back, its bloody teeth exposed in a feral growl. Pumash was undeterred. Deemu was his, his last fellow living soul, and he would not lose him.

The undead looked as if it might pounce, but Pumash held firm, standing over his servant and daring the creature to attack them. Then a gasp sounded from the stairs behind them. Pumash glanced away from the undead, back to the stairs where two women stood. One was more mature than the other, a warrior by her mien and accoutrements. The younger one was quite fetching and had a noble appearance.

While the younger woman remained by the stairs, the warrior strode forward. Pumash only noticed as she got within a few paces that she held a sword. Which one of them was it meant for? In that moment, Pumash didn't care. He welcomed an end to this existence.

"Deemu," he whispered. "Don't let me become one of those things."

"Yes, Master," came the faint reply.

Don't die, Deemu. You must live to see me interred in the proper style as befits my station.

Even as the thought crossed his mind, he realized how ridiculous it was. He cared not what happened to his body after he was gone. He only sought to an end to the horror. An eternity of oblivion sounded divine.

The undead threw itself at the warrior woman in a flurry of grasping talons and gore-stained teeth. She met it with the point of her sword. The blade bit deep into the creature's stomach, spilling black blood on the floor. Still, the thing kept going, clawing at her arms as it pulled itself closer, jaws snapping toward her throat. The woman tried to fend it off for a moment, and then, perhaps sensing it was impossible, she twisted her hips and threw the creature to the floor. With a boot on its chest, she yanked her sword free. A decisive downward stroke half-severed its neck, and a second chop ended it for good.

Pumash braced himself to be next. *Please let it be now. Release me from this existence.*

Instead of a sword thrust, he was greeted with kind words.

"Are you all right?"

SUN AND SERPENT

The warrior woman knelt beside Deemu and pressed her hands against his ruined shoulder. Blood continued to flow freely down his arm.

"Princess," she said. "We need clean bandages to bind him."

Princess? Pumash stared at the younger woman, who was digging in a canvas bag as she approached. He couldn't believe he hadn't recognized her. "Princess Dasha?"

"You must be important, to have an imperial rescue party," the warrior woman said, and Pumash realized she was making a jest.

"Highness? Where did you come from? Is the rest of the imperial family . . .?"

"Dead," the princess answered as she frowned at Deemu's injury. "They were killed in the attack. As for Elia and I, well, that's a longer story. Right now, we have to move. Fast."

Pumash was distracted as the bodyguard picked up the bottle. He watched as she cut out the cork with a dagger, and then winced as she poured the amber liquor into Deemu's wound. Pumash could smell the rich bouquet. His manservant stiffened in pain, but then relaxed. *Such a waste of good alcohol.*

Then he remembered the princess was talking to him. "Move? Where?"

She looked back to the steps, where more footsteps were echoing. Many of them. "I'll let the commander explain. But be at ease. You're safe now."

Safe? Pumash wanted to laugh, but he was too stunned. *No one here is safe, least of all you.*

Men in armor ascended the stairs. Pumash froze as he sighted them. A dozen or so in all, they were all painted silver as if they had been dipped in the metal. He had never seen such a thing before. They fanned out as they entered the chamber, some moving to the narrow windows while others surrounded him and Deemu.

The princess knelt on Deemu's other side and helped the warrior woman bind his wound with strips of cloth. Pumash could only stare at Her Imperial Highness, close enough for him to touch. He was tempted, just to make sure she was real, but kept his hands by his sides. Was it fear or apathy? Fear that all this was a dream. Or, worse, that this was real, and he would be blamed if he was found in their company?

While the princess and her companion tended to Deemu, a large man with mahogany-brown skin strode over. His cheek bore the four diamond brands of a murderous slave. "You found survivors?"

As the ex-slave turned to him, Pumash found himself wanting to step away, so forceful was his presence.

"How are you here?" the huge man asked. "Are there others? We were led to believe the city was dead."

Pumash swallowed and found his voice. "Yes, dead. I'm afraid it is, save for Deemu and myself. To be honest, I'm not entirely sure why we've been allowed to live."

"Allowed? Who allows it?"

Pumash was about to lie, to use his gift of persuasion to spin a tale of desperate survival among the capital's ruins, but he was too exhausted to care. *The Master can spin his own webs. I'm done with it.*

"He calls himself the *Manalish*. He was once a man, though. His real name is Astaptah."

"So Astaptah *is* here."

The statement was spoken by another man, a man with pale skin. A Westerner, then. Realization washed over Pumash. "You are Horace of Erugash. The one they call the Stormlord."

The new arrival frowned, mirroring the large commander's expression. "Where is Astaptah now?"

The big man glanced at the Western magician. "You cannot sense him?"

"He's close," Horace replied. "But I can't determine more than that." He looked to Pumash. "Do you know where he is? A tall man with burning gold eyes. You would remember if you saw him."

"I remember," Pumash said, his voice faltering.

"Master . . .," Deemu said weakly.

"It's all right, Deemu. These people are here to help us."

"We're here to end the threat," the commander said. "Tell us what you know."

Pumash made a decision, based on nothing more than the feelings buried inside him. His life would be forfeit the moment he spoke. *That will be a blessing. One I have not earned, but I shall welcome it just the same.*

"The *Manalish* spends his time in the temple of Nabu," he replied.

Both men frowned.

"Why?" Jirom asked. "What occupies him there?"

Horace answered before Pumash had the chance. "The last Seal."

"He is close to breaking it," Pumash said. Then, as both men turned their hard gazes on him, his boldness retreated. "He has often summoned me to his side. To gloat of his accomplishments and fill my mind with visions of the future to come."

"Who are you?" Horace asked. "What have you done?"

"I am no one. What I have done is too monstrous to tell. I have walked the streets of Epur, Chiresh, and Nisus, where only the dead now roam. I am the harbinger of destruction."

The commander seized him by the arm and yanked him closer. "You're his servant. *You* did this!"

Pumash did not resist. He nodded to the men. "A slave to his dark will, but I accept responsibility for my role in this apocalypse. I should have died in Nisus with my people. That would have been a fitting end to a life. Not this living nightmare."

He braced himself for savage blows, or least recriminations of his complicity. His longing for death was complete. He could not summon the smallest shred of pity for his fate. He would get what he deserved. *As will we all.*

"Bring him with us," Horace said.

"The risk is too great." The commander lifted his sword to Pumash's throat. "We'll kill him here and now."

Yes, please.

Horace gestured, and the sword was pulled away. "No, Jirom. We may need him."

The commander turned his glare on the foreign magician. "We need nothing from this monster. Better to kill him now, before he does any more harm."

"Humor me. I have an idea."

Horace stepped up to Pumash and looked his directly in the eyes. "You know what I can do. You've heard the stories. Betray us, even once, and I'll rip the skin from your bones."

Pumash felt a slight relief. "I understand, Stormlord. I will do nothing to betray your mission. Just tell me what to do."

Horace gestured toward the stairs. "Let's go."

"What of my servant? He is not fit to travel."

Deemu waved from the floor. The princess and her guardswoman had wrapped his shoulder and chest in crude bandages. "I am fine, Master. Please, do as they say."

Pumash winced at the plaintive tone in the servant's voice but nodded. "Very well. Lead on, sirs."

The silver men and women descended the stairs to the main floor of the tower. As Pumash reached the bottom step, green lightning flashed in the windows. Once, twice, three times, in quick succession, almost blinding him with their brilliance. The palace shivered as the thunder struck, its discordant rumble sounding as if it were tearing off the roof.

Pumash glanced behind him to the magician.

Horace pointed past the silver warriors to the tower entrance. "Keep moving."

At the top of the stairs, coming down, the ex-slave commander eyed Pumash with obvious loathing. *Yes, it would have been better to kill me outright. But I will be true to my word. I won't betray you. I don't need to. The* Manalish *is aware of all that happens within his new empire, as you shall soon find out. Alas, I do not believe he will grant any of us a quick death.*

Heeding his captors, Pumash walked toward the sundered door.

The undead man's head exploded in a shower of brains and bone fragments to Suh's falchion in front of Three Moons. One of Horvik's axes chopped down through the shoulder and into the chest of another black-eyed corpse that used to be a woman, and the other axe hacked into her forehead. Black blood sprayed over Three Moon's legs as the undead collapsed beside him, to be finished off by an earth spirit drilling into her temple and climbing inside.

Three Moons called the spirits to heel. The rest of Ralla's company surrounded him in a ragged circle, keeping him safe as he worked his craft. The blood-lusty spirits proved more efficacious than he had imagined, as they found inventive ways to destroy the undead. Water spirits froze the brain, making the ghuls fall to the ground in violent spasms. Fire spirits leapt inside skulls and exploded, until flames jetted from oozing ear holes and eye sockets. Children of the earth and air simply entered the head and dug out the gray matter in runny scoops.

The army's push into city had ground to a halt only three blocks inside the gates as more and more undead poured out of the surrounding streets to clog their path. For every undead they slew, three more appeared to take their place, drawn by the din of the battle and the flickering torchlight, until the army was encircled by a seething mass of monsters in human form. Conflicting orders came from Emanon's command, instructing the army to push outward in different directions. Sometimes counterorders reached them to halt a particular surge. Sometimes not. Three Moons could almost feel Emanon's desperation. Their leader was getting frantic, frustrated by their lack of progress, and no doubt worried about Jirom's fate.

The company stayed together amid the chaos and slowly hewed its way up the main boulevard. Three Moons thought he would have run out of energy, or blood, long before now, but every time his reservoir of power dried up, he found more surging inside him. It made him feel omnipotent, but it also scared the shit out of him. Power was never free. He was sure he would pay for this somehow, and the toll kept climbing higher.

Captain Ralla pulled back from the line as a messenger appeared. Three Moons tried to listen in, but he couldn't hear anything over the fighting and the roar of the rain. After a few seconds, Ralla sent the messenger back.

"Listen up!" she shouted. "We're pushing for the palace again. This time, we lead the charge."

"Aw, fuck," Yella said as he cut down an undead youth before him and kicked the corpse away.

Corporal Suh stepped back from the melee to shake the gore from his falchion. "We'll never make it, Cap."

"Emanon knows that, but we're making the attempt anyway. The farther we plunge into this cesspool, the more heat we pull away from the commander."

Her words steeled the rebels. Three Moons saw it in the renewed intensity of their efforts as they extricated themselves from the melee. Wounds were quickly bound up, ripped armor strapped together as best they could, and then the company pushed forward through the army's ranks toward the southern front, where they immediately carved out a place for themselves at the center of the Thuumian frontline. The rebels fought with cool economy compared to the frantic efforts of the Akeshians, for whom every strike and block seemed to siphon away part of their will to resist the enemy. Three Moons had seen it before, in battles that appeared hopeless. The mind could crumble in the face of certain defeat. He smiled as Ralla tried to put some backbone into their allies.

"Form up that sagging line!" she shouted. "Spears forward! Forward, you idiots! Set shields for the next surge!"

The rebels' appearance proved a tonic for the flagging Thuumian troopers. Their resistance stiffened, and they began to push back the undead.

Beside Three Moons, Yella smiled a wide grin. Rainwater mixed with dark ichor ran down his face. "I think today we look into the eyes of death for the last time."

"About fucking time," Three Moons replied. "I'm too old to keep doing this. My system can't handle the strain."

Yella spat onto the blades of his long knives and rubbed them together. "Don't worry, old man. I'll carry you across the threshold into the underworld myself if I have to."

"You're all heart."

"You know it."

They were preparing for the signal to charge forward. Far before them, over the rising arc of the broad avenue, rose the hill upon which sat the imperial palace. Although not as tall as the palace in Erugash, and its once-pristine turrets and domes marred by the stains of fire and storm, it was a structure that inspired awe nonetheless. Three Moons was summoning his strength when he heard the horns, blaring from the rear. *That's not the signal. The rebels don't use horns.*

Heads turned, his included.

A new force had appeared under the stone arch of the city gatehouse. Lines of marching pikemen in shining mail, a thousand strong and more, coming through the open gates. They marched under a strange banner, a glowing icon set atop a tall pole. Three Moons squinted. The object looked like a miniature sun. Rays of golden light streamed from its golden surface, cutting through the storm's gloom. A cadre of sorcerers in crimson robes surrounded the standard-bearer. This had to be the promised reinforcements from Yuldir. Three Moons felt the power of their *zoana* roll past him and couldn't help feeling relief.

Shouts echoed across the army as the undead horde fell back, snarling and clawing at the air as if trying to fend off the oncoming rays of light. For a brief moment, Three Moons had a hope they would break and flee. Then, an ominous rumble came down from the sky. The city shook like a beast in mortal terror. A heartbeat later, sharp green lightning flared overhead, forcing him to shut his eyes. More thunder boomed in a series of concussive strikes, and with each strike the street's pavestones shifted under his feet. The rebels staggered into each other, and Three Moons felt half-smothered in the middle of the throng. Finally, the din of the storm subsided back to a roar in the background.

As the coruscation faded, Three Moons cast his gaze back to the gate. More than half of the Crimson Brothers had fallen, their bodies incinerated to nothing more than ash and pieces of fluttering cloth. The rest crowded around the icon, which had lost much of its glow, the radiance becoming dreary and faint under the pall of the storm. Emerald lightning struck their position again, and another pair of sorcerers fell. Shouts arose once again on the southern front where the undead had regrouped. They attacked in a massive wave that almost overwhelmed the human line in the first few heartbeats. Only the savage battling of the rebel troops kept them at bay, and that only barely. Ulm disappeared under an avalanche of living corpses, and when they were beat back, he was gone, leaving no trace except one of his hooked swords lying on the street.

Three Moons glanced at Ralla. A troubled expression creased the captain's brow. *Aye, lass. It's over. Either we retreat, or we die here. Maybe both.*

The army made a slow withdrawal, back to the gate where it joined up with the Yuldirans. The addition of fresh troops allowed Emanon to bolster his flagging lines, but Three Moons could see it was only a stopgap measure. The undead were still coming in increasing numbers. It was only a matter of time before the combined armies were overrun.

Three Moons looked back to the city's center, to the palace compound now barely visible through the haze of mist and rain. Jirom was out there somewhere. Holding onto that hope, Three Moons got back to work keeping his brothers and sisters alive.

CHAPTER ELEVEN

Rain sluiced through the streets, its swirling current littered with refuse. Just down the hill from the imperial palace was the Forum, flanked on four sides by smaller hills, each crowned with high marble buildings. A wide public square stretched in its center, rows of pillars extending upward as if holding up the slate-gray sky. It was all so familiar to Dasha and yet so alien. It made her want to cry.

Past the Forum, they traveled along the Noble Way, which merged the imperial ward with the temple district. The fierce beat of water on pavement and rooftops was almost deafening, and it was difficult to see more than fifty paces in any direction, making Dasha feel as if she and the rebel strike team were traveling inside a hazy bubble. She wore a soldier's cloak that was too long for her. Its back dragged through the water, making the neck clasp pull against her skin, but it kept her dry for the most part.

Every few steps she looked over her shoulder, bothered by a feeling she couldn't shake off. They were being watched. Beside her, Elia was so tense she seemed to be on the verge of jumping out of her own skin. The bodyguard's eyes never stopped moving. Her sword, however, was perfectly still, never wavering an inch as she walked. Rain ran down the bright blade and poured in a tiny stream from its point.

The rest of the mercenaries were much the same as Elia. Watchful to the point of obsession and ready to lash out at the slightest provocation. Dasha had learned a little of what they had gone through, and it was remarkable to her that any of them managed to survive. The destruction of Erugash, hounded across the deep desert, the battle at Thuum. Now they were risking their lives again. *They are not rebels, but heroes. I will remember this, should I survive this war.*

Dasha watched the survivor, who walked in front of her. His name—Pumash—was vaguely familiar, but she couldn't remember meeting him before. She felt he must be a noble, by his once-fine clothes and the way he carried himself. She had wanted to find out if he knew anything about her family, but Jirom insisted they needed to move quickly, so she'd been forced to hold her questions. Still, she kept a close eye on him. She had the uneasy feeling there was much he hadn't told them.

Niko, at the front of the line, seen vaguely through the haze, halted and held up a hand. The team stopped at once. Those on the sides hugged the walls of the buildings on either side of the street. Shivering in the rain as she strained to hear any sounds of danger, Dasha was struck by how much her life had changed. It seemed unreal that, just a month ago, she had been living in luxury, with tutors and parties and no larger concerns than this season's fashions and which noble son she might someday marry. That life seemed so sheltered, it bordered on perverse. She had learned a lot about the world in these past several weeks, painfully. And those lessons were not lost on her. *I will rebuild Akeshia. I will make it a better world than it was before.*

"What is it?" she whispered.

Elia shook her head. Her sword had risen to a warding position. Then word was passed back. Dasha heard "undead" and couldn't stop a shiver from running through her. The wind suddenly felt icy cold, penetrating her soaked garments. Her hand stole to the belt around her waist. Elia had taken it from a fallen guardsman and put it on her. A long knife hung from the belt in a leather sheath. The weight felt strange, as if she were wearing a costume. She slowly drew the weapon. A wavy pattern ran through the blade. The single edge looked quite sharp, as did the tip. Dasha looked at how Elia held her sword and tried to emulate it.

"Keep it low," her bodyguard whispered with a hiss. "Bringing the point up from a longer distance adds power to the stab. If someone, or something, attacks you, aim for the underside of their chin."

"Not the heart?" Dasha asked.

The lady Silver Blade named Jauna chuckled softly from Dasha's other side. "Don't try to get fancy, girl. You might stab a body ten times and not hit the heart. Aim for the easy parts that cause the most damage. The throat, the eyes, and the groin."

Dasha thought about stabbing the knife into someone's groin and it almost made her sick. "Under the chin. Got it."

Niko waved forward before dropping his arm, and the team started off again. As they reached the next intersection, Dasha saw remains of several bodies lying in ankle-deep water, all badly mauled as if they had been torn apart by wild animals. Blood pooled into the trash-clogged gutters. Everything was silent.

"It's empty," she said, not realizing she had spoken aloud.

"What is?" Elia whispered.

"My city. My empire. It's all gone, isn't it?"

"We're still here, princess. My pa used to say, 'while there's still breath, there's hope.'"

"But it is hopeless. All these people dead. Why? What purpose does such wanton death and destruction serve?"

"I've seen it all my life, girl," Jauna said, pausing to survey the bodies. "Maybe not on this scale, but it's just the same. Killing is all some people do, and most of the time they don't even need a reason. And the destruction goes hand in hand with the killing. Haven't you ever felt that rage and it just needed to come out? It don't matter how. It just has to be."

Dasha shook her head within the rain-drenched hood, trying to comprehend the magnitude of the rage required to kill hundreds of thousands of people, and then the cold fury to bring them back to a horrid semblance of life. It was beyond her capacity to understand. "No, and I never want to feel it either."

Jauna nodded, still looking down at the bodies. "Then you're the fortunate one, girl."

A crash echoed behind them. Dasha turned, teeth clamped to keep from making a sound. A door had slammed open down the street behind them. A tide of undead poured out and rushed into the ranks of the Silver Blades. Several of the living corpses fell almost at once as half a dozen crossbows fired at point-black range. Then the Blades drew hand-to-hand weapons and engaged. Swiftly slaying the undead nearest to them, they formed a solid line and began to wheel back toward the main body of the team.

SUN AND SERPENT

Jirom ran past Dasha and charged into the melee at a flagging spot near the line's left flank. His tulwar flashed, the steel blade etched in green incandescence as lightning rippled across the sky. Two undead fell immediately to his onslaught, one with a severed neck leaking black blood and the other with its skull half caved in from the sideways blow to the temple. Jirom never stopped moving. He went from one enemy to the next. A scrawny girl in a tattered sarong jumped on his back. Jirom reached back over his shoulder and dragged her off by her filthy hair, flung her down and drove the point of his blade into her forehead. Dasha winced as the top of the girl's head exploded in a fountain of black gore.

Several undead had surrounded Ino and Ivikson. As the two mercenaries tried to fend off the horde, Jirom plowed into the midst, hewing on both sides of him like a grain thresher gone mad. Dark blood flew and spattered all around. One fiend grabbed Ivikson by the arm, its jaws extended, but before it could bite down, Jirom's tulwar split the thing's skull from the back and flung it aside.

To Dasha, the rebel commander seemed invincible. Nothing could stand before him. Then she felt ashamed. This was her city, not his. She should be the one who protected it, who brought it back from the Dark King's defilement. She took a step toward the melee.

"Whoa!" Elia pushed her back with her free hand as she watched the fighting. "Where do you think you're going?"

Dasha pointed the dagger at Jirom. "We should aid him."

The bodyguard shook her head, the ends of her wet hair whipping across her shoulders. "Get too close and he's liable to take off your head before he knows it's you. No, just stay put, Princess. Let them do their work."

Dasha fumed at the instruction, but she obeyed, if only because she hadn't considered that Jirom or the others might harm her by mistake. So, she held her knife tight and watched. With Jirom providing a solid anchor, the silver fighters were able to make an orderly withdrawal. But the undead kept coming, leaping down from windows and scurrying out of alleyways, more and more of them with each passing heartbeat.

Dasha turned from side to side, expecting to be attacked at any moment.

Fear crept up into her chest, squeezing her lungs and setting her heart to race faster. The Blades had formed a solid cordon across the width of the street. They fought with methodical precision, retreating step by step without breaking or panicking. Dasha marveled at their restraint. But where would they go? Did they intend to fight all the way to the temple? There had to be a better way.

Then she saw it. The high walls to the south belonged to Imperial Park, which should be empty. Better yet, it had a direct route into the temple district.

Dasha grabbed Elia by the arm. "Jerovan Concourse!"

"Aye. That may work."

Dasha called to Jirom as she pointed to a closed gate fifty yards down the avenue. "We have to get inside the park! There's a way to the temple!"

The commander looked back over his shoulder, blood smeared down the side of his face. With a frown, he waved his fighters forward. Dasha and Elia remained near the center of the squad, jostled together with Pumash. The man looked miserable, as if he were marching to his own execution. His hands were clutched together in front of him, so tight his knuckles showed white.

As they approached the parkland, Dasha could see it had not gone unscathed in the city's sacking. One of the ornamental gates hung open, while the other was torn off its hinges and lay on the street. A corpse was pinned beneath the fallen gate. As the fighters got within a few steps of it, the body's head lifted. Bedraggled ropes of wet black hair hung from the skull, obscuring the features so Dasha could not tell if this was a man or woman, but the bestial way its jaw yawned open told her this person was no longer truly alive. It reached out toward the team, broken and bloodied nails scrambling across the pavement. Without ceremony, Niko thrust the point of his dagger through the fiend's forehead, and it went limp with a shudder.

Thunder boomed. Through the storm's fury, Dasha heard a sound that made her blood run cold, a terrible screeching roar that wasn't the wind. Everyone looked up and to the south. Beyond the bent trees and rain-stained monuments of the imperial park rose the great towers of the temple district.

SUN AND SERPENT

Atop the temple of Nabu's singular tower perched a monstrosity. At first, Dasha took it for an impossibly huge vulture, black and lean, hunched over of the steeple. But then the thing spread its wings and its reptilian nature became apparent. The jaws at the end of its sinuous neck opened, and a titanic roar issued forth with the force of a hurricane. Icy dread filled Dasha as she tried to look away but could not. This was a thing out of legend, out of time and place, a thing that did not belong. Everything about it struck her with a sense of incredible wrongness.

"What the fuck is that?" one of the Blades asked behind her.

Horace stepped ahead of the group in the monster's direction. "Astaptah must have summoned it. Jirom, get your people out of here."

The rebel commander pulled back from the melee. Dark blood covered his arms and dripped in thick lines down his chest. He had a few scrapes and claw marks, but otherwise appeared uninjured, and Dasha found herself strangely glad for that. *What do I care for him? He's a barbarian and a would-be conqueror. He means nothing to me, except as a convenient ally.*

She told herself these things, even as a small voice in the back of her mind whispered otherwise. *You can try to deny it, but you like him. He's strong and honest, completely unlike anyone else you've ever met. Certainly nothing like the strutting fools who used to stalk you around the court, all seeking your hand and the power of your family.*

"No," Jirom said over the din of the fighting. The Blades had formed a semicircular cordon around them that kept the undead at bay. For now. "We stand together. Niko! I want crossbows on the rooftops."

Horace went over and said something to Jirom that Dasha couldn't hear. Whatever it was, Jirom shook his head and continued placing his fighters. There were fewer undead in the street now, a testament to the skill and ferocity of the Silver Blades. The gutters were piled with unmoving bodies, covered in gore and grime. It made Dasha sad to look at them, but she forced herself to do it. *These are your people. Evil did this to them, and you must find a way to make it right.*

Horace stood alone in a cleared section of the street. Even Jirom had left his side as the young foreigner faced the monstrosity atop the temple, his eyes closed. Dasha wanted to say something to him—perhaps a word of encouragement, for he fought for her people now, whether he understood that or not. Before she could speak, another great roar shook the city, followed by the thunderous flap of great wings as the beast left its perch.

Somehow, a pair of Blades had gotten onto the roof of a two-story building fronting the street. Faint twangs echoed from their position as they fired their arbalests in the creature's direction. The missiles looked pitiful compared to its vast bulk. Indeed, they failed to penetrate the scaled hide of its underbelly. The beast flew higher, like a condor seeking prey. Then, when it was over the parkland, it folded its leathery wings and dropped from the sky with frightening speed.

Jirom now stood close to her, on the other side from Elia. Both warriors clutched their weapons in tight grips, but what could mortal muscle and steel do against such a monster? Dasha tried to stand tall as she watched her death approaching. *You are the daughter of an emperor. You will die like one.*

The monster opened its jaws, and Dasha saw something flicker within. Black flames tinged with golden-red tongues. However, before the thing could unleash death upon them, it was wrenched sideways as if it had been struck by a flying ship. But there was nothing there. Then Dasha felt the wave of power erupting behind her, where Horace stood. The energy seared her senses like standing beside a bonfire, so fierce she couldn't imagine it. She had been surrounded by *zoanii* her entire life, including some of the most potent magi in the empire, but she had never felt anything even approaching such raw power. It was terrifying to witness.

The monstrous beast skewed to the side past the park's walls, but soon righted itself. Screaming in draconic fury, it launched itself at their small party again. And again, the monster was struck by an invisible force and sent off course before it could reach them. Because she was prepared for it, Dasha felt the incredible explosion of *zoana* from Horace. She allowed herself to sink into a light trance, and there—on the edge of the spectral world—she Saw these events as they really occurred. The force striking the monster appeared to her as gigantic fist wrapped in bands of iron armor. The monster, too, appeared differently in her Sight. Far more startling, she glimpsed the mote of infinite darkness lying at its heart. With every blow from Horace's magical fist, that black heart flickered momentarily like a candle in a strong breeze. Each time, it recovered to blaze anew. Was there no stopping it?

On its next pass, Dasha summoned her own *zoana*. It was a mere taper next to Horace's blazing sun, but she couldn't stand idle any longer. Since Mordab was her strongest dominion, she fashioned her power into a spear of ice. Taking aim, she flung it into the dragon's path with as much mental strength as she could muster. She was shocked to see what materialized. The ice spear she had created was as tall as two men standing on top of each other and as big around as a tree trunk. She had never created something so monumental. Just before the missile struck, the monster opened its maw and out jetted a gout of black fire. Ice spear and fire met in an explosion of frosty slivers that fell to the ground. Trembling from the power she felt, Dasha reached again for her *zoana*.

Before she could create another spear, the dragon shuddered in midflight. Its course wavered, and then turned into a sharp decline. As it fell, Dasha saw a gaping wound down the length of its underside, as if a giant knife had sliced it open from collarbone to genitals, but she had Seen no mystical blade. Confused, she watched as the beast landed inside the park with an impact that shook the street.

"Princess, remain still," Elia said.

The bodyguard held up Dasha's arm. Lines of blood ran from a long cut down the inside of her left forearm. She hardly felt it at all. While Elia bound the wound in tight layers of bandage fetched from her rucksack, Dasha looked at Horace. The aura of his power was diminishing as he closed his *qa*, but she could still feel the energy lacing the air around him. From what she had Seen and felt, he was easily as powerful as her father's entire court combined. How could one person hold so much *zoana*? And he bore no immaculata. The idea staggered her. *Is this a gift from the Gods, or something else?*

"What was that?" Jirom asked, clearly aiming the question at Horace.

When Horace shrugged, Ino answered in a deep growl, "It was a dragon! A fucking dragon, coming right at us. What the fuck is going on?"

"It came from beyond the Veil," Horace said. "I have to go."

"What do you mean?" Jirom said. "We're all going."

"No," Horace said, shaking his head. "Astaptah will just summon more horrors. I have to go now, alone. I have to end this."

"Horace—"

A tremor ran through the ground with a sound like cracking stones. Dasha covered her ears as the street's pavement ripped open in a long, jagged crack. The chasm widened to several man-lengths across within seconds, forcing the team to quickly move to the sides to avoid falling into the yawning abyss. Rainwater ran over its sides—a mixture of clay, earth, and raw stone. At the same time, she felt something tearing inside her head, like part of her brain was being pulled apart by invisible forces. Out of the corner of her eye, she saw Horace stumble. His hands were clasped to his temples, his face twisted in obvious agony. Jirom was by his side in an instant.

"What is it?"

"The Seal," Horace replied through gritted teeth. "It's breaking open." He looked up at Jirom. "I'm sorry. There's no time."

With those words, Horace vanished. A rent of darkness opened beside him, and he simply stepped through. The aperture closed after him.

Dasha couldn't stop the yelp that escaped her lips. One moment, the magician was right in front of her. The next, he was gone.

"Hell's fire!" Elia murmured. She had finished dressing Dasha's arm.

Dasha flexed her fingers. The bandage was already sodden from the rain, but tight. A little blood seeped through the wrapping.

Niko and Jauna came over to Jirom, who stood near her.

"There's fighting to the west," Jauna said.

"Lots of lightning coming down over there, too," Niko added. "It could be the main force, coming in through the city gates."

Dasha watched as Jirom peered in that direction, squinting as if he could pierce the rain and gloom through sheer force of will. Then he called Captain Paranas over. "Take the princess and set out for the north gates. Join up with the main force if you can. If not, find a place to hunker down until Emanon gets through to you."

Paranas had taken off his helmet. Rain ran through his close-cropped hair. "No, sir, I don't think so."

"You're refusing an order, Captain?"

"Well, Commander, first of all, we haven't been paid in months, so the Blades aren't technically under contract anymore. Second, Three Moons would skin me alive if I left your side before this is all said and done. So, if you don't mind, let's just get this finished. All right?"

"I agree," Dasha said. "We all set out on this mission together. We will end it together."

Jirom looked from the captain to her with a gaze as hard as granite, but he nodded. "As you will. Come on then. We've no time to waste."

Elia's eyebrows were raised as they all turned to follow the rebel leader into the park. Dasha didn't give an explanation as she hurried along after him. She didn't have one, just a feeling that she needed to prove something. *I only hope this newfound bravado doesn't get us killed. If we don't survive this, please forgive me, Elia.*

Drenched in the storm's heavy tears, they dashed down the paved walkway.

Instead of transporting him to the temple as he wished, the mystic portal dumped Horace into a cold, dark place. The ground was perfectly smooth under his hands and knees, slippery like a plane of polished glass. He couldn't see a thing, nor See. All around him was complete blackness. Even the air tasted strange, cool and dry in his throat with a metallic tang. Moving carefully, he stood up. *Where am I?*

The question hung in his mind like the queasy aftertaste of a bad meal. This place, the darkness and the cold, reminded him too much of his vision of the Outside. He tried to summon a magical light. The *zoana* flowed through him, but nothing happened. He remained blind. He tried again, this time to create a ball of flame. The magic flowed but nothing appeared. No light, no heat. Panic welled up inside him.

Steeling himself, he took a short step, and then another, feeling ahead with his toes before he trusted each stride with his full weight. There could be a pit in front of him and he wouldn't see it. Step by step, he moved through the darkness.

After a couple minutes, a new fear occurred to him. What if he had transported himself into some other world, something like the Otherworld that the Silver Blades had described? After all, there could be any number of other realms in existence. What's to say he hadn't inadvertently entered one? Three Moons said they had found a doorway that brought them back to their own world, said it had called to him like a fiery beacon. Horace stopped walking and closed his eyes. Concentrating, he tried to extend his magical senses outward, seeking something, but he felt nothing. Only emptiness, spreading out forever in every direction.

From right beside him came a deep laugh. "Greetings, old friend. Did you really believe I would not be waiting for you? That I would not control every avenue to the heart of my power?"

Horace turned but saw nothing. He could feel Astaptah's presence, though he knew the man was not here in body. More tricks. "This—whatever it is—won't hold me forever. I'm coming for you, Astaptah."

The laughter continued, amused now and coming from several directions. "It's already too late, Horace. You and your friends have merely arrived in time to die. I'll take them first, and then return for you at my leisure. Perhaps I shall make you my slave. You can sit at my feet and witness my eternal triumph."

"I will find you and kill you first!"

The *zoana* surged within him. Horace tried to lash out with whips of fire and ice, but nothing manifested. More laughter floated down to him, this time from high up and far away.

Horace spun around. He couldn't be trapped here. *If he lured me into this place, there must be a way out. Just keeping searching.*

Taking deep breaths to calm himself, he started walking again, arms extended before him in the dark. As he stumbled onward, slowly making his way across the smooth floor, encountering nothing, feeling nothing but cool air on his face, despair began to creep over Horace again. He couldn't stop thinking of his friends, alone in the capital, facing Astaptah without him, and suddenly it seemed that his entire life had been one long string of failures. *Sari and Josef. Washing up in Akeshia. Slavery. Losing every friend I made, even Byleth, to the darkness. Then . . . Alyra. Now I have nothing left.*

Then, another voice spoke in the darkness. It didn't come from any one direction but seemed to emanate from all around him.

You have everything you need, Horace.

Horace swallowed hard. The voice belonged to Mulcibar. He wanted to believe it was him in truth, but he didn't trust his senses anymore. "You aren't here. You're dead."

Yes, Horace. Yet you still live.

"For now. Until Astaptah comes to finish me off, after he's done destroying the world."

You do not understand. Horace, I failed to recognize the threat before it was too late, but you saw. You are more than what you appear. I always sensed that. However, it wasn't until I died that I could truly appreciate that knowledge.

Horace was beginning to think he was going mad. *Maybe I've been insane since the day Sari and Josef died. Maybe all of this has been one colossal delusion, and any moment I'll wake up in a sanitarium, trussed up so I won't hurt myself.*

You are not insane, Horace. And you are not lost.

Horace snorted, unable to help himself. "Really? I don't know where I am, and I can't get out. The magic isn't responding. So, unless you have a plan to get me out of here . . ."

Mulcibar's voice was closer now, more substantial. *You hold a light inside you that can never be extinguished. You must let it out in order to find a way through.*

"I can't make a light. I can't do anything. The power is there. I can feel it, but it won't obey me."

Then another voice spoke to him. *It is not a light for the eyes, Horace. But for the spirit. Seek the spaces in between.*

"Ubar?"

Horace squeezed his eyes shut and pressed his palms to them, wanting to dig his fingernails into his face. *I should have died back in Tines. Or off the shore of this accursed land. Why am I here? What do you want from me?*

The Woman's voice spoke to him from the dark, whispering softly in his ear as sultry as a desert breeze. *The world is an illusion, Horace. Seek the spaces in between.*

With his eyes still closed tight, he opened his senses to See.

The spaces in between.

At first, there was nothing. Just the cool air on his skin and a faint tickle in his hair. He felt the tension in his muscles, the desire to move, to exercise their strength, to escape. But the path out wasn't a physical one. *I entered this place through the void, by slipping through the space in between the elements. But there's nothing in the void. Is there?*

He looked deeper, extending his Sight farther, not outward but inward. Into himself. He didn't know what he was looking for until he found it. A kernel of light buried deep inside, burning brighter than a thousand suns.

Just as if he were accessing his *zoana*, he reached for it. The power flared until even his mystical senses could not withstand it. Then, his ethereal grasp closed around the light. Power, pure and unadulterated, crashed through him. Horace opened his mouth, but no sound emerged. He was seized in an electric paralysis. It lasted only a moment, a fraction of a heartbeat, but he felt like an entire lifetime could have been lived within that span.

He blinked, and he was himself again. A disc of dazzling white light rested in his hand.

There isn't much time, Horace.

Mulcibar/Ubar/Woman spoke, and the void shuddered.

The enemy is approaching his goal.

He nodded, as much to himself as to any other presence. He was ready. He knew what to do. All his doubts had burned away.

Raising the disc, he cut a hole in the darkness and stepped through.

The void thrust him from its pitch-black womb onto a stone floor. Horace blinked as his eyes adjusted to the dimness. The disc of light no longer appeared in his hand, but he felt its connection, like a hot metal wire leading back to his *qa*. He opened his hand, and the disc appeared.

The light pushed back the darkness around him to reveal a small, plain chamber about six paces on each side. The air smelled of old incense. A single narrow window was situated high up on the wall above his reach. A closed door was before him.

Getting up, he took a moment to center his concentration. The *zoana* pulsed within him. There was no hiding his presence now. No more games. It was just him and Astaptah. He pushed open the door and entered a nightmare. He had come to the right place.

Horace had never been inside a temple to the god Nabu, but he knew a little about the cult. Enough to know the interior of this temple had been altered. Tormented. Every visible surface—the floor, walls, and ceiling—was blackened as if a great fire had raged within the structure. He reached out to the nearest wall and felt the rippled texture, like melted wax. The floor was uneven under his feet and slightly sticky. Then he turned a corner and froze.

A body hung on a massive black spike jutting from the wall. The corpse wore the remains of a robe, which may have once been pristine white, but now was stained with blood and ash. The corpse's features were withered and dark, as if it had been fired in a kiln. It must have been a priest, possibly the temple's last defender against Astaptah's incursion.

According to the texts Horace had read during his time in Erugash— which now seemed a lifetime ago—Nabu was the patron of scriveners and archivists, known as the Keeper of Secrets. The creation myth of Akeshia stated that the world came out of chaos, a detail that now had added meaning to Horace. The Gods had managed to defeat the chaos using special weapons they had created from secret knowledge, passed down to them from their Sky Father. At the time he'd read these myths, Horace hadn't paid much attention to the details, but now he wished he had. Apparently, the Seals that held back the chaos resided in Nabu's temples. What other 'secret knowledge' did they hold?

The corridor continued past the impaled cleric through several rooms. None had furnishings, merely walls and floors of dark gray stone with the occasional high-set window looking out onto a darker sky. The only light came from occasional flashes of lightning through those narrow portals. The sound of his footsteps echoing through the empty chambers set his nerves on edge. He kept a tight grip on his power, ready to unleash it in any direction.

The more he explored, the more he believed the temple was empty. Whatever had scoured these halls with fire and shadow had departed, leaving only a vast emptiness.

Horace halted in an empty hallway. A vast emptiness. He focused his magical senses until he could See the internal structure of the temple. There it was, a web of void energy woven into the stonework so subtly he had missed it. This was something new. As his Sight followed the lines of power, Horace marveled at its scope. The void encompassed every room and corridor, but why? He couldn't determine a purpose to the enchantment. He walked deeper into the structure, searching for an answer.

A chamber led to another hallway, wider and taller than any he had seen in the temple so far. The walls were carved in raised patterns of interconnecting lines. Horace thought the intricate engravings must be poignant, but their meaning escaped him. A tall, silver door stood at the end of the antechamber.

Horace reached out with his power. He was prepared to batter down the door, but it opened with a brief touch, swinging on silent hinges. Beyond lay a dark chamber. Every surface was jet-black stone, without any flecks or veins, making the chamber feel like a vast empty space around him. Near the far wall sat a long block of the same stone, which pulsed with Shinar energy.

Horace took a step into the chamber and was jarred to a stop as a vast quake shook the temple. A voice rumbled in his head, sending lances of pain through his skull.

YOU HAVE ARRIVED TOO LATE, FIRST SWORD. THE LAST SEAL IS CRUMBLING, AND SOON THE GATES OF DEATH WILL OPEN. ALL THAT YOU KNOW AND LOVE SHALL BE DESTROYED.

Horace pushed back with a mental shove. "You will be the first to fall, Astaptah. I'm coming for you."

The vast chuckle echoed in his mind.

COME THEN, MY OLD FRIEND. I AWAIT YOU.

The presence left his mind. There was a doorway behind the altar block. Horace could See it clearly now, and beyond it was a circular stairway winding down deep into the earth below the temple's foundation. He started to approach, but another tremor shook the chamber, and a fierce itch burned down the back of his neck. Horace stepped back as six huge shapes flowed out of the walls around him. Twice his height and hulking, with gigantic hands that ended in sharp talons, they were ink-black to match the stone from whence they emerged. Their faces were masses of wriggling protuberances beneath a multitude of fiery red eyes. A horrible stench preceded them, making Horace gag as he sought to escape, but he was boxed in. With lumbering strides, the creatures attacked.

Horace threw open his *qa* and wove webs of fire and wind. The demons ripped them away as if the magical constructs were strands of papyrus. The first one to reach him lashed out with both paws. Horace ducked beneath the attacks and reached out with the disc of light, running its edge along the creature's midsection. Black flesh parted as easily as cheesecloth, spilling dark bile. Horace punched out with his other hand, wrapped in power. The demon's flesh was rough and pitted, like thick hide wrapped over iron-hard muscles and bone. Bones cracked beneath his strike, and the fiend was hurled back into the wall behind it. The chamber trembled from the impact. Horace stumbled for a moment as he sought to keep his balance, and that moment almost proved fatal as heavy footfalls sounded behind him.

Without looking back, Horace opened himself to the void and stepped inside. He tried to transport himself back to the hallway, where he thought he'd have a better chance to fight these colossal creatures. A wave of vertigo crashed on him in transit, and he tumbled out of the darkness in a corner of the same room. The demons turned to find him.

Still woozy from the failed transportation, Horace hurled rays of fire and ice. The attacks deflected off the demons' thick hides to gouge holes in the black stone walls. Horace was reaching for more power when two demons approached him. Both bent down and thrust their faces toward him. The stench intensified as the hundreds of writhing feelers covering their chins and mouths reached for him.

He swung the disc of light in a swift arc. Deafening bellows resounded from the walls as the demons lurched backward, bleeding from the loss of masses of severed tendrils. Inspired, Horace dropped to one knee and rested his free hand on the floor. He drew upon the Kishargal dominion and felt the strength of the solid granite floor flow into him. Sending a burst of power through the floor, he flung the demons away. More titanic crashes filled the chamber.

The rest of the creatures closed in on him before he could stand up. Horace barely had time to erect a shield of hardened air around himself before he was knocked around by a barrage of claw attacks. The demons surrounded him, battering his shield. Tremendous pain pierced Horace's skull as the pressure built, straining his grasp on the *zoana*. He looked for an escape, but the pain made thought difficult. His shield was on the verge of collapse, and when that happened, he would be crushed. Then he remembered his days back in Erugash—specifically, the night he was attacked in his home by a creature from the Outside. It had been vulnerable to only one thing.

Shinar.

Drawing as much power as he could, Horace invested his shield with a stream of pure void energy. Incandescent sparks sizzled outside the barrier as the demons staggered back. Their roars shook the chamber. With eyes glowing a deeper hue of red, they attacked the shield with renewed fury. More sparks flew, and a cloud of violet smoke filled the chamber. The shield held, but maintaining it was draining Horace of strength. He needed to take the fight to the enemy. Focusing his will, he diverted the void energy from the shield and split it into six channels. The demons pounced on him as the Shinar vanished from his protective barrier. Fighting the tide of agony, Horace released the channels. They shot out from him, each one penetrating straight into the chest of a demon.

The pressure vanished.

Horace lowered his hands. Oily puddles filled with corrupted body parts stained the floor where the demons had stood. Through the haze of putrid smoke, he watched the organs and bones collapse and the pools dry up, leaving hardly any trace that the fiends had ever existed.

Horace breathed a shallow sigh in relief. Then, a quake ran through the floor. A rasping growl echoed from behind the altar block. Horace stepped back as a new shape came through the wall.

SUN AND SERPENT

It had the same coal-black flesh and overall appearance as the demons, but the new arrival was much larger, and a wreath of flames hovered above its head like a crown of fire. Awful majesty dwelt in its burning eyes, such that Horace felt an impulse to drop to his knees before the creature. He steeled himself and held his ground. The demon lord opened its maw, and an immense roar shook the chamber.

Horace struck at once, hurling the disc of light. The demon lord swatted it away with the back of its hand as it stepped over the altar. With its every stride, the floor shook. Horace retreated to keep his distance. He launched a volley of attacks from all the dominions—javelins of ice and stone, fiery blasts, chains of air. The demon lord shook them off as they were no more than gnats buzzing around its head. For all its bulk, the beast was swift. Horace barely had time to erect shield around himself before tusk-long claws swung in his direction. The talons sliced through the warding barrier with hardly a pause.

Their tips cut across Horace's body from shoulder to hip, drawing lines of fiery pain as he was flung backward. He hit the wall with a muffled thud. Legs shaking, he stood up straight. Blood ran down his chest and stomach.

Horace combined flows of air and fire to produce a jet of smoke, which he projected up into the demon lord's face. Then he darted to his left to get around behind the monster. The demon lord turned to track him, not fooled by his trick, and swung another massive paw at his head. Horace called upon the Kishargal dominion to cover his arms in shells of granite. He raised those arms, suddenly empowered with gigantic strength, to block to attack, and shuddered as the blow shattered his stony armor and sent him reeling back.

Horace continued his barrage of elemental attacks, aiming them at the demon lord's face. He knew they wouldn't harm the creature. They were only meant to distract it while he created a separate channel of *zoana*, one of pure Shinar. A direct attack hadn't worked, but he had an idea. These demons, these things from another world, seemed to be made of void energy fused into physical form. So, what would happen if he unbound the Shinar within them? As the demon lord closed in on him, Horace put up the strongest shield he could manage. Hoping it would be enough to keep him alive, he stood in the monster's path. *Just a little closer.*

266

When the demon lord's massive fists crashed down on him, Horace opened a conduit between them. For a moment—a moment that seemed to last for hours—he and the beast were joined. He felt the intense rage churning inside it, and beneath that something worse, an insatiable hunger that never subsided, a bottomless pit within the beast that had fed on other life-forms for millennia, even devouring entire worlds. It destroyed everything it encountered. How could such a creature come to be?

Using his Sight to penetrate inside the demon lord, Horace saw its inner workings, a chaotic jumble of conflicting forces. At first, he couldn't make sense of it. The thing had nothing that resembled vital organs, only layer over layer of muscle and tendons. What kept it alive? Then he Saw the source of its power, deep within the beast's torso. A sphere of absolute darkness, which throbbed at irregular intervals like a malformed heart.

As he reached out with his magical senses, Horace felt a shudder run through his physical body. The shield was on the verge of collapse. The strain of holding it together was tearing him apart. With no more time to explore, Horace summoned the disc again and thrust it deep into the demon lord's mass. Crimson light flashed as the cutting edge bit into the sphere, almost blinding him. The heart beat faster. It had a stony exterior, but Horace kept his power focused on it, slicing away the thick shell bit by bit.

Agony drilled through his right shoulder as the demon tore at him. Jarred from his Sight, Horace fell back on the floor. All was dark around him, but he could feel the presence of the demon lord above him. His entire left side was drenched in blood, and he could no longer feel that arm. He reached up with his other hand, afraid of what he would find. A wave of nausea came over him as his questing fingers found a bloody socket. The ends of bloody tendons hung loose, but the rest of his arm was gone. He tried to push the tattered ribbons of flesh back into the empty socket. *This can't be real. It can't be.*

A roar filled the chamber, followed by a loud crunch that sounded ominously like fangs snapping bone. A huge foot crashed down beside him. The stench of the beast wrapped around Horace as he tried to stop the river of blood flowing from his shoulder. He would be dead in a few heartbeats.

Summoning the last of his strength, Horace plunged his consciousness back inside the demon lord. He fashioned his *zoana* not into a disc this time but into a radiant spear, and rammed it into the black heart. The power bit deep. Incandescent light exploded around him as thunder roared in his ears. He was flung away, unable to stop his flight, and struck something hard.

Horace lay still and strained to breathe. He could feel his blood pumping out from the stump of his severed arm. His entire left side was cold. *I'm going to die here. Astaptah has won.*

Anger rekindled inside him. No, he wouldn't just lie here and let it happen. *Fuck him.*

His *qa* trembled with the forces straining behind it. Horace opened it gently, and a wave of blackness crossed his vision. Fumbling with the strands, he wove the *zoana* into a net of the four basic elements: earth for flesh, water for blood, air for life, and fire to fuse them all together. Bracing himself, he released the power into his wound. Pain flooded his brain, so bad he wanted to slam his skull against the floor. It subsided after a few seconds, leaving behind an intense throb, but the bleeding had stopped. *That's the first step. Now for the hard part.*

Slowly, he drew himself up into a sitting position. There was nothing left of the demon lord except a steaming pool of dark ichor and a foul stench.

Gritting his teeth, Horace pushed himself to his feet. For a few seconds, he held onto the wall with his remaining hand for support, then stepped away. His sense of balance was off, but he managed to walk around the altar to the doorway behind it.

A cold wind blew from the aperture, making him shiver. Taking one step at a time, he passed through.

CHAPTER TWELVE

The temple of Nabu rose in tiers of dark gray stone. Sheets of rain ran down its smooth outer face, forming tiny waterfalls at the ledges of each tier. The temple's corners were rounded and the stonework carved with deep grooves, lending a strange texture to the edifice unlike anything else in Akeshian architecture. Narrow, rectangular windows yawned in the upper floors.

The Blades spread out at the entrance, crossbows in hand, eyes sweeping across the nearby rooftops. The scouts dipped inside the temple yard, skulking like a pair of shadows.

As she and Elia followed Commander Jirom to the front gates, Dasha considered what she would do when they confronted the Dark King. She held her borrowed dagger, and it seemed like paltry protection against the horrors that roamed her city. And now she was plunging into the heart of the corruption. *Gods save us. We need a miracle.*

Jirom paused at the gate, which hung open, before going inside. Dasha looked around. Why was everything so quiet? She felt exposed out here. The Blades crouched, ready for anything, but Dasha could see they were exhausted, their superhuman reserves of strength finally being tapped. Not a single one of them sat down to rest or even so much as lowered their weapon. They could have been cast from metal, in truth, for all the weakness they showed.

Pumash, their new addition, stood off by himself beside a lamppost, with his arms wrapped around his body. What was his role in this? Apparently, he and his manservant were the only living souls left in the city, but why had they been spared? Every so often, he would glance in her direction with a look that made Dasha anxious. *He is not to be trusted. He knows what is going on here, and I would bet my sandals he is part of it.*

Lightning flashed. A heartbeat later, Jirom shouted from beyond the gate, his call followed by a sharp ring of steel against stone and the unmistakable sounds of battle. Several of the Blades rushed inside. Seconds later, the dull twangs of firing crossbows sounded.

Elia moved to the entryway. "Stay behind me," she said as she headed inside.

A large courtyard extended around the temple proper in a flat lawn, which had turned into a muddy swamp, decorated with a scattering of leaf-less trees. A stone path led to the doors of the temple. Jirom and the team of Silver Blades stood midway down the track, surrounded by a pack of undead. Elia rushed to aid them.

Their swords flashed in the flickering lightning like tongues of living fire, cutting deep into cold flesh with every swing. Jirom stabbed a fiend through the neck, and Elia hacked her weapon deep into its forehead. As the undead dropped, they wrenched their weapons free and turned to find new targets, and there were more than enough to choose from, with more undead appearing from around both corners of the temple yard. Within moments, the warriors were swamped within a widening mass of implacable foes. Captain Paranas shouted for more support, and the rest of the Blades ran into the courtyard. Still, they seemed far too few to hold back the rising tide of undead.

So far, the creatures had left Dasha alone, standing in the lee of the temple gate, rigid with fear. *I must help them! But how? I'm no soldier. I can't do anything.*

The dagger in her hand seemed ludicrously insignificant.

In the midst of her hopelessness, she heard her father's voice. Its warm, reassuring tones washed over her, driving away the icy rigor that held her prisoner. *You can, Dasha! You have the power within you. Let it out! As you honor me, honor and trust yourself. Be free, my daughter!*

Dasha looked at the dagger in her hands. One of her father's favorite maxims came to mind. *Not all wars are won with spears and arrows.*

Dasha drew a deep breath and closed her eyes. As always, it took her a few moments to find her *qa*. It quivered on the edge of her inner senses, seemingly too remote to access. She clawed her way toward it until the mystic doorway stood before her, shining bright in her mind's eye. Shudders ran through her body in time with the quivering of the portal. *I must do this.*

With a steady grip, she opened the portal. Intense energy poured into her.

For a moment, she floundered in its powerful flow, unable to hold on. Then she grasped a thread. The magic gleamed brightly in her inner Sight. More confident, she gathered the rest of the threads until she had tamed the wild river. Opening her eyes back to the physical world, Dasha witnessed the battle with a new perspective. Elia and the rest of the team were pillars of bright energy amidst the crowd of undead, which appeared to Dasha's Sight as empty husks radiating cold malice. She reached out with the *zoana*, sending weaves of Imuvar and Girru through the unliving crowd. The power seared the flesh from their rotten bones, burning away tendons and ligaments, and finally exploded their bones in showers of smoking meal. When she was finished, she allowed the power to leave her, and blinked as the sorcerous patina dropped from her eyes. Elia and the commander stood, wreathed in smoke, over piles of ruined bodies. Both had suffered wounds, but they appeared minor. The warriors turned to her, and Dasha saw new regard in their eyes. She was the first to look away, flustered by their attention.

"If I had known you could do that . . ." Jirom said.

Dasha shook her head. "I didn't know I could."

"I did." Elia tore off another long strip from her tunic and started binding Dasha's right forearm, which also now dripped blood from a fresh *immaculata*. "You just had to find your strength, Princess."

Everyone gathered at the temple's inner doorway. Off to the left lay the twisted remains of a huge statue. Dasha felt a chill as she saw it, not just for the sheer impiety its destruction represented, but because it felt like everything she had taken for granted—the things she thought were permanent in this world—had been stripped away. Her family, her people, and even her gods.

The temple door was closed, but not secured. Jirom pulled it open easily. Beyond was a broad corridor with a high ceiling. Dasha couldn't see much from the outside.

Jirom was about to lead them through the doorway when two quick whistles sounded from the courtyard outer gate. Jauna stood in the lee of the arched entryway and flashed her open hands several times, before she disappeared out into the city street.

SUN AND SERPENT

Captain Paranas swore under his breath. "There's another group of hostiles coming. At least a hundred head."

Jirom repeated the curse. Dasha couldn't help from shuddering, considering where they stood. This was supposedly holy ground, or it had been. Now, she felt this parcel—like the entire city—had been tainted. She hoped the stain wasn't irrevocable.

As Jirom stepped toward the compound entrance, Paranas stopped him with a raised hand. "We'll handle it," the mercenary captain said.

"No, we will fight them together."

"With all due respect, there's no time. Horace is inside, right? He'll need help. You go, sir. We'll hold the line."

Jirom made as if to argue, but Ino interrupted him from behind Paranas's shoulder. "We'll hold the line," the large Isurani said.

Pie-Eye said, "We'll hold the line."

One by one, the rest of the Silver Blades repeated those words. A powerful feeling of affection surged inside Dasha, but also sadness. She knew what these men were saying. They were ready to lay down their lives to ensure the mission succeeded.

By his expression, Jirom knew it, too. He nodded as he clapped a hand on the captain's shoulder. "All right. We'll see you on the other side."

Paranas returned the nod. "On the other side."

Dasha looked at the gathered warriors, these men and women who had fought so hard, spilling their own metallic blood, to save Akeshia. She wanted to hug them fiercely and thank each of them, but she respected the solemnity of this moment. *I respect your sacrifice. May you find shelter and solace in the houses of the Gods for all time.*

Looking back to Jirom, this powerful man covered in the blood of the dead, surrounded by comrades who were willing to lay down their lives for him, something tugged at Dasha's heart. Far from the primitive savage she had first taken him for, she now saw him as these others did—a leader who cared for those who followed, a man willing to fight, and even die if necessary, to do what must be done.

Without another word, Jirom turned and passed through the temple entrance. With a heavy heart, Dasha followed him, with Elia at her side. Pumash trailed behind them as silent as a wraith.

Past the threshold, the dark walls of a long antechamber closed around them like the inside of a tomb. Dasha fought back a shiver. The stone surfaces of the floor, walls, and ceiling were warped and twisted, scorched in many places. She reached out to the near wall and quickly pulled her hand away. The stone had an oily texture that made her feel ill just touching it. A heavy odor hung in the air, like the stink of the burned undead outside but also something else, some scent she couldn't identify but that made her uneasy. This place had been horribly corrupted. *It's been resanctified to a new purpose. An evil purpose. And we enter like flies into a spider's lair.*

Beyond the entry hall was a short corridor that ran straight for a score of paces before it branched into a four-way intersection. Jirom paused at the crossway, glancing quickly to his left and right, and then continued forward, deeper into the building. Dasha did likewise. Both side hallways were of a similar appearance, with more doorways leading to different chambers. Narrow windows pierced the walls at the end of either hallway, giving glimpses of the storm-cast sky. Gazing at the window to her right, Dasha walked into Elia's back. Her whispered apology echoed from the misshaped walls around them. Then she saw why her bodyguard and Jirom had stopped.

A few yards away, a long spike thrust out from the wall at the height of Jirom's shoulder. A body hung from the spike. Its flesh had been seared away by a tremendous heat, along with most of a previously pristine white robe. "A priest," she said softly.

Elia shrugged. "Perhaps. We're likely to see more in similar condition."

Jirom cocked his head as if listening for something. Dasha held her breath and listened, too, but there was nothing except for the beating of her pulse in her ears and the soft beat of the rain outside, punctuated by occasional rumbles of thunder. Every sound inside the temple was muted, as if the walls soaked them up, leaving only a faded remnant. Her anxiety was so fierce she felt it grinding in her joints, pulling taut every nerve and sinew. She couldn't remember what security felt like, without the constant fear that something horrible was about to happen.

Jirom padded forward, his shoulders hunched and sword held ready. His coiled posture made Dasha even more anxious. *If he's afraid, then I should be terrified. No. He's not afraid. He is prepared, completely, for whatever comes.*

Envious of his courage, Dasha attempted to emulate it as she followed him and Elia down another short corridor. The darkness of the temple's interior had swallowed them, as the dim light provided by the infrequent windows faded. A silver doorway yawned ahead. Dasha couldn't control a shiver as she passed through. The air within was electric with currents of *zoana*, mingled with that same unfamiliar odor. She couldn't see anything in the gloom. On a whim, she tried to conjure a globe of light, and jumped when it appeared beside her. The power had come with surprising ease.

All the surfaces in this huge chamber were solid black sheets of jet. At first, just standing in the room made Dasha feel strange, as if she were floating through the night sky. Something had happened here recently. She didn't know precisely what, but it had been violent. Things had died here.

Her companions looked around cautiously, as if they could not see as clearly as Dasha. To be helpful, she said, "There is a doorway behind the altar, and stairs beyond."

"What altar?" Elia asked.

Jirom had crossed the chamber. He reached out with his sword until the tip clinked against the long block of black stone. Dasha was about to join him when an icy cold enveloped her like an arctic wind. The floor at her feet was stained with a broad smudge so dark she had missed it. Powerful energy radiated from the stain. Powerful and dark. Its corruption clawed at her skin. With a trembling step, she backed away and went around it, only to find more stains. Seven in all, with the last by far the largest, right under Jirom's feet at the foot of the altar. The commander took no notice, and Dasha wondered how he couldn't feel the evil seeping into his boots.

"We should leave," she said. "Quickly."

Jirom's head swiveled to the doorway behind the altar. "More undead?"

"No. I just want to be out of this room."

"You'll get no argument from me," Elia said. "The place makes my scalp crawl."

They were approaching the doorway when the chamber shook. Not a simple tremor like they had experienced before. It was a full-blown quake that shook the walls and made the ceiling groan as the vast weight of stone shifted above their heads. Dasha's heart pounded as she felt a tremendous burst of energy. It came from far beneath the temple. She quailed at the thought of what could be causing it. All the *zoanii* in her father's court, working in concert, couldn't have produced even close to that much raw power. It was terrifying in its immensity. *And Horace is down there. I know it.*

"Hurry!" she shouted.

Jirom leapt through the doorway. Elia waited for her. Dasha swallowed hard as she stepped over the dark threshold. A low moan echoed through the passage ahead, carrying her forward with its sibilant whisper.

Power played across his soul like the movements of a symphony, rising and falling in a lulling rhythm that belied its deadly intent. Horace became lost in the sensation, trusting his feet to carry him down the long spiral of stairs as he descended into the earth beneath the temple's foundation. The power called to him, and he followed its resonating tones. He lost track of time. Even the pain of his shoulder receded, drowned out by the siren's call below.

The stairs were smoothed in the same half-melted texture as the temple hallways above. Lines of scorched stone ran down the walls to pool in the joins where they met the floor. After a long descent, spiraling like a dead helix, the steps ended at the head of a tunnel with a high, arched ceiling. The way ahead was dark, but he could See walls and floor of rough bedrock just like the catacombs beneath the queen's palace. He was confused. When had he returned to Erugash? The power throbbed here, so thick Horace could feel it dancing in the overheated air.

The tunnel bent in a downward curve. His footsteps echoed against the decrepit stone. About a hundred paces from the stairs, the tunnel stopped at a large archway. Its door, huge and made of black iron, stood open. A thick bar of the same metal, now twisted almost in half, lay on the floor against the opposite wall. Strange lights flickered from within. As Horace steeled himself to approach, a familiar voice sauntered from the opening.

"Come in, my friend, and see what I have wrought."

Horace walked to the doorway. He had been expecting to see a vast cavern like the one that had sat below Byleth's palace, with a molten magma lake and an island with a metal machine, but instead he stood at the entrance of a large, long chamber. Its high walls rose to a series of vaults more than thirty feet above his head. Like the sanctum chamber above, every surface was smooth, black stone. Dozens of figures in gray shrouds stood against the side walls. Horace Saw their true forms—demons, every one of them, with elongated heads, pebbled gray skin, and hooked talons dangling from their fingers. Their huge, yellow eyes watched him.

His Sight also pierced through the gloom cloaking the far end of the chamber, where a dais rose in two tiers of steps. Above the platform, a large frieze was carved into the back wall, reaching most of the way to the ceiling. Horace couldn't make out the design, but he got an impression of entwined coils and sinuous curves. Fear grew inside him as he Saw past the frieze's physical representation to its true self. The carving was a window into another realm, the realm he had seen once before in a vision. The Outside. He could feel its gelid horror from where he stood, knowing what lay beyond that barrier. And the Seal was weakening. Its skin was thin, wavering as it struggled to hold back the power trying to break through from the other side.

Astaptah stood facing the frieze with his back to the door, but Horace recognized him at once. The skin of the former vizier's head and neck was rippled with dark scars.

The Dark King turned as Horace entered. His gaze went to Horace's left shoulder. "It appears you are missing something."

Horace swayed slightly. Exhaustion and pain were leaching away his strength. "There's more than enough of me left to put an end to you."

Astaptah glanced back to admire the frieze. "It's far too late for that, Horace. But, perhaps, not for you. Behold the final Seal. Soon, we shall witness the birth of a new era. The world's *last* era. I'm glad you are here to see this.

It is fitting, don't you think? You and I, standing here together at the end?"

Horace took another step into the room. The air was denser around him, making movement more difficult. He opened himself to his power, allowing it to fill him to the brink of his capacity. "No more offers, Astaptah. No more cajoles or threats. It's time to finish this."

Astaptah's shoulders rose and fell in a shrug. "As you wish."

There was no build-up of power. One moment Horace was standing inside the chamber's doorway, and the next he was flung back into the hall by an invisible punch. With his head spinning, he started to get up, but another blast caught him in the side and slammed him into the wall. Horace fell to his knees. His vision dimmed for a moment as he tried to catch his breath. He barely had time to put up a shield of Shinar before the next attack landed. His shield shuddered under the impact. Then he was picked up completely off the ground and pulled back inside the chamber. Before the next blow landed, Horace launched an attack of his own. Weaving together a tight ball of all five elements, he hurled it toward the dais. Astaptah lifted a hand, and the missile exploded harmlessly before it reached him. Horace sent a second attack and a third, but each time they failed to reach his foe.

All the while, the shrouded demons watched from their perches against the sides of the chamber. Horace could feel their malice directed at him. They wanted to tear him to pieces and feed on his remains, but they stayed in place like well-trained hounds.

Astaptah came over to the edge of the dais and looked down at him. "You are pathetic. You could have had everything. Power and glory, a seat at my side. Yet you cling to your myopic notions of morality. Don't you see? We are beyond such things, Horace. We could be the new gods of this world, masters of all."

Horace stood up slowly, holding his shoulder, which throbbed fiercely. "Slaves, you mean. Ruling over a dead realm, while your true overlords hold the leash."

With a glance of annoyance, Astaptah lifted a hand, palm up. The section of stone under Horace's feet broke loose from the rest of the floor and launched itself toward the ceiling. A similar section of the ceiling dropped down from above his head. Horace instinctively raised his remaining arm as he reinforced his shield. A grating rumble echoed through the chamber as the two blocks of stone slammed into him from above and below, squeezing him in between. Pain exploded in Horace's head from the intense pressure. He gasped as he fumbled to find the structural vertices of the stone surfaces. His Sight was darkening along with his normal vision. Finally, he located the nodes of *zoana* within each block and unbound them. He fell as the stone crumbled but caught himself in a web of Imuvar. A cloud of black dust billowed around him. He sensed the next attack too late before it slammed into his shield, catapulting him backward. He lost his grip on the flows of air and fell once more. Twisting, he managed to avoid landing on his severed stump and instead hit the floor on his back, rolling and sliding across the smooth stone until he came to stop near the entrance.

Looking up, Horace could see only a hazy figure on the far dais. Head swimming, he got up, slowly and painfully. He spoke through bruised lips. "Is that the best the new god of Akeshia can do?"

Horace started walking toward the dais, feeling his muscles cry out with every step. "Surely the emissary of the Ancient Ones can defeat one insignificant man. Or have they abandoned you, Astaptah, to stand on your own? Do they see what I see, the fearful heart underneath those black robes and scarred flesh?"

With each stride he gathered his power. It came to him in drips and dribbles, seeping past his *qa* like water through the leaky hull of an old ship. He thought of the *Bantu Ray*, the last ship he had been on, and the storm that had raged overhead on the night it sank. Much like the storm roiling above at this very moment. He couldn't see the ghoulish green lightning lancing down to the city's streets, but he felt each forked bolt in his bones. They were now as much a part of him as his own skin and blood. He reached up through the earth and stone, up to the storm. Its chaotic power cascaded around him, battering him like a ragdoll caught in the current of a powerful river. He surrendered to the power and rode the storm.

Astaptah's answer came as a barrage of black bolts. The first one pierced through Horace's shield as if it wasn't there, and he narrowly ducked in time to avoid catching it with his face. He deflected the rest with small bursts of Shinar, flinching only slightly as they ricocheted and disintegrated holes in the walls. Fueled by the storm's power and his own fury, Horace shot back with a wave of energy. It surrounded Astaptah in a coruscating gray-white nimbus. Bright sparks flew from the contact, amid a stench of burning flesh. A tremor ran through the floor. A heartbeat later, the chamber was filled with bright light as the power rebounded toward Horace. There was no time to defend himself. Hunched over with his arm wrapped across his face, he groaned as the power tore into him, ripping into his skin and sinking its claws into the muscle and bone underneath. It was too much to resist. He felt himself backing away as droplets of his blood pattered on the floor. Then, he stopped himself. No more retreating.

Horace sent his *zoana* coursing throughout his body, reknitting the degenerating tissues as fast as he could. At the same time, he tried to move forward, into the brunt of the attack. He wanted to get closer to Astaptah, to grapple face to face with this adversary who had plagued him for so long, but he couldn't make any headway against the fierce tide of magic. He was stuck in place, neither retreating nor gaining ground, but how long could he hold out? Astaptah showed no signs of weakening. The force of the destructive energies pouring out from his foe had redoubled in intensity, chewing at Horace faster than he could restore himself. The corruption entered his veins, scouring him from the inside. He felt his muscles begin to sag under the onslaught.

Astaptah's voice rose above the tumult. "I am the new herald, reborn in the fire of the void. I am the First and the Last, and my word shall be the law of the new order."

With jaws clamped together and muscles locked, Horace gave up trying to protect himself and focused all his power on a retaliatory strike. He created a lance of Shinar as narrow as possible, folding layer upon layer of his *zoana* into the weapon until it shone like a diamond in the sun. Then, he hurled it at his foe. An explosion rocked the chamber. The concussion threw Horace back onto the floor, where he rolled over several times before coming to a stop.

He struggled on the edge of consciousness. His thoughts were unclear, and a high-pitched tone rang in his ears. He rolled over to see Astaptah standing before the frieze, arms spread as if to accept an embrace. The gateway pulsed, its every throb warping the stone walls around it, sucking them in and out like a vast maw breathing.

Horace started to climb back to his feet. He had to stop this now, or never. But before he could fully stand up, the demonic minions were upon him. They seized him by the legs and arm and tore at his skin with long claws. Horace shoved them away with blasts of hardened air, but the demons were relentless. He burned holes in their bodies and froze their head in blocks of ice, drove stony spars through their bodies and lashed them with gale-force winds. Some feil, writhing in their death throes, but their numbers were too great.

Beyond the vicious melee, Astaptah's voice rang out. "Come, Masters of Void and Time! We welcome you into the new world!"

Through the maelstrom of violence, Horace felt the veil between worlds dissolving, but there was nothing he could do to stop it. Hands closed around his throat. As they bore down, Horace thrashed and tried to invoke his power, but everything was falling away. A gray haze settled over his vision, and his thoughts slowed like they were encased in mud.

The temple shook as if caught in the throes of an earthquake. Catching himself time and time again before he fell, Jirom raced down the broad stairs two at a time. He was covered in sweat, but not from the exertion. Esoteric energies played across his skin, making him want to drop his sword and shield and scratch until he dug runnels in his flesh. Shaking away the image, he continued his descent.

With every step, he felt himself delving into another world. It wasn't just the warped stone around him. There was a current running through the air, alien and horrifying like a gust of wind from another world. His senses, physical and otherwise, begged him to turn around and flee, but he continued onward, forcing himself to follow Horace's trail.

The stairs ended in a long, winding tunnel. Jirom jogged down its lengths, not waiting for the others. The princess's mystic light tagged along a few paces behind him, casting its stark illumination ahead. A large doorway yawned at the end of the tunnel. Its ancient, black-metal door hung open. The sounds of sorcery echoed within, a terrible orchestration of sizzling elements and grinding stonework, punctuated by blasts that shook the bones of the earth. Jirom hesitated, as his sense of self-preservation made one last attempt to stop him from plunging into the maelstrom that awaited. Then, steeling himself, he flung away his fear and stepped up to the opening. Part of him quailed at what he saw beyond.

A large hall had been carved from the raw bedrock under the temple. The wall at the far end was some kind of tableau but the stonework writhed and twisted like a living thing in agony. A gaunt figure stood on the raised platform in front of the display. Cloaked in night-black robes, his skin was terribly marred, as if it had melted and then reformed in dusky waves. Bright amber eyes pierced the chamber's gloom from that deformed visage.

Jirom tore his gaze from that dread specter to the battle on the chamber floor. A score of hunched-back men in gray robes grasped and tore and pummeled at something within their midst. Jirom remembered these creatures as the same ilk he had discovered in the twisting warrens under the palace at Erugash when he and Alyra had rescued Horace. Revulsion climbed up his throat as he saw them attacking a lone individual. He could not see Horace, but he knew his friend was at the bottom of that pile, and anger shoved his disgust aside. He ran into the scrum, tulwar slashing from side to side. Its keen edge sliced through gray fabric and gray, wrinkled flesh with equal ease. Blood, so dark it was almost black, spurted sluggishly from the wounds he made and coated the blade of his weapon. Some of the gray-cloaked men, those nearest to him, looked up from their prey and pierced him with their feral eyes. Snarling without a sound, three of them leapt at him. Jirom cut them down with heavy strokes, reveling as his sword opened their throats and stomachs.

When more turned on him, the princess's bodyguard was at his side. Together, they dispatched the silent minions and sent the rest stumbling back with the ferocity of their attacks. A ghoulish minion stabbed at him with a long-bladed dagger. Jirom caught the thrust on his shield and buried his tulwar in the woman's forehead. As she toppled over, Jirom saw a familiar form lying on the floor beneath the weight of several gray men. Trusting Elia to guard his back he waded deeper into the press until he was standing over Horace. His friend was battered and bleeding. Shock registered through Jirom's battle fury when he saw the empty stump where Horace's left arm had been torn away at the shoulder. Despite the tremendous damage he had suffered, Horace still lived. He fought like a man possessed, and Jirom felt a grim smile of pride twist on his lips.

Then he resumed the battle, cutting down foes as the old battle hymn thrummed in his blood.

A voice whispered to him. *Come back to us, Horace. We've been waiting for you!*

Tears leaked from his eyes as figures emerged from the fog. His wife Sari, holding their son. Josef reached out toward him with his little hands, fingers grasping. With them walked Alyra, smiling with a pure joy he'd never seen when she had been alive. And more people he knew behind them—Mulcibar and Ubar and even Byleth, looking as radiant as she had in life. The images started to fade as a dark veil descended over the scene.

The clawed hands holding Horace loosened, and then let go. Harsh sounds of battle echoed in his ears. His vision returned slowly, to see Jirom standing over him, defending him with sword and shield. Dasha and Elia were at his sides, the three of them forming a triangle amidst the demonic horde. The bodyguard flailed about with her sword and a long knife, while the princess froze the enemy with clouds of ice crystals and shattered them with concussive blows of Kishargal. Dead minions lay piled upon the floor at their feet.

Horace fought to get up, wanting to help. Pain tore at him with every movement, but he pushed it aside. He reached for his *qa*. It wavered for a moment, refusing to allow him access, but he wrenched it open and ignored the psychic damage he was inflicting on himself. All that mattered was stopping Astaptah. Horace sent out multiple bolts of fire and lightning, raking the fell energies across the crowd of minions behind his guardians, until an aisle of dead bodies formed down the center of the chamber. At the far end, Horace could make out Astaptah atop the dais. The frieze bubbled outward as if something was pushing through from the other side. Something huge. In his mind's eye, Horace Saw the eldritch creature trying to enter their world. Once it did, this battle was over. They would all die, if they were fortunate.

"Go on!" Jirom shouted as he cleaved in the skull of a demon who had strayed too close. "We'll guard your back."

Horace exchanged glances with his friend. In that brief moment, he tried to pour all his admiration and respect into his gaze. What he saw reflected back was enough to give him strength. "All right. Be ready to retreat and fast. I don't know what's going to happen."

Dasha turned to look at him with a distraught glare. "What other choice do we have?"

Horace shrugged with his one good shoulder as he strode out from behind their protective screen. He gathered his magic again. His *qa* ached like a strained muscle, but he pinned it open regardless and pulled through as much power as he was able. It didn't feel like enough for what he had in mind, but there wasn't anything he could do about that. Jirom and the others had bought him time. Now he needed to finish this, and he finally knew how. It made sense. If what Eridu had told him was true, if Astaptah was his polar opposite in the Shinar, then he could never win. They would forever cancel each other out. However, there was another way.

Astaptah stared down from the platform, his eyes blazing in the gloom. "I have expended enough power on you to level a mountain range. Yet, you endure. What secret do you possess, Horace? I wonder if I shall find it written upon the folds of your brain once I have pried your skull open."

Horace launched a dozen separate attacks in fire and ice and wind, but they were only distractions. As Astaptah deflected them each with ease, Horace got closer, until he was climbing the dais steps.

"Yes," Astaptah said in a low voice, almost crooning. "Come to me.

SUN AND SERPENT

Embrace your demise. No need for threats, as you said. Just one last embrace between old friends."

The Dark King glowed with a dark aura, like a gleaming god freshly risen from the underworld. The shine hurt Horace's eyes, but he forced himself to keep his gaze upon his foe. His vision quivered as a lance of vertigo shot through him. Horace blinked, and suddenly Astaptah's gaunt form was replaced by a gigantic serpent with glittering black scales. Its amber eyes blazed as it reared back, long fangs glistening with venom. He also felt a change within himself and risked a glance downward. In place of his jacket he wore an armored breastplate of bright gold. A skirt of the same material fell past his knees, and his shins and feet were clad in golden greaves. In his hand was a sword that shone like the sun. Even more shocking, he no longer stood on the floor of the subterranean temple but floated in the sky. Storm clouds raged around them, ominous witnesses to their battle. Far below, he saw the rooftops and ramparts of Ceasa. What was happening?

In that moment, he saw how this battle had happened before, many times, stretching back to the dawn of the world's creation. Light against darkness, serpent and sun.

Lightning crackled as the serpent lunged. Out of pure instinct, Horace lifted his sword to block, and the huge beast recoiled with a rumble of thunder. The golden sword blazed brighter as he pressed a counterattack, swinging its blade at his foe in a long arc. The serpent-Astaptah glided sinuously under the blow and sprang at him again, and the sword swept down to deflect the attack once again. The force of their colliding power knocked him back a step.

Horace heard faint cries behind him and understood that his material form was still standing in the long chamber under the temple, hemmed in by its shadowed walls and vaulted ceiling, but he couldn't spare a glance to make sure his friends were all right. He lifted his sword as the serpent reared back, preparing for another strike. At the monster's center, beneath the scales and corded muscles, pulsed a tight mass of infinite darkness. It was like what he had seen at the heart of the demon lord, but infinitely deeper and more powerful. Astaptah was filled with the negative half of the void, almost to the point of bursting. Horace knew that sensation. The heady rush, the feeling of invulnerability. But what if the power continued to grow within you? What if you couldn't stop it? It would consume you until nothing remained.

It was one hell of a gamble, but Horace had nothing left to lose. He dropped his defenses and directed all his *zoana* at Astaptah—not as an attack but as a mystical funnel.

Astaptah's eyes widened as Horace poured his power into him. Down in the temple's lower hall, the former vizier lifted his hands to marvel as the magic played across his skin in incandescent skeins. His laughter shook the chamber like thunder.

"You have my gratitude." Astaptah twitched, and a powerful gale roared through the chamber. "Now I am unstoppable!"

Horace advanced, both in his astral form floating in the sky and his physical form beneath the earth, focused on getting closer while he continued to transfer his power into the former vizier. Astaptah gestured, and Horace was pushed down to the ground, until his face was shoved against the steps. He tried to get back up, until a sharp pain pierced his chest. Horace looked down to see he was fully back in his own body again, the golden armor and sword vanished. A spar of black stone had shot up from the floor to impale him. Blood poured from the wound to pool underneath him.

Astaptah laughed again. "Bow before me, insect. Bow before your master and beg for my mercy."

As his vision grew darker by the moment, Horace clung to his link to Astaptah.

CHAPTER THIRTEEN

Dasha sent a gray-clad henchman reeling back with stone shards embedded in his face and chest. She paused from her magic-weaving to take a deep breath. Though she had not been touched by a foe—Elia and Jirom kept the mob at bay—blood ran down her arms from scores of cuts. She could feel more immaculata along her ribcage and across her stomach, oozing blood to stain her tunic. Despite the pain, she had never felt so alive. The zoana flowed through her like a lover's touch, awakening feelings she had never suspected she possessed. The power was seductive, and she knew therein lay the danger.

She lifted her gaze past her protectors and their shrouded foes to the dais at the far side of the chamber. There, on the steps of the platform, stood Horace and the gaunt Dark King, arms locked onto each other in an immobile struggle. They didn't move at all, but Dasha felt the immense power of the eldritch energies clashing around them, erupting in flashes of light and spots of inky darkness. Sensing how much *zoana* was flowing between the two combatants, she wondered how they could keep going. The ground rumbled ominously, and wide cracks had spread up the chamber walls, reaching to the vaulted ceiling.

Jirom cut down the last of the hooded minions. As it fell, snarling, at his feet, the rebel commander leapt over it and advanced on the dais. Elia looked back to Dasha. Her face was covered in sweat and spattered beads of blood. Dasha pointed to Jirom, Elia nodded, and they both followed the man.

As she stepped past the fallen bodies on the floor, Dasha felt a growing pressure. The maelstrom of magical forces concentrated at the other side of the hall buffeted her senses, making every step more difficult than the last. Before she was halfway across the chamber, the pressure became so intense she had to stop. She shielded her eyes and tried to view the conflict through the lattice of her fingers. Elia had stopped, too, leaning forward with her head down as if she were trying to walk through a hurricane. Only Jirom kept going. With his black shield raised before him, he fought through the mystic storm, step by step. Finally, even he was halted, a few steps from the base of the dais steps, as the titanic powers surrounding the two sorcerers grew to a fevered gale.

Suddenly, Horace was thrown back onto the floor by an explosion that shook the chamber's foundation. He fell onto his stomach and was transfixed by a spear of stone thrust up from the ground. The Dark King stood over him, triumphant. For a moment, Dasha Saw them as something else. Horace's torn and bloodied clothing was replaced by brilliant golden armor. Where his foe stood reared a massive black snake, coiled and ready for a lethal strike. She blinked, and the images were gone, but the memory of that brief glimpse into the astral plane was seared into her brain. Cold dread flooded her body. *It cannot end this way!*

She was assaulted by the acute understanding that this battle was about more than the empire. The Dark King represented forces inimical to all of humanity, to life itself. She gazed at Horace, lying on the floor, dying. He was their last, only chance.

Jirom took three excruciating steps, fighting through the magic until he reached the stairs. The rim of his shield glowed red-hot, and the stench of burning flesh permeated the chamber. With a primal growl, he surged forward to attack the Dark King. The gaunt sorcerer lurched backward to avoid the sweeping blow, and in that instant, Dasha could see Horace take a deep breath. He was still alive. Her elation was short-lived as the Dark King flung Jirom back with a blast of green fire. The blaze would have incinerated the warrior if not for the black shield, which somewhat stifled the flames. Even so, Jirom was hurled off the dais steps and slammed against the wall to the right.

With tears welling in her eyes, partially obscuring her vision, Dasha opened herself to as much *zoana* as she could hold and unleashed it all. She sent spears of barbed ice and jagged stone hurtling toward the enemy and had the brief satisfaction of watching them tear into his flesh. He did not fall, did not even stagger. With a look of sheer contempt in those amber eyes, the Dark

King waved his hand. The rest of her enchanted missiles exploded in midair. Then he clenched his fingers into a fist. Dasha gasped as an insurmountable force surrounded her, crushing her within its iron-hard grasp. Then she was flying through the air. She had one final glimpse of the battle, as Elia bowed beneath an invisible power with her forehead nearly touching the floor, and Horace writhed on the blood-soaked steps. The last thing she saw was the Dark King, standing above them all. Then the back of her head struck something, and darkness claimed her.

Pumash pressed himself tighter against the wall. The stone, chalky with the dust of centuries, vibrated harshly beneath his touch from the violent powers being tossed about the chamber. Cracks had appeared in the walls, thin at first but widening with every passing minute, some of them running all the way from floor to ceiling. *Yes, keep killing each other. And bring a million tons of stone down upon all our heads. Let us die here together.*

With every passing moment, he saw that his wish was becoming less and less likely. The *Manalish* was handling the foreign magician and his allies with ease. This Horace from the West was lying prone on the dais steps, pierced through his stomach by a spear of solid rock. The other members of the rescue party had been flung back like so much flotsam. He almost felt bad for them. They had come with such proud hopes. He almost wished they could have succeeded. It would have been a pleasant thought as he died, knowing the empire would return to its former splendor, but they were doomed to fail. *I should have known. This pitiful few wouldn't be enough to defeat the Master's supreme power.*

He inched along the stone wall, and even as he moved forward, Pumash wondered why he was bothering. This fight was over. Within moments, the last Seal would open, and the Master's victory would be complete. Still, he advanced, one small step at a time, and tried to make himself beneath notice. *I am an insect, not worthy of your divine attention, Great Master.*

SUN AND SERPENT

As he moved, the handle of the knife under his robe dug into his stomach. He had no plan, no cunning stratagem, not even a hope of one. He only knew he couldn't retreat any farther. He had to go forward. Perhaps if he were fortunate, he would die quickly. He was looking forward to an end to the pain, and the guilt. *Cleanse me with your unholy touch, Master. Release me from this world.*

Stealing quietly up the dais steps. Pumash looked over at the foreigner. Somehow, despite having lost an arm and being spitted like a duckling for the roasting pit, he still lived. Pumash could not help but be impressed by this young magician's fortitude. It was obvious he would fight to his last breath. *Such courage. Too bad it is a wasted effort. I tried to tell them. Their quest was futile from the start. Still I will join you in your pointless endeavor. I, too, will take one last chance to strike at the one I hate, and I will die for the effort. At last.*

"I am glad you are here, my servant."

Pumash froze on the final step, terror pulling at him like a riptide. The *Manalish* hadn't turned, hadn't even moved his gaze from the enemy at his feet. Pumash stepped forward, out of the shadows. "I am here, Master."

"I want you to bear witness to this. Do you know what you are seeing?"

"Your victory, Master."

A smile spread across the *Manalish*'s scarred lips. "That is correct. Come closer."

Pumash tried to appear calm as he came over to stand beside the *Manalish*. Looking down, he fought back a gasp. Seeing Horace up close, the stone point protruding grotesquely from his lower back, smelling the fresh blood pouring from the man's body, was almost too much to bear. He steeled himself. He had, after all, seen far worse over these past few weeks.

The *Manalish* held out his hand. "Give me your knife."

"Master?"

"The knife belted inside your robe. Give it to me."

Of course, he knows. He sees every corner of your soul, fool.

Willing his hands to remain steady, Pumash reached inside his robe and drew the knife. He laid it in the *Manalish*'s palm gently, as if with great reverence.

The *Manalish* examined the knife for a moment, turning it over in his hands. "Such a primitive thing. Just a piece of ore pulled from the ground and shaped in fire. You have learned, haven't you, Pumash?"

"Master?"

"The true meaning of power."

Pumash lowered his head. "Yes, Master. True power is control over life and death."

"Precisely. When death is no longer an obstacle, then all things are possible. Are we ready to see the birth of a new world?"

His gaze focused on the floor at his feet, Pumash did not trust his voice to reply. A powerful feeling was building inside him. More than rage, deeper than despair, it burned hotter than the sun. Trembling, he fought to keep it tamped down.

The sky crackled. Jagged bolts of lightning etched the midnight cloud, painting them in stark shades of green and white as they passed back and forth. Three Moons frowned as he watched the display. *The fucking gods are at war, and we ants have to scramble not to get squashed underfoot.*

Bolstered by the Yuldirans, the combined army had managed to carve out an island of relative security. They had taken over a city block of tall tenement buildings surrounding a small park. After scouring the buildings clean of undead, they had barricaded the doors and windows at the street level. Every possible entrance was guarded by a platoon. So far, their defenses had kept the enemy at bay.

Looking down over the edge of the rooftop where he stood, Three Moons tried to estimate the number of ghuls clogging the street below, but soon gave up. Tens of thousands.

Behind him, the commanders of the combined forces were conversing. Their discussion was low, but he could hear their words clearly. They were scared—no, terrified—and the troops were in a similar state. Only sheer exhaustion kept anyone from panicking, but that was also only a matter of time. As the noose tightened around their throats, and every last refuge was stripped away from them, the units would lose their cohesion as every individual sought to survive as long as possible. He had seen it before. The memory of Pardisha loomed over him.

The remaining half-dozen Crimson Brothers huddled at the far corner of the rooftop. Bedraggled, their fine robes stained and sodden, they looked even more miserable than the commanders. One young sorcerer still bore the golden icon. His forehead rested on the oaken staff holding the relic, eyes closed as his brethren stood around him in a loose circle. The nimbus of their protection spells was dim, almost nonexistent.

Turning back to stare down at the seething masses in the street below, Three Moons hawked and spat over the side of the roof, watched as the spittle stretched into a thinner and thinner line until it broke, the thick wad of phlegm dropping like an egg yolk into the mob.

"Moons," Emanon said, sounding more than a little like Jirom.

Three Moons turned and joined their convocation, though it didn't make him feel any less lonely. Now, at the end, more than ever, he wished he was with the Blades.

"I don't have an answer," he said without preamble. He had to fight the powerful urge to punctuate his words by spitting at their feet. "I don't know where Jirom and the others are. There aren't any spirits left within five miles of here, so I'm just as blind and deaf as you—"

He flinched as several bolts of lightning crashed down a hundred yards from their position, and a riot of thunder exploded overhead. In that moment, he saw an impossible image against the dark backdrop of the sky. It was Horace, but as huge as a titan and clad in gilded plate armor. In his hand he held a vast sword, shining like the sun. He was falling, and over him stood a vast serpent, its jaws spread wide as it prepared to strike again. The blazing sword's light faltered like a guttering candle, swallowed by the ravenous storm clouds.

"Moons?" Emanon said.

A shudder ran through Three Moons. He shook himself as he tore his eyes away from the fading vision. "Is this the end?"

Emanon stepped closer, concern written across his features. He started to reach out as if to grasp Three Moons by the shoulder.

Suddenly, the golden icon atop the staff blazed with renewed radiance. Its light shoved back the gloom covering the rooftop, the beams stabbing up to shred the clouds above. At the same time, Three Moons felt a burst of mystical energy like a tidal wave, coming from deeper in the city. He turned toward the temple district, only half-seen through the haze of rain, and a sliver of hope pushed its way up from the dregs at the bottom of his heart.

"Come on," he whispered. "Get up, lad. Get up and fight."

An inky haze surrounded Horace. It clouded his eyes and wafted into his mouth, threatening to suffocate him. He struggled to clear it away, but he was too weak. He couldn't move because of the stony spike impaling him. He felt blood dribbling from the wound, felt himself dying drip by drip. *This is it. This is how it ends.*

Through the miasma, he sensed Astaptah's presence over him, a nexus of dark energy. Horace maintained his psychic connection to his foe, holding onto it like a lifeline. It was the only thing keeping him from sinking into unconsciousness. Beside Astaptah stood the man they had found in the palace, like a loyal servant. *What kind of creature could serve an evil like Astaptah? Maybe I should have killed him when we met.*

Then Astaptah was leaning down. He held a knife in his hand. With a sardonic grin, he aimed the blade at Horace's left eye. Horace struggled but the spike held him fast and he was too weak to move away.

"I wonder what you will see," Astaptah said, "without your eyes, Horace. I suspect it will amaze you."

Suddenly, Astaptah dropped the knife and flinched back as a long blade of steel flashed toward his head. Jirom rushed at Astaptah. His sword cut through the air, and the dark-robed sorcerer retreated. In that moment, Horace dared to let himself hope. However, Astaptah recovered as quick as a jungle cat. Emerald flames leapt from his hand, and Jirom disappeared from Horace's view amid a stench of burning leather and flesh. Gritting his teeth, Horace took a deep breath.

Then, Astaptah was attacked again, this time by a swarm of flying ice and stony shards. Horace could feel Princess Dasha channeling *zoana* behind him. Although the magical assault was fruitless—Astaptah merely waved it away—it gave Horace time to gather what little strength he had left. With a low grunt, he managed to push himself off the spike. More blood poured from him, but he hardly felt it. He was having trouble concentrating. He didn't have much *zoana* left, but he gathered it all and pushed it through the connection into Astaptah. *Just a little more. Dig, Horace. You're almost there.*

Astaptah looked down and his triumphant smirk faltered. "That's enough. No more! I can't . . ."

The Dark King's face contorted. He clutched at his robes and tore them away. Underneath, his body was writhing as if thousands of serpents wriggled beneath the skin. Spots of inky blood appeared as the flesh broke open and wept.

"It's too much!" he cried out. "Take it back! Take it from me!"

His eyes bleeding, Astaptah thrust his hands down toward Horace. However, the power had raged beyond his control. Dusky beams exploded around him, carving channels in the floor and walls. The chamber shook.

Gathering his legs under him, Horace steadied himself. He couldn't see clearly, but he knew Astaptah was standing directly in front of him. Behind the Dark King, the frieze pulsed with frantic energy. Horace took a breath and held it. Then he propelled himself forward with all his strength. He struck Astaptah, chest to chest, and they tottered toward the back of the dais.

Three steps . . . four . . . The writhing frieze loomed before them. Their momentum slowed to a halt as Astaptah recovered his balance. He was far stronger than he looked. He grabbed Horace by the temples and began to squeeze. Horace hissed in pain as pure power stabbed into him, threatening to crush his skull. He had a choice. He could use what was left of his *zoana* to defend himself, or he could continue to feed it to Astaptah, but he couldn't do both. He pushed it out, into his enemy, knowing it was the last thing he would ever do, and hoping it was enough. But Astaptah did not budge. Although his body rippled and twisted with the over-burgeoning of energies, he held on, too. They were locked in a fatal embrace, but Horace knew he could not outlast his foe. His power was fading fast.

Astaptah staggered as something leapt onto his back. Looking up through the fog clouding his mind, Horace saw Pumash clinging to the Dark King's shoulder. With animalistic savagery, Pumash sunk his teeth into Astaptah's neck. Blood spurted as the flesh tore open. Astaptah lifted his hands and dark radiance exploded from his palms. Pumash was thrown off him with a shriek, but Horace saw his chance. He rushed Astaptah again. His shoulder caught Astaptah in the midriff, and he wrapped his arm around his adversary's waist. Astaptah struggled in his grasp, but Horace held tight and drove with his legs. Together, they collided with the frieze.

The stone carving was rubbery to the touch. As his hand and forearm made contact first, Horace felt intense cold, and a hungry pulling as hundreds of tiny appendages reached out from the gateway to latch onto him. Astaptah must have felt it, as well. His struggles became frantic, kicking and clawing to get free. Fierce heat burned down Horace's back as light blazed behind him, but he ignored it. All his focus was on pushing Astaptah, and himself, into the portal between worlds. It was the only way, he had reasoned, to Seal it once more.

"No!" Astaptah shouted.

Horace held onto his foe tightly as they pushed through the gateway's frigid membrane. It engulfed them. Horace turned for one final look into the chamber behind him. Jirom and the two women were running toward him. He saw at once what they intended to do. Horace shook his head, but he wasn't sure they could see him anymore. He and Astaptah had passed most of the way through the gateway. His muscles and joints were locking in place from the icy cold, but his mind remained active. *This must be done, but you can survive.*

As his friends charged up onto the dais, Horace used the last of his *zoana* to fashion an enchantment. With a smile, he let it go. A moment later, Jirom, Dasha, and Elia vanished. Horace's view of the temple chamber disappeared as he and Astaptah passed through the veil. There was still one thing he had to do. The rift between worlds throbbed behind them like an angry wound. He had to close it for good, but he was spent as the last dregs of power had drained out of him. However, Astaptah blazed above him like a black sun. The Dark King's withered flesh felt like old paper, his bones a bundle of dry sticks, but the *zoana* pulsed within him like a living thing. Horace reversed the direction of their mystical tether and drew forth the power. Astaptah spasmed, but Horace ignored it as he wove his spell. Bracing himself, he let it go in the direction of the rift.

Scintillating light exploded all around him. Images flashed before his eyes. He saw his wife Sari in the wedding dress she and her mother had sewn, walking down the aisle of the old church in Tines where they had been married. His heart ached to hold her again. Another flash, and he was in the front room of their modest house as the midwife handed him Josef for the first time. Tears wet his eyes as he held his newborn son. A small cry escaped Horace's lips as the light flashed again. He stood on the deck of the *Sea Spray*. Shouts filled the air. Horace turned to see Sari and Josef on the deck beside him, neither noticing as the burning mast started to fall behind them. Terror and grief dueling in his chest, he lunged toward them, but the light flashed again. The slick deck of the *Bantu Ray* rolled beneath his feet. Horace fought to keep his balance as the storm tossed the vessel about. Green lightning crackled overhead as a great wave came over the gunwales. It picked him up and tossed him over the side. He hit the water like a stone and sank into its icy embrace. The lightning continued to play above him as he drifted down into the depths. His lungs burned. One final flash of light.

He and Astaptah floated in a black void. No light to be seen, not even stars. But Horace sensed other presences in the vast nothingness. The rift had closed. The portal between worlds was Sealed once again.

Astaptah's voice echoed inside his skull. *You have killed us, Horace.*

No, he answered. *We shall live eternal in the Outside. But your dream is dead. The world will live on, without you or your gods. And if you try to reach for the gate and sunder the Seal, I will be here to stop you. Every time.*

Astaptah's power raged, and Horace felt his own energy returning. They rotated until they faced each other again. Horace smiled as the *zoana* bloomed and they resumed their battle.

Forever and ever. A worthy price to pay. Goodbye, my friends.

The undead surged around the combined army of rebels and Akeshian troopers in a rising tide, a force of feral hunger driven by dark sorcery. Several of the barricaded doorways of the tenement block had been sundered, and the troops were fighting inside those buildings, trying to hold back the inevitable.

From his vantage atop the roof of the southeast corner building, Three Moons surveyed their impending defeat. Retreating into this complex had bought them some time, but now they were spread out. The soldiers and rebels were being overwhelmed with alarming swiftness, entire platoons decimated and devoured in a span of minutes, collapsing under the weight of bodies. It was over.

A Thuumian company tried to break out of the containment, exiting their assigned block house on the east flank. They got into the open street and then lost all cohesion. They were slaughtered and torn apart within a dozen heartbeats, with a scant few even reaching the end of the block.

The remnants of Emanon's paltry command staff watched from the rooftop. *Pradi* Naram had gone below a half a bell ago to fight alongside his soldiers. Runners came with news and left with orders, but none of it made much difference. They had no reinforcements, and their enemy gained strength with every passing minute. Three Moons watched the way Emanon stroked the haft of his spear and knew what the man was thinking. Any minute, he would leave this perch and find a place to sell his life. Like the *pradi*, he would choose a warrior's death among his comrades. A noble death.

Three Moons tried to laugh, but it came out as a dry cough. *Noble death? There's no such fucking thing. Just a series of bad choices compounded by useless gestures.*

The din of the fighting lessened in his ears, becoming almost silent as he watched the swords rise and fall, the undead leaping into the wall of blades again and again, the savage ferocity writ on their bestial faces. Lifting his gaze to the east, he couldn't make out the palace any longer through the haze of rain and darkness. Somewhere out there, the Blades were likely fighting for their lives, too. *I'm sorry, Jirom. We couldn't get to you. With any luck, I'll see you in the next life.*

The main doorway below him gave way with a dreadful crack, and the undead poured in. Shouts echoed in the tenement's rooms and hallways where Ralla's company was positioned. Three Moons made up his mind. It appeared that Emanon did, too, at the exact same time. Three Moons followed him inside the building and down the stairs. At the bottom they found the fight.

Ralla had retreated from the front of the ground level to give her troops some space. As the undead flooded in through the doorway and front windows, the rebels cut them down with arrow fire and flung javelins. That dropped a few but then the undead swarmed into them. Swords and axes cut into cold flesh with heavy thuds like they were chopping wood.

Three Moons followed Emanon to the front of the defense, where Ralla and her first squad stood as a bulwark, against which the undead tide crashed again and again, flinging blood instead of spume with each contact. While the Akeshians on either side of them fell and were dragged away, the rebels remained steadfast in their resistance. Three Moons knew they would eventually be overcome, outnumbered and surrounded. He had seen many battles in his years, seen thousands die bloody, horrible deaths—tens of thousands— but the reek of dark sorcery hanging over this slaughter sickened him worse than anything he'd ever witnessed. He couldn't help thinking this is how humanity would end, dragged down into extinction by the dead.

A pair of ghuls scrambled past the front line. Dragging weapons stuck in their cold flesh, they leapt toward Three Moons. He called to a spirit out of instinct and was amazed when two broken boards tore themselves from the wall. The fiends' heads exploded in showers of brown and gray. A pair of air elementals spun across the ceiling, delighting in the chaos. Another undead attacked from a doorway to his left, sprinting through the line. Three Moons summoned an ember and sent into the fiend's gaping mouth. A moment later, its skull erupted in flames. Staggering, clawing, the thing fell and curled in upon itself. Rebels surrounded it, chopping the thing to pieces.

Apparently, the spirits weren't quite done with him yet. Three Moons took full advantage of that. He called to all the ghosts and goblins he could muster and formed them into a whirlwind of destruction, targeting only dead flesh. Wiping the sweat from his eyes, he turned to survey the battle. The rebels were holding, but the undead closed around them like a noose, slowly choking the army to death. *This is it. No grand speeches. No eternal glory. Just a cold death and my bones left for the vultures to pick over.*

He was preparing to expend the last of his magical energy in one last burst of defiance against the powers assailing them when a tremor ran through the floor underfoot. As he staggered to keep his balance, a burst of light exploded in the street outside, as if the night had suddenly lifted and sunlight poured down. The potent radiance blinded him for a moment as raw power—more than he had ever felt before—erupted somewhere to the east in a single, tremendous burst. Then, it was gone.

Three Moons was blinking furiously to clear his vision when he heard the shouts arise. *It can't be. Can it?*

As he rubbed the last afterimages from his sight, what he saw drained the blood from his face. Jirom had appeared in the street, along with the Blades, the Akeshian princess, and her bodyguard, all of them looking as stunned by their sudden appearance as he was. Jirom turned away, ignoring the enemies ringed around him as he looked back to the east.

He pointed. "It's Jirom! They're back!"

With a shout, Emanon led with troopers through the press in a desperate charge. Three Moons followed close on their heels, flinging the last scraps of his magic to aid Ralla's company as they cut their way through the press of undead. He also kept an eye on the rear, but the remaining Akeshian infantry had stepped up to hold the line, preventing the enemy from streaming into the gap behind them. But for how long? Already he saw the lines further shrinking as soldiers fell to filthy claws. Even worse, some of those fallen men and women rose again to the fight as black-eyed monsters, intent on killing their former allies.

SUN AND SERPENT

Finally, the company burst out of the building. They surrounded the tight knot of mercenaries, using their bodies to make a wall between them and the undead.

"It's about time you showed up!" Emanon shouted.

It was clear that Jirom wasn't listening. He still faced eastward. Up close, Three Moons saw their commander was covered in cuts and scratches. The princess knelt on the ground beside another man that Three Moons didn't recognize. Half his face was burned away, revealing red muscle and bone. The bodyguard stood over the princess. All of them looked as if they had walked through a meat grinder. "Sarge?" he said, hoping for a response. "It looks like you've been doing some damage on your own, but we've got a real scrap here. We could use a little guidance."

Emanon reached out with his free hand. "Jir?"

Three Moons was about ask where Horace was when a second quake shook the earth, followed by a sudden rush of undead clogging the street on both sides of them. Ghuls dropped from rooftops and windows to land on the pavement, breaking bones in the process but dragging themselves toward the living troopers with frightening intensity.

Three Moons called to the spirits of earth and stone and set them to work on the mortar holding together the brick walls of the storefronts on the far side of the street. A brisk wind blew down the avenue as air spirits lent their strength. He was rewarded with a sudden crackle of breaking cement before those walls collapsed outward, burying that side of the street in a mountain of rubble. Then he slumped to the ground, exhausted. He couldn't do any more. He was spent.

Struggling to get enough air as the battle seethed around him, Three Moons glanced over at the princess and the man she was watching over. She had his head in her lap, heedless of the blood streaming from his horrendous wounds. "Who is he?"

The princess replied without looking over. "I don't really know. But I think he saved us all."

Saved us all from what?

Three Moons looked around. The crowd of undead was growing.

Emanon and Captain Paranas led their fighters in a furious defense, but they didn't have the numbers to hold out. Piles of corpses were heaped all around them. There was no time to pull a wounded comrade back from the fighting. Every moment and every breath were spent just trying to stay alive. Against a mortal foe, they might have been able to turn the tide, but the dead felt no fear. Even as they fell by the dozens, more poured in to take their place. As Three Moons watched, he was suddenly very glad he wouldn't die alone.

But we all die alone, soldier. You know that. You've watched enough of your sisters and brothers take that solitary path. Seven decades spent in this world, and what have you got to show for it? Flat feet and a wagonload of sorrows. But maybe I redeemed myself here at the end. Finally, I found a cause worth dying for.

Yella fell, and Three Moons reached through the forest of legs to drag him back from the fighting. While he pressed a hand against the ragged bite wound gouged in the younger man's side and looked through his bag for a semi-clean rag to bind it, a tremendous eruption of thunder shook the sky. He knelt over Yella instinctively as the ground bucked beneath them. Most of the troopers fell to the ground around him, and Three Moons looked up with fear. *What new deviltry is this?*

A bright glow limned the fog over the east end of the city. Troopers stumbled as they tried to regain their footing, ready to resume the battle. They looked about, by their expressions unsure whether to believe what they saw. Thousands of undead sprawled around them, unmoving.

Three Moons reached out with his mind. The spirits concurred with his observation. The undead were . . . dead, again. The dark magic that had animated them was gone, leaving nothing behind but empty shells. The storm clouds dissipated, revealing a gray sky streaked with bands of red and gold. Above the western horizon, the wan sun was fixing to set. Three Moons took a deep breath and let it go. As he exhaled, a great weight lifted from his chest, and with it went the adamantine control he had kept over himself for these past few years. Tears formed and ran down his cheeks.

Jirom was on his knees, his sword dropped from his hand. Far in the distance, more rumbles sounded, not from the sky but the ground. A structure was collapsing in the temple district, and with its demise, Jirom seemed to contract within himself.

Emanon stayed a step back from his lover. He asked without turning, "Moons?"

Three Moons silently asked the spirits for their aid in reaching out further with his senses and found what he had feared and hoped. The entire city was dead, truly dead now. "It's over. Whatever you did, it worked."

Jirom took a deep breath, looking as if he wanted to sob, but the moment passed. Slowly, as if he were stiff from toes to crown, he stood up, but he didn't touch his fallen sword. Taking that for a good sign, Emanon took the final step and wrapped his arms gently around Jirom. "You are a fucking good sight to see. Are you hurt?"

Three Moons watched as the two men took a moment to examine each other, like they were seeing each other for the first time in years. *It seems like a lifetime. Is it really over?*

As the commanders embraced, the rest of the army lost the last vestiges of organization. Soldiers dropped to their knees beside dead comrades, tears running down their dirty faces. Swords and spears were dropped as others wandered off, including some officers. No one tried to stop them. Captain Paranas sat alone off to the side of the street, helmet off, staring up into the deepening sky. The rest of the Blades stood around, milling listlessly. Pie-Eye kept opening his mouth as if he wanted to gripe about something, but no words came.

Once Yella's wound was bound, Three Moons pushed himself to his feet and went over to Jirom and Emanon.

"I bet you have one hell of a story to tell, Sarge," Three Moons said. "What say you we go find a couple bottles of wine and compare notes?"

Jirom nodded wearily over Emanon's shoulder. "Sounds good to me." Then he frowned. "But first we have to secure the city. We'll need food supplies and fresh water. And we have to sweep the houses, block by block. There's no telling what might be hiding in the dark corners."

Emanon grinned and playfully swiped at Jirom. "That's my man. Always thinking of the practical matters. So, tell us, Commander. What are we to do after we've filled our bellies and made sure everything is safe?"

Jirom was gazing up at the sky. "I honestly don't know."

"I have a few ideas."

They turned to Dasha, who stood a few paces away with her bodyguard. Both women were smeared with grime and blood. Jirom studied them with a thoughtful look.

I'll bet you do, Princess. I'll bet you do.

EPILOGUE

The throne that symbolized the power of the emperor over all Akeshia was covered in gilt. Thousands of people had abased themselves before the seat over the centuries, in awe of its majesty.

Jirom kicked it over. He took a momentary satisfaction from the cracking of ancient wood as he stood in its place. *I'll have Emanon find a camp stool. That suits me better.*

As if summoned by the thought, his lover's voice echoed from the chamber entrance. "The locals aren't going to like that. Are you ready?"

Jirom turned, mindful of the costly raiment that draped him. A tunic and long skirt of white silk, trimmed in gold. A matching cape held in place by a thick gold chain. Jeweled bands on his wrists and upper arms. He felt like a Mehulhan whore. "I suppose so. Tell me, why am I doing this again?"

"It's the best option." Emanon was also dressed in white silk. "You know I'm right."

Three nights ago, just after the first sunset of the new era, Emanon and Dasha had come to Jirom together. "We need to talk to you," Emanon said first, with a look that had made Jirom uneasy. "It's about the empire."

"More precisely, who is going to rule it," Dasha added. "And how."

"We have an idea," Emanon said, "but you might not like it."

And so, they explained their plan to him. After hearing them out, Jirom was tempted to toss them both out on their backsides. "You want me to marry her?" He asked this looking straight into Emanon's eyes.

His lover nodded without a trace of hesitation. "I do."

Jirom looked at the princess. "You know he and I are partners in love. But you want to marry me anyway?"

She nodded as well. "I do."

"Stop it," Jirom said. "This isn't funny."

"Think about it," Dasha said. "We fought so hard to save this world and sacrificed so much. I don't want to see it fall apart again, but I cannot hold it together on my own. I need your strength."

Emanon said, "We have the strength, you and me. But we don't have the legitimacy. And without that . . ."

"We would be just another couple of warlords," Jirom finished for him. "Ruling at the point of a sword."

"Exactly."

Jirom looked from Emanon to Dasha and saw the resolve in their eyes. "Em . . ."

"I know. It's not how we envisioned the future. But it's just a political arrangement."

"Absolutely," Dasha said.

Now, Jirom found himself on the verge of getting married to the princess. "It's not too late. We could slip out the back, grab a couple horses, and be out of the city before they notice we're gone."

Emanon put an arm around his shoulders. "We'll make this work. I promise you. It's just a matter of logistics."

Jirom glanced at the toppled throne. "For the good of the empire."

"For the good of the people."

Jirom kissed him on the lips and held it for several tender heartbeats. Then, "Damnit, you always know the right thing to say."

"Come on, Emperor-to-be. Let's go get you hitched."

Together they walked the long hallway to the palace atrium, where they were greeted by a company of rebel fighters. Captain Ralla stood with her troopers, looking resplendent in a new suit of armor, sword at her hip. She saluted smartly, and her soldiers repeated the gesture. The sound of a hundred fists slapping against steel breastplates reverberated through the grand chamber.

Jirom gestured to the outer exit. "All right. Let's get this over with."

The huge doors swung open, and the sunlight poured in. Jirom allowed himself a moment to bask in the warmth. Such a simple thing, and yet it felt like a renewal of spirit to him.

Emanon nudged him in the ribs. "That's no way to speak on your wedding day."

"Keep it up, and I swear I'll punch you right in your pretty face."

"Promises."

"Just don't forget what I told you."

At the end of their late-night talk, after Jirom had agreed to go along with their scheme, he delivered an ultimatum to Dasha and Emanon, one he meant with every fiber of his being.

"You don't have to remind me," Emanon replied. "It's what I always wanted."

Jirom suppressed a grunt. "So you say now."

They exited the palace and looked out onto the capital. Reconstruction was already underway. No one had had to give the command. In the days following the battle, his fighters and the Akeshian soldiers had pitched in together to start rebuilding the damaged city. It would take years, maybe a lifetime, but it was a beginning.

The palace grounds had avoided the brunt of devastation. A couple of the compound towers toppled, and swathes of grass were burnt to crisp, but the broad path leading up to the gates was pristine. Every living person in Ceasa was assembled, which amounted to a little more than two thousand souls. His rebel fighters stood beside the last three companies of Thuumian soldiers, flanked by the Yuldiran reinforcements. Jirom's stomach quivered as all their eyes settled on him. With a deep breath and release, he stepped out to meet them.

At the edge of the broad portico, Emanon turned to him and bowed. Jirom caught the smile his lover didn't bother to hide as he stepped away. They had choreographed this moment, but it still felt incredibly awkward, especially as Jirom was left alone on the palace's front steps. He had thought long about what to say to these men and women who fought so bravely, but he hadn't been able to find the words. They had lost friends, brothers and sisters, in this battle for freedom. All his thoughts felt hollow in the face of such sacrifice. However, he needed to say something.

Then soft footsteps echoed behind him. Elia walked her charge to the edge of the portico, with Dasha following behind her in a lace veil. With one hand on the pommel of her sword, the bodyguard gave Jirom a hard glance, and then she stepped away, giving space for the princess to come to his side. Dasha looked up at him through the veil. She appeared completely serene. *Of course. She was born for this.*

With a poise beyond her years, Dasha slipped her arm through his, and together they faced the crowd. There were no more priests alive in the city, so they spoke the words of the ritual alone. As he intoned his vows, Jirom kept wanting to look to Emanon, but he forced his eyes forward, his stance as rigid as if he were a cadet standing for review. As they spoke the final words, a hush fell over the courtyard.

Dasha pushed back her veil and addressed their audience. "My people!"

The cry faded as the soldiers and rebel fighters strained to hear her.

"My people," she repeated. "We have won a great victory! Light has defeated darkness. We saw the dead rise again, but they have been put back down into the earth's hallowed embrace for good. We have won, and now we shall have peace, all of us living and working side by side to build a new Akeshia."

Scattered applause echoed through the courtyard. Jirom considered her words. Yes, the dead had been put down once more, but the cost had been steep. So many lost. He had heard a few rumors about what happened in the temple district. Somehow, word of Horace's sacrifice had spread among the ranks. The stories of his battle with the Dark King ranged from fiendish to messianic, with some saying he had given his life to save the world, while others insisted he'd been in league with the Dark King from the start. Jirom had instructed Emanon to quash the rumors, but he didn't hold much hope that anyone would obey his orders.

"They just went through Hell," Emanon had said to him the other night, as they lay together in the royal chambers. Jirom studied the way the lamplight fell across his lover's body, creating a rippled pattern of shadows across the hills and valleys of his musculature. "They need something to believe in, Jirom. So it all makes sense in their heads."

"I miss him, Em. I feel like I've lost the better part of myself."

"He died defending his friends. That's a good death, Jir. The best a man can hope for. Someday, maybe, the truth will be known. But if not, the fact that we're still alive is the greatest testament to his sacrifice that could ever exist."

Jirom didn't disagree. He just wished these men and women could have known Horace the way he had. *Emanon's right. Let them have their hero, or villain. I know the truth.*

"Tonight," Dasha continued, "let us celebrate the future together."

Jirom held his breath, unsure of the response this pageant would receive. Looking out over the sea of faces, he saw expressions of confusion among his warriors, and consternation among the Akeshians. His ultimatum for accepting Emanon and Dasha's bargain had been simple.

"If I am to be an emperor," he had told them, "then I won't be a figure-head or imperial consort. I will be emperor in power as well as name."

Emanon agreed at once, and, after a moment's consideration, the princess consented as well. Yet, even having their agreement, Jirom had been dreading this moment, when the survivors of the battle got their chance to weigh in on this decision. If they didn't accept him, then this fledgling alliance would fall apart before it ever became a reality.

A cry went up. "Hail Empress Dasha and Emperor Jirom!"

The words reverberated like the cracking of a dam, and then everyone in the courtyard dropped to one knee, heads bowed. Their reaction made Jirom feel odd. He wanted to shout for them to get up and stop making such a show, but a gentle tug on his arm from the princess reminded him of his new station. *No, not princess any longer. She is an empress now.*

He kept his gaze on the people. This was the performance they needed to heal.

After another minute of adoration, he and Dasha turned and went back into the palace. As they passed through the grand archway and the doors closed behind them, she dropped his arm. Jirom stepped away.

"You did good," Emanon said, returning to his side.

"It felt strange. I kept wanting to reach for a weapon."

"See, marriage is already agreeing with you."

Dasha nodded at something Elia whispered to her, and then faced the two men. "There is a delegation of engineers gathering in the north hall."

Emanon gave a short laugh. "Engineers? Jumped-up sappers, you mean."

"Regardless," she replied, "I should meet with them. And a group of military officers is waiting to see you at the main audience chamber." She added with a faint smile, "Your Imperial Majesty."

Jirom felt like he had swallowed a live snake and it was twisting around in his gut. "Already?"

"Yes, the wheels of bureaucracy never cease. But together we are going to forge a new empire on top of the ashes of the old."

"Just remember your end of the bargain," Emanon said.

"You'll learn that I never forget."

Jirom watched as she hesitated a moment, her hand hovering as if she were about to reach out and touch him. But instead, she left with Elia.

"This is going to be confusing," Emanon muttered.

"You're telling me?"

Emanon threw him a grin. "My apologies, Your Imperial Majesty. Shall we saunter to the audience room so a bunch of grunts can kiss your royal ass?"

Jirom seriously considered punching him. "Let's go."

Ralla's troopers escorted them to the hall, and once more Jirom entered the seat of Akeshian power. Four guards posted around the chamber made him frown, but a pair of short, sturdy chairs on the raised dais lightened his mood. The gaudy imperial throne was nowhere to be seen. Jirom climbed the platform and sat in the right-hand seat. When he was ready, Emanon opened the outer door and ushered in a cadre of officers, half from the Akeshian units and half from the rebels. Another of Dasha's ideas, to mix the forces and include both in all decisions, in an effort she called a demonstration of unity. *She'll make a good ruler, I think. I'm the one out of place.*

Jirom kept the meeting brief, as he already knew most of these men and women. He listened to their expressions of congratulation, gave them their orders, and then sent them on their way. The rebel fighters would remain in Ceasa to protect and rebuild it. He was sending the rest to Semira and all points west, to exterminate any undead remnants they found and aid any survivors they came across. He didn't envy them. It was a duty that would take months, if not years, to complete. Emanon went with the captains when they left, speaking with emphatic gestures.

Jirom sat back in the chair. He had been emperor for only half a bell, but he already wanted to run away. The responsibility of his new position was too monumental to consider. He almost jumped out of his chair and grabbed for the sword he wasn't wearing as someone came out from behind the ornately carved screen at the rear of the audience chamber. "Mezim? Damn you, I almost jumped out of my skin. What are you doing skulking back there?"

The former secretary bowed as he shuffled forward. "Pardon, Your Majesty. There is a hidden viewing room at the rear of the hall. I thought you knew."

"I had no idea. What do you want?"

Mezim held up a rolled scroll and a writing kit. "Earlier, you said you wanted to draft an edict, sire."

Jirom eased back in the seat once more. "Yes. My apologies. I had forgotten in all the . . . excitement."

"Of course, Majesty." Mezim set himself up at an elaborate writing desk against the wall. After unrolling the scroll, sharpening his pen, opening and stirring the ink, and getting himself situated, he looked up to Jirom. "Whenever you are ready."

Jirom had decided what his first law as emperor would be in the wan hours of the morning before his marriage, as the first hint of dawn crept into the chamber he shared with Emanon. He owed Emanon everything, and now he would begin to repay that debt. He cleared his throat and began to recite the words that had come to him in that hazy hour between night and day.

"I, Jirom, Emperor of Akeshia, son of Khiren, born of the Muhabbi Clan, hereby proclaim that it is forbidden for any person to own another as property. Neither for reasons of debt nor the circumstances of their birth, nor even in a time of war. All men, women, and children are free henceforth and for all eternity.

"Furthermore, no one—no matter their station or rank—is permitted to take the property of another by force without fair compensation."

Mezim looked up from his writing. "Pardon me, sire. That one may require further explanation, particularly in the definition of what is considered fair."

Jirom rubbed his forehead in anticipation of future headaches. "Compose some thoughts on the matter after we've finished here, and I'll read them later."

"Yes, sire. Was there more?"

"Aye. From this day forward, all peoples of Akeshia shall be permitted to worship whatever gods they desire without punishment or prejudice."

"That may be difficult to enforce," Mezim mumbled.

"Just write it down. Oh, and add a tax on the temples."

Mezim glanced up again, this time with no little amount of alarm. "Sire? The temples of the cults have always been sacrosanct against imperial levies and fees. They will not be pleased to see that changed."

Jirom shrugged as he stood up, rubbing his lower back. "There aren't many priests left alive to complain. Those who do will be eager for assistance in rebuilding their houses of worship, and they'll either accept this or they can preach from a gallows pole, for all I care."

Mezim finished his dictation and then packed up his kit. "Yes, Your Majesty. I shall write out a formal copy for your perusal."

As Mezim left, a silver figure emerged from behind the screen. This time Jirom wasn't surprised as Three Moons walked into the chamber.

"That was deftly done," the sorcerer said as he came over to the dais. A single cut marred the side of his face, but already it was little more than a fading scratch. "But what about external threats? Your empire is empty, ripe for the plucking, and Akeshia has many enemies."

"Envoys were sent to all the neighboring countries, warning their merchants to stay away on account of a plague."

Three Moons nodded as he stroked his chin. "That could work. For a while."

"One day at a time."

"Paranas says you wanted to speak to me."

"I'm sending the Blades with the expeditionary force, but I need a court wizard. And with Horace gone . . . Well, you're the only candidate."

Three Moons made an unpleasant frown. "I thought I'd earned a little peace and quiet. But you intend to work me until I drop dead, don't you?"

"You and me both."

"At least you got a blushing new bride in the deal." He looked Jirom in the eyes and shrugged. "Sorry. That came out crueler than I intended. How is Emanon handling it?"

Jirom waved the apology away. "It was his fucking idea. He and the empress cooked it up together, and I'm just supposed to go along with it like we're all getting what we want."

"You want to rule?"

"No, I want to hang up my sword and retire, just like you. I thought Horace would take over once this fight was done. Remember? But he's gone, and there's no one left to hold the reins."

"What if no one rules? What if we let it all go?"

"Then the empire will collapse. The larger towns will die off without the support of the city-states. People will scatter. Anarchy will run rampant, resulting in disease, banditry, and famine. And then, at the end, a warlord will arise to take over and start the whole process of empire over again."

"I see you've thought this through."

"I have."

"All right, you've convinced me. So, where do we begin?"

Jirom thought of how this had all started for him, when he was chained to a slave coffle in front of a pale-skinned prisoner of war. On that day, he'd had no idea of what lay before him, or how events would change his life. He thought of the friends he had lost. One in particular. *Are you dead, Horace? Or trapped in some other world? I don't think I'll ever see you again, but at least I hope you have found the peace you never had in life.*

"We start at the beginning. We rebuild Akeshia one stone, one tree, and one person at a time. We make it strong, but we also make it just and good. For all people, not just those with wealth and power."

"It sounds like a dream," Three Moons said.

"It is. It's up to us to make it a reality."

The door opened, and Emanon returned. "Are you two going to jaw all day? There's work to do. We have burial crews to assemble, storehouses and armories to inventory, repair plans to finalize, and someone just spotted a sinkhole big enough to swallow a wagon and team in the temple district."

Jirom glanced at Three Moons, and they both chuckled as they followed Emanon out of the throne room.

A warm wind blew in from the Midland Sea. Stirring up the turgid waters of the Typhon River delta, it followed those ancient banks inland, past towns and fishing villages where people struggling to rebuild their lives paused at the sharp tang of salt in the air.

Gathering strength, the gust swept over the ramparts of Erugash and flowed through the great city until it found a once-fine estate not far from the palace ruins. The tattered remains of curtains stirred in the window of an office on the second floor. Papers swirled beneath a dusty wooden desk. The decorated sword hanging on one of the office walls rattled as if trying to lift itself from the pegs holding it. A couple inches of the blade slid out of the scabbard.

A heartbeat later, a soft emerald glow emanated from the room and shined out through the window like a beacon. It briefly flashed across the sky, with its low-hanging clouds, and over the rest of the city. Then it subsided, and a fierce wind blew down from the open sky, carrying the scents of a new world in its gusty embrace.

Far to the west, an old man in a borrowed cloak left the capital of Ceasa by its southside gate. The entrance was unguarded, one gate propped open by the bloated, fly-covered corpse of an ox.

A mile from the gates, the old man stopped at the top of a rise in the road and looked back. His shoulder still ached from the bite wound, but it would heal in time. He had buried his master in an unmarked plot in the pauper's boneyard. Not the most dignified resting place for Lord Pumash et'Luradessus, but it was the best he could do. He had a mission to complete. There was a new Power rising in the south, far beyond Akeshia's borders, and he intended to be among the first to bow at its feet.

With a weary sigh, Deemu turned southward and resumed his journey. Pumash might be dead, and the Dark King cast down, but the war continued. For ever and ever and ever.

HERE ENDS THE BOOK OF THE BLACK EARTH.